THE YADA YADA PRAYER GROUP® GETS ROLLING

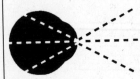

This Large Print Book carries the
Seal of Approval of N.A.V.H.

THE YADA YADA PRAYER GROUP® GETS ROLLING

NETA JACKSON

THORNDIKE PRESS
A part of Gale, Cengage Learning

GALE
CENGAGE Learning

Detroit • New York • San Francisco • New Haven, Conn • Waterville, Maine • London

GALE
CENGAGE Learning™

LIBRARY OF CONGRESS CATALOGING-IN-PUBLICATION DATA

Jackson, Neta.
  The yada yada prayer group gets rolling / by Neta Jackson.
    p. cm. — (Thorndike Press large print Christian fiction)
  ISBN-13: 978-1-4104-3379-4
  ISBN-10: 1-4104-3379-X
  1. Women—Illinois—Fiction. 2. Female friendship—Fiction. 3. Christian women—Fiction. 4. Chicago (Ill.)—Fiction. 5. Prayer groups—Fiction. 6. Large type books. I. Title.
PS3560.A2415Y3375 2011
813'.54—dc22   2010040203

Published in 2011 by arrangement with Thomas Nelson, Inc.

Printed in Mexico
1 2 3 4 5 6 7 15 14 13 12 11

PERMISSIONS

Scripture quotations are taken from THE HOLY BIBLE, NEW INTERNATIONAL VERSION ®. © 1973, 1978, 1984 by International Bible Society. Used by permission of Zondervan Publishing House.

The Holy Bible, New Living Translation, © 1996. Used by permission of Tyndale House Publishers, Inc., Wheaton, Illinois 60819. All rights reserved.

The New King James Version®. © 1982 by Thomas Nelson, Inc. Used by permission. All rights reserved.

The King James Version of the Bible. Public domain.

Selected song lyrics are taken from the following:

"I Go to the Rock" by Dottie Rambo, © 1977 John T. Benson Publishing Co.

5

To the Yada Yada Prayer Support
Team . . .
Pam Sullivan
Karen Evans
Julia Pferdehirt
Janalee Croegaert
Cynthia Wilson
Sue Mitrovitch
Janelle Schneider
Becky Gansky
Jodee Vragel
Sherri Hopper
Dawn Ashby
who committed themselves to pray for
the writing of every Yada Yada
novel, prayed me through writer's block
and family crises,
rejoiced with me when I met my
deadlines,
and encouraged me with e-mail
prayers —

even though a few of these precious
sisters are readers I've never met!

And to Terry-Ann Wilson,
bookstore owner in Essex, Ontario,
who provided the name for . . . well,
you'll find out!

PROLOGUE

A surge of energy flowed through the wire, a cocktail of adrenaline greedy for power. The Spark flexed, pushing at the cord that gripped its life force, holding it in, always holding it back, harnessing its urge to jump free, to feed, to grow . . .

"Girl! You be careful with that outlet. You got too many cords plugged in there."

"Nah. It's okay . . . look at that, will ya? The kids are gonna love those lights. Kinda skimpy though. We could use a few more strings."

"I dunno. Looks okay to me. What else we gonna put on it?"

"The kids can make stuff — paper chains, snowflakes. String popcorn. That's what I used to do as a kid."

"Ha. You were never a kid. Bet you never made one of them paper snowflakes, neither."

"You don't know what you talkin' about.

Gimme a sheet of paper, I'll show you. Scissors. We got scissors anywhere?"

Constrained, the Spark quit struggling and resigned itself to keeping the strings of Christmas lights lit on a meager diet of fifteen watts . . . Jolted awake, the Spark gulped air frantically. Zzzzzt. Zzzzzt.

"Ow!"

"Mikey! You know you ain't s'posed to touch no electric cord."

"I jus' wanted ta turn the tree on. But it bited me!"

"Nuthin' bit you, stupid."

"Did too. Like *that*."

"Ow! Let go! I'm gonna tell Mama, an' she whip your butt good."

"But you dint believe me. Had to show you."

"You didn't have ta show me nuthin'. 'Sides, your fingernails all dirty! What if you broke my skin, huh? You gonna give me rabies!"

The Spark laid back down. Hunger nibbled at its belly, but there was nothing to feed on. Might as well sleep . . .

On. Off. On. Off. On. Off . . .

The Spark had nearly given up its quest for bigger and better things.

"When we gonna take down this tree? It's

already past New Year's. We always took our tree down New Year's Day."

"What? Ain't you never heard of the Twelve Days of Christmas?"

"That's just a song. One of them counting songs, sing it over an' over till ya wanna puke."

"Nah, nah, it's for real. Christmas Day's just the beginning. Some churches got stuff goin' for weeks, before an' after. Saint Lucy, or somebody, wears candles in her hair and gives out real homemade pastries. And Boxing Day — don't know what that one is. Three Kings Day — that's in January when we really s'posed to give gifts like the Wise Men brought to baby Jesus."

"How do you know all this stuff?"

"Oh, I get around. Girl, just pour some more water in that bucket."

"What for? Tree's too dead. Ain't drinkin' up anymore. Next year when I'm outta here, I'm gonna get me one of them artificial trees. I'm tired of sweeping up all these needles."

"Ha. We used ta leave ours up till *all* the needles fell off."

"What? Your mama put up with that?"

"Nah. My grandma raised all six of us. And she didn't see too good. Here . . . plug in the tree an' dim the other lights. See?

11

Still looks like we just put it up."

The familiar jolt. The Spark licked hopefully . . . and was rewarded. A small frayed piece of the cord. Just a taste. Sizzled on its tongue and disappeared.

"You smell somethin'? Somethin' hot?"

"Ha. Hope so. Maybe the heat's come back on."

The Spark laid low, nibbling its way along the frayed cord. The more it nibbled, the more its hunger grew. Urgent now, it smoldered and smoked, pushing its way into the dark. And then . . . tinder.

Fragrant. Green. Dry.

The Spark consumed the fallen pine needles, its hunger glowing into a small flame. But there was more. More! With utter abandon, the Spark became a blaze, leaping and crackling and climbing the brittle branches. Feeding and fueling, the Spark flashed into a full bonfire. Glorious light! Nothing could stop it now!

Feeling its power, the Spark — fat and full, dancing and darting — leaped from the charred tree to the overstuffed furniture, consuming the frayed fabric and matted stuffing, licking its way up the walls and across the ceiling, finally embracing the whole room in a fiery feast —

"Fire! Fire! Everybody out!"

"Oh my God! Oh, please God!"

"Keep low! Keep low! Don't take anything — just go! Go!"

"My baby! My baby! Where's — ? I gotta go back! Let me go!"

Screams. Cries. Coughing and gagging.

"Mama! Maaaamaaaaa!"

"I got you! I got you! Run!"

1

Stepping over Willie Wonka's inert body sprawled on the floor, I groped in the shadows behind the Christmas tree for the electric cord, felt for the outlet, and plugged it in. Instantly, a glittering fairyland replaced the early morning gloom. Framed neatly by the bay window in the front room of our first-floor apartment, the six-foot fir tree we'd found at Poor Bob's Tree Lot winked and twinkled its multicolored minilights like little blessings.

Shivering, I pulled Denny's robe tighter around me and drank in the sight. If I had to choose between Christmas presents or a Christmas tree, I'd take the tree any day. Memories hung from every branch. Orange-juice-lid ornaments the kids made when they were in kindergarten bobbed nobly on the front branches. The ornaments we'd given both kids each year had multiplied until they actually filled up the tree. I

15

smiled. That was a tradition I'd brought to our marriage from my family, who had carefully packed up *my* ornaments as a wedding present when I got married. As we would do when Josh and Amanda —

My smile faded. *Ack!* Didn't want to go *there.* I dreaded the Christmas our tree would be denuded of our kids' ornaments.

I heard the coffee gurgling its last gasps as the pot filled. Scurrying back to the kitchen as fast as the stiffness in my left leg would let me, I poured my first mug of the day and then settled into the recliner facing the glittering tree for a few quiet moments before our Saturday began. It had been a nice Christmas — nothing spectacular, but nice. Leslie Stuart, our upstairs neighbor and one of my Yada Yada sisters, had invited her parents to visit her for a few days — a Christmas miracle big enough to warrant a few angels singing, "Glory! Hallelujah!" if you asked me. We'd met the senior Stuarts briefly when they'd arrived at our shared two-flat on Christmas Eve, but we'd officially invited the three of them for supper tonight.

Which meant I had to get everything ready this morning, since Ruth and Ben Garfield had also asked us and the other Yada Yadas to their house for baby Isaac's *brit mila* this afternoon.

"Brit mila? What's that?" I'd blurted when Ruth called me the day before Christmas.

"Brit mila — the ritual circumcision ceremony. A newborn Jewish male is joined to the Jewish people on the eighth day. Read your Bible, Jodi."

I had ignored the dig. *"Don't they do that in the hospital nowadays? With Josh —"*

"Is your Josh Jewish? Didn't think so. So, are you coming?"

"Wait a minute. The twins were born almost a month ago. What happened to the eighth day?"

A long pause. Not like Ruth, who usually filled up gaps in conversation like rainwater flowing into sidewalk cracks. I had immediately regretted my blunt question and started to apologize, but Ruth had just sighed. *"Pediatrician said we had to wait. Preemies, you know. But . . ."* Her voice had brightened. *"All is well. Havah and Isaac came home from the hospital on their due date — last Saturday. So this Saturday is the 'official' eighth day. The eighth day of Hanukkah too. See? God is good."*

"All the time," I'd agreed. *"Sure, we'll be there."*

Should have checked with my family first.

17

"Mo-om," Amanda had wailed. *"That's gross! If they gotta do that circumcision thing, at least do it in private. Not with everybody gawking at that poor naked baby. He'll be so embarrassed when he's thirteen and we all say, 'My, how you've grown! I was at your circumcision.'"*

I had ignored her. Sixteen-year-olds are embarrassed by everything. But even Denny had blanched. *"Uh, I dunno, Jodi. I'm kinda squeamish. What if I faint?"*

Josh, however, was the only one with a real excuse. *"Sorry, Mom. We're doing a Christmas party at Manna House for the kids."*

Now it was Saturday. The Big Day for Ben and Ruth. I sipped the hot coffee, feeling its lingering warmth. The sky beyond the bay windows — more visible in winter through the bare tree branches lining our narrow street on Chicago's north side — had begun to lighten. *Well, God,* I thought, *this year is almost over, a new one about to begin. Didn't I tell You I could use some "dull and boring" last year about this time? What happened, huh?*

Huh. Fact was, it had been a tough year for the Yada Yada Prayer Group all the way around. Nonyameko's husband, Mark, beaten up after that racist rally . . . Chanda

18

finding out she had breast cancer . . . Florida's boy arrested and locked up in the juvenile detention center . . . Avis's daughter ending up at the Manna House shelter for abused and homeless women . . . Ruth — childless, on her third husband, and pushing fifty — discovering she was pregnant with *twins* . . . Josh, our firstborn, refusing to go to college and falling in love with an "older woman" . . .

Didn't I walk with you every step of the way? The Voice in my spirit spoke gently but firmly. *Have I brought you this far to leave you now?*

"Yes, Lord, thank You," I whispered. "And . . . I guess it's a good thing You don't show us everything that's going to happen ahead of time." Because if this coming year was anything like the last year and a half since I'd met the rest of the Yada Yadas at that Chicago Women's Conference, change was in the wind.

Just then, Willie Wonka wheezed noisily to his feet and pushed his wet nose into my lap, rear end wiggling impatiently. Translated: *I gotta go out — now.*

Yeah, well. Some things *never* change.

By the time the three of us Baxters squeezed into the Garfields' compact living room that afternoon, there wasn't much room to sit. Amanda — as I'd suspected — wouldn't dream of being left behind, though her face fell when she realized Delores and Ricardo Enriquez had left all the kids at home. Amanda never missed an opportunity to show up when Delores's sixteen-year-old son José might be there.

I spied Ruth standing by the front window holding one of the twins; Delores, standing beside her, was patting the other twin over her shoulder. Had to be the boy. Even from across the room I could see the large red birthmark covering a third of the baby's face. I winced, not yet used to such a conspicuous raspberry.

I quickly counted Yada Yada noses. Besides Ruth and Delores, I spied Hoshi Takahashi and Nonyameko Sisulu-Smith sitting on the couch — but not Nony's husband, Mark, who was still recovering from his head injury. Yo-Yo Spencer, who'd been taken under the Garfields' wing when she got out of prison after doing time for forgery, perched on the arm of the couch . . . was that *it?* Only five of us? Well, six, counting myself. Where was everybody?

But I only had time to give the couch sitters a quick wave before a bearded man wearing a prayer shawl began to chant a

20

prayer. Voices immediately hushed all around the cramped living room. This must be the *mohel,* who, according to Ruth, would perform the ceremony. *"An expert he is, trained to do the circumcision with minimal discomfort,"* she'd told us on the phone. Then she'd muttered, *"He'd better be."*

After the prayer, the *mohel* called out, "Kvatter!"

Heads turned as Ruth nodded to Delores. "Delores Enriquez is *kvatterin,* the child's godmother," she announced with that stubborn tilt of her chin, daring anyone to disagree. My mouth dropped in delight, and I saw our Yada Yada sisters exchange astonished smiles as Delores, blushing up to her hair roots, tenderly cradled the little boy and made her way toward the other end of the room where she handed the baby to her husband, Ricardo.

"And Ricardo Enriquez is *kvatter,* the child's godfather," Ruth announced.

Again, little gasps of surprise and pleasure circled the room. *Well, well,* I thought. *No one deserves it more than Delores; she stuck with Ruth through this pregnancy like white on rice.* But Ricardo. *That* was a surprise — though, sure, it made sense to have husband and wife be the godparents. They were hardly Jewish, though.

21

As Ricardo took the baby, the *mohel* with the prayer shawl said, *"Baruch haba,"* while Ruth and several others responded, "May he who cometh be blessed." And then the *mohel* offered another prayer, mentioning God's covenant with Abraham, the sign of which was circumcision. ". . . and through Abraham's seed, all nations will be blessed." And we all said, "Amen."

The *mohel* took the baby from Ricardo Enriquez and handed him to someone sitting in a straight-back chair. Craning my neck, I saw Ruth's husband, Ben — a brand-new daddy at sixty-something — take his tiny son and place him on a large pillow on his lap. Ruth, coming up behind me, muttered in my ear, "Huh. Would Ben let anyone else hold his only son for his *brit mila?* Lucy would let Charlie Brown kick the football first."

I had to stuff my fist against my mouth to keep from laughing.

"— Oh Lord, King of the universe," the *mohel* was praying once again, "who has sanctified us with Thy commandments, and commanded us concerning the rite of circumcision." And then there was murmuring and rustling. Backs closed in around Ben and the baby.

This is it! I thought, looking away. I steeled

myself for —

A wail broke the hush in the room. Ruth was fanning herself big-time. I could hear Ben's growly voice soothing and shushing his child as the *mohel* finished his administrations. As Isaac's wail subsided, sighs of relief and whispers filled the room.

Then the *mohel* lifted his voice once more. "Creator of the universe, may it be Thy gracious will" — I leaned forward, trying to hear — "and give a pure and holy heart to *Yitzak,* to be called Isaac, the son of Ben and Ruth Garfield, who has just now been circumcised in honor of Thy great name. May his heart be wide open to comprehend Thy holy Law, that he may learn and teach, keep and fulfill Thy laws."

Ben's "Amen!" boomed out over all the others. I caught Denny's eye — and saw that he had his handkerchief out and was blowing his nose. At least he didn't faint.

"One moment, please," the *mohel* added, finishing the ritual and actually smiling. "Today we have a double privilege, the honor of blessing and naming Isaac's twin sister. Ruth, can you join us?"

Beaming now, Ruth elbowed her way to the *mohel* and surrendered the baby in her arms. The bearded man took her gently and then held her up for all to see. A pink headband circled the tiny head, the bow on top matching the just-woke-up rosy cheeks. An *ahh* seemed to squeeze from the room, like the sigh of an accordion. And then the *mo-hel* prayed, "Lord of the universe, who created us both male and female, we ask your blessing on this little girl, to be called Havah, which means *life.* Help her to grow in joy and understanding of your gift of life to all people, even as she herself is a gift to her parents."

Again we all cried, "Amen!" accompanied by much applause and laughter.

And like all Jewish festivities Ruth had introduced us to, the *brit mila* was soon followed by food — lots and lots of food, spread out on the dining room table like its own deli. I sidled up alongside Yo-Yo, who was filling her plate. "Hey, Yo-Yo," I grinned. "Wasn't that a neat ceremony?"

"Yeah. I guess." Yo-Yo shrugged inside the bulky cotton sweater she was wearing over her overalls and moved to the other side of the table.

I frowned. *What was that about?* But Yo-Yo ducked out and headed for a seat, just as Ruth appeared with little Havah in her arms. Clucking ladies — clones of Ruth, I thought — gathered around, oohing and ahhing over the pretty child, passing her from

24

hand to hand. "Two minutes older than Isaac, she is," Ruth bragged.

Ben, I noticed, anchored the straight-back chair in the other room with Isaac on the lap pillow, as if daring anyone to pluck away his son.

After urging platefuls of macaroons, rug-elach, and mandelbread on everyone — "Jewish biscotti, only better," Ruth said about the latter — Ruth followed several of us Yadas as we finally headed for the bed-room to retrieve our coats piled on the bed. "So," she said, "does this count as our Yada Yada meeting? Everybody in town was here — or else up to their eyeballs in family shtick."

Yada Yada normally met on second and fourth Sundays, and this was the last week-end of the year. But she had a point. Stu's parents were still here. Avis's daughter and grandbaby were "home" for the holidays. (Avis couldn't bear the thought of Rochelle and little Conny spending Christmas at the women's shelter, where they'd been since Rochelle left her abusive husband a month ago.) Becky Wallace probably had Little Andy for the holidays, and —

"What about Chanda's birthday?" Yo-Yo piped up. "She complained that we missed her birthday last year 'cause it falls between

25

Christmas and New Year's."

"Do not worry about Chanda. She decided at the last minute to take the kids to Jamaica." Nony's cultured South African accent made it sound like the queen of England had gone abroad. "Since her sister moved back to the island, Chanda has been — how do you say it? — sick for home."

"Oh, *sí,* Jamaica!" Delores closed her eyes dreamily. "Sunshine. Tropical breezes. No ice storms . . . Can't blame her. Every Chicago winter I get homesick for Mexico."

"Yeah, me too," Yo-Yo muttered. "And I've never been out of Illinois." We all laughed.

"So, we cancel?" Ruth pushed, handing out the last of our coats.

"Uh," I stalled. "If we don't meet tomorrow, it'll be *another* two weeks before we get together — practically a whole month since our last real meeting." Didn't we all need a lot of prayer going into the New Year?

"Excuse me." My husband poked his head (swathed in the overly long scarf my mother had knit him for Christmas) into our little huddle. "I hate to state the obvious, but why don't you Yadas just meet the next week? Try first and third Sundays for a while. Half of you were complaining about meeting second Sundays anyway."

Which was true. Now that Uptown Community Church and New Morning Christian had merged, half of us Yada Yadas were in the same church, and second Sundays already had a combined church potluck and business meeting until we ironed out all the bumps in the road.

But I whacked him with my glove anyway. "Isn't it a burden to be *right* all the time, Denny Baxter?"

2

The clock said 4:30 when we got home. Ack! Stu and her parents would show up for supper in less than two hours. Did I have time to finish supper and send an e-mail to Yada Yada suggesting the new time? Not that most of us looked at our e-mail on a regular basis, especially around holidays. I'd probably have to call people so they wouldn't show up at . . . whose turn was it, anyway?

I looked at the Yada Yada list taped inside one of the kitchen cupboards. Yo-Yo's turn to host next.

What was up with Yo-Yo, anyway? I thought, opening the fridge and pulling out the lasagna spinach roll-ups I'd made earlier that day. I thought she'd be all over those babies, as close as she and her brothers were to Ben and Ruth. But she'd seemed . . . indifferent. Never once saw her hold one of the twins or even talk to Ben and Ruth, except when Ruth cornered us about our next meeting. *Weird.*

Oh well. Maybe she just felt out of place. There had been a lot of people today at the *brit mila* I didn't know either.

While the oven was heating, I called up e-mail and typed a quickie to Yada Yada saying, "It has been suggested" — didn't have to say *who* suggested — "we (a) cancel our fourth-Sunday meeting tomorrow, and (b) consider changing our meeting times to first and third Sundays to avoid schedule conflicts at Uptown–New Morning Church. That would mean we could meet NEXT week, the first weekend of the New Year."

I frowned at the message. If anybody didn't like this, *I* was the one who was going to hear about it. How did I end up being the group secretary, anyway?

I could just hear Stu answer that one: *"Because you* do *it, Jodi. If you don't want the job, just say so!"*

But as a precaution, I signed it, "Ruth, Nony, Hoshi, Delores, Yo-Yo, and Jodi," and thumped the Send key. I was pretty sure no one would complain about canceling tomorrow. And I'd let Avis, our unflappable group leader, handle the other one. After all, didn't elementary school principals have to major in Scheduling Changes Diplomacy?

By the time our front doorbell rang — *Stu must be on her best behavior,* I snickered to myself; she usually came sailing through our back door without knocking — I'd dragged Amanda off the phone long enough to set the table, Denny had buttered some garlic bread, and I'd tossed together a green salad. While Denny was greeting Stu and her parents in the front hall, I was still wondering whether to put out wineglasses. We usually splurged on wine with Italian food. But *my* parents would die if I served wine, with or without Italian food. Any kind of alcohol was *verboten* in the little Bible church I grew up in.

Better not risk it. Should've checked with Stu first.

I scurried into the living room to greet our guests. The resemblance between Stu and her father was striking. Tall. Angular face. Strong nose. "Hi, Jodi," Stu said. "You met my folks the other day, right? Lester and Luann Stuart . . . Jodi Baxter."

I smiled and stuck out my hand. "I'm so happy you guys could come for supper." *Ack! "You guys"? Why did I say that? But what am I supposed to call them? Lester and Luann? Or is that too familiar? They're Stu's* parents, *for pity's sake. Should I call them Mr. and Mrs. Stuart?*

30

Stu's mother, a sixtyish woman with short blonde hair, smiled and shook my hand. "Mrs. Baxter. You are very kind to invite us. You and your husband have been so good to Leslie . . ."

Okay. That answered that.

Mr. Stuart presented a slim bottle of red wine with a fancy label. "I hope you can use this. A small token of our appreciation."

I smiled, trying not to giggle. *And that answered that.* Oh, right. They were Lutherans. Real wine at Communion.

Stu and I left Denny to small-talk with the Stuarts while we set out the food and added wineglasses to the table. "How's it going?" I whispered, climbing on the kitchen stool to get a basket for the garlic bread.

She idly twisted a long strand of her straight blonde hair. "Pretty good, I guess . . . well, okay, kind of weird. I mean, until Thanksgiving we hadn't even talked to each other for four years! But yesterday we went to the Museum of Science and Industry and had dinner at Bubba Gumps on Navy Pier. Not too bad if we keep busy."

"Bubba Gumps! I'm jealous." We'd never been to the popular seafood restaurant named after the boat in the *Forrest Gump* movie. I struck a match, lit the green tapers nestled in some fake holly in the center of our red holiday tablecloth, and dimmed our modest chandelier. Even in the candlelight, Stu's eyes carried a sadness that the holidays only intensified. "Can you . . . you know, talk about stuff?"

She snorted. "You mean about the abortion? The grandchild they don't have? They know about it, sure — we got it all out on the table at Thanksgiving. We all cried buckets. But now it's like a big elephant standing in my living room that we're all pretending isn't there. No one wants to bring it up."

I gave Stu a squeeze. "Give it time. I'm humbled by your courage, Stu. Took guts to break the ice after so many years."

The back door opened and slammed shut, letting in a surge of frigid air. "Yo! I'm home!" Josh announced, shrugging out of his winter jacket. "What's for — oh. Hi, Stu." Josh surveyed the candlelit table. "Whassup? We got company?"

I held up a warning finger. "Read my lips," I breathed. "Stu's parents are here. Go meet them. You are not surprised. You are pleased to meet them. You speak English." I raised my voice sweetly as he meekly headed for the living room. "Call everyone to the table, will you, Josh? Your sister too."

Stu snickered. "I'll get another plate. You

forgot to set a place for him."

I rolled my eyes. "Huh. Never know when Josh will show up for dinner. We still get mail for him, so I think he still lives here." I was only half kidding.

But ten minutes later, as we passed around the lasagna roll-ups, I breathed a prayer of thanksgiving that Josh had showed up. He kept the conversation rolling with tales from the Christmas party at the Manna House women's shelter. Mrs. Stuart seemed especially interested.

"— and you should have seen the crazy decorations the kids made for the Christmas tree. Somebody donated a tree *after* Christmas, but hey. We went all out anyway. Paper chains out of magazine pages, newspaper snowflakes — even raided the kitchen for measuring spoons and tea balls. We tried to string popcorn, but most of it got eaten. Maybe ten or twelve lonely kernels got on the tree itself."

We all laughed, but I felt a twinge. *Sheesh.* I could've sent tons of colored construction paper. Why didn't he *ask?*

Stu's mother leaned forward, fork delicately held in her manicured hand. "And how did you happen to get involved in this charity, Josh?"

Josh had used the laughter to finish off a

piece of garlic bread. He chewed thought-fully. "Kind of a long story. But if you're coming to church tomorrow, you'll hear a little more. Edesa and I are recruiting volun-teers."

"Edesa?" Mrs. Stuart asked sweetly. Josh's ears turned red.

"She's in our prayer group," I put in. "Also volunteers at Manna House."

I eyed Stu across the table. *Are you going to bring your parents to church?* Uptown Community had been "an interesting expe-rience" when my parents had visited a year ago. But the Uptown–New Morning amal-gamation? We hadn't yet ironed out all the booby traps inherent in merging two churches — one mostly white, one mostly black — in an unfinished new building smack-dab in the middle of a shopping mall. That might be a stretch for a couple in their sixties from a mainstream church in Indianapolis.

Stu must have read my mind. She slipped a grin and mouthed, *"Sure. Why not?"*

"On second thought," Stu murmured to me the next morning as we surveyed the rapidly filling storefront sanctuary at the Howard Street Shopping Center, "I forgot about these awful folding chairs. My dad will be

34

squirming in no time."

New chairs were probably at the bottom of the list of things to be decided by our new congregation. "Maybe we could make a case that padded chairs are a necessary tool for shopping center evangelism," I murmured.

Stu rolled her eyes. "Ha. Good luck." She moved off to rejoin her parents. "Pastor Clark, Pastor Cobbs," I heard her say, "these are my parents, Lester and —"

"Hey, Jodi. How ya feel?" Florida Hickman peeled off her winter jacket and knit hat, shaking out the coppery corkscrew curls that nearly matched her skin. "Man, it's hot up in here."

I nodded. "Yep. Temps in the forties today. Not what you expect from a Chicago winter." Florida looked good but didn't sound like her usual high-octane self. "How was —"

"*I* wannit ta *snow.*" Nine-year-old Carla Hickman, hair done in matching corkscrews, folded her arms in a pout. "Daddy said I could build a snowman when we got us a house."

"Of *course* you want it to snow," I teased. "You're *nine.*" I'd made it through half a bumpy school year with Carla Hickman in my third-grade class at Bethune Elementary; maybe we'd make it through the rest of the year. I leaned down and whispered in her ear. "Tell you what. If it snows after school starts, we'll build a snowman in the playground, how about that?"

She cocked her head at me. "Cross your heart and hope to die?"

Might as well live recklessly. "Promise." I got a rare Carla-smile in return before she skipped off. I turned back to Florida. "So, how was Christmas in your new house?"

Florida sighed. "Decent, I guess. Carl got us a tree, tried to keep our spirits up on account of Carla and Cedric. An' it was fun havin' Becky and Little Andy with us."

Ah, yes. *Becky*. Ex-con Becky Wallace had moved out of Stu's apartment and into the Hickmans' upstairs studio back in November when she got off house arrest. Trying to make a home of her own so she could get custody of Little Andy.

"But . . ." Florida wagged her head. "My insides was all torn up, knowin' Chris is locked up at juvie." Then she brightened. "But God is good, know what I'm sayin'? Carl an' me got to go see him that evenin', an' we goin' again tonight. They don't let kids in, though. Oh, hey!" She waved across the room. "There's Nony an' Mark. Mark's lookin' good, don't ya think?" Florida made

36

a beeline for the Sisulu-Smith family.

The worship band and praise team were warming up, and Denny beckoned me to come sit down. But as I headed his way, I did a quick gander around the room to see if any other Yada Yada sisters were there . . . yep. Avis Johnson-Douglass and her husband, Peter, sat in the second row. Avis's daughter Rochelle sat beside her — a beauty, just like Avis, with that trim figure, smooth nutmeg skin, and fall of long, raven-colored, wavy hair. Two-year-old Conny was crawling all over his stepgranddaddy's lap. *Hm.* The Christmas visit must be going well.

My attention was diverted by Becky Wallace grabbing for Little Andy, who was chasing the Sisulu-Smith boys across the six-inch-high platform and dodging musicians — and I had to snicker when I saw Hoshi Takahashi, the Northwestern University student who lived with the Sisulu-Smith household, snag Marcus and Michael and march them to their parents. *Ha.* Mild-mannered Hoshi obviously didn't put up with any nonsense from her charges.

So that was Avis, Stu, me, Flo, Becky, Nony, Hoshi, and — wait a minute. Edesa Reyes just came in, getting a huge hug from our sixteen-year-old Amanda. I poked Denny. "Look. Edesa's here," I whispered.

37

Even though seven of us from Yada Yada had ended up here after the Uptown–New Morning merge, Edesa was a member of *Iglesia del Espíritu Santo* on the West Side, had been ever since she came to the States from Honduras on a student visa.

Denny nodded. "Yeah. Recruiting volunteers for Manna House, remember?"

Oh. Right. Josh had said . . . *Ack!* I twisted my head, trying to catch a glimpse of my son. *Did Josh wear those tattered jeans again?* It was one thing to sit at the back with the sound equipment and look like something that's been through a paper shredder, but to get up front —

Pastor Clark, our pastor from Uptown, and Pastor Cobbs, New Morning's pastor, both stepped onto the low platform to signal the beginning of the worship service. They made a funny pastoral team: salt and pepper, tall and short, widowed and married. And to be honest, Pastor Clark's quiet demeanor was usually no match for Pastor Cobb's vigorous style. But as Pastor Clark kept saying, *"God is doing a new thing."*

"Good morning, church!" Pastor Cobbs boomed.

"Good morning!" bounced back from all over the spacious room.

"Our hearts should be bursting with joy

38

this morning, for this week we celebrated the birth of the Christ child —"

"Thank ya, Jesus!" "Praise God!" "Hallelujah!"

The congregation was definitely awake. I fully expected the worship band and praise team to swing into a rousing gospel version of "Joy to the World!" — the usual carol to kick off the Sunday after Christmas. But Pastor Cobbs simply started to sing from somewhere deep, slowly, majestically . . .

O come, let us adore Him
O come, let us adore Him
O come, let us adore Hi-im . . .
Chri-ist the Lord.

All the instruments were still except the saxophone, rich and resonant. I forgot about Josh's jeans. I forgot about Stu's parents and whether they were squirming on our awful folding chairs. The words pulled at my heart . . .

O come, let us adore Him . . .

We sang no verses, just the chorus, again and again . . . until I longed to get down on my knees, like the shepherds of old, and just worship the Christ, Immanuel, come to live among us . . .

But I didn't. Too chicken.

3

The praise team finally wound up the time of worship with a get-down version of "Joy to the World," causing Sunday morning shoppers to peer in the windows. A few even stepped inside the door to listen, though they skittered back outside when Pastor Clark — wearing a skinny red tie that ran up and down his white shirt like a fever thermometer — stood up to welcome visitors and give announcements. "Don't forget our next business meeting and potluck on the second Sunday of the New Year —"

"What? No New Year's Eve service?" I whispered to Denny. He ignored me.

"— Also, volunteers from the Manna House women's shelter here in Chicago would like to bring an announcement. Josh? Edesa?" Pastor Clark waved them up.

I was relieved to see Josh was clad in a pair of jeans with no skin showing. Edesa, as usual, glowed like polished mahogany.

She was the first Spanish-speaking black person I'd ever met. Even with all my textbook education about the ugly slave trade on both American continents, it had somehow eluded me that African descendants peppered Central America too — until I met Edesa. Nationality: African Honduran.

But as the two of them stood up there in front of the whole church, my heart bounced back and forth between affection and anxiety. Josh, our eldest, was a recent high school graduate, with no plans — yet — to go to college; he wanted "life experience first." Edesa, three years older, had recently changed her study track to public health at UIC — and had been one of *my* Yada Yada prayer sisters ever since God threw the twelve of us together at that Chicago Women's Conference a year and a half ago.

Josh and Edesa. Everywhere I turned lately, they were doing some kind of youth group thing together. They'd helped chaperone a group of Uptown teens at the Cornerstone Music Festival last summer. Taken kids to Six Flags Great America. (Huh! In *my* book, nineteen-year-old Josh was still two hairs shy of being an adult.) Now they were volunteering at a homeless women's shelter, of all things!

Josh, of course, admired Edesa. Who didn't? The Honduran student was a vibrant young woman — one of the sweetest I'd ever met. Thoughtful. Caring. Like a daughter to Delores Enriquez and her brood. Still, I nearly swallowed my tongue when, in a rare moment of vulnerability, my son had told me, *"Mom. I . . . love . . . Edesa Reyes."* And in an even rarer moment of motherly grace, I'd actually asked, *"Have you told her?"*

No. She'd never encouraged him that way, he said. They were "just friends."

Right.

"Buenos días, church!" Edesa's bright yellow sweater and yellow cloth headband added sunshine to the rather gray day outside. "I bring you greetings from *Iglesia del Espíritu Santo,* my home church on the West Side. I am delighted to be with you this morning — and I see many familiar faces here." She winked at Little Andy, who hid his face and giggled.

Josh picked it up. "Edesa and I are volunteers at Manna House, a women's shelter in Chicago, less than a year old." He sketched the beginnings of the shelter, "home" to two dozen women with children, more or less, who were homeless or — in some cases — victims of domestic abuse who needed a

42

place of safety.

"Right now," Edesa said, "we have only one full-time paid staff member — our director. Our office manager is part-time. We desperately need more volunteers — especially on the weekends, to give the staff a break — including those who would be willing to spend one or two nights simply being *un amigo* to the women, doing activities with the *niños,* and simply being a 'presence.' " She smiled at the gaggle of kids on the front row. "But maybe the best thing would be to hear from one of the current residents."

Who? Rochelle? Only a few people here knew Rochelle was a "current resident" at Manna House. Wouldn't it be risky to go public? She didn't want Dexter to find her. Besides, I thought Rochelle was still so mad at Peter "You're Not My Dad" Douglass for sending her to a shelter when she showed up at their apartment a third time, I couldn't imagine she'd plug Manna House — not in front of her mom's new husband!

But Rochelle didn't move. Instead, Edesa took a letter from her pocket, unfolded it and began to read. *"To whom it may concern: To tell the truth, I never imagined that I would end up in a women's shelter. But I never imagined I'd be afraid of my husband either, so here I am . . ."*

Did Rochelle write the letter? Sounded like her story. She whispered something to Conny, as if not paying attention. Avis's eyes were closed, her lips moving soundlessly. Praying, no doubt.

"The shelter isn't much," Edesa read on. *"The space could use a lot of sprucing up."* Josh rolled his eyes in agreement; the kids on the front row giggled. *"But I'm so grateful the staff and volunteers have been there for me and my baby. They've loved on us, accepted us, given us legal help, and been a safe haven when we needed it most. Of course, we don't want to stay here forever! But for now, we are blessed. And if you can do anything to keep the shelter going, I know you will be blessed too."* Edesa looked up. "Signed by one of our residents."

The congregation clapped spontaneously. When the noise died down, Josh said, "Uh, I think that speaks for itself. We're hoping to get enough volunteers so your time would only be one weekend per month. So . . . if you have any questions, please talk to us after the service. We can give more details at that time."

Before Josh and Edesa went back to their seats, both Pastor Clark and Pastor Cobbs laid hands on them and prayed for this new shelter. I noticed Denny fishing in his pants pocket for a handkerchief and blowing his nose.

When the prayer was over, Josh and Edesa finally left the platform — and then suddenly Josh turned back. "As long as I have the floor —"

My head jerked up. *Uh-oh.* What was my unpredictable son going to do *now?*

"— we've had a tradition at Uptown Community on New Year's Day —"

Oh no. He's not going to bring that up in the middle of a worship service!

"— a Polar Bear Swim down at Loyola Beach. I know we're a 'new' church now, and all the old things are on the shelf till we get things decided, but, hey, just wanted to invite anyone, especially the teens and anyone young at heart —"

Oh, brother. He's actually inviting people to that crazy Polar Bear Swim right here in the middle of worship! And Stu's parents are visiting too! I saw a few New Morning adults shaking their heads. *Ack! What are people thinking!*

"— noon sharp, 'cause I know everybody's gonna stay up late the night before seeing the New Year in. So —" Whatever Josh said after that was drowned out by the whoops and enthusiastic catcalls of several teen-

45

agers, both black and white.

I was afraid to look at Pastor Cobbs's face. I mean, there was nothing remotely *spiritual* about a Polar Bear Swim! And we were the newbies in this church — after all, we *were* meeting in New Morning's new space, and —

Beside me, I felt Denny shaking. I looked at him, startled.

My husband had his head down, laughing silently.

"What you so uptight for, girl?" Florida rolled her eyes at me after church as we walked away from the coffee table, Styrofoam cups of hot, black liquid in our hands. "Thought you was gonna turn into a frog, the way your eyes bugged out when Josh did that Polar Bear thang." She grinned at me unsympathetically.

"I know, I know," I moaned. "It's just that . . ."

Just what, Jodi Baxter? said the Voice in my spirit. *Worried about what people will think? Hm, haven't we been there before, you and Me?*

Well, yeah, but —

And what's "unspiritual" about the Polar Bear Swim? After all, Scripture says, "Do all things to the glory of God."

46

Well, yeah, but —

Stop worrying about what people will think, Jodi, and start looking for the possibilities. Like your son.

Like my son. I looked around until I saw Josh — in the middle of a knot of kids, laughing and talking. Huh. I doubted they were signing up to be volunteers at Manna House. But just then I saw Pastor Cobbs thread his way through the mob of youthful bodies and shake Josh's hand. Josh's face lit up. Even from where I was standing, I heard him say, "That'd be great! Wow."

Nanoseconds later, Amanda, butterscotch hair falling out of a butterfly clip perched on the back of her head, bounced over to me. "Hey, Mom. Guess what? Pastor Cobb thinks the Polar Bear Swim thing is great. He encouraged all of us kids to invite other teenagers, then bring them back here to the church for hot chocolate and music and stuff. Cool, huh?" She bounced off. Amanda rarely waited for an actual dialogue.

I closed my eyes and shook my head. *Sheesh.* When was I ever going to learn that God was a whole lot bigger than me and all my ought-tos and fear factors and what-ifs? Was God giving me a word for the New Year?

Look for the possibilities, Jodi . . .

4

So once again I found myself standing on the beach on New Year's Day along with Stu, filling cups of hot chocolate for the shivering teenagers who had just come up out of the water after their mad dash into — and out of — Lake Michigan. The lake, which hugged the long eastern shore of Chicago like a wet, soggy blanket, rolled in unhindered. No ice this year; it'd been too warm. Not that I felt warm, standing on a beach in forty-degree weather, hunched inside my winter jacket, wishing I'd worn a sweatshirt underneath to cut the wind.

Clad in dry sweats over wet bathing suits, the teenagers piled into an assortment of minivans and cars and Uptown's old fifteen-passenger van, driven by — bless him — a beaming Pastor Clark. I waved good-bye as the cars headed back to our shopping center church, glad that Pastor Cobb, Pastor Clark, and Rick Reilly — Uptown's youth group leader before the merge — were going to take it from there.

"And that's that," Stu said, loading the two big Igloo coolers we'd lugged down to the beach. "Quite a few kids I'd never seen before. Our kids must have invited them . . ." She looked at me sideways. "Or was that the whole idea all along?"

"Maybe." I climbed into the passenger seat of her silver Celica, blowing on my hands, and waited for her to get in. "All I know is Pastor Cobbs jumped on the idea and saw it as a youth outreach . . . Turn on the heat, will ya?"

"Who's doing the food back at the church?" Stu steered the car up Sheridan Road until we came to Lunt Avenue, our street.

I shrugged inside my jacket. "Dunno. Rose Cobbs got on it" — I still wasn't used to calling her First Lady Cobbs, the term of respect New Morning members gave to their pastor's wife — "and asked somebody to do it. Say, did you get any feedback from your folks about their visit to our nameless church? Sheesh. Hope we do something about that soon. Can't keep calling it 'Uptown–New Morning' forever."

"Ha." Stu pulled into the alley behind our two-flat, hit the garage door opener, and drove in. "I think my folks were a little shell-shocked. You've gotta admit, we're not exactly a liturgical church."

We headed for the house through our tiny backyard, and parted as Stu turned up the back steps to her apartment. "Hey," she called back, "has anyone heard from Chanda? Are she and the kids back from Jamaica yet?"

I blinked. "Ack! Chanda! . . . No, I haven't heard if she's back, but school starts on Monday, so she's gotta get home this weekend. But it was her birthday yesterday — New Year's Eve, remember? She was complaining it never got celebrated because of all the holidays. We gotta do something for her at Yada Yada this weekend."

"Piece of cake — pun intended." Stu laughed. "I'll make a cake. I think we should give Becky's lopsided creations a rest, don't you think? And you do your meaning-of-the-name thing, Jodi. Think you can dig up a meaning for Chanda?"

I made a face and unlocked our back door. Willie Wonka was whining on the other side. "Huh. It's not exactly 'Sue' or 'Mary,' but I'll give it a go. Oughta be interesting . . . okay, okay, Wonka. Come on out. Go pee. But hurry it up, will ya?"

As if the poor deaf dog could hear a thing

I said.

"Ah, the miracle of the Internet," I murmured, staring at the computer screen. I'd been trying for an hour to find the meaning of Chanda's name — putting off the job of taking down the Christmas tree, the major chore on my to-do list the Saturday after New Year's Day — but kept running into dead ends. It wasn't listed in any of the usual "Baby Name" sites; searching Jamaican names turned up nothing; ditto African-American. Finally, I'd just Googled "Chanda . . . name . . . meaning" . . . and there it was.

"CHANDA. Hindi, meaning 'dignified.' "

From the Hindi language? *Huh. Wonder where her Jamaican parents got* that *from?* I couldn't help smiling. Dear, funny, fussy Chanda was a lot of things, but "dignified" didn't come to mind. On the other hand, it was amazing the significance God seemed to squeeze from the meaning of our names —

"Mom?" Josh's voice behind me interrupted my thoughts. "You got a minute?"

"Sure." I suppressed a smile. My nineteen-year-old actually wanted to *talk* to me? I had sixty minutes!

Josh, dressed in a rumpled T-shirt and

sweatpants that had seen better days, sprawled into a dining room chair. He ran a hand over his tousled hair. "Well, we didn't get that many volunteers last Sunday at church . . . three, I think. A girl — well, young woman — named Karen somebody, and Mr. and Mrs. Meeks."

"Debra and Sherman Meeks? I mean, aren't they too old? Sherman's got asthma; he has to use an inhaler."

"Mom." Josh dialed up his patient voice. "Young, old — age doesn't matter. Anybody can volunteer if they've got the right heart. Which is why I wanted to talk to you. Edesa's going to ask again at your Yada Yada meeting tomorrow night, but I thought, if *you* volunteered, maybe some of the other Yadas would too. You gotta pass a background check, but no sweat." He must have seen my eyes widen, because he threw up his hands. "Only one weekend a month, I promise! You can bring your own sheets and pillow if you like."

If I *liked?* It hadn't even occurred to me to volunteer. I was blithely assuming others would, single people probably, without family responsibilities, without —

Think of the possibilities, Jodi.

The phone was ringing. "Uh . . . let me think about it, Josh. Okay?"

52

"Sure!" Josh unwound his body and hopped off the chair like a human Slinky. "Thanks, Mom." He grabbed the kitchen phone. "Baxters . . . Yeah, she's here." He handed me the receiver and headed for the refrigerator.

"Hello, this is —"

"Sista Jodee, is dat you? We back from Jamaica! Mi mama *so* happy to see de t'ree kids — first time to see de girls! An' dey got to play wit all dey cousins, an' swim in de ocean, an' milk a goat. Yah, a goat for true . . ."

Chanda giggled, giving me an opening. "So glad you had a good trip, Chanda. We're all jealous, you know! But we missed you. Hey . . . are you coming to Yada Yada tomorrow? It's Yo-Yo's turn to host." If we were going to do this birthday thing, it'd be handy to know if she'd be there.

"Oh, *yah mon.* Such a good time we had. Got mi a nice tan too." She giggled again. "*Irie, mon!* Yah, mi be dere." And the phone went dead.

I blinked, still holding the receiver. Why in the world did Chanda want a tan? She was already brown! And was it my imagination, or had her Jamaican *patois* thickened up like chicken gravy?

■ ■ ■ ■

It snowed six inches that night, burying the Christmas tree we'd dragged out to the curb the day before. Our first real snow of the winter. But salt trucks and snowplows had cleared most of the major streets by the time Stu and I headed for Yo-Yo's apartment Sunday evening in her Celica. Stu cautiously navigated the slick side streets, while I balanced the cake carrier. We'd be lucky to get her three-layer red velvet cake there still layered.

"Sorry." Stu grimaced. "If I'd known it was going to snow, I'd have made brownies or something."

But somehow the two of us and the cake made it in one piece, and so did most everyone else. Everyone except Ruth.

"Aw," Chanda pouted, shrugging off her winter coat and boots and twirling to show off a bright turquoise-print Jamaican dress, which she filled out. "Mi wanted to see dem babies. What are dey — six weeks? Dey must be so big now!"

"Shoulda met at your house, then," Yo-Yo muttered. "Mine's probably not clean enough."

She was kidding, right? I tried to read her

face with no luck. But Adele Skuggs, who styled funky cuts on everybody else at Adele's Hair and Nails, shook her short, no frills, black-and-silver afro. "Don't think we'll see Ruth for a while — an' clean ain't got nothin' to do with it, Yo-Yo Spencer. MaDear always said, 'Got one, you on the run; got two, you make do; got three, there you be.' An' if you ask me, two at the same time probably *feels* like three."

"She should just leave 'em with Ben," Stu said. "He's the daddy. He can take a turn."

Adele snorted. "Yeah, right."

We all laughed. Yeah, it was a bit of a stretch imagining white-haired Ben Garfield juggling both babies by himself all evening.

By that time, we'd all found something resembling a place to sit — on Yo-Yo's salvaged-from-the-alley couch, a few mismatched table chairs, and the floor. But our first meeting of the New Year felt more like a party than a prayer meeting. Even Avis and Nony and Florida, all struggling with huge family challenges, just seemed glad to be there, their burdens a bit lighter in the company of sisters who knew and still cared. And, well, it *was* a party. We surprised Chanda with the red velvet cake, Adele had picked up a mixed bouquet of cut flowers, and I presented Chanda with the birthday

55

card we'd all been secretly signing as people dribbled in.

Chanda beamed — until we cut the cake. "Dat cake! Why she so *red?*" Her eyes rounded, as if suspecting someone had bled into it. But Stu cut a huge bite from the slice on Chanda's paper plate and teased her into opening her mouth. And then . . . *"Mmm."* Chanda's eyes rolled back in blissful delight at the velvety chocolate taste.

Four enormous bites later, she handed her plate to Stu for a second slice and opened the card. I'd used a sheet of pale gold vellum and a pretty script font, trying to find something that expressed "dignified." But as she read silently, tiny frown lines pinched between her brows. She looked up. "Dis no joke? Me name mean 'dignified'?"

I nodded. "I looked for a name spelled C-H-A-N-D-A. It's Hindi."

"Hindi! What's dat?"

"India's official language — or one of them."

The frown deepened. "Oh." A pause. "Guess dat explains it."

Now I was surprised. I'd expected her to protest that she wasn't from India, that there had to be a mistake. But now we all looked at her, curious. "Explains what?" I blurted.

Chanda shrugged. "De mon from India, dey like Jamaica. One mon come, soon all de brothers and cousins come too. *Yah, mon.* All de family. Own all de jewelry stores, all de shops for tourists in town. Some peoples tink dey take all de jobs. But me mama, she 'ave a good friend . . ." Another shrug. "We kids called her Missus Siddhu. But mi tink Mama maybe name mi after she friend."

"Read the inside," I urged. I'd found a perfect quotation about *dignity* in *Bartlett's Quotations* and was feeling smug.

No race can prosper till it learns
That there is as much dignity
In tilling a field
As in writing a poem.
— Booker T. Washington

I thought Chanda would be pleased, but her lip quivered. "You just making fun of mi. Mi know what you tink — Chanda some kind of fool, get rich quick, just a cleaning woman dressed in fancy clothes."

I started to protest, but Avis got up quickly, moved behind Chanda, resting both hands on her round shoulders, and began to pray. "Lord, Your Word says that You created us in *Your image.* That means Chanda has the stamp of God on her life, giving her

57

a dignity that no one can take away from her. Help her to see herself as You see her, Lord — beautiful, dignified, worthy, noble, Your highest creation!"

Nony carried the prayer. "Yes, yes! And this is a special birthday, Father, because the breast cancer was found early and You have given our dear sister another year of life! — to praise You, serve You, and be a blessing to all of us, her sisters and her friends. Help her to hold her head up high, with dignity, for she is Your daughter, Your child, Your precious creation."

This was followed by a chorus of "Amen!" "Hallelujah!" and "Thank ya, Jesus!"

Chanda said nothing. But her eyes glistened as she fished in her bag for a tissue and blew her nose.

Resuming her seat, Avis said, "As long as we're praying, do we have other prayer requests? What about your boy, Florida? Has he had a hearing yet?"

Florida's forehead puckered. "Some good news. Peter Douglass — Carl works for Avis's husband, ya know — found a good defense lawyer who's gonna represent Chris pro bono. Says he believes Chris's story, that he just caught a ride with those gang-bangers, didn't know nothin' about the robbery that was gonna go down. Smucker's the name." She rolled her eyes. "At least I ain't gonna forget his name."

The rest of us snickered. We weren't going to forget it either.

"But what's next?" Yo-Yo asked. "Chris had a prelim yet?"

Florida shook her head. "That's comin' up. But what worries me is, the perp that robbed that 7-Eleven was eighteen, is bein' charged as an adult. The state's attorney is hot to charge *all* those boys as adults, rather than juveniles." Tears collected, threatening to spill. "Chris only fourteen! If they find him guilty under that accountability law an' he goes to prison . . . oh, Jesus!" She buried her face in her hands.

"Uh . . ." Becky Wallace, our other ex-con, cleared her throat. "I'm not so good at prayin' out loud, but I'd like to pray for Chris." And she did, stumbling here and there, but asking God plain and simple to keep Florida's boy in the juvie system.

I thought we were going to close our prayer time, but Edesa waved her hand. "Sisters, Manna House needs our prayers. Not only prayers, it needs warm bodies — several more volunteers willing to give a day or two every month." She lowered her dark lashes a moment and leaned forward, clasping her hands. "I — I don't want to put pressure on anyone, but I'd like to ask if any of you would be willing to volunteer."

Ack. There it was again. I could hear Josh's voice in my ear. *"Mom, if you volunteered, maybe some of the other Yadas would too."* I looked around the room. *I don't need to go first — maybe several others will volunteer and that will be enough.* My eyes alighted on Avis. *Like Avis. Good grief, why not? She's got a daughter at the shelter, for heaven's sake!*

As if my thoughts had appeared on my forehead in an LED readout, Avis spoke up. "I've given it a lot of thought, since my own daughter and grandson are at Manna House. But to tell you the truth, I think that's why I *shouldn't* volunteer. It puts both Rochelle and me in an awkward position — and things are awkward enough. Maybe there is some other way I can help."

Becky Wallace waved her hand. "I'd like to volunteer. Could do it Saturday — Bagel Bakery's closed for Shabbat. But not Sunday. That's the day I get Little Andy."

"I dunno, Becky," Yo-Yo said. "You're still on parole. Might not go over so good with your PO. Better check it out."

The room was quiet. I knew Delores worked weekend shifts at the county hospital . . . Chanda had little kids at home . . .

Nony's husband still needed nursing care . . . Saturday was the busiest day at Adele's Hair and Nails . . . even Stu had DCFS visits to make on the weekends . . .

That pretty much left me.

Think of the possibilities, Jodi.

The Voice within my spirit was surprisingly gentle. Beckoning. As if this wasn't something I *ought* to do, but a privilege, an adventure. The next step in the God-journey I was on — though I had to admit it felt more like a roller coaster than a mere step.

But I raised my hand. "Um, Edesa? I'd like to volunteer . . . I think."

5

Winter vacation slam-dunked to a finish by dropping temperatures to a mere five degrees Sunday night, and the ever-cheerful weather guy said Chicago could expect more snow and below-freezing temps all week. As I spooned hot oatmeal into bowls for the Baxter crew Monday morning, I batted my eyelashes at Denny. "Any chance I can get a ride to school on your way?" If flirting didn't work, I could always use the rod in my leg — left over from my car accident a year and a half ago — as an excuse.

"Me, too, Dad." Amanda flopped into a dining room chair, dropping her book bag on the floor. "It's *murder* out there. Wonka told me so, didn't ya, baby?" She scratched Willie Wonka's rump before dumping a mountain of brown sugar on her oatmeal.

"Hey!" Denny said, grabbing the sugar bowl.

Good, I thought. About time Denny did

some of the nagging.

". . . Leave some for me!" he finished, matching her brown-sugar mountain granule for granule. I rolled my eyes. They were both hopeless.

Gulping his oatmeal, Denny glanced at his watch. As the new athletic director at West Rogers High School, he didn't like to be late. I knew dropping me off at Bethune Elementary a few blocks away was one thing; but Lane Tech College Prep was at least two or three miles out of his way — in rush-hour traffic on slick roads. But leave his little princess standing at a bus stop in weather like this? *Ha.* "Okay," he said. "Everybody in the car in three minutes."

So I got to school forty-five minutes early. Not a bad thing. I had time to organize my lessons for the day, hunt up chalk and erasers, which had somehow disappeared over Christmas vacation, and best of all, walk up and down the rows of desks, praying for my third-grade students by name.

The laminated names taped to each desk were a little dog-eared but still readable. "Lord, bless Abrianna this semester. Help me encourage her when she wants to give up, when she thinks she can't do it . . . and Caleb. Oh, Lord, he's so bright! But he needs a little humility too. The other kids tend to avoid him because of his bragging. I think he's lonely . . . Thank You for Mercedes, God. She is Your special creation, even though the kids tease her because of her weight. I've seen Big Mama, too, so it's no surprise . . . and Carla, Lord. That little girl's been through so much! Now her big brother's been arrested. When she lashes out, help me to remember that she's scared . . ."

Because of the cold weather, the kids lined up in the gym instead of on the playground when the bell rang. Carla was first in line, the pink fur of her jacket hood framing her dark eyes and creamy brown face. "Miz Baxter?" She tugged on my sweater. "Miz Baxter!"

Two boys started pushing at the back of the line, and the kids were standing so close to each other I was afraid they'd all go down like dominoes. "Lamar! Demetrius! Stop that! — not now, Carla."

By the time I'd herded the kids into our room, marshaled coats, boots, and mittens into the general vicinity of the coat pegs, and collected the take-home folders, I'd totally forgotten Carla's question. But she obviously hadn't. She appeared beside my desk, jiggling impatiently, but I held up my hand, palm out, as the office intercom came on and a fifth grader led the whole school — remotely — in the Pledge of Allegiance.

"— withlibertyan'justiceforall," Carla gushed. "Miz Baxter?"

"*What,* Carla?"

"You said if it snowed, we could build a snowman." She pointed a finger at the bank of windows running along the classroom wall, a miniature prosecutor pointing out the culprit in the courtroom.

"Oh, Carla." I had, hadn't I. What was I *thinking?!* I walked over to the windows, ignoring the noise level rising around me. The six inches of snow that fell on Sunday had been trampled Monday morning by the diehards who had started off "back to school" with a rousing snowball fight. "I don't know, honey . . . the playground is pretty much a mess."

Carla's eyes narrowed. "But you *promised.* Crossed your heart and hoped to die."

Right. I glanced at the thermometer outside the window. Nudging slowly upward, a whopping fifteen degrees now. Maybe we'd get more snow by the end of the day . . .

I leaned close to Carla's ear. "All right," I whispered. "We can try. But don't say anything to the other children, or the deal's off." Mention snowman making and I'd be nagged to death by short people all day.

At lunchtime, Carla blocked my way, arms folded, giving me The Look. I shook my head, stalling. What should I do? Keep Carla after school? Wait until the other kids had gone home?

My slower readers were parked on the Story Rug after lunch, plowing in jerks and starts through *Charlotte's Web,* when Carla yelled from her desk, "Look!" The telltale finger pointed toward the windows. A curtain of powdered-sugar snow sifted past the glass. "*Now* we can make a snowman!" she announced.

An immediate stampede to the windows ensued. "Yea!"

I took a deep breath and glanced at the clock. Two-ten. If I took my class outside to build snowmen before the last bell, other classes would probably hear them and mutiny. Even if I wasn't censured for ignoring the no-early-dismissal policy, the other teachers would be mad. But I couldn't keep all the children after school. After-school childcare buses would be waiting; parents would show up, impatient to drag their progeny off to violin lessons or ice hockey.

But I was reluctant to extinguish the eager anticipation shining in the eyes of the kids. Here in the city, how many of them had ever built a snowman? If we just plowed on with our reading lesson, this day would simply melt into the pool of all the other school days. But if we built a snowman, we'd create a childhood memory that might linger for years. A memory like . . .

I was in third grade, chewing on my pencil and trying to do my sheet of division problems, when my teacher tapped me on the shoulder. "Your father is here." I looked up, startled. Was something wrong? But he stood in the doorway, hat in hand, smiling. I grabbed my lunch box and followed him to the car; my two brothers were already slouched in the back-seat. What was going on? They shrugged. Daddy was mum. Didn't say a thing. Just drove to the Veterans Memorial Auditorium in Des Moines, surrounded by enormous bill-boards shouting, "CIRCUS!" with pictures of gold-and-black tigers jumping through flaming hoops and clowns in whiteface and bushy red hair.

It was one of those magic memories of child-hood. Funny thing is, I don't remember much about the circus. What still makes me giggle is that Daddy took us out of school *just to have fun . . .*

"Everybody! Come to my desk. No talking." Wide-eyed, the children crowded around my desk. I'd never called them to come around my desk, all at the same time.

Something was up and they knew it. I lowered my voice and we made plans. Wait another twenty minutes. Then *quietly* get on our coats and boots. *Silently* tiptoe down the hall and out to the playground, like mice creeping past a big cat. By then, I figured, there would only be ten minutes before the bell rang. By the time the other students or teachers heard us, it'd hardly be worth complaining about.

By three-ten, three lopsided snowmen stood in the school playground. Two were sightless, since we only found two small rocks to use for eyes. One had a branch sticking out of its side for an "arm." But all three wore brightly colored knit caps and scarves, donated by junior Good Samaritans who insisted the snowmen needed *something.* I'd have to rescue the hats and scarves before leaving the school grounds, but for now . . .

"They *bee-yoo-tee-ful,*" Carla breathed. She was the last kid to leave.

I grinned. "Yep. But off you go. Cedric picking you up?"

She shook her head. "Nah. I walk by myself. Mama be home soon." Her eyes lit up. "Maybe now Daddy help Cedric an' me build *another* snowman at home! We got us a backyard now, you know." She ran off, her backpack bumping on her rump like a loose saddle.

I stopped in at the school office, took off my gloves, and knocked on Avis's inner office door, which was slightly ajar. She was on the phone, dressed in black slacks, white silk blouse, and black-and-white costume jewelry, dark hair neatly wound into a French roll. She held up a finger to wait. I loitered by the bulletin board in the main office, reading the school lunch menu for January: chicken tenders with muffin, cheese or pepperoni pizza slice, peanut-butter sandwich with fruit cup, turkey hot dog on bun . . . until I heard her say, "All right . . . Thursday. Yes . . . me too. Bye."

I slipped into her office and closed the door, unzipping my down jacket. "I'm here to confess before you get a complaint."

She put down the phone and glanced in my direction.

"I took my class outside ten minutes before the last bell and we built snowmen. Guilty as charged." I grinned, fishing a tissue from my jacket pocket and swiping my still-icy nose. "Call it outdoor education."

"Jodi Baxter," she snapped. "What *are* you talking about?"

"Uh . . . snowmen." Her tone of voice caught me completely off guard. I thought

Avis would be my ally in this minor flouting of school dismissal policy. "Took my kids outside before dismissal and . . ."

Her eyes wandered. I could tell I'd lost the connection. She was frowning at the phone. *Sheesh, Jodi.* I felt like slapping myself upside the head. I'd just blundered into her office, didn't even ask if it was a good time — and now that I thought about it, her last few words on the phone had sounded personal.

"Sorry, Avis. Uh . . . are you okay? Is something wrong?"

Avis sighed and sank down into her desk chair. "Yes. Maybe . . . I don't know, Jodi." She propped her elbows on the arms of the high-backed desk chair and pressed the tips of her fingers against her temples. "That was Rochelle . . ."

I waited.

She finally looked up at me and shook her head. "Just when I think God's answering our prayers, we get blindsided from a different direction."

This sounded like *Are-you-sitting-down?* news. I pulled up a cushioned chair.

"Manna House routinely asks residents to get HIV testing. No big deal. We knew that." Avis blew out another breath. Her voice

70

dropped to a whisper. "Rochelle's came back positive."

6

"*Positive!* But . . . I mean, how could . . ." I stopped, embarrassed. But my mind churned. Dexter was the one who'd been running around on his wife. Nobody would be surprised if *he* turned up HIV-positive. But sweet Rochelle? "Is that for sure?" I finished lamely. "I mean, isn't there such a thing as a false positive?"

Avis shrugged. "We can hope. Rochelle insists it's impossible, says she's never been unfaithful to Dexter. She's going back for a retest on Thursday. Wants me to go with her — though I'm not sure why. She won't get the results for another week." She smiled weakly. "But at this point, it's enough that she *wants* me to go."

"Oh, Avis." I could hardly imagine hearing that kind of news about my daughter. People with HIV were at risk for AIDS, and people with AIDS often died a terrible, lingering death. I suddenly felt like throwing up.

Avis took a deep breath, as if collecting herself. "So . . . what's this about a snowman?"

I snorted. "Nothing." Which was the truth. Here today, gone tomorrow. I reached for her hand across the desk; she put both of hers in mine. What could I say? If she were in my shoes, Avis would probably offer a comforting scripture or pray. But what did one pray in a situation like this? *Oh Lord, make it go away! Heal Rochelle! We know You're going to do it!* . . . I couldn't. The words seemed hollow. Dishonest. A cliché. I didn't know what God would do.

So all I offered was a whisper. "Oh Jesus. Help us." She squeezed my hands.

The snowmen met a violent death sometime before the first bell. Stomped on. Kicked to smithereens. Anger boiled in my gut as I surveyed the damage from my classroom window. "What kind of deranged person would destroy a kid's *snowman?*" I muttered.

Huh. I sounded like my mother. Mom Jennings just couldn't understand anyone who would talk back to a teacher or drop a candy wrapper on the ground, much less bump off a snowman. Her world was populated by hardworking men, dutiful women, and polite children — or she thought it ought to be.

I traced a frowny face in the fog on the window. No wonder I'd had such a hard time owning the fact that I was "just a sinner," like everyone else. Funny thing, it was such a relief not to be perfect. To know I could mess up and still be forgiven. To begin to understand what *grace* was all about. Yep. Jodi "Good Girl" Baxter had ugly thoughts, did things she regretted, didn't do things she should —

Ack! My hand flew to my mouth; I peered out the foggy window. Not only had the snowmen disappeared, but the hats and scarves they'd been wearing had too! I'd totally forgotten to bring them in before going home last night. *Blip,* right off my radar screen. And it was starting to snow again . . .

I pulled on the jacket and boots I'd just taken off and ran out to the playground. Most of the early birds were heading for the warm gym. But Bowie Garcia and Lamar Pearson stood looking at the lumps of snow that used to be snowmen, muttering dark threats. "Man, I find out who kicked our snowmen, I'm gonna pop 'em," Bowie said. He made his gloved hand into a pistol.

"Pow! Pow!"

My own anger turned to alarm. But now wasn't the time to talk about "disproportionate response" — though, hm, it might be a good life lesson for my third graders. *"Snowmen can be remade; people can't."* Right now, my own forgetfulness was getting buried deeper in new snow.

Several of my other third graders appeared on the playground. "Oh no!" "Who did that?" Followed by a few nasty expletives they probably heard at home.

"Sorry about the snowmen, kids," I said. "But with this good snow, we'll be able to make bigger and better ones, whaddya say?" Their scowls slowly turned to grins. "But tell you what, how about a contest? Whoever finds one of those hats or scarves in the snow gets a bag of Skittles. For each one!"

We found two hats and one scarf buried in the snow and I was out three bags of Skittles. The lost scarf belonged to Mercedes LaLuz and she shrieked. "My mama said she gonna *kill* me if I lose another scarf!" Which hopefully was an overstatement. But to placate the situation, I brought in the handmade knit scarf my mother had made me and gave it to Mercedes the next morning.

Josh and Amanda thought the whole episode was hilarious. "I'll donate *my* scarf to your next snowman," Josh said, faking a straight face. "My sacrifice to a good cause." *Yeah, right.* He had yet to wear the overly long and rather garish scarf his grandmother had crocheted for *him.*

Ruth Garfield, on the other hand, was full of advice. She called midweek to ask how the first week back at school was going. With the phone cradled between my shoulder and ear, I moaned about the vandalized snowmen in the schoolyard while trying to fry up some hamburger and peel potatoes for a Baxter version of shepherd's pie.

"Vandals? A lesson from us you should take. Havah and Isaac's snowman —"

"*Havah and Isaac's* snowman?" I snickered so hard the phone lost its precarious perch and crashed to the floor. I snatched it up. "Oops. Sorry. Ruth, *what* are you talking about? Havah and Isaac are . . . what? Six weeks old? You didn't take them outside to —"

"Six-and-a-half. Very bright they are too. Looking around, taking in everything. Ben decides to make a snowman so the twins can see it from the front window —"

"*Ben* made a snowman? Ben 'I'm-Too-Old-to-Have-Kids' Garfield?" Now I was

76

laughing out loud.

"What are you, my echo? Don't be a *shmo*. I'm trying to help you, Jodi Baxter. Ben knew the little *nudniks* on our block would knock over anything in the front yard, so he sprayed the snowman with the garden sprayer. Froze solid overnight. Any juvenile delinquent who tries to kick down *that* snowman is going home with a broken toe."

"Love it!" I hooted. I had visions of young thugs hopping around the schoolyard bawling like branded calves. But my ecstasy was short-lived. "On second thought, if we did that, the school would probably get sued for erecting 'dangerous structures' on public property."

"Humph," Ruth sniffed. "You could always melt the evidence — wait a minute."

In the background, I heard Ben yelling. A minute later, Ruth was back. "Blind as a bat, he is! Turning everything upside down looking for a pacifier. I show him, there it is, pinned right to Isaac's sleeper. Does he say thanks? No. Tells me, why don't you put it somewhere I can find it? Such a klutz."

"Uh-huh." I dumped the peeled potatoes into a pot of water and turned on the gas burner. Ruth plunged on, though she lowered her voice.

"But here's the good news. 'Ben,' I say, 'I

want to go to Beth Yehudah services on Saturday.' So Ben considers. I see his brain working. If I go by myself, he's stuck with the twins all morning. If I *take* the twins, he'll worry I can't manage car, car seats, baby carriers, diaper bags all by myself. So he says, 'All right, all right, I'll drive you.' " I could hear the chuckle in her voice. "Once we get there, he'll have to help me take the baby carriers inside, and once he's in-side . . ."

"Ruth! You're shameless!" But I laughed. The good people at Ruth's Messianic Jew-ish congregation would fall all over them-selves, oohing and ahhing over the twins. A good number had been at Isaac's *brit mila* and baby naming. Proud daddy Ben would eat it up and hang around, not wanting to miss a minute of adoration. "Well, that's one way to get Ben Garfield to church."

She sighed. "He might go to church more often if he could hang out with Denny or Peter Douglass or Carl Hickman or Mark Smith. He respects all those guys . . . wait a minute. All those Yada Yada husbands ended up at Uptown when it merged with Mark and Nony's church, didn't they! Maybe we ought to come visit you some Sunday . . ."

"That'd be great, Ruth! Just don't call it Uptown anymore. We're meeting in New

Morning's new space, which makes it kind of awkward. Guess we need a new name in a hurry. We have a business meeting this Sunday to talk about it."

"Yachad," she said. An infant started wailing in the background.

"What?"

"Yachad! A good name for your church."

"Yachad? What kind of name is that? What does it mean?"

The wailing was now a duet and rising in intensity.

"Yachad. It's Hebrew. Look it up — sorry. Feeding time. Talk to you later!"

It was Saturday before I had time to "look it up," as Ruth ordered.

Almost a foot of snow fell that week, and my class and I tried to build some new snowmen during Thursday lunchtime. Kids from other classes joined us, which is probably why the new snowmen lasted *two* days. *Snowmen* was a bit of a misnomer, though; the hapless creations looked more like "snow bumps with eyes." This time I donated the black and red checkers from our old checkerboard at home for eyes, along with a bag of carrots from the Rogers Park Fruit Market for noses. Even bought a disposable camera and shot the whole roll.

I dipped into the school office Thursday afternoon to update Avis on Bethune Elementary's snowman project, but her inner office was dark. "Oh, Mrs. Douglass left at one o'clock," Ms. Ivy offered, fiddling with the temperamental photocopy machine. "Said she had an appointment."

Ouch. That's right. Rochelle's retest . . .

Almost decided not to call Avis about the retest. What was the point? They wouldn't know the results for a week anyway. But on Saturday morning — I still had two weeks until my turn came up to volunteer at Manna House, hallelujah! — as I stuffed laundry into the washing machine in the basement of our two-flat, it hit me: waiting is sometimes harder than knowing.

I called Avis on my next trip through the kitchen. Peter Douglass answered. "No, Avis isn't here. She drove down to Manna House to take Rochelle shopping."

Shopping. Yeah, I bet. More likely Rochelle needed some propping up. There was nothing in Peter's voice to indicate that Avis had told him about the HIV diagnosis, though. Maybe she was waiting for the second test; probably didn't want to get him all upset until they knew for sure. Or maybe it was Avis who needed propping up! Mother-daughter shopping could be a good emotional Novocain.

Peter's voice plowed into my thoughts. "I was just about to call your house anyway. Is that man of yours there?"

"Nope. Gone to a basketball game over at West Rogers High. Intramurals. You know Denny; he's got coaching in the blood."

"Yeah, well. Tell him to give me a call when he gets home."

I hung up, feeling a strange warmth. What was it — appreciation? Well, yes. But more than that. Feeling blessed . . .

My mind lingered on Avis's new husband as I trekked back down to the basement to change laundry loads. When Peter first started courting Avis, we Yada Yadas were like a bunch of schoolgirls. *"Ooo, girl, that man is fine!"* We started making her a wedding quilt before he even popped the question! Then . . . I started worrying that Peter might take Avis away from Uptown Community Church. He seemed uncomfortable being the only African-American male in the congregation; came only because his ladylove was a member and worship leader there. But when New Morning Christian Church, which was mostly black, started using our building for their worship services, Peter Douglass was one of the first people to articulate that "God had a reason."

Now, with the extraordinary decision to merge Uptown and New Morning, Peter had jumped in with both feet. "Thank You, Jesus!" I said, dumping a capful of detergent into the washing machine and pushing the Start button.

Hiking back up the basement stairs with a basket of hot, fluffy towels, however, I knew the blessing was bigger than just "not losing Avis." God not only brought Peter Douglass into Avis's life, courting and winning her after several years of widowhood — the first wedding I'd ever been to where the bride and groom "jumped the broom"! — but He'd brought Peter into our lives too. A seasoned businessman, Peter had not only found a job at Software Symphony for Carl Hickman, Florida's husband, but took Josh on, too, when our son decided *not* to go to college this year. But more than that, Peter and Denny seemed to respect each other, even though the two men couldn't be more different. Peter — serious, thoughtful, businesslike, always practical. Denny — the sports-crazy kid who never grew up. But it was Peter Denny had talked to when struggling with whether to take the job of athletic director at the high school. Peter who had said, *"It's not just about what you like to do. Where can you be the most influence on those*

82

kids' lives?"

"Wonder what he wants to talk to Denny about?" I murmured, stepping over Willie Wonka's inert body at the top of the basement stairs. The dog opened one eye at me but didn't move. The dog rarely moved these days. Slowing down. Waaay down. *One of these days, I'm going to trip over that dog and kill myself.*

I set the basket of clean towels on the dining room table and began to fold. Maybe Peter wanted to talk to Denny about the men's breakfast next Saturday . . . or the church business meeting tomorrow. We were all supposed to come with ideas for a new church name —

"Yachad."

My telephone conversation with Ruth earlier that week popped into my head. Ruth had just thrown that word into the ring and told me to look it up. Not sure why I should bother. *What a weird name for a church.* Maybe it meant something in Hebrew. Might be a nice name for a Jewish synagogue or a Messianic congregation. But the hodgepodge that was Uptown–New Morning? *Nobody* would know what "Yachad" meant.

Still, curiosity got the better of me. I dumped a towel in midfold and booted up the computer. Took me a while to Google it, but finally I found it in an online Old Testament Hebrew lexicon. *"Yachad . . ."*

"Whoa!" I said. Then, "Wow." I moved my cursor to Print Current Page, typed in "20" copies, and hit Print.

7

"So what did Peter Douglass want yester-day?" I had given Peter's message to Denny when he got home Saturday afternoon. They'd spent a good thirty minutes on the phone, with Denny saying stuff like, *"Yeah, I agree . . . Good point . . . Man, wish I knew . . . I'll see what I can find out."* I might as well have been Willie Wonka for all I learned from Denny's side of the conversation. I gave up and took the dog for walk, but even that didn't last long. Poor Wonka. Every time we found a cleared sidewalk, he'd lifted first one paw, then another, and looked at me with that pitiful rumpled brow. The salted sidewalks stung his cracked pads.

By the time we got back to the house (finally cutting through the alleys, which were *never* salted and *never* plowed, creat-ing a mishmash of stuck cars like a destruc-tion derby pileup), Denny was engrossed in a basketball game on TV. I knew I'd only get *"Huh?"* and *"Can it wait?"* if I tried to strike up a conversation while "da Bulls" were scoring. So I'd given up on curiosity and tackled a major molehill: what to take to the Second Sunday Potluck tomorrow.

Josh, who'd done a twenty-four-hour shift at Manna House, said he'd take the el and meet us at church this morning. Now I pulled the big bowl of hot calico beans out of the back of the minivan and stood aside while Denny locked the car before following Amanda, who'd already disappeared into our "new" shopping center church. "You guys talked long enough," I added.

"Oh yeah." Denny took my arm to steady me as we mushed through the icy parking lot. "He's concerned about Carl. Seems depressed on the job. Can't blame the guy. I'd be depressed, too, if my kid was locked up in juvie. Anyway, Peter was trying to pick my brain about what we could do to support the Hickman family right now — or Chris for that matter. But the only visitors allowed at the JDC are parents or guardians — not even siblings."

Huh. And I thought they were hashing over new names for the church. "You come up with any ideas?"

"Peter thinks a bunch of guys need to be there for Carl on a regular basis. Let him vent his feelings, pray with him, get him out with the guys now and then — stuff like that. I mean, Florida has you Yada Yadas for support, but . . ."

I cringed. *Florida has you Yada Yadas for support.* It'd been a week since our last meeting at Yo-Yo's. Had I even called Florida this past week to see how she was doing? Had I called *anybody* except Avis — and I didn't get her even then. Ruth had called me, but . . .

Sheesh, Lord. You're so faithful! But I always seem to fall down on the job. It's hard being Your hands and feet in this Body You've put us in.

Denny held the glass door open as I carefully carried the hot beans inside and headed for the half-finished kitchen on the other side of the "sanctuary," trying not to bump into anyone.

I dunno, God. Maybe You can be there for a zillion people at once. But I'm only one person — with thirty kids on my job, two almost-grown teenagers at home, a prayer group of twelve sisters whose lives keep getting snarly like a dozen cats in a yarn shop. How am I supposed to —

"Yo, Jodi." Becky Wallace stood in front of me and peered into my face. "The kitchen's back that way. You planning on storin' that

87

dish in the ladies washroom or something?"

I sighed and pushed back my paper plate. That morning's worship — get-down praise and a good word from the Word from dear Pastor Clark, who'd seemed energized by the congregational talk-back of "Amen!" and "That's right, brother!" — had satisfied my soul. The potluck — a glut of greens, macaroni and cheese, fried chicken, hot wings, calico beans, potato salad, and green salad — had satisfied my stomach.

Now it was time for the church business meeting. Would it satisfy my spirit?

Tables were pushed back, chairs replaced into rows, and cleanup left until later. I chafed at the rows of chairs. Wouldn't a circle, even several layers deep, be more welcoming? Maybe I'd work up the courage to suggest it next time.

Some of the younger teens took the little kids and babies into one of the back rooms, while most of the older teens, like Josh and Amanda, elected to stay in the meeting. Pastor Joe Cobbs opened the meeting with prayer.

"Father God." The fifty-something pastor's booming voice always took me a bit off guard. "You led Your people across the Red Sea. You provided manna and meat in the wilderness. You gave them clothes that didn't wear out, even though they wandered around in that wilderness for forty years. You told them that if they followed Your commandments, You would make them into a great people. And then You brought them victorious into the Promised Land."

"That's right! That's right!"

"So, Father God. We *know* You are going to lead us through the deep waters we're facing —"

"Hallelujah! Jesus!"

"We *know* You are going to provide the ways and means to survive our challenges and be nourished along the way —"

"Jesus! Thank You!"

"And we *know* that if we listen to Your Word and obey the voice of Your Holy Spirit, You are going to make us into Your people, right here on Howard Street!"

By this time, people were on their feet, hands raised, shouting hallelujah, thanking God. Not exactly how most business meetings started, but the hope and confidence in the prayer squeezed the anxiety out of me. "Yes, Lord!" I cried, adding my voice to the hubbub. "We know You have a plan for us, to give us a future and a hope!"

Praying Scripture was still new for me, but thanks to Yada Yada, I was beginning to memorize more of God's promises, so that they came pouring out when we needed them. Like now.

Nonyameko must have had the same prompting, because as the general praises drifted to a hush, I heard her voice lift above the others. " 'For I know the thoughts that I think toward you, says the Lord, thoughts of peace and not of evil, to give you a future and a hope. Then you will call upon Me and go and pray to Me, and I will listen to you. And you will seek Me and find Me, when you search for Me with all your heart.' God's Word from Jeremiah chapter twenty-nine, verse eleven. Amen."

As we resumed our seats and took up the agenda, I was surprised at how quickly a number of potentially sticky issues were cared for. But the first recommendation oiled the gears: all decisions made today would take effect for one year, giving the congregation more experience with one another, at which time all decisions would be reviewed. That one passed unanimously. "Smart," Denny murmured. "Very smart."

Next, the double congregation affirmed that Pastor Joseph Cobbs and Pastor Hubert Clark were copastors, with mutual responsibility for teaching and preaching, but with a division of administrative oversight for the various ministries according to their gifts and strengths. (*"Hubert?"* Florida hissed in my ear from the row behind me. "No wonder that man keeps his given name under his hat!")

I wondered how we'd deal with the next level of leadership, though. We didn't know each other well enough to elect new elders from each previous church. But the current crop — three from Uptown and five from New Morning — was too many for a church our size, seemed to me. Peter Douglass cleared his throat and stood up.

"I realize I'm not a voting member of this congregation . . . yet." He smiled. "A fact I intend to change at the first opportunity." A burst of applause and laughter erupted. "But I'd like to make a suggestion about elders. Why don't the current elders from both congregations draw lots. Half would serve the first six months of this year; half would serve the second half. Then at the end of the year, we can have a new election."

A murmur rippled among the rows of chairs. But Peter held up a hand to continue. "That way, we honor our current elders, giving us the benefit of their experience as we begin this marriage." Several people laughed. "But it also gives an opportunity to raise up new leaders in the near future."

"Amen, brother!" More clapping.

Denny stood up. "I like that suggestion. But I have to confess, I don't know who we're talking about — from New Morning, at least. Could we have the current elders from Uptown and New Morning introduce themselves?"

More clapping. Pastor Clark introduced Uptown's current elders: Rick Reilly, Tom Fitzhugh, and David Brown. Pastor Cobbs said New Morning had deacons, not elders, but the function was probably similar. He called on Debra and Sherman Meeks, Carrie Walker, Rommel Custer, and Mark Smith to stand.

I beamed at the Meeks, who'd been so warm and welcoming from day one.

"Hallelujah!" Florida exclaimed behind me. "All right now!" Then I heard her hiss in my ear again. "They got *women* on they board!"

I watched as Nony's husband stood with the other deacons, gripping the back of the chair in front of him. The Northwestern University history professor whose head had been bashed in with a brick last summer was still a looker, in spite of the weight he'd lost during his convalescence. The black eye patch he wore over his left eye gave him a debonair, mysterious air — especially with that trim goatee outlining his chin. I poked Denny. "Did you know Mark was a deacon at New Morning?" I whispered.

He shrugged. "Not surprised."

But I saw Nony's face tilt upward, watching him, brows knit in concern.

Mark raised his hand. "Pastors? If I may say something?" He spoke clearly, just a tad slowly. Easy to miss if someone didn't know what he'd been through.

The room quieted. People leaned forward.

"I think Peter Douglass's suggestion is excellent, and under normal circumstances I would be glad to serve. But as you all know, I haven't been able to carry out my responsibilities for the last six months, and I think it best to step down at this time. God has brought me a very long way . . . but I also want to be realistic. I don't think I need to explain." He sat down. Nony put an arm across the back of his chair, resting it there.

Pastor Cobbs stroked his chin thoughtfully. "We could assign you to the second six months if that would make a difference, brother."

Mark just shook his head. My heart was aching. Why step down? Give the healing process another six months! Was stepping down accepting defeat?

But we moved on. Peter's suggestion became a motion, which was carried by the "ayes." Then and there, the seven remaining elder-deacons drew slips of paper, four of which had X's on them. Our first set of elders was Debra Meeks, Rommel Custer, Rick Reilly, and Tom Fitzhugh. The second set would be David Brown, Sherman Meeks, Carrie Walker. I noticed no one said anything about the disproportionate number. Maybe Pastor Cobbs was leaving the position open on purpose, just in case . . .

The last item on the agenda was a new name for the church. Now I was getting excited. I fished the papers I'd printed out from my tote bag. Wasn't sure what the procedure for introducing new names would be, but I was ready. The pastors passed out a sheet with a few possibilities. All were a combination of the old names: *Uptown New Morning Church . . . New Morning Community Church . . . New Community Christian Church.*

The discussion was spirited.

"How we gonna decide whose name goes first?"

"Does it matter?"

"Sure it does. Uptown's been around twenty years. If we want people to know we're still around, the name ought to be in there somewhere."

"I like that 'New Community' one."

"We're not voting yet."

Becky Wallace waved her hand. "Uh, seems ta me we oughta come up with a new name. New church, new name." Her head swiveled at the murmurs that rippled around her. "Or maybe not. What do I know?" She shrank into her seat.

"Maybe the old names aren't important to *some* folks." A big woman eyed Becky over the top of her skinny reading glasses. "But for those of us who've been around awhile, the name is important. Preserves our history. It's part of our identity."

Murmurs of assent this time.

"Heh-heh-heh. This is like John Smith-Brown gettin' hitched to Mary Jones-White," a man cracked. "Whatcha gonna call the *next* generation? Smith-Brown-Jones-White?" That got a laugh — but I could tell the tension had risen.

Silence descended over the room. My insides were churning. Seemed like some combination of the old names would win the day. My idea was probably dumb anyway. Nobody else had mentioned any new names —

"Could I say something?" Avis Johnson-

Douglass stood up, her Bible open. "I don't disagree about the importance of history, of celebrating our identities. But I find it interesting that God often gave a *new name* when He was doing something new in the lives of His people. Abram was changed to Abraham. Jacob was changed to Israel. Simon was changed to Peter. Oftentimes there was a prophetic quality to the new name — a promise of something new, something *God* was going to do. Here, let me read . . ."

My eyes widened. *Prophetic.* That was the word. That was what had excited me about Ruth's off-the-cuff suggestion.

Avis read from Revelation chapter three. " 'He who overcomes, I will make him a pillar in the temple of My God, and he shall go out no more. I will write on him the name of My God and the name of the city of My God, the New Jerusalem, which comes down out of heaven from My God. And I will write on him *My new name.* He who has an ear, let him hear what the Spirit says to the churches.' " Avis closed her Bible. "I don't have a name to suggest, but Pastor Clark often says, 'God is doing a *new thing.*' A new wineskin, so to speak, for new wine. So I'd like to suggest we add some new names to this list. Something that expresses what God is doing among us. Or" — she smiled — "what God will do among us if we let Him."

I felt like shouting. *Thank you, Avis!* But I still hesitated. Didn't want to be the first one.

To my surprise, Hoshi Takahashi stood up. "Avis spoke my heart. Thank you, dear sister. I have a name to suggest: All Nations Church. Because we want people of all nations to be welcome here."

I saw a few heads bobbing, as well as a few frowns. But Hoshi's courage strengthened my own backbone. I stood up. "Thank you, Hoshi. I like your suggestion. But I also have a suggestion. You might think it sounds funny at first — I did. But the more I thought about it, the more I realized —"

"Just tell us the name, Jodi," Stu piped up.

For a moment, I felt flustered. "Okay. *Yachad.*" I heard a few snickers, so I rushed on. "*Yachad* is a Hebrew word, found in the Bible, which means 'together in unity' or 'in one accord.' It has the prophetic quality Avis was talking about. Like Jesus' prayer in John seventeen, when He asked God to make us one, just as He and the Father are One. That's our prayer for this merger, too, I think. I've got a page here explaining the

97

meaning if anyone's interested."

I sat down, feeling the heat in my face. Comments flew all around me. "Yachad what? Yachad Community Church?" "Sounds like a mosque to me. We'd get a bunch of Muslims showing up." "So? Maybe that's good." "She said it's Hebrew, not Arabic." "Still, nobody would know what it means." "But people would ask and we could tell them — like a witness, you know." "I kinda like it." "I don't know . . ."

But a sense of peace lapped quietly at my frazzled nerves. In spite of the voices all around me, I heard a still, small Voice in my spirit. *Now let it go, Jodi. You planted the seed. You were obedient to speak the Word. Let it go.*

8

My watch said 3:10 by the time Josh pulled our minivan into the garage after the marathon worship, potluck, and business meeting. I groaned, shedding my coat as I dragged myself from the back door to the coat tree in the front hall. "I am *so* glad we changed Yada Yada off second Sundays. I just wanna chill tonight and go to bed early."

"Oh." Denny, following me to the front of the house, sounded disappointed. "I thought maybe we could go out or something, take advantage of a free Sunday night."

I locked eyes with him. "Why not Friday? Why not Saturday? Why wait till *Sunday?* We've both got to go to work tomorrow morning."

He tossed his London Fog with the flannel zip-in liner over the top of the coat tree, making it look like a football pileup. "Okay. Except we *didn't* go out Friday or Saturday this weekend, and now it's Sunday. Besides, you know Fridays are bad. A night game or something usually keeps me at school late."

"You're not coaching now, remember? You don't *have* to be at every game." I headed back to the kitchen. I needed a cup of hot tea.

"Whoa, whoa, whoa, what's that about?" Denny was right behind me. "I said I'd like to go out with my wife tonight, and now we're talking about my *job?* C'mon, Jodi."

Josh was standing at the refrigerator, pulling out bread, mayo, cheese, and lunchmeat, in spite of the fact we'd had a megapotluck only two hours ago. Irritated that I was sandwiched between my son and my husband, when what I really wanted was a cup of tea and a good book, I flipped on the gas under the teakettle. "Fine."

Denny stopped in the kitchen doorway. "Yeah. I know what 'fine' means. It means I haven't heard the last of this yet."

Josh stared at us, hands full of sandwich makings. "You two need a time-out?"

"Mind your own business, buster." I turned off the stove, marched out of the kitchen, and headed for the bedroom.

"So much for *yachad!*" Denny yelled after me.

I slammed the bedroom door behind me. Hot tears stung my eyes. What did he mean by *that?* That he wasn't going to vote for the name I suggested for the church, just because I didn't want to go out tonight? How mean was that!

Shedding my nylons, skirt, and sweater, I crawled under our wedding quilt in my slip and punched the pillow into submission. How did Denny and I end up fighting five minutes after coming home from church? Yeah, I'd been kind of nervous to nominate a name for the church . . . but nobody got upset at me. The pastors suggested we have a preliminary paper vote between all the names in two weeks, then a discussion and final vote of the top two at our next business meeting. That was cool. So why did I get all hot and bothered the minute we got home from church?

I had no idea. Still, it had already been a long day. Maybe I just needed a nap.

But as I lay in the bed, willing my churned up emotions to calm down, I heard Denny's comment again in my head: *"So much for yachad!"* . . . and I boiled up all over again, mad tears wetting the pillow. Maybe I had been short with Denny, but *that* was downright mean.

Jodi, My child. Are you sure? Denny may be a lot of things — but mean?

I listened. Was the Holy Spirit talking to

me? I mean, it was like a thought in my head, and yet . . . more than a thought. Something deeper down, nudging my spirit.

It was true. Whatever faults Denny had — huh! *Clueless* came to mind — "mean" wasn't one of them. So what was he implying?

Now I was wide awake. I got out of bed, pulled on a robe, and quietly opened the door. Competing music came from behind Amanda's and Josh's closed bedroom doors. Down the hall, I could hear the TV . . .

I snuck into the dining room, found my Sunday tote bag I used to carry my Bible and other stuff, and pulled out one of the sheets I'd photocopied. *"Yachad . . . together in unity . . . in one accord."*

My eyes teared up again. That's what Denny meant. *So much for 'together in unity' . . . so much for being 'in one accord.' "* Touché. Yeah, it hurt — but he was right.

Darn it. I sighed. Why was I the one who always had to say I'm sorry? On the other hand, wasn't I learning that "I'm sorry" and "Please forgive me" were steps toward healing and freedom? The sooner the better, before we made mountains out of molehills.

I sucked up my pride and headed for the living room.

■ ■ ■ ■

Denny not only forgave me (as I knew he would), but said we could have a night "in," make something yummy like quesadillas after Amanda went to youth group, and just watch TV together. But as it turned out, every single station — we didn't have cable — was running specials on the "Presidential Primaries 2004" kicking off in high gear. Channel 2 . . . 5 . . . 7 . . . 11 . . . all blabbing opinions about the chances of the president's reelection. Followed by cozy magazine formats on the various candidates' backgrounds and dissecting their political careers (or lack thereof). Commentators nodded soberly at their monitors showing reporters in the field, following presidential wannabes like rock-star groupies. We even tried channels 32, 38, and 50, but only got a rerun of *The Good, the Bad, and the Ugly*, some big-haired TV evangelist I'd never heard of striding around a platform, and a motivational speaker talking about turning your money into millions. Yeah, right.

Denny finally jumped in the car and rented a video. We both fell asleep on the couch and had no idea how the movie ended, waking only when Amanda came in after being dropped off after youth group. Well, at least Denny and I had zoned out "in one accord."

If the kickoff of the presidential primaries had taken over our Sunday evening, it consumed the teachers' lounge at Mary MacLeod Bethune Elementary that week. No *yachad* here, though. A couple of the staff bellyached loudly about the current administration, complained about the war in Iraq dragging on when we'd been promised the US would be "in and out," and enumerated a long list of election promises from 2000, which still eluded fulfillment. A few defended the president. Most of us kept our mouths shut. In fact, I did my brave Jodi Baxter thing — I began avoiding the teachers' lounge altogether. Maybe I could return when the election was over next November.

Florida called me Tuesday evening while I was recording math homework scores in my grade book. "Jodi? Girl, I got a big favor to ask ya."

My mind was still calculating scores. *Lamar is falling too far behind . . . I need to get him some extra help . . .* "Uh, sure, Flo. What's up?"

"Chris got a hearing tomorrow down at the JDC, know what I mean? Smuckers, the new lawyer Peter Douglass lined up for us, he gonna try and get the charges thrown out. Says Chris don't have no priors, was just in the wrong place at the wrong time. All the other perps are two, three years older; the perp who pulled the job is gonna get tried as an adult. Smuckers says it's a long shot, but he wants to keep Chris out of adult court at all costs. This would be a prelim hearing; if it don't work out, then they schedule a hearing to decide whether he gets tried as a juvie or an adult."

She had my attention now. "Oh, Flo. Want me to get the Yada Yadas praying? I could send out an e-mail, make some calls —"

"Well, yeah. That too. But what I wanna ask is, can Carla come home from school with you tomorrow? The hearing's at two — but regardless of what happens, Smuckers says he wants to meet with Carl and me afterward. We both takin' the afternoon off work. Don't know when we get done. I'd feel better if I knew Carla had someplace ta go."

I hesitated. Teachers weren't supposed to take kids home — for obvious reasons. But given my personal relationship with Florida, this wasn't exactly a normal situation. How could I *not* be there for my friend? "Uh, sure! Not a problem."

Should I let the office know what was going on? Like, do it officially? I decided no. I'd write Avis a note and leave it in her box to cover my butt.

Which is how Carla Hickman ended up at my house Wednesday after school, cooing over Willie Wonka while I made hot chocolate. Wonka, stretched out on the floor by the window radiator in the dining room, patiently put up with the child kissing his nose, stroking his silky ears, and yelling into the kitchen, "Isn't Willie Wonka a boy dog? How come he got those nipple things on his belly?"

I took two mugs of instant hot chocolate out of the microwave and brought them into the dining room. Carla hopped onto a chair and took a sip. "Eww. It's too hot!"

"Sorry 'bout that. I'll put some cold milk in it."

Carla seemed satisfied with the cooled-down chocolate but eyed me over the rim of her mug, her three wiry ponytails peeking out top and sides. "Got any cookies? My other mama always had cookies to go with hot chocolate."

I winced. How many times did Florida have to put up with *"My other mama always . . ."*? The Department of Child and

Family Services had taken the Hickman kids into state custody and put them in foster care for five years. That was *before* Florida got "saved an' sober." Now the Hickmans were trying to put their family back together again. And they'd come a long way, praise Jesus! They'd found the missing Carla, whose files had somehow been "misplaced" in the DCFS system. Peter Douglass had offered Flo's husband a decent job at Software Symphony. They'd just moved out of a crowded apartment in the Edgewater district into a rented house here in Rogers Park. And Florida had been clean for six years now. Things had really been looking up . . .

Until Chris got arrested, hopping a ride after school with some gangbanger who "just happened" to rob a 7-Eleven at gunpoint while Chris waited outside in the car.

Carla was still waiting for an answer about the cookies. "Sorry, kiddo. Don't have any cookies — but tell you what. Why don't we make some? What kind do you like?"

Carla's eyes rounded. "Really? Can we make a whole bunch of cookies?" She hopped off her chair. "Oatmeal raisin chocolate chip! That's what I wanna make."

I did a mental run-through of the cupboards. *Oatmeal — check. Raisins — check.*

Chocolate chips — maybe. I scrapped the idea of parking Carla in front of some kid video while I graded homework papers. "Let's do it." I headed for the kitchen, expecting Carla to follow me, but turned back to see her still standing by the dining room table. I paused at the doorway. "You okay?"

"It's my birthday Saturday," she blurted. "I'm gonna be ten."

"Why, that's right. Amanda and I came to your birthday party last year." *A party Florida would rather forget.* I wondered if there would be a party this year.

"Since we gonna make cookies, can we make enough to take to school on Friday? Ya know, like some of the other mamas do when they kids have birthdays?"

How easy to say, *"Sure. No problem."* But was it a problem? How would Florida feel if I stepped in and did her mama thing? Except, I reasoned, given everything going on at the Hickman household, I doubted cookies for Carla's third-grade classroom was on the priority list. Second problem. If my class found out the *teacher* made cookies for Carla, was I setting myself up to make cookies for *all* the kids' birthdays? If not, would I be accused of playing favorites?

But I grinned at Carla. Life was slippery;

didn't fit neatly into all the pigeonholes. We had to take risks — if the risk was about love. "Tell you what. Sure, we'll make cookies you can take to class on Friday. On one condition." I leaned close to her ear. "You can't tell *anybody* at school that you made them at my house. Deal?"

We found half a bag of chocolate chips — some lowlife chocolate fiend had snacked away the other half, and it wasn't Willie Wonka! — giving us enough goodies to make four dozen oatmeal-raisin-chocolate-chip cookies. Carla counted and recounted the cookies, making sure we saved enough so every kid in the class could have two, then insisted we leave those at my house. "Otherwise, they be gone by Friday," she said darkly. "Cedric eat 'em all his own self."

I wasn't sure they'd be any safer at my house, but I promised I'd guard them with my life — having to "cross my heart and hope to die" again.

Denny took the call saying Hickmans were home and could we bring Carla? "What happened at the hearing?" I asked him. Denny just shrugged and shook his head.

Men! Denny in particular was missing the curiosity gene. Which is why I took Carla home. I mean, did the case get dropped or not? Probably not. Wouldn't whoever called have been praising God and yelling with joy if Chris's case had been thrown out?

Florida confirmed my fears, after sending Carla inside and closing the front door behind her, leaving us standing out on their front porch in thirty-degree weather. She lit a cigarette and blew smoke into the frosty air, eyes smoldering. "Judge turned down the petition. Said Smuckers could argue 'not guilty' at Chris's trial. So that's the next thing we facin' — another hearing to decide if he gets tried in juvie or in adult court. 'Cept they don' call it a trial in juvie — a *disposition* or somethin'. No jury either. Just the judge, decidin' my baby's whole life." She frowned at the cigarette. "Huh. Tryin' ta give up these things, but it ain't easy, not with all this crap goin' on."

I felt tongue-tied. *Sheesh!* What could I say? I blew on my hands to warm them, then thrust them back into my jacket pockets. "How can I pray, Flo?"

She sucked on the cigarette again and shook her head. "Don' really know, Jodi. Sometimes it feel like my prayers just bouncin' off the ceiling, know what I'm sayin'?" She flipped the cigarette stub into the darkness and sighed. "Maybe pray that Carl an' me, we can just keep hangin' on ta God's hand." She reached for the door handle. "Guess I'll see ya Sunday. Thanks for keepin' Carla."

I opened my mouth to ask if they were planning anything for Carla's birthday on Saturday, but the door closed abruptly behind her.

The TV news that night flashed the attractive face of a Palestinian woman who blew herself up along with four Israelis. Watching the news felt like a punch to the stomach. *Oh God, not a woman!* I didn't understand the hatred that drove suicide bombers to throw their lives away to kill "the enemy." But a woman? Women were *life-givers!* Weren't we? Didn't women keep the world sane when all hell was breaking loose?

I felt so sick about it, I almost forgot to bring Carla's cookies to school on Friday — I'd "hidden" them upstairs in Stu's apartment to thwart the Baxter cookie monsters — but thankfully *she* remembered and dropped them off at the back door on her way to work. "Count 'em. They're all there." She grinned at me under her red felt beret and headed for the garage.

Monday would be a school holiday — Dr. Martin Luther King Jr.'s birthday — so we had a nice all-school program that Friday morning commemorating the civil rights leader. Back in our classroom, I mentioned that Carla Hickman *almost* shared a birthday with the famous African-American and had brought everyone a treat. Carla, true to her word, kept mum about the cookie origins, beamed happily as we sang "Happy Birthday" to her *and* to Dr. King, and only threatened to punch Lamar one time, when he started to help himself to the last four cookies, left over because two students were absent.

"Those cookies are for . . . for Miz Douglass, ain't that right, Miz Baxter?" Carla thrust the plastic container with the four orphan cookies at me. "You give 'em to her, okay?"

Which gave me a lovely excuse to drop into Avis's office at lunchtime, avoiding both the noisy cafeteria and the teachers' lounge with its nonstop droning TV. But the moment I saw the tightness in her face, the missing smile, I remembered. Rochelle was supposed to get results back yesterday from the HIV retest.

I shut the door to her office and sank into a chair. "Bad news?" I whispered.

Avis nodded. Sudden tears glistened in her eyes and she grabbed a tissue from the box on her desk. "No question. Rochelle tested positive for the HIV virus." The tears spilled and she blew her nose.

"Oh, Avis." I could barely grasp the reality of it. What did it mean? What was going to happen to Rochelle? Was there anything that could be done? How —

Avis stood up abruptly and paced behind her desk, then turned back to me, her voice low and intense. "I am *so angry,* Jodi! So angry I could spit. Do you know why? Rochelle says Dexter is the only man she's ever slept with, that she's been faithful to him from day one." The side of her mouth twisted slightly. "Well, she didn't say whether day one was *before* or *after* their wedding day . . . but I believe her. Which means . . ." Avis gulped for air, as if she couldn't breathe.

I watched pain and anger twist Avis's beautiful face into something almost terrifying.

"Which means," she finally breathed, "that *Dexter* is the one who infected her. That pretty-boy Don Juan has not only been abusing my daughter, but he's going to kill her too."

9

I was tempted to snuggle deeper under the covers the next morning when my inner alarm woke me up at six. Why couldn't my body clock tell the difference between weekdays and weekends? But the memory of Avis's muffled tears wetting my shoulder as we just held each other in her office the day before, got me out of bed and shuffling toward the kitchen to start the coffee. I needed some time alone to pray, to talk to God, to ask Him how in the world this made any sense!

Ten minutes later I was in the recliner in the front room where the Christmas tree had stood, flipping open my Bible in the glow of the floor lamp. Denny's warm robe and the hot coffee soothed my body, but I missed the glittering Christmas tree lights, as if cheer had been snuffed out from my spirit too.

The Psalms . . . that's what I needed.

Good ol' King David somehow got away with ranting at God when *he* was upset. Yeah, Psalm 69 — that was a good one. I'd pray it on Avis's and Rochelle's behalf. Maybe mine too. I took a breath and spoke aloud in the stillness, my mind paraphrasing the verses even as I read.

"God, it's Jodi here. This news about Rochelle feels like floodwaters rising clear up to their necks, about to drown them. Avis is sinking right now into the mud, unable to keep her feet on solid ground. She's overwhelmed, God! I'm sure she's worn out calling on You for help, calling until she has no voice left! She's looking for You, God — trying to understand why this is happening. Why aren't You answering?"

My eyes skimmed part of the chapter until I came to verse 13: "But I'm praying to You, O Lord, looking for Your favor. In Your great love, O God, answer me! Answer Avis! Answer Rochelle! Answer with your sure salvation. Rescue them, O God, from the muck. Don't let them sink! Don't let these floodwaters, this terrible disease, swallow them up! Don't just throw Rochelle's life away into a pit. Answer us, O Lord, out of the goodness of Your love! Answer quickly, because Avis and her family are in trouble, Lord, and it hurts — it hurts all of us who love them . . ."

I heard Denny clear his throat behind me. "Uh, sorry to interrupt, babe. Just want to let you know I'm heading over to the church. Going to pick up Carl on the way."

"What?" I squinted at my watch. "It's only six-forty! Doesn't men's breakfast start at eight o'clock?"

"Yeah." He came over to the recliner, bent down, and kissed my nose, smelling like mint toothpaste. "But Peter Douglass talked to Carl about the men at church praying for Chris, and for him and his family. Carl was kinda shy about it, said he'd rather do it with just a few guys he knows instead of the whole men's breakfast. So a few of us are getting together ahead of time to pray with Carl." I saw him grin in the glow of the lamplight. "I asked Ben Garfield to come. Said he would. Mark Smith is coming too."

"Really?" For a moment I forgot I was mad at God. "That's great!" I chuckled. "God's got Ben in His sights, for sure . . . oh! Let Wonka in, will you? He's been out there quite a while."

When the back door closed behind Denny a few minutes later, I squeezed my eyes shut. *Thank You, God. Thank You for reminding me that You are answering our prayers. Maybe not on our timeline, but we've been*

116

praying for Ben a long time, and there he is, joining the guys for a Jesus prayer meeting. I giggled to myself. Knowing Ben, half the reason he'd agreed to come was probably to get out of the house for a couple of hours, escaping baby duty. But who cared? Didn't Ruth say Ben might go to church if he could hang out with Denny and the other Yada husbands?

On the way to the coffee pot for a refill, I passed the kitchen calendar and realized I had one other thing to be thankful for this morning. I still had a whole week before I had to show up for overnight duty at Manna House.

"He *what?*" I started laughing as Denny reported the morning's events while he threw stuff into a small duffle bag. "He brought *Isaac* to the prayer meeting?" I still couldn't get used to the image of white-haired Ben Garfield walking around with a baby in a baby carrier. Would wonders never cease?

"Yep. Fed him a bottle, burped him, put him to sleep over his shoulder. Gotta tell you, Jodi, that guy is nuts about that kid."

My grin faded. "Yeah. *Isaac.* Wish he paid that much attention to Havah. I think he overcompensates with Isaac because of that birthmark on his face."

Denny shrugged, hunting for his clip-board. "Don't worry about it. They've got *twins,* remember? Makes sense for them to divvy up the childcare."

Yeah, maybe. But I pushed the thought aside, following Denny back into the kitchen. "How was the prayer time with Carl? Did he stay for the men's breakfast too?"

He rummaged in the refrigerator. "Yeah, it was great. Just five of us — Peter, Mark, Ben, me, and Carl. Well, and Isaac." He chuckled. "Gave Carl a chance to just talk about how he feels with his boy in lockup — he hides a lot of that, you know. He's scared, big-time . . . Jodi? We got any more bottles of water in here?"

I pulled one out of the refrigerator door, right in front of his nose.

"Oh. Thanks." He threw it in the duffle bag and shrugged into his down jacket. "But no, he didn't stay for the men's breakfast. Mostly because we all encouraged him to go home and take Carla out for breakfast for her birthday. Told him it was important not to neglect his other kids in his worry over Chris."

"Great idea!" Hopefully Ben Garfield would take the hint too.

Denny headed for the back door. "Varsity game's over by three. I should be home by four." Pulling open the door, he waggled his eyebrows at me. "Anything happening tonight I should know about? Or can we go out? See? I'm asking early."

"Hm. I'll think about it, see if I get any better offers . . . Just kidding! Close the door! No, wait." I pulled Denny back inside and shut the door. "Did Peter Douglass mention anything about Rochelle? I mean, did you guys pray for her too?" I had told Denny the news about the HIV test and how devastated Avis was.

He shook his head. "He didn't say anything, and I hesitated to ask. You said yourself you didn't know if Avis had told him yet. Look, I gotta go."

I leaned against the door after Denny left. I didn't get it. Avis was a strong woman. She knew how to lean on God front and center, especially since Conrad died and left her a widow. But this thing with Rochelle was tearing her up! She needed the support of her new husband. Maybe she had told him, and Peter just didn't want to bring it up, afraid it would take away from the focus on praying for the Hickmans.

"I dunno, Wonka," I muttered to the dog, stepping around his bulk as I headed for the basement to switch loads in the laundry. "I can't figure Avis out, sometimes. But guess it's not easy getting married in your fifties. Trying to merge your old family with your new one." Down in the basement, I pulled a load of whites out of the dryer and stuffed wet wash-and-wear into it. But I knew one thing — I was gonna get on her case. She couldn't keep this all bottled up inside. She needed support! And Rochelle did too.

"It's not that easy, Jodi." Avis spoke quietly into the phone. No tears now. "Rochelle isn't ready to tell the world. People . . . react funny when they find out you have HIV or AIDS. You know that."

I did know that. Did I want someone who was HIV-positive or had AIDS to check out my groceries? Handle my money at the bank? Teach my kid at school? It was hard to let go of the myths about how HIV could be transmitted when it got in-your-face personal.

"And the minute someone says they are HIV-positive," she went on, "everybody's thinking, 'Oh, are you gay?' Or, 'Must've been sleeping around, *tsk tsk*.' "

Exactly.

"But to defend herself, Rochelle would

have to point the finger at Dexter — and she's not ready to do that. He hasn't even been tested yet."

"Why in the world would she want to protect *Dexter?*" The cad.

"I think" — her voice got tight — "she's hoping they could work it out, get back together. He is Conny's daddy, you know."

I stifled a snort, cradling the phone in my ear while I pulled a clean towel out of the laundry basket and started folding. When I could trust myself, I got to the point: "The thing is, Avis, how can Yada Yada pray for Rochelle and Conny — and you! — if you keep this a secret? In fact, did you tell Peter yet?"

A silent beat hung in the air. Then, "Yes. Yes, I did. Last night. He . . . didn't say much. Just held me and let me cry."

Well, good. That was a start. I glanced at the clock. Almost four. "I better go, Avis. Denny wants to go out tonight and I still gotta do something with this rag-mop hair. See you tomorrow at Yada Yada? We're meeting at . . ." I looked at the list posted on one of the kitchen cupboard doors. "Florida's house. Wait — do you think that's a good idea? I mean, what they're going through with Chris and all that?"

"Flo's not shy. She'd say something if it's

not okay. Besides" — Avis's voice took on the old, familiar "everything's under control" tone — "didn't Becky say the next time Yada Yada met at the Hickmans, she wanted an apartment blessing for her squirrel's nest on the second floor? And seems like it's somebody's birthday . . . who did we celebrate last year in January? Not Chanda — we missed her last year. Somebody else . . ."

I groaned. Now I remembered. *Nony.* Why didn't we celebrate both Chanda and Nony at our last meeting? Well, I knew why we hadn't. Chanda needed her own celebration. But who was going to bake a cake *this* time? Get a card for all of us to sign? Why in the world didn't we *plan ahead* for this kind of stuff!

"Well, I'm not going to stay home tonight to pull it together," I sniffed, knowing I sounded like a snit.

Turned out Hoshi Takahashi had everything under control. She pulled me aside at worship on Sunday morning, said she had ordered a cake from the Bagel Bakery and Ruth and Yo-Yo were going to bring it. "You already did the meaning of Nony's name last year, correct?" she said softly. She smiled, dark eyes twinkling. "So this year I have a little surprise we can give her. Not exactly a birthday card, but something we can sign and give to her."

My snit melted. I even felt ashamed. Why had I gotten so aggravated, assuming that if I didn't do it, nobody would? But we really did need a birthday maven to make sure *somebody* was on top of the Yada Yada birthdays. I'd bring it up at Yada Yada tonight —

I smiled and shook my head. *There you go again, Jodi!*

Denny was laid back about me going off to Yada Yada Sunday evening. We'd had a great time the night before — went out to dinner at the Davis Street Fish Market in Evanston, tried *not* to talk about all the trials of various Yada Yada sisters, spent way too much money ("It's Jamaica Jerk Café next time," Denny groused good-naturedly), and laughed at my squeamish attempt to eat one of the oysters he'd ordered. We ended the evening with some behind-closed-doors hanky-panky, given that Amanda had a late-night babysitting job and Josh was "out."

I hitched a ride to Yada Yada with Stu, who seemed kind of quiet on the way over to Hickmans. Dirty ice and snow humped in ugly patches along the streets. It was time

123

for a fresh snowfall to brighten up winter's gray rags. "You okay?" I said.

She shrugged. "Just tired. I might leave early. We'll see."

We arrived at the little frame house before Nony and Hoshi got there. But Becky Wallace beckoned us furtively into the Hickmans' narrow kitchen. A baby carrier on the floor contained baby Havah, sound asleep just under a pretty bakery cake on the counter. But Yo-Yo, Ruth, and Florida were crowded around a box lid on the other counter. My eyes widened. Sitting in the box lid were at least a dozen exquisite origami shapes folded from bright colored paper. A star, a butterfly, a rose, an owl . . .

"Hoshi smuggled 'em to me after church," Flo said. "Said we were supposed to each pick one and sign it for Nony."

"Hey. I like that frog on a lily pad." Yo-Yo picked it up. "Do we hafta give 'em *all* to Nony? Man, this is cool."

"Don't be a *shmo,* Yo-Yo," Ruth sniffed. "Sign the frog." She lifted the paper butterfly from the box. "This one I like. I will sign it from Havah and Isaac, one name on each wing."

Chanda called while others were still arriving. "All three of her kids got the flu," Flo announced when she hung up. "She

124

said Adele ain't gonna make it either. MaDear's got the flu too. They had to put her in the hospital. Worried about pneumonia."

The prayer list for tonight was getting longer.

But Nony, wearing a blue-and-gold tunic over a black turtleneck and wide, black pants, was utterly delighted with the origami shapes and touched that we had remembered her birthday. I eyed Avis. *Ha.* If it weren't for Hoshi, we'd be up a creek without a paddle. I was touched by Hoshi's unselfish spirit, providing a gift for all of us to give Nony.

"So, Nony. How old are you? I wanna be like you when I grow up." Yo-Yo was serious. Ruth rolled her eyes and stuck a pacifier in Havah's mouth.

"I am thirty-eight this week," Nony admitted in her cultured South African accent. "Do you think I will know what I am supposed to do with my life by the time I am forty years?" Her tone was light, but I suspected her words betrayed a trace of frustration. Six months of playing nursemaid to her husband recovering from head trauma had sapped some of her fire.

After demolishing the bakery cake, we tromped upstairs to Becky Wallace's studio apartment at the back of the Hickmans' house. The two rooms — combination kitchen/living area plus a bedroom with a single bed for Becky and a youth bed for Little Andy — were somewhat bare but neat and clean. The closet-size bathroom even had a scented candle burning on the sink. Stu poked me and muttered in my ear, "Maybe she picked up some household tips living with me after all, you think?" Avis brought out her anointing oil, and we prayed that God would fill the apartment with His love, His laughter, His protection, His hope. The prayers didn't take long, but Becky sniffled and had to blow her nose.

Half our time was gone already, but back downstairs Avis led us in singing, "Jesus, Your Name is Power." I was gripped by the words, *"Jesus, Your name will break every stronghold . . ."*

We all sat quietly after the song, each one probably grappling with the words. Did I really believe Jesus had the power to break strongholds? Free every captive? Give life?

To my surprise, Avis broke the silence. "I've been singing this song in my heart all day," she said, "holding on to the words. Because, I confess, Satan seems to have established a stronghold in my family that threatens to devastate us."

Ten pairs of eyes stared at her.

"I . . . did ask Rochelle's permission to tell you this, but I'd like to ask that it not leave the room." And then Avis said it, flat out. "Rochelle has been diagnosed with HIV."

Shock and disbelief registered on every face, like freeze-frame photography. But Nony literally lifted right out of her seat, hands clenched toward the ceiling. "Nooo!" she wailed. "No! No! No!" Then she burst into tears.

10

I was startled by Nony's outburst, even though I'd had the same inner reaction when I first heard the news. But she practically flew to Avis, fell to her knees, and grasped Avis's hands in her own. "Oh, my sister! The devil is afoot, stealing the health of our own daughters, right under our noses. It is her husband, yes?"

Avis, slightly taken aback, nodded silently.

"O God, how long will the wicked be jubilant? They pour out arrogant words! Evildoers are full of boasting!" Nony's head was thrown back, eyes tightly closed, even as she still kneeled in front of Avis. I knew she had to be praying one of the psalms, but I didn't know which one. "They crush Your people, O Lord! They oppress Your inheritance — even one of our own precious daughters! They slay the widow and the alien; they murder the fatherless. They say, 'The Lord does not see; the God of Jacob pays no heed.' "

The rest of us reached out for one another's hands, making a circle as she prayed.

"O Lord God who avenges, shine forth! Rise up, O Judge of the earth; pay back to the proud what they deserve." With this, Nony's chin fell to her chest. She seemed spent. After a few moments, she got to her feet and returned to her chair. She looked around the circle. "Forgive me, my sisters. But you know that AIDS is killing my people in South Africa at a terrible rate, leaving thousands of orphans. It has troubled my spirit for years, and I have often felt God calling me to respond in some way. But Rochelle . . . Oh Jesus, Jesus, have mercy." Tears rolled down her smooth cheeks. "It is as if a spear has pierced my own child, child of my own body. That beautiful girl . . . Oh Jesus."

Avis's calm had been rattled by Nony's intense emotion, and she dabbed at her eyes with a tissue.

We moved on with our meeting, gathering prayer requests and covering each other with prayer and words of encouragement from Scripture. But as we hugged each other goodnight, I noticed that Nony's eyes had a new fire in them. If I had to guess, the call of God on her life was roaring in her ears.

Amanda was on the phone in the kitchen when I got home, still wearing her jacket after getting home from youth group. "Why not?" she was saying. "It's a holiday! . . . José! You played with your father's mariachi band on Saturday! Why do you have to do it again tomor—" She rolled her eyes, leaning against the doorjamb between kitchen and dining room as she listened, totally ignoring me as I squeezed past. "So? That's in the evening! We could do something earlier in the day — go roller-skating or something . . . What? . . . *Practice!* What do you need to practice for! . . . Fine! *Fine!*" Amanda slammed the phone into the wall set and stormed past me, heading for her room.

The door slam shook the whole house.

Denny poked his head into the dining room, where I was still standing with my coat on. "What was *that?*"

"Uh, a fight with José, I think. Did you pick her up from youth group?"

"Yeah. We just got home ten minutes ago. She was fine."

I sighed. Seemed like Amanda had inherited my ability to go from zero to eighty mood-wise when it came to reacting to the men in our lives.

I decided to ignore my daughter's little tiff. Let them work it out. I was tired. What I wanted to do was crawl into bed, turn on the electric blanket — if we had one, which we didn't; a hot water bottle would have to do — and read myself to sleep on a cold winter night. It was supposed to get down to seven degrees tonight. Even if it was a school holiday the next day, thanks to Dr. King . . .

But as I lay in bed, feet propped on the hot water bottle under the covers, trying to concentrate on my novel, I rather regretted that Amanda hadn't been able to talk José into going roller-skating tomorrow. I used to love to roller-skate — the "good Christian girl" alternative to going to dances when I was growing up. I'd gotten pretty good too. Skating backward, leaning around the corners, waltzing with my partner . . .

I smiled. Maybe I could talk Denny into going skating sometime. Wondered if Amanda and José would come with us . . . maybe Josh and Edesa too . . .

I closed my book. Okay, that was weird. Triple dating with your own teenagers.
Nah.

Maybe it was because we only had four

school days that week. Maybe it was because the president gave his State of the Union address on Tuesday, heating up the opinions dividing the school staff into liberal, moderate, conservative, or head-in-the-sand. Maybe it was because I had a lot on my mind, worried about my friends who seemed to have a *lot* on their plates. Not just Florida with her boy locked up on charges of armed robbery — and he hadn't even done the robbery! . . . Not just Avis, learning that her own precious daughter had been diagnosed with HIV . . . but Adele, too, worried about her ailing mother, who already suffered from dementia and was now in the hospital with pneumonia . . .

Whatever it was that stole my attention, suddenly it was Saturday. The *fourth* Saturday of January. The day I'd agreed to be an overnight volunteer at Manna House.

Hoo boy. I wasn't ready.

"Mom." Josh eyed me over the rim of his glass of orange juice as he slouched in the kitchen, backside propped against the counter, legs crossed at the ankle like an urban cowboy, arms folded except for the hand holding the glass. "It's going to be fine. You'll love it. The kids are great. Besides, the staff will give you a tour and an orientation the first time you volunteer."

132

"Uh-huh." I opened cupboards, doing a quick inventory so I could make a shopping list for Denny and Amanda. "Twenty-four hours, you say?"

"Well, give or take. They usually let us off a couple of hours early Sunday morning so we can get to church . . . There, see?" He slapped the counter. "The shelter needs a *van* so we can bring some of the women and kids to church! Know anybody who has a van they'd like to donate? They could get a tax write-off."

Had to admire Josh's dedication to Manna House. How my nineteen-year-old son got so immersed at a *women's shelter* still seemed odd to me. Although . . . Edesa Reyes had changed her college major to public health last year, and Manna House, a new and struggling shelter on Chicago's north side, was crying out for public health volunteers. And where Edesa was, you could pretty well count on Josh showing up too.

Oh Lord, I prayed silently as I stuffed sweats for sleeping, slacks and a sweater for Sunday, and my toothbrush into my backpack. *I hope You've got that "first love" thing under control.* At Josh's suggestion, I left all jewelry except for my wedding ring at home, along with my wallet and purse, tucking only my driver's license and ten bucks into my jeans pocket.

At least Josh was going with me. He and Edesa and one of the other new volunteers — Karen from church — were also scheduled for this weekend. We nobly took the elevated train down to Belmont so Denny could have the car. *Correction,* I thought, shivering inside my winter jacket while we waited on the platform at the Morse Avenue el station. *Denny already has the car over at school, leaving me no choice.*

I was a bit taken aback when Josh said, "Well, this is it," after getting off at the Belmont el stop and walking four or five blocks. We stood in front of a small, rather dilapidated, brick church building shoehorned between two larger buildings, complete with ancient stained-glass windows and a short steeple, badly in need of paint.

"Wow," I said. "You didn't tell me Manna House was housed in a *church.* Do they still —"

"Nope. Congregation moved out to the suburbs years ago. Some little Missionary Baptist Church met here for several years, I'm told, but it was mostly elderly people who couldn't meet the mortgage payments, so the bank foreclosed. Not sure how Manna House got hold of it."

Beside the warped and damaged wooden

doors hung a church sign — the kind you could slide letters in to post worship times or change the name of the sermon each Sunday. Blank. "There's no sign that says Manna House. How would anyone know —"

"Because it's a safe house, Mom. We don't exactly want to advertise to every Tom, Dick, and Harry. C'mon." Josh took my arm and steered me around to a side door, located in a little gangway that measured five feet at best between the church and the ugly brick building next to it, which housed at quick glance a Korean grocery, a Pay-Day Loan, and a twenty-four-hour Laundromat on the street level, topped by five floors of apartments. *Who in the world would do their laundry at three in the morning?*

We went down five steps into a small stairwell, where Josh tapped a numeric code into the automatic lock and then opened the door. In spite of the almost clandestine entryway, I was pleasantly surprised by the brightly lit basement room, even more delighted by the bright, colorful walls — orange, yellow, and blue. A Christmas tree that had seen better days dominated one corner of the room, decorated with dozens of handmade decorations and strings of mismatched lights. Nearby, a teenage girl and two smaller boys — all African-American — played a noisy game of Ping-Pong. Several cozy sitting areas had been created with overstuffed couches, armchairs, and braided rugs, none of which matched, while another corner functioned as an office or reception area, complete with a large desk, computer, two large file drawers, and an overflowing wastebasket.

The young woman sitting at the desk looked up. "Jodi Baxter! *Hola!*" Edesa Reyes scurried from behind the desk to give me a big hug. Out of the corner of my eye, I saw Josh beaming at her. No wonder. Edesa's wide smile lit up her whole face, like gemstones laid out on velvety soft mahogany. As usual, her ebony curls bounced behind a sunny headband of three-inch cloth, tied at the base of her neck.

Edesa's eyes danced. "We are so excited to have you join our volunteers! And *I* get to give you the tour and the orientation." She motioned to the Ping-Pong players. "Mikey! Jeremy! Come here! I want you to meet someone. You too, Sabrina."

The two boys put down their paddles and ran over. The girl followed more slowly, seemingly indifferent, but she said hello, then flopped on one of the couches and flipped open an ancient issue of *Allure* magazine. But the boys, maybe eight and nine, tugged on Edesa's hands. "Let us give her the tour, Miz 'Desa!"

The younger boy, Mikey, looked suspiciously up at Josh. "Is that lady really your mama, Mr. Josh?"

"I dunno," he said with a straight face. "She and the guy she's married to let me sleep at their house, though."

I backhanded his shoulder. "Watch it, buddy."

The two boys nodded at each other knowingly. "Yeah, she his mama," they chorused in tandem.

Josh disappeared somewhere, lugging a bucket with tools in it, while Edesa and the two chatty boys gave me a tour of the building. Another brightly painted basement room was set up as a playroom, with tables and small chairs, large pads of newsprint clipped to painting easels, dolls and doll furniture, several potty chairs, and shelves of toys. Two heavyset white women with frowzy hair chatted in a corner while several children bounced around the room.

We passed an office door — locked — marked "Director," peeked into a kitchen where three women, two Latina and one black, were doing dishes at one end of the room, and another was wiping tables — six long ones with four chairs along each side.

"How many residents do you have?" I asked Edesa.

"Right now, twenty women and about that many *niños*."

Where are they all? I wondered as the boys led us up some narrow stairs to the main floor. We peeked into the sanctuary, which was just that — a small sanctuary, complete with pews, platform, and a pulpit. In the dim light that made its way through the dusky stained-glass windows, I saw the shadowy form of someone sitting in a far pew.

"We use this as a prayer room," Edesa whispered. "Women can come here to be quiet, get away from the common rooms. We have a prayer meeting on Saturday mornings, and sometimes a music group or drama troupe lead worship service on Sunday evenings. No one could bear to turn it into a dormitory."

But finally we did get to the sleeping rooms both on the sanctuary floor and the second floor — what were once Sunday school rooms, I presumed, now containing six to eight bunks each. Edesa introduced me to every woman and child whose path we crossed, and I was greeted for the most part by friendly smiles. *Nametags would be helpful,* I thought ruefully, knowing I'd never remember all the names. Well, I'd just have to suck it up and keep asking until I learned a few. Mikey and Jeremy and Sabrina . . . at least that was a start.

Back in the basement common room, the two boys grabbed both my hands. "C'mon, Miz Jodi, play Ping-Pong with us!"

Edesa laughed. "Go ahead. We can show you where you'll sleep later."

I let the boys drag me away, but I called back over my shoulder, "I didn't see Rochelle. Is she here?"

Edesa looked at a sign-out book on the desk. "She's out. Avis often comes down on Saturday and they do lunch or go shopping or something with Conny." She gave me a meaningful look. "Rochelle's kind of fragile right now, because of . . . well, you know."

Yes, I knew. But I didn't have any time to dwell on it, because Jeremy and Mikey started slamming Ping-Pong balls at me from their end of the table. It'd been a long time since I'd played Ping-Pong — almost as long as my roller-skating days — but I was surprised at how quickly it came back. Laughing and giggling, we slammed the little white balls back and forth until Josh came tromping back through the room with a plastic pitcher and tried to pour water into the Christmas tree stand.

"Huh. Still full," Josh muttered.

"Okay, okay, that's enough," I told the little boys, raising my hands in surrender. I joined Josh at the Christmas tree and rubbed one of the branches between my fingers. Needles fell off like a spring rain.

"Josh," I hissed. "This tree is too dry. You really should take it down." The boys hovered nearby, so I didn't add, *It's a real fire hazard.*

He scratched his head, which sported another couple of inches of sandy growth. "Yeah, guess you're right. The kids keep begging us to leave it up, but . . . maybe we'll do it tonight, make a game out of it or something."

"Just don't tell them *I* suggested it," I whispered under my breath. "That's all I need my first weekend here is to be the Big Baddy."

11

Avis, Rochelle, and Conny trudged in the side door, stamping snow off their boots, just as Mikey ran up and down the stairs ringing a bell for supper. I got a tired smile from Rochelle and a damp hug from little Conny, who wanted to show me the colorful "bug" he'd made at the Children's Museum at Navy Pier from different "bug parts." Avis, wearing a hat trimmed with fake fur that matched the collar of her hip-length winter jacket, bent down to get a good-bye hug and kiss from her grandson, but I butted in. "Why don't you stay for supper, Avis? — if that's okay," I amended hastily, realizing I had no idea what the rules might be about dinner guests.

"*Sí, sí!* The more, the merrier." Edesa laughed, grabbed Conny's hand, and headed for the kitchen/dining room.

"Thanks, but I need to get home. I told Peter I'd be home by dinner. Bye, baby!

Grammy loves you!" She blew Conny a kiss.

Rochelle rolled her eyes, gave her mother a peck on the cheek, and disappeared in the direction of the washroom. I followed Avis to the door. "How's Rochelle?" That felt lame. How *should* someone be who just found out she had HIV?

Avis glanced away, absently pulling on her gloves. "We've got an appointment at the HIV clinic next week. Conny needs to be tested. They strongly recommend that other family members come, too, to learn what the treatment options are. 'How to live with HIV,' as the brochure says." She sounded weary.

My mouth went dry. Surely not Conny too! I swallowed. "What about Dexter? Has Rochelle told him yet?"

Avis shook her head. "We're going to get some advice about that too. Peter thinks we should phone Dexter, tell him we need to talk, then all meet together. But . . ." Her mouth tightened. "Don't know if I can do that. Right now I just want to strangle him." Suddenly she pulled me into a tight embrace. "Thank you, Jodi. For being here. Knowing Rochelle and Conny are with you and Edesa and Josh this weekend helps. I just wish . . ."

She didn't finish. Just turned and disappeared out the door. Snow fell gently into the narrow stairwell, the monster flakes sliding down light beams cast by the hundred-watt bulb just outside the door. Behind me, a wobbly *a cappella* rendition of the Doxology floated from the dining room. I shut the door and scurried in that direction.

The other new volunteer — a young black woman named Karen, whom I'd seen at church — turned out to be the cook that night. She'd done a passable job making enchilada casseroles for forty-plus hungry appetites, along with a chopped salad and brownies for dessert. The director, a stocky white woman with cropped salt-and-pepper hair, wire rim glasses, and a firm handshake, dropped by in time for dessert and coffee, and to meet the new volunteers. Karen and me, that is. She introduced herself as Liz Handley, but I noticed everyone else called her "Reverend Handley."

Okay, so I was curious. "Uh, Reverend Handley, do you pastor a church?"

She smiled, grabbed a passing kid, and gave her a tickle-hug. "This is my parish now." The child dissolved in laughter and pulled away.

For some reason, her comment put a lump in my throat. *Whatever you do for the least of these, you do for Me.* Jesus had said that. And here I'd come, mentally dragging my feet and wishing I was anywhere but.

You're here, Jodi. Don't beat yourself up. Think of the possibilities . . .

Well, might as well start with the dirty dishes. Maybe the equivalent of "washing feet" here at the shelter. I joined the dish crew, drawn to a talkative young woman named Precious who had something to say about everything. "Gonna be a mild winter. All that global warmin', ya know . . . Man, wish I could get myself down to Houston to see them Panthers play at the Super Bowl. My people come from Carolina, ya know . . . Wait, wait! Girl, don't dry those dishes wit' *that*." She snatched the dishtowel from my hand. "Get that boilin' water off the stove, pour it over them dishes in the rack, then let 'em air dry. They be dry in a minute." She plunged her hands back into the soapy dishwater and tossed her braids — twenty or more skinny ropes hanging halfway down her back. "My grandma only got a third-grade education, but she taught me that much."

I complied, wondering how a woman named Precious — someone, somewhere, had loved this girl enough to call her "precious" — had ended up homeless in a women's shelter. "Do you have any kids?" I

144

asked, stacking the hot, dry plates onto a rolling cart.

Precious jerked a thumb toward the common room, where we could hear the *whack, whack, whack* of a Ping-Pong game. "Sabrina. She's my girl. She fourteen."

I couldn't contain my surprise. "You don't seem old enough to have a teenager!"

She grimaced. "Yeah. Got myself pregnant, not much older than she be now." She busied herself scrubbing one of the casserole dishes. "Sure did want a better life for my baby, but . . ." For the first time since we'd started doing the dishes, Precious fell silent.

Later that night, curled up in a lumpy comforter on a lower bunk in one of the Sunday-school-rooms-turned-dormitories, I listened to the assorted breathing in the other bunks. I'd asked if I could spend the night in Rochelle and Conny's room. In fact, while Josh was getting whupped by Mikey and Jeremy at the Ping-Pong table and Edesa played cards with other Manna House residents in the common room, I'd volunteered to read Conny a story and put him to bed. Rochelle shrugged and said sure, but stayed in the room with me buffing her nails. I read *Goodnight Moon,* which

I'd tucked into my backpack at home, then tiptoed out after Conny fell asleep. I'd been hoping I could talk to Rochelle, get to know her a little better, but though she was friendly enough, she stayed distant. Probably because I was her mother's friend.

I was tired now, but sleep eluded me. I felt so out of place. So . . . homesick. I wanted my own pillow and my crisp sheets and my husband's comforting sprawl in the bed next to me. What a wimp I was! I had volunteered to stay here one measly night per month. Precious and her daughter, Sabrina . . . Mikey and Jeremy's mom, Margo . . . and the other women I'd met that night — Estelle and Nikki and Bonny, to name just a few — didn't have that choice. Whether for six weeks or six months, this *was* home.

Oh God! Why did You put me here? What am I supposed to do?

The Voice in my spirit responded, *First things first, Jodi. You can start by praying for them. Pray for the women and the children by name. Precious . . . Sabrina . . . Estelle . . .*

And so I did, picturing each one's face that I'd met that night. Mikey's delighted giggle when Josh let him plug in the Christmas tree lights one last time. Conny cuddling close to me while I read, *"Goodnight room . . . *Goodnight moon* . . ." Precious dispensing her grandmother's dishwashing wisdom. Sabrina absorbed in *Allure* magazine's teenage fantasies, where no teenager was homeless or had to wear clothes from the Salvation Army. Estelle deftly knitting a bright blue sweater vest with skill and an eye for pattern and design. Each with her own story, stories I didn't know yet. But if Avis's daughter was just one example, how many others had been betrayed, abused, rejected? How many had turned to drugs or alcohol to dull the pain? How many dreamed of a day when they could sleep in their own bed. At home. Safe. Loved.

Oh God, help me to see these women as You see them. Like Precious, each one precious in Your sight . . .

Blaaat! Blaaat! Blaaat! Blaaat! . . .

I groaned and turned over. Was it morning already?

Wait a minute. That wasn't my alarm clock —

"Fire! Fire! Everybody out! Now!"

I sat up, eyes wide in the dark. That was Josh's voice yelling from below!

Thudding feet on the stairs. "Oh my God! Oh, please God!"

I leaped out of bed, fishing for my gym

shoes. I grabbed them and ran for the door. Smoke was drifting up the stairs.

"Keep low! Keep low! Don't take anything — just go! Go!"

"My baby! My baby! Where's — ? I gotta go back! Let me go!"

Screams. Cries. Coughing and gagging. Bodies pushing down the stairs.

Edesa stood at the bottom of the stairs. "Go out the sanctuary door — *don't run*. Ladies! Don't run. Don't push. But hurry! Hurry!"

Wait. Was everybody out of the room? Where were Rochelle and Conny? I turned and started back up. Two bodies pushed past me on the stairs, knocking me against the railing. But I finally gained the top and practically fell into our sleeping room.

"Mama! Maaaamaaaaa!" Conny was sitting up in his bunk, screaming.

Rochelle sat on the edge of her bed, a dazed look on her face. "Rochelle!" I screamed. "It's a fire! We have to go!" I pulled at her arms. "Get up! Get up!"

She let me pull her up onto her feet. Bare feet. What was the matter with this girl? Had she taken a sleeping pill? Drugged herself?

"Maaaamaaaaa!" Conny screamed again.

I pushed Rochelle out the door toward the stairs and grabbed Conny into my arms,

148

blanket and all. "I got you, I got you, sweetie." Putting the blanket over his head and pushing Rochelle ahead of me, we stumbled down the stairs.

Five minutes later I found myself standing outside the old church on the sidewalk in my wet socks, holding Conny wrapped in his blanket and staring at the smoke pouring from windows, doors, the steeple, and hundreds of other cracks in the structure. I vaguely remember Josh grabbing my arm. "Mom! Thank God you're okay. Is everybody out of your room? Yes? Good!" And then he disappeared again.

Why don't I hear any sirens? Didn't someone dial 9-1-1? I could do it. Where's my cell? . . . I shifted Conny to one hip and slapped at my sweatpants. No pockets. No cell phone. It was upstairs in my backpack, probably melting down into a glump of plastic and computer chips. That's when I realized I didn't have my shoes either. Hadn't I grabbed my shoes? Must have lost them when I went back for Conny and Rochelle.

I heard sirens then. Thank God! *Somebody* called the fire department.

Josh appeared again. I suddenly realized he was bare-chested and barefoot, wearing only sweatpants. Two inches of fresh snow were soaking through my socks, but Josh, Rochelle, and several others didn't even have socks. "Everybody, into the Laundromat," he croaked. "We have to count noses, make sure everybody's out." His voice didn't sound like Josh. Stretched with strain. Had he swallowed smoke?

Numbly we followed Josh, the only male among the herd of females and assorted children, into the Laundromat. *Oh, hallelujah, thank You, Jesus, for Laundromats that stay open all night!* My throat caught at the unexpected blessing. It was warm. It was dry. It was empty — no, an old gentleman in a rumpled golf hat sat in a corner, babysitting a tumbling dryer, staring at us as we came in. A clock on the wall said 1:40.

The bundle in my arms squirmed. "Mama!" I found Rochelle, who still seemed in shock, pushed her into one of the molded plastic chairs, and plonked Conny into her arms. Several fire trucks roared up outside. Men in big boots and heavy coats jumped off the pumper, grabbed axes, and ran for the church. Others grabbed huge, pythonlike hoses, and pulled them toward a fire hydrant. The long hook-and-ladder backed into place, beeping warnings.

"Listen up, everybody." Josh's voice was firm, though to my mother's eye, he looked like he was about to cry. "Is *anybody* missing? We have to know *now*. We have to tell the firemen if there's anybody inside. Estelle? Everybody out of your bedroom? Margo?"

"Precious! I don't see Precious or Sabrina!" someone cried.

"I saw 'em heading for the alley door. Couple others too."

Josh sprinted for the glass door of the Laundromat.

"Wait, son!" The old man in the corner moved with surprising speed from chair to door. He peeled off his faded jacket and pushed it at Josh, who wiggled his long arms into it. Then the man took off his shoes that had seen better days. "Good thing I got big feet," he chuckled.

Stuffing his bare feet into the old leather shoes, Josh flew out the door, laces undone. In two minutes, he was back, herding a small group of women and children who had been coming out of the alley on the far side of the Laundromat. Cheers went up from the crew crowded around the window, watching the drama outside.

We counted noses again. And again. I felt helpless, because I didn't know everyone and couldn't have said if anyone was missing. But Josh and Edesa and the others finally seemed satisfied. Everyone was out.

Several of the women broke down crying. Others shouted. "Praise Jesus!" Children clung to the closest adult. Someone muttered, "We sure is homeless now."

The fire chief pushed open the door of the Laundromat and asked who was in charge. Edesa spoke up. "If you'll let me use your cell phone, I'll get our director down here."

Fifteen minutes later, Rev. Handley arrived. Shock at what she'd seen outside had tightened her face into a grim mask, but she quickly kicked into gear, huddling with the fire chief, Josh, Edesa, and Estelle, who at fifty-something seemed to be the senior resident of Manna House. I sank into a plastic chair and watched. The adrenaline of fear was wearing off and cold reality was settling in.

Manna House was gone. What were all these women and children going to do?

A mad started to build up inside my gut. I knew without asking where the fire had started. *That tinderbox Christmas tree.* I *knew* it was a fire hazard. Josh had known it too! I glared at his back, looking slightly silly with his long arms sticking out of that too-small jacket. He was still a kid. Nineteen. His good intentions outweighed his wisdom.

But the director, that Rev. Handley — *she* was responsible too. She should have told them to throw it out weeks ago.

Estelle's voice rose above the rest. "Yessir, praise Jesus, every one of them smoke detectors was working. That's why we are all *here* and not in *there*." She pointed dramatically in the direction of the burning building next door with her knitting needles. I stared at the wad of bright blue yarn clutched in her hand . . . and started to laugh. Estelle had run outside shoeless, coatless, and wearing nothing but a shapeless, flannel bag of a nightgown. She'd just lost every possession down to her toothbrush.

But Estelle had come out carrying her knitting!

12

The fire chief clicked his cell phone shut. "People? Can you all hear me?" Sniffles quieted; murmurs died away. The old man pulled open the door of the big dryer so it would stop rumbling. "The Salvation Army will be here in thirty minutes with blankets, food, and some warm clothes. But their shelter is on overload tonight. We, uh, we'll try to find a place for you all to go, but for now just sit tight. It might take —"

"Uh, chief?" Josh glanced at me, as if he wanted confirmation. "I think I know a place we can take these women and children for the night."

My mind spun. *Of course!* "That's right." I got off my duff and joined my son. "Our church is only twenty minutes from here. But we need to make some calls . . ."

Rev. Handley mutely offered her cell phone to Josh. The old man — who gave his name as Rosco Harris — shuffled over with half a roll of quarters. His laundry money. "Pay phone over there." He pointed.

"Bless you," I whispered, giving him a hug. "You are definitely a Good Samaritan."

He waved it off. "Hey. I still got a roof over my head, lady."

I didn't know Pastor Cobbs's or Pastor Clark's numbers by heart and neither did Josh. So we started with the numbers we did have. Denny. Avis and Peter.

"Dad," I heard Josh say. "We're *okay* . . . yeah, she's okay too. Look, we need a place to take these women and children for the night. Could you call —"

The pay phone was ringing in my ear; then I heard someone pick up on the other end. I glanced at Rochelle, arms wrapped around Conny, rocking and crying silently in a corner of the brightly lit Laundromat. No, I was not going to ask Avis or Peter to make any calls. "Peter? It's Jodi Baxter. There's been a fire down here at Manna House. Everybody's okay. But you and Avis need to come *now.*"

The Douglasses were the first to arrive. Peter jerked open the door of the Laundromat, searched faces, then strode to the corner where Rochelle and Conny still huddled. The big man knelt beside his stepdaughter and pulled her and the child in her lap into a big embrace. "Oh, Rochelle, baby." His voice, though muffled against Conny's blanket, was more like a groan. "I'm so sorry, baby . . . so sorry. I never should have —" His shoulders began to shake.

Avis also knelt beside her daughter and put her arms around them all. Some of the other women respectfully moved away, giving the little family a scrap of privacy.

Peter finally helped Rochelle to her feet, took Conny into his arms, and made for the door. Avis hesitated before following her husband and daughter out into the night. "Jodi? Edesa? Should we take anyone else?"

"No, no! Go." Edesa gently pushed her out the door. "We'll be fine. Others are coming."

The Douglasses had no sooner left than a Salvation Army van squeezed past the police barricades. A man and three women in navy blue uniforms quietly and efficiently carried in armloads of colorful fleece blankets, baskets of sweet rolls, jugs of hot coffee, and boxes overflowing with sweatshirts, hats, mittens, socks, children's boots, and adult gym shoes. In one way or another, all of us got fitted with something to keep body and soul together for the next few hours.

The clock on the wall said 2:45. My eyes burned with unshed tears.

While the Salvation Army people were gathering names, ages, and contact information for any relatives in the local area from the Manna House residents, Pastor Clark showed up, rail thin even in his bulky parka and big rubber boots. He asked no questions, just said, "The church van is around the corner. I can take fourteen people. Several other church members with minivans are coming. The Cobbses are over at the church, making calls and collecting blankets, food, and air mattresses."

I wanted to throw my arms around Pastor Clark and hug him. But Denny arrived, ashen-faced, unshaven. He looked terrible. He looked wonderful. He held me a long time. "You okay, babe?" he whispered into my hair. "You sure?" I nodded my head against his chest but couldn't speak.

Finally, he gently pushed me away. "Let me go see Josh, okay?"

I nodded again. For the first time I noticed Josh sitting in one of the ugly plastic chairs, elbows on his knees, head in his hands. Denny sat down next to him, stretched an arm across his son's bent shoulders, then . . . just sat without speaking. My heart ached as I watched my two men sharing a silent pain.

Edesa didn't sit. She joined Pastor Clark as he made his way from person to person, touching one. Hugging a child. Whispering something to another.

But within the next half hour, several other members from Uptown–New Morning Church arrived with minivans and SUVs, lined up just outside the barricades. Josh, Edesa, Karen, and I managed to park our feelings and assigned small groups of women and kids to the various cars, agreeing all would meet at the church building in the Howard Street shopping center. Rev. Handley said she'd stay with the Manna House residents until they got situated. Pastor Clark promised to stay in touch with the Salvation Army people, and we moved amoebalike out of the safety of the twenty-four-hour Laundromat into the night.

Most of the women, dead tired, wrapped in blankets and assorted sweatshirts, plodded silently behind their assigned driver toward the cars. But, like Lot's wife, I turned and looked back at the smoldering remains of Manna House. The stained-glass windows were broken. Smoke had blackened the outside bricks and still rose in stubborn ribbons from holes chopped into the roof. Leaking water from the hydrant and drips from the broken windows were turning into ghostly icicles. The wide sidewalk, steps into the church, and the front of the church itself glistened like sheets of ice.

Unlike Lot's wife, I didn't turn into a pillar of salt. But the image of the shelter — shattered, broken, no longer a refuge — burned itself into my spirit, especially as Precious and Sabrina, and Mikey, Jeremy, and Margo climbed into our Caravan for the trip up an empty Lake Shore Drive toward Howard Street. From somewhere in my memory, the words of the psalmist floated to my lips. "God is our refuge and strength," I murmured. "Our ever-present help in trouble."

"I know that one," Precious said from the back. "My grandma used ta say it. 'God is our refuge and strength, a very present help in trouble. Therefore, we will not fear, though the earth be removed, and though the mountains be carried into the midst of the sea. Though the waters roar, though the mountains shake . . .' Somethin' like that."

"Huh," Margo muttered from the third seat. "Don't say nothin' 'bout no fire."

"Yeah, but there's another one. Lord, Lord, my grandma knew 'em all! Somethin' 'bout passin' through the waters —"

"I said *fire*," Margo grumbled. "An' keep

it down. Mikey's asleep."

Precious was not deterred. "I'm gettin' there. Mr. Denny, you know what one I'm getting' at?"

Denny kept his eyes on the drive as the tall streetlights passed over us like gentle waves. But I saw the tightness in his face soften slightly. "Uh, think so. The one that goes, 'When you pass through the waters, I will be with you; and through the rivers, they shall not overflow you . . .' " He glanced at me, as if asking for help.

Now I knew the scripture Precious was remembering. " 'When you walk through the fire, you shall not be burned, nor shall the flames kindle upon you. For I am the Lord your God . . .' "

"Yeah." Precious blew out a long sigh. "That's the one."

Pastor Joe Cobbs and First Lady Rose cheerfully welcomed the stream of homeless women and children as if the shopping center church were always open at five in the morning with the temperatures outside hovering at fifteen degrees. A small crew of volunteers — I saw both Uptown and New Morning people among them — had stacked up the chairs in the large meeting room, and assorted "beds" had already been laid out. More blankets and air mattresses were in some of the back rooms used as Sunday school rooms. "Get some sleep," Rose Cobbs urged the bedraggled band, giving hugs to as many women and children as time allowed. "We'll be back at nine o'clock with breakfast."

Oh yes, God. Sleep . . . Suddenly I felt as if all my body parts might disconnect and clatter to the floor if I didn't lie down somewhere.

Pastor Cobbs pushed the church keys into Josh's hand and herded the drivers and other volunteers out the door. I hesitated. Rev. Handley was spreading blankets on the floor as a makeshift bed for herself. Should I leave? Could I live with myself if I did? After all, my twenty-four-hour volunteer stint wasn't up yet. But Pastor Cobbs tapped a finger on Denny's chest. "Brother Baxter, take your wife home. Reverend Handley, Josh, and Sister Reyes can stay with these people. But you'll both be more helpful sorting things out for these women if you go home and get some sleep."

I didn't protest. I didn't even look back this time as I numbly shuffled behind Denny across the icy parking lot to the car. But when I crawled into the front seat and Denny turned the heater on full blast for the one-mile trip to our house on Lunt Street, I cried all the way home.

13

Willie Wonka nosed my hand and whined. Blearily, I opened one eye and tried to focus on the bedside clock. Eight-thirty . . . *Eight-thirty!* No wonder Wonka was whining. I slid out of bed, groped for Denny's robe, and followed the dog to the back door, my eyes at slit-level, hoping I could remain half-asleep and fall back into bed.

Then it hit me. Rose Cobbs would be showing up at the church with breakfast for the fire victims at nine o'clock. *I should be there.* After all, I wasn't the only one short on sleep. *And Josh . . . how is he doing? Did he get any sleep at all?* I'd hardly spoken more than a few sentences to my son since the fire alarm went off. Frankly, I'd let him and Edesa shoulder the primary responsibility for the Manna House residents.

A pitiful whine from outside broke up my reverie. Stuffing my feet into a pair of clogs by the back door, I darted outside into air so brittle it felt like it would break and hauled the arthritic dog up the icy back steps and into the house. Then I stumbled toward the bathroom mumbling, "Sleep can come later . . . sleep can come later." But I had to admit, I felt worse now than I did before I fell into bed three hours ago.

A shower and a strong cup of coffee helped a little. But I pulled on my sweats from the night before. No way was I going to dress up for church. I was tempted to just take the car and let Denny and Amanda come later with Stu. But a call upstairs nixed that idea. Stu was headed out the door herself to pick up Little Andy Wallace on Chicago's west side.

Sheesh. She's still doing that? Why hasn't she asked —

"What's going on?" Stu demanded. I told her in twenty-five words or less. "A fire at Manna House! Why didn't you call me?"

"Later, Stu," I mumbled and hung up.

Reluctantly, I woke Denny and offered to come back and pick him up, but he gamely got out of bed. He even woke up Amanda with the promise that all she had to do was throw on her sweats. Fifteen minutes later, we all piled into the car with travel mugs of coffee — though we had to wait while Amanda doctored hers with lots of milk and sugar. "Cool," she said. "Wish we could dress like this every Sunday."

Her eyes widened when we pulled up in the shopping center parking lot and she saw the crowd of homeless women and children milling around inside the big open room we used as a sanctuary. True to their word, Pastor Joe and Rose Cobbs, along with Debra and Sherman Meeks, were handing out bagels with cream cheese, jam, hard-boiled eggs, apple, and orange juice, while a crowd-size pot of coffee perked away in a corner. Several of the young children were still sleeping on blanket pallets in spite of the chatter among the adults, while others were sitting up and rubbing their eyes as bright daylight streamed into the room from the bank of windows along the front.

The director of Manna House, still grim-faced, and a representative from the Salvation Army were huddled in a far corner with Pastor Clark, comparing lists, frowning. Two women in Salvation Army uniforms were opening boxes of donated clothing and passing out jeans, sweats, tops, sweaters, and socks.

Taking her cue from Edesa, who was taking some of the children to the bathroom, Amanda pitched right in with the kids — getting them washed up, sitting them down with bagels and juice, cracking the hard-boiled eggs while making little jokes. I greeted Precious and Estelle with a hug, then assigned myself to serving coffee as soon as the big pot stopped gurgling.

Josh was nowhere to be seen.

I snagged Edesa, but she shook her head. A moment later, little Mikey tugged on my sweatshirt. "You lookin' for Mr. Josh?" He pointed toward the parking lot. "He said he goin' for a walk."

Wearing what? I thought. He'd run out of the burning building with no shirt and bare feet. The last I'd seen him, he was still wearing the old man's coat and shoes . . .

We were still cleaning up after breakfast when people began arriving for our usual ten o'clock worship service. Mattresses and blankets still dotted the floor, the chairs had not been set up, and the room was full of strange women and children in an assortment of rumpled nightclothes.

"Come in, come in!" Pastor Cobbs beckoned the bewildered members of our Needing-a-New-Name Church into the warmth of the big room. "Grab a chair and a cup of coffee, or sit on the floor. Church is going to be somewhat different this morning."

The sound crew and musicians cleared a

166

little area at the back and the front of the room for their equipment — and with extra hands, it didn't take long to stack the mattresses and blankets along one wall. The women and children from Manna House looked a bit overwhelmed as the room filled with men in suits and ties and women in dressy coats and high-heeled boots. Mothers drew their children close.

As folding chairs were set up at random, Pastor Cobbs took a handheld mic and explained the emergency situation as briefly as possible. "What we have here, brothers and sisters, is an opportunity for us to worship God not only in spirit but in truth. Let the Word of God speak for itself." He flipped open his Bible and searched for a passage. "In the Gospel of Luke, chapter three, John the Baptist said, 'Every tree that does not produce good fruit will be cut down and thrown into the fire.' So the people asked him, 'What shall we do then?' He answered and said to them, 'He who has two tunics' — make that two coats — 'let him give to the one who has none; and he who has food, let him do likewise.' " More page flipping. "And in the book of Romans, chapter twelve, the apostle Paul said, 'Share with God's people who are in need. Practice hospitality.' "

Pastor Cobbs looked up from his Bible, and made his way to where Margo was sitting with Mikey in her lap. He lifted the little boy — still in his pajamas — into his arms. "But maybe the most important word of all was spoken by Jesus. 'Whatever you did for one of the least of these brothers and sisters of mine, you did for Me.'"

Sherman Meeks stood up. "All right, Pastor. Say it now."

Pastor Cobbs let Mikey get down. "Thank you, Brother Meeks. What we need, church, are temporary homes for these women and children until the Salvation Army or another shelter can find a more permanent place for them. But while you're thinking about that, we're going to thank the Lord God Almighty —"

"Hallelujah! Oh, thank You, Jesus!" At first, I thought it was Florida, but then I saw Estelle on her feet, still in her nightgown with a worn sweater over it, arms lifted in praise and tears running down her cheeks.

Pastor Cobbs's voice caught. "That's right, sister. Let's thank the Lord God Almighty for all His goodness and mercy in saving every single life from that fire last night. Praise team, can you do 'We Bring a Sacrifice of Praise'?"

As voices joined in a hearty rendition of,

"We bring a sacrifice of praise into the house of the Lord!" I saw Josh slip inside the double doors, blowing on his bare hands. I sidled over to him and slipped an arm around his waist. He was shivering.

I could've kicked myself. *Why didn't I bring some of his warm clothes from home? Socks! Boots! Gloves! His own coat, for heaven's sake.* Under cover of the music, I whispered, "Josh, honey. You're freezing. Let me take you home —"

He shook his head and pulled away from me. He looked down at his sockless feet, stuffed into the old, scuffed shoes. Then he said in a hoarse whisper, "The old man . . . I took his jacket and shoes. How . . ." His lip twitched. "How am I ever going to find him to give them back?"

By the time our unusual "worship service" was over, a table had been set up where Pastor Clark, Major Lewis from the Salvation Army, and Liz Handley coordinated the matching process, assigning Manna House residents to the homes of various church members. Denny and I agreed to take Precious and her daughter Sabrina. Stu, grinning, said she'd take Estelle. Rochelle and Conny, of course, were already with Avis and Peter, who didn't make it to church that morning. Who could blame them?

I was surprised, though, when the Hickmans agreed to take Margo and her two boys. I pulled her aside. "Flo! You guys don't have to do this. With what you're going through with Chris, don't you guys have enough on your plate?"

"Like nobody else does? Look, girl, we got us an empty bedroom now, don't we? And them two little boys, they don't have *nothin'*. 'Sides, Becky Wallace said they mama could bunk up with her."

I backed off, feeling like I'd just had my mouth washed out with soap.

All the host families were told to remember that Manna House had been a "safe house" for several of these women and our homes needed to function in the same way. "Do not talk publicly with your coworkers or neighbors, even your extended families, about who you are hosting," Rev. Handley said. "Do not take any phone calls for your guests except from Major Lewis, Pastor Clark, or myself. If you have questions, feel free to call me at any time on my cell. One of us will let you know as soon as we have found more permanent shelter for the Manna House residents — hopefully within the week. If you have e-mail, we will send a daily report about our progress."

Josh insisted on taking Edesa home after dropping us off at home. I figured they needed to debrief after the stressful events of the past twelve hours, but he was home sooner than I expected. He seemed relieved that his sister had already given up her room for Precious and Sabrina, turned down the sandwiches we'd thrown together for lunch, and disappeared into his room.

"I think we all need a nap," Denny said.

I lay beside Denny in the darkened bedroom, feeling awkward with strangers under my roof. I envied Stu and her guest room upstairs, beautifully decorated in muted green and rose. All we had was Amanda's bedroom, which looked like a geometric black-and-yellow puzzle with one thousand loose pieces, though at least I was able to put clean sheets on the double bed.

Today's the last Sunday of January . . . thank goodness Yada Yada isn't meeting on the fourth Sunday anymore! . . . but something was supposed to happen today . . . can't remember what . . . Oh, yeah.

"We didn't take the paper vote."

"*Huh?* What paper vote?" Denny's voice was muffled by his pillow.

"For the church name. We were going to take a paper vote today to narrow it down.

Final vote at the next business meeting."

Denny raised his head an inch from the pillow, eyed me with a look that suggested I'd just entered a not-guilty-because-of-insanity plea, and turned over.

I got up at five, worried that I wouldn't get any sleep that night if I napped too long. Under other circumstances, I would have told my family "you're on your own" for supper, but with two guests, I ransacked the cupboards and threw canned beans, chopped vegetables, a can of tomatoes, and macaroni into a soup pot that was supposed to resemble minestrone.

Precious, dressed in her "new" clothes from the Salvation Army boxes, raved over the soup, as chatty and bubbly as if there'd been no fire the night before. But Sabrina kept her eyes down, stirring the soup with her spoon and mostly nibbling crackers. She cringed warily every time Willie Wonka wandered through the dining room. I finally had to shut the dog in our bedroom.

"Um . . . what grade are you in, Sabrina?" Amanda asked.

"Ninth. But . . ." Sabrina shrugged. "Ain't got no school clothes now. An' don' know how I'd get there."

"Maybe you could wear something of

mine." Amanda eyed her enviously. "Though you're smaller than me, lucky you."

Lucky you? I hoped the irony was lost on Sabrina.

"Hey! Let's go shopping tonight." Amanda brightened. "I've got some babysitting money — we could get one outfit at least. If we went to Target or A. J. Wright, anyway." She turned on Denny. "See why I need my license, Dad? Then you wouldn't have to drive us!"

Her father waggled his eyebrows. "You know the drill, kiddo. Finish driver's training, come up with your share of the insurance, *then* you get your license."

"What about youth group tonight?" I asked. "Maybe Sabrina would like to go."

Sabrina shook her head emphatically even before I finished. Amanda rolled her eyes. "Don't sweat it, Mom. Come on, Sabrina. I'll find you something to wear to the store."

Shopping. Huh. Why didn't I think of that? Surely Precious could use some more clothes — underwear, at least. "Precious, do you want to go with — ?"

"Nah. Let them two go. Maybe 'nother day." She watched the girls disappear. "She sweet, your Amanda."

"Mm. She can be. Would you like some more soup?"

14

The girls came home with a pair of fashion-faded jeans, bikini underwear, a bra, two clingy tops, and two pairs of socks. Denny pleaded no contest. "Uh, no way was I going to hang around women's intimate apparel."

"Dad got the shoes, though," Amanda said, giving him a hug. She didn't seem the least bothered that she'd just spent all her babysitting cash.

But as it turned out, Precious decided not to send Sabrina to school the next morning until she talked to Rev. Handley about train fare and figured out the route. Couldn't blame her. I'd probably do the same thing in her shoes. Still, I felt uncomfortable going to work the next morning, leaving two strangers in my house all day with only Willie Wonka on duty. And Sabrina still whimpered every time Wonka came within three feet.

Bethune Elementary office was in an uproar when I got to school. All the school computers had been shut down as a precaution against the MyDoom virus, supposedly wreaking havoc on millions of computers nationwide via the Internet. Teachers wanted lesson plans, now locked in the school's digital brain. The office staff wanted the weekly schedule, the lunchroom rotation list, and a flyer for the upcoming Fall Festival. "The Fall Festival isn't even on the Internet!" snapped Ms. Ivy, the chief school secretary.

But Tom Davis, second-grade teacher and the closest the school had to a computer guru, was adamant. "No one gets on a computer until we've blocked the virus."

I called Denny at his office. "Do we have virus protection against this MyDoom 'worm,' or whatever they call it?"

He sighed. "Just don't open any e-mails when you get home. I'll ask Peter what we should do. Or Josh. Maybe he knows."

Sabrina and Precious were both watching afternoon TV when I got home, Wonka zoned at their feet. Guess girl and dog had made their peace. Precious glanced up, then crowed as the contestant failed to win his round. "Girl, I knew that! They should get *me* up on that show!" But when the show ended, she bounced into the kitchen, where I was frowning at the open refrigerator, trying to think what to feed our expanded family. "Miz Estelle came down, said the Stuart lady invited us all upstairs for supper t'night. Nice of her, ain't it?"

Downright nice. I let the refrigerator door close with a sigh of relief.

Stu seemed almost giddy having company. She and Estelle had obviously hit it off big-time, laughing and joking. Josh, however, came upstairs reluctantly and excused himself from Stu's table early, saying he was going to do a search-and-destroy on our computer in case MyDoom was lurking somewhere.

"I think we're clean," he reported when the rest of us trooped downstairs half an hour later. "But I deleted all our incoming e-mails just in case one of them was infected."

"What?" I jerked a thumb at Precious and Sabrina. "Reverend Handley said they were going to keep us updated by e-mail! How are we supposed to know —"

"*Mom.*" Irritation spiked Josh's voice. "These worms aren't pretty. Do you want us to be protected or not?" He stomped off to his room.

Denny and I exchanged glances. Why did

177

I suspect this wasn't just about a computer virus? But I was frustrated too. I'd wanted to send an e-mail to the rest of Yada Yada, to tell them what had happened. Now I was going to have to make calls.

Sabrina had no homework — yet — but Denny hogged the TV for Monday night football, so the fourteen-year-old sprawled on Amanda's bed listening to CDs while Amanda did her calculus. I listened to the decibels shake the windows for two minutes before marching in and handing Sabrina a set of earphones. Amanda would thank me later.

Precious went back upstairs to Stu's apartment to hang out with Estelle while I spread out my February lesson plans on the dining room table. This was my third year at Bethune Elementary, which helped. I could build on my previous syllabus, tweaking as needed: introduce fractions and word problems using measurements in math . . . highlight "Main Idea" and "Fact vs. Opinion" in language arts . . . tackle early Illinois history, Abraham Lincoln, and Black History Month in social studies . . . construct simple machines and focus on home safety in science. Add test-taking skills somewhere —

"Mom?"

I looked up. Josh leaned against the dining room archway in his favorite pair of shredded jeans and a sweatshirt with the sleeves ripped off. His disheveled sandy hair hung over his ears and down his neck. I was beginning to think the bald look he used to sport was better.

"Got a minute?"

"Sure. Time for a tea break. Want some?"

He shook his head. I turned on the tea water and sat back down at the table.

Josh didn't look at me, just sank into a chair and hung one arm over the back. He sighed. "Okay. I deleted all our incoming e-mails, like I said. But . . . I did scan through some of the senders and subject headings. One was from the Manna House director —" He sucked in his breath and let it out. "Calling a meeting this coming Saturday to debrief about the fire."

I nodded. "Makes sense." Huh. I needed a meeting next Saturday like I needed sand in my shoes. "But . . . you didn't open the message."

He shook his head again. "Guess we should call to get the details."

I waited. He said nothing. Just fidgeted with his hands.

I cleared my throat. "So are you going to call, or do you want me to?"

"Oh. . . . Yeah, would you?" More fidgeting.

God, help me here! I'm not sure what's going on.

The Voice in my spirit said, *Just ask him, Jodi. He came to you. That was an invitation.*

I reached out and laid a hand on his. "Josh, what's going on? It's natural to feel upset after a fire like that. *I'm* upset! Everybody is. Just give yourself some time . . ."

He pulled his hands away, jaw muscles working. "It's — it's not that."

Oh, great, Jodi. You not only asked, you supplied your own answer. This time I kept my mouth shut.

Finally he sighed. "I don't want to go to that meeting Saturday. Because everyone wants to know what happened. And you and I" — he finally looked at me, eyes tortured — "we both know how that fire started. Mikey and Jeremy, they begged and begged me to keep the tree lights on one more time. So I gave in. And then . . ." His head sagged into his hands. "I forgot to turn them off. That fire's my fault, Mom. *My fault!*"

Josh's shoulders began to shake.

"Oh, Josh." My heart squeezed so hard I could hardly breathe. I got up and put my arms around my son. "Don't . . . don't cry. It's all right. Nobody's blaming you."

He jerked out of my embrace, nearly vaulting out of his chair. "That's not true! *Edesa* blames me. I can see it in her eyes! And she won't talk to me." With that, Josh strode out of the room and slammed his bedroom door.

I told Denny about my talk with Josh. He frowned. "I'll talk with him." But it wasn't easy. Josh left early for work, worked late, went out in the evening, or stayed holed up in his room. Not to mention that with two extra people in the house, juggling our schedules took extra energy and time.

Denny drove Precious and Sabrina to the Morse Avenue el station early the next morning so Sabrina could get to school on time. Had to hand it to Precious, who decided to take Sabrina and pick her up each day from school until they got re-settled, rather than leave her daughter to navigate the new route on her own.

As for Yada Yada, I was sure Edesa would have called Delores first thing. But I finally managed to call Chanda to tell her about the fire, and she promised to call Adele and Yo-Yo. "Why you wait t'ree days to call mi?" Chanda scolded. But she seemed pleased that I called her first and asked her to call the others.

I called Ruth myself. Had to check on the twins, anyway.

"*Oy! Oy!* I read about that fire in the paper!" Ruth said. "An abandoned church, the paper said. Or maybe they said it no longer had a congregation. But they didn't mention Manna House. Rochelle and her little boy are okay? No one was hurt? Praise to Jehovah-Rohi, the Good Shepherd! You were there, Jodi? Gray hair it would give me! You need something to help you lighten up. Come to our party on Saturday."

She actually left space for me to speak. "Uh, what party, Ruth?"

"The twins' birthday party! They're two months old this week. Ben says, why wait a whole year to celebrate? Every month they change so much. Did you know, Jodi, that babies change more in the first year than —"

"Uh, sorry Ruth. I have to go to a meeting on Saturday. The volunteers and staff of Manna House."

"A meeting? Why? You were there two minutes, the place burns down, end of story. Come on, come to the party. You should see Havah lift her head, straight up on her arms. Like a gymnast she is!"

End of story . . . I wished. I hadn't even finished my volunteer training, so what did

182

I have to contribute? I sighed. "I'd love to, Ruth. But I was there when the shelter burned down, so I better go."

Stu popped in Thursday night while Denny and I were doing dishes, looked into the dining room to make sure no one else was about, then leaned against the counter. "I'm thinking of asking Estelle to stay, to be my roommate. Housemate. Whatever." She liberated a cookie from the cookie jar. "Whaddya think?"

I stared at her. "Are you sure, Stu? It's only been a couple of months since Becky moved out. Weren't you looking for some peace and quiet?"

She nibbled on the cookie. "Yeah. But . . . I miss the company. Miss having someone there when I get home." She looked at Denny. "What do you think, Big Guy?"

He frowned. "How well do you know Estelle? I mean, she's been living in a shelter for some reason. No money. No job. Will you be giving her a free ride? How can she pay her share of the expenses?"

Stu rolled her eyes. "How well did I know Becky Wallace? At least Estelle never robbed me, isn't a drug addict, and isn't under house arrest. So far, we've hit it off great. She's got a great sense of humor. Like living with an older sister or favorite aunt."

"Sounds like you've made up your mind." I knew that sounded tart, so I softened. "Just give yourself a little time before committing yourself, Stu. Maybe invite her to stay for a few weeks as your guest, you know, to give her a breather from living in a shelter. You can decide to invite her longer if it works out."

"Huh. Now *that's* a good idea. Glad I talked to you guys . . . Oh, your phone's ringing." Stu bopped out the back door as quickly as she'd come.

The answering machine had kicked in by the time I found the cordless phone tucked between the couch cushions in the living room, where Precious and Sabrina were watching sitcoms on TV. "We're here! . . . Oh, hello, Reverend Handley. . . . Yes, she's here."

I handed the phone to Precious and headed back to the kitchen, but not before I heard her say, "Yeah, okay . . . That's good, I guess." A few minutes later, she showed up in the kitchen doorway. "Uh, Reverend Handley says Salvation Army has room in they shelter for Sabrina an' me, if y'all can take us down there Saturday morning." She shrugged. "Or we can take the el if that's

184

too much trouble. We ain't got that much stuff."

"No trouble. Be glad to take you." Denny smiled as he turned on the dishwasher. "Glad something is getting worked out. Sabrina will be closer to school too."

"Yeah." Precious leaned against the kitchen doorjamb. "It's been nice here, y'all. Real nice. Someday me an' my girl gonna have a nice apartment like this. Just gotta get me a job, save up some money." She started to go, then turned back with a wry smile. "Heard Estelle might be stayin'. Lucky Estelle." And then she was gone.

I looked at Denny. Had Precious been hoping we'd let her stay permanently? Impossible. Completely impossible!

15

Chicago got a dump of snow that Thursday — an accumulation of five inches. My third graders wanted to build more snowmen. I rolled my eyes. "You're on your own, kiddos." A few diehards charged bravely into the playground at lunchtime, but they were back in five minutes. The high that day was only ten degrees above zero. Add the wind off the lake and it felt like tiny ice picks hammering away at your face.

Josh emerged from his hole Saturday morning to say he'd drive Precious and Sabrina to the Salvation Army shelter. Amanda also wanted to go along. We packed up as many warm clothes, boots, jackets, and blankets as we could find to fit the mother and daughter, using Pastor Cobbs's John-the-Baptist guideline: "If you have two coats, share with the one who has none." But our guests looked so forlorn as we hugged them good-bye that guilt nibbled away my smile. *Just washing your hands of it, aren't you, Jodi? You're glad they're gone. Now maybe things can get back to normal. But how would you like to be heading to a shelter with your teenage daughter for who knows how long?*

I stood in the kitchen long after the minivan disappeared down our icy alley. It was true. I felt relieved that they were gone. The week had gone smoothly enough, but it had been taxing having two extra people in the house — people whose life situation was so starkly different from ours. Homeless. Poor — no, not poor. *Destitute.* No relatives in Chicago to take them in. Sabrina's father had abandoned them long ago. Since then it had been hand to mouth, shelter to SRO "by the week," back to a shelter. Then the fire, wiping out everything but the clothes on their backs. Literally. Now another shelter.

Should we have invited them to stay, like Stu invited Estelle? Wait. Here I was wrestling with those questions in good old Jodi fashion. Stewing. Going around and around. I needed to pray. Didn't the Bible say we could ask God for wisdom?

I heard Denny turn on the shower; now was not a good time to wash the sheets from the "guest bed" anyway. Willie Wonka fol-

187

lowed me stiffly as I grabbed my Bible and another cup of coffee, and settled into the peace and quiet of the living room. I reread the scriptures Pastor Cobbs had mentioned on Sunday morning: Luke 3:9–11; Romans 12:13; Matthew 25:40. Definitely stretched my comfort zone, but Scripture was clear: we needed to not just be "concerned" about the poor but give practical help. *Okay, Lord, what are You saying here?* I really didn't want to put it into words, but I gulped and prayed: *Were we supposed to ask Precious and Sabrina to stay?*

The Voice in my spirit seemed to speak right up. *Why are you assuming you have to fix it for Precious and Sabrina all by yourself, Jodi? You did what was needed: you gave them a place to stay until another could be found. You gave them food and clothing.*

Huh. Was that the Holy Spirit speaking to me, or just wishful thinking?

I know. But look at Stu. She's going the extra mile, asking Estelle to stay.

The Voice continued, *So? Are you Stu? Do you have room in your home for another grown woman and her almost grown teenager for the long haul?*

Well, no. Amanda had had to sleep on the couch all week. She was a good sport about

188

it, but it wasn't a permanent solution.

Guilt isn't helpful, Jodi. Neither is over-responsibility. But that doesn't mean there isn't more you can do. Look for the possibilities, My daughter. And ask for My direction. Because My yoke is easy, and My burden is light.

"Jodi?" Denny poked his head into the living room, swathed in knit hat, long scarf, and several sweatshirt layers. "I think I'll jog over to the Hickmans'. Been wanting to talk to Carl about something. Give me some exercise too. Oh — when's your meeting?"

"One o'clock. At the church. Josh promised he'd be back in time to pick me up. I think he's going to pick up Edesa first while he's down that way. Isn't it too icy out there to jog?"

"I'll be fine." He came into the room, bent down, and kissed me on the lips. He smelled good. Irish Spring good. "Just one thing, Jodi. Don't feel like you have to take the world on your shoulders, just because this situation with Manna House presents a lot of needs. Whatever they ask you today, it's okay to think about it. Take time to pray about it. Talk about it with me. Okay? Promise?"

I nodded sheepishly. "Thanks. I needed that."

"What? The kiss or the lecture?"

189

I grabbed his shirt and pulled him closer, kissing him back. "Both. Believe me."

The Manna House meeting started at one and ended at three. To my surprise, the group was small — just Rev. Handley and the other staff person, an African-American woman named Mabel, who served part time as office manager, resident coordinator, and volunteer organizer, plus the four volunteers who had been there that night: Josh, Edesa, Karen, and myself. I thought all the volunteers would be there to get hyped up about "what next."

The fire marshal showed up to report on the inspection. The fire had started in the basement, probably an electrical short, intensified, of course, by the dry Christmas tree. Josh kept his eyes down, his face pale. "But it was a fire waiting to happen," the fire marshal added, "Christmas tree or no Christmas tree. The wiring in that old building should have been totally replaced before getting a permit to use it as a shelter." He glared pointedly at Rev. Handley. "I'm not saying anything illegal happened here, but we are investigating who did the safety inspection for your permit and whether city negligence is an issue."

Rev. Handley nodded, visibly upset.

The verbal reports we had each given the night of the fire had been typed up. The marshal asked us to read them over and sign our names if we stood by our reports. I was afraid Josh would scrawl over his, *"It's all my fault!"* But like the rest of us, he read his report tersely, then signed.

The fire marshal stood up to leave. "You people are trying to do a good thing here. But if you manage to get a building and start up again, now you have a chance to do it right. That's what I want to say to you. No shortcuts. *Always* put safety first." He solemnly shook hands all around, then headed for his official car, parked like a red cherry in the snowy parking lot.

We all just looked at each other. Rev. Handley finally cleared her throat. "Well. Mabel and I will be meeting with the board to discuss the future of Manna House — or even if we have one. Right now, however, I want to commend each one of you volunteers for responding quickly and responsibly during the emergency. I've talked to all the residents, and they have nothing but praise for you four helping to get them all out of the building. Josh, I especially want to thank you for taking charge —"

"That's right!" I wanted to cry out. *"He did!"* But Josh was shaking his head miserably. I

bit my lip, my throat tight, knowing my son was in pain.

Rev. Handley pursed her lips thoughtfully. "Son, I know you're beating yourself up because you turned on the Christmas tree lights that night. But all of us — myself included — knew that tree was nothing but dry kindling. We let cozy feelings — trying to create a homey atmosphere for Manna House residents — override our responsibility to put safety first. And you heard the marshal. All the electrical wiring was compromised. As director of Manna House, I take full responsibility for what happened."

I stared at the short, stocky woman with the salt-and-pepper cropped hair and wire-rimmed glasses. Admiration for her eased the tightness in my throat. She could so easily have dumped blame on someone else . . . on my son. She'd only been there briefly that night; wasn't anywhere around when the fire started. But she took responsibility without mincing around. *Huh. If only more leaders displayed that kind of leadership . . .*

Liz Handley sucked in a deep breath, hands on her knees. "We've learned something the hard way. But God in His mercy protected all lives . . ." The director seemed to have a hard time getting any more out.

"*Sí.* That is what is important." Edesa

leaned over and gently touched the director's hand. "I think we should pray and thank our heavenly Father for His mercy." She didn't wait for confirmation but moved right into earnest prayer. "*Oh Dios, nuestro Padre, gracias por tu misericordia! . . ."*

"You didn't talk about the future of Manna House? Nobody asked you to do anything?" Denny couldn't hide his surprise.

I shook my head. "That's all it was — a debriefing after the fire. Reverend Handley reported that all the residents have been moved to other shelters — except for a few, like Rochelle and Estelle, who are staying put — and then we just prayed for them all." I fished a sheet of paper out of my jeans pocket. "I asked for the list so I could continue to pray for them all. By name." I grinned at him impishly. "Didn't think I needed to talk to you or pray about praying."

Denny scratched his chin. "Uh-huh. Well then, guess I don't have to ask *you* if it's okay if I invite all the guys over here tomorrow afternoon for the Super Bowl. Twenty or thirty is all —"

"What?" I snatched a dishtowel and flipped him good. "You didn't!"

He threw up both hands. "Hey! Just kidding! Carl Hickman and I both nixed our homes; our TVs aren't big enough. We're asking Mark Smith. They've got one of those monster screens in their family room."

"Wait just a cotton-pickin' minute." I opened the cupboard door where I kept the Yada Yada list. Tomorrow was February first. Super Bowl Sunday. *And* Yada Yada was supposed to meet . . . where? I ran my finger down the list.

Adele. Perfect. At least she didn't have a sports fanatic hogging the living room or hollow-leg teenagers emptying the food cupboards on Super Bowl Sunday like most of the rest of us.

Ruth and Yo-Yo struggled out of the Garfields' big green Buick in front of Adele's apartment building, each one lugging a baby carrier, just as Stu and I parked across the street. "Where's Ben? Doesn't he usually drop you off?" I asked as we huddled in the small entryway of the apartment building, waiting for Adele to buzz us in.

Ruth rolled her eyes. "Does he usually let me drive? Never. But today, drop *him* off at the Sisulu-Smiths early, he says. Huh. Doesn't want to miss even one Super Bowl commercial, that's what."

"He was going to teach *me* to drive so I

could get my license," Yo-Yo grumbled. "But that was B.B."

I started to ask what "B.B." meant, but I figured it out: *Before Babies.*

We had a good turnout that night, in spite of chilly temperatures. February had shuffled in like a hobo in dirty clothes — no exciting snowstorm, no cleansing thaw, just leftover piles of dirty snow along the plowed streets. I thought Stu might bring Estelle, but she said Estelle was busy sewing up some new clothes for herself from material Stu once bought but had never done anything with.

Rochelle didn't come with Avis either. Avis wasn't happy about leaving her and Conny alone on a weekend. "What if Dexter finds out where she is now? But Peter took himself off to the Super Bowl Bash at Nony's house, so someone had to stay with Conny. Rochelle said she'd love a quiet evening alone anyway." Avis shrugged. Seemed to me Avis's usually joyous face had a permanently strained look these days.

After the traumatic events of last weekend, it felt good to see my Yada Yada sisters chirping away like sparrows on a telephone wire. We teased Nony about leaving her lovely home at the mercy of the guys. She rolled her eyes and laughed. "I know, I know. But

Mark was so excited, we managed to get rid of anything on the first floor that said 'Convalescent Lives Here.' "

But even as we attacked the banana bread Adele brought out right from the oven and passed the babies around, fussing over them like blithering idiots, something seemed amiss. Was someone missing? I counted noses, stopping at Edesa. It occurred to me that Josh had taken her home after the meeting yesterday and had *not* come right home. What was going on with those two? Well, that was neither here nor there right now. I finished going around the circle. All present and accounted for. *So what . . . ?* And then I realized what it was.

MaDear's wheelchair was empty.

16

"Adele? Where's MaDear? Did your sister take her for the weekend?" Immediately heads turned, and the chatting and munching hushed to a whisper. Adele snorted. "My sister? That hussy? Don't know what's gotten into that girl! Sissy's so busy huntin' for a man, she's likely to forget MaDear's at her place and go dancin' all night." She jerked a thumb toward the small bedroom in the back. "Got MaDear in the bed. She's still gettin' over that pneumonia, you know. But don't know what I'm gonna do, y'all. I can't leave her here by herself all day. Gotta get her up an' take her to the shop." Adele sank into a chair and sighed from deep inside, like a slow leak in a truck tire. "Might have to put her in a nursing home. Hate to do it, though. My people take care of their own."

"Girl, I know what you sayin'," Flo agreed. "Just don't seem right, how we treat our

197

elders these days. But I hear ya. Ya gotta do what ya gotta do."

Delores spoke up. "*Sí.* But maybe we should pray that God would provide another way for Adele and MaDear."

Avis smiled. "Sounds like we're ready to begin our prayer time. Why don't we worship the Lord for a few minutes, get our focus right, before we gather up our other prayer concerns." She followed her own suggestion and led out with a familiar hymn . . .

My hope is built on nothing less
Than Jesus' blood and righteousness!
I dare not trust the sweetest frame,
But wholly lean on Jesus' name.

Even Becky and Yo-Yo, who didn't seem to know the words to the verse, picked up on the chorus:

On Christ the solid Rock I stand!
All other ground is sinking sand;
All other ground is sinking sand.

We helped each other through the next few verses and heartily sang the chorus once more, followed by some spontaneous praise. "Thank ya, Jesus! — for being my Rock in the middle of this storm!" "*Sí! Sí! Dios,* You are the anchor we cling to." "Yeah. Thanks, Jesus, for keepin' me from drownin' in my own mess."

Some quarterback must have made a touchdown at Reliant Stadium in Houston just then, because people in the apartment above Adele started yelling and stomping their feet. "Or maybe they tryin' to drown *us* out," Becky smirked. We laughed.

Most of the prayer requests that night were updates on on-going concerns. The Manna House fire and displaced residents . . . a second hearing coming up for Chris Hickman . . . Ricardo Enriquez still looking for a job . . . Becky groaning about the "loop-de-loops" DCFS was putting her through to regain custody of Little Andy . . . whether Stu should ask Estelle to be her housemate . . .

"Avis," Nony cut in, two furrows gathered between her brows. "What about your daughter? You are not sending her back to a shelter, are you? I am very concerned about Rochelle. This is a critical time for her, and the fire is one more trauma on top of everything else."

Avis shook her head. "Rochelle and Conny are going to stay with us for the indefinite future. In fact, Peter says he was wrong to send her away when she needed us most."

She let slip a wry smile. "Kind of nice to see him grovel."

We all laughed again, even harder this time. How many of us had squirmed uncomfortably when Peter put his foot down but kept our mouths shut, not wanting to create more tension in Avis's new marriage?

A loud wail from one of the baby carriers joined the laughter. "Awake she is now," Ruth pouted. "Yo-Yo, see if Havah will fall back asleep if you walk her."

Yo-Yo didn't move. "Walk her yourself," she muttered.

My mouth nearly fell open. Ruth glared at Yo-Yo, but unbuckled the baby from the carrier and headed for Adele's hallway, murmuring, "Shh, shh, *mamela.* Don't pay any attention to that *nebbish.*"

Avis did not seem to notice the interruption. "There is one piece of good news, sisters. The HIV clinic tested Conny, too, but" — her voice dropped to a choked whisper — "praise God! His test came back negative. We are so grateful!"

"Thank ya, *Je*sus!" Florida cried. Others joined in the praise while some looked shocked, as though they hadn't even considered that possibility.

When the room quieted, Nony leaned forward. "Avis, do you think Rochelle would be comfortable talking with me? I would very much like to help her get the help she needs to live with her HIV diagnosis. It is not hopeless, you know. But . . ."

"Thank you, Nony. I — I would appreciate that very much. Let me talk to her." Avis looked at her lap, absently twisting her wedding ring. "In fact, I think all three of us need some help to live with this diagnosis."

In the silence that followed, the only sound was Ruth jouncing the baby over her shoulder and muttering who-knows-what in Havah's tiny ear.

"Well." Avis raised her head and looked around, back to business. "Have we heard from everyone? Hoshi. You've been very quiet tonight. Is everything all right? How is your new semester going?"

Hoshi nodded, her straight hair falling like black silk over her shoulder. "It is very good. But hard. This is my last semester at Northwestern, you know."

Her last semester! How had that snuck up on us? I felt a sudden pang. Would Hoshi go back to Japan after graduation? Would Yada Yada lose her? And what would the Sisulu-Smith family do without her? She had been an incredible help to them during the difficult time of Mark's injury and convalescence.

". . . but most of all, I would like prayer for Sara," she was saying.

My attention snapped back. Sara. "The girl in the sundress" who had caught my eye at the racist rally at Northwestern last spring, part of the White Pride group. The girl God had prodded me to pray for, even before I knew her name. The girl who had defied her racist friends and named the men who had attacked Mark Smith and left him for dead. The girl Hoshi had unknowingly befriended at Northwestern and brought to a Yada Yada meeting at the Sisulu-Smith home one night last fall, tearing the peace of that home to shreds and smashing the fragile friendship between the gentle Japanese student and the mixed-up white girl from Chicago's North Shore.

We all leaned forward. Even Ruth stopped jouncing the baby and tuned an ear.

"Sara transferred out of my history class, so I do not see her as often. But our walkways keep crossing anyway." Hoshi smiled. "Nony calls them 'divine appointments.' "

"Hallelujah, Jesus," Nony murmured.

"We had coffee at the student center last week, and I invited her once more to Yada Yada, at a different home this time. But . . ." Hoshi shook her head. "I do not think she will agree."

This was met with sympathetic murmurings. "Well, girl, you tried," Florida said.

"Yeah," Yo-Yo chimed in from her perch on a floor pillow. "That girl's a hard case. Maybe harder than me."

Hoshi's volume hiked up a notch or two. "I do not agree. It is not time to give up on Sara. Why has God put her in our way if He does not want to show her how much He loves her? Haven't we often said, 'God's ways are not our ways'?"

Whoa. Hoshi had some backbone!

Hoshi's voice softened. "I . . . there is a Christian student group on campus. I am going to ask Sara if she would like to attend. They share a meal together, then have a Bible study and discussion. She may say yes if I go with her. She's very lonely."

Delores Enriquez patted Hoshi's hand. "We will pray that she will go with you."

Hoshi lowered her lashes. "There is only one thing. It meets on Sunday evenings."

"Sunday evenings?" I groused to Stu as we walked from the garage to our back porch. Stu's lights were on upstairs, but my house was dark. "Do you think Hoshi will start going to this campus group rather than coming to Yada Yada?"

"Possibility, I guess." But I could tell Stu

was distracted. "Adele said she has to take MaDear to the beauty shop with her, even when she's sick. But, you know, I wonder . . ." She ran up the back stairs and I heard her call out, "Estelle? How's the sewing going?" before the door shut.

I unlocked our door. Wonka rose stiffly from his post just inside the door to greet me, snuffling. Otherwise, the house was silent. So Amanda wasn't back yet from youth group. But surely the Super Bowl was over. Maybe Denny and Josh were giving rides home to some of the other guys.

I suddenly had an inkling of how Stu felt coming home every night to a dark house.

I shed my jacket and turned on the flame under the teakettle. Wonka just stood in the kitchen, whining faintly.

"What's the matter, Wonka? Want to go out?" But the dog was facing me, not the door. "Hungry?" I looked in the dog's bowl. Still full of kibbles. Hadn't been touched. How strange was that? "Just lonely, huh?" I scratched the dog's ears. "You don't like it when we all leave the house, do you?"

I glanced at the clock. Still had a couple of hours before bed. I should probably finish my lesson plans. February was Black History Month. I already had my class reading books about Mary McLeod Bethune, the inspiring African-American teacher our school was named after. But I felt weighted down by all the concerns we were carrying in Yada Yada. *MaDear's illness . . . Chris Hickman locked up at the JDC . . . Rochelle needing to "live with HIV," as Nony put it . . .*

I knew we were supposed to take our burdens to God and leave them there. But I still felt like I had sand in my gears. Maybe it was just the winter blues. While we had been sending up desperate prayers for our loved ones that evening, the guys had probably been laughing, cracking jokes, and yelling at their Super Bowl bash. Plain old fun.

That's what we Yadas needed! Some good old-fashioned *fun.*

I looked at the calendar in the kitchen, ignoring the whistle of the teakettle. Our next meeting in two weeks would meet upstairs at Stu's place. That Saturday was Valentine's Day . . . and the following Monday was a school holiday: President's Day. We should do something fun that weekend! Something everyone could do, not just the "couples" on Valentine's Day. But what? Something like . . .

I grinned. *That's it!*

"Wonka, old buddy," I said, as I plonked myself down in front of the computer and booted it up, "it's too bad you have four feet, because I don't think they make roller skates for dogs." A few minutes later, I was typing furiously.

To: Yada Yada
From: BaxterBears@wahoo.com
Re: A Roller Party

Sisters! Anybody up for some FUN in the midst of all the serious stuff life throws at us? How about a roller-skating party on Valentine's Day! That's a Saturday. Bring the kids! Bring a friend! (Hoshi? Do you think Sara might come?) Oh, yeah. We might even let the guys come if they behave themselves and don't act like a bunch of adolescent showoffs. So . . . what do you think?

Love, Jodi

All three of my family members looked at each other as though sharing a terrible secret: Mom had gone completely off her rocker. Denny backpedaled. "Uh, Jodi. It's been twenty years since —"

"It's like riding a bike. You never forget!"

Amanda rolled her eyes. "*Kids* go roller skating, not . . . not *old* people." She flounced off to her room.

"Watch it, kid. I could skate circles around

206

you!" Denny called after her.

Oh, so Denny was on my side now?

Josh shrugged noncommittally and hauled out the city phone book. "Mom? You got a number for the Salvation Army?"

So much for roller-skating. "Uh, think I do." I flipped through our address book. "Who're you calling?" *None of my business, but so what?*

"Precious. She's gotta be bummed."

"What? You mean . . . ?" Guilt over letting Precious and Sabrina go to the Salvation Army shelter popped up again and danced like a gremlin on my conscience.

"I *mean*" — Josh grinned wickedly — "the Carolina Panthers lost to the Patriots 29 to 32 tonight. I'm calling to rub it in."

The first week of February slogged its way across the city, with snow flurries upping the snow cover to about seven inches. At least it blanketed the dirt-encrusted ice clumps that made walking as treacherous as downhill skiing. Still dangerous, but not so ugly. One out of two wasn't bad. But I felt like a triathlon athlete every time I made it to and from school with no broken bones.

A couple of days in a row, I saw Estelle leaving with Stu in the morning. On the third day, I poked my head out the back door. "What's up with you two? Estelle going to work with you?"

Stu laughed. "Better than that! Estelle is taking care of MaDear at home so Adele doesn't have to take her to the shop."

Estelle, bundled against the cold, smiled big. "Ain't the Lord good? That MaDear is the sweetest thing. And Ms. Skuggs is paying me, too, so I can contribute to my room and board while I'm here."

I wouldn't have called forgetful, feisty MaDear "the sweetest thing," but I whooped, "Hallelujah!" anyway. "What a great idea! I'm so glad for Adele — and you, too, Estelle. Keep warm!" I quickly shut the door against the frigid air, then pulled it open again. "Stu! Did you get my e-mail about the roller-skating party?"

"Count me in!" she yelled back.

"Count me out!" laughed Estelle.

But as the week wore on, I got several more positive responses to the roller-skating party idea. Florida said she was game, also Cedric and Carla, but she couldn't vouch for Carl. Chanda and her tribe said they'd come, so did Becky, Yo-Yo, and Edesa. Delores said it depended on her work schedule, but she knew Ricardo had a gig that night. Well, that was a good start, so I Googled a list of roller rinks in the Chicago area and started making calls to find the closest rink. It didn't matter if everyone got on board. The rest of us could have fun.

But I was worried about Willie Wonka. I fed him in the morning as usual before leaving for school, but more often than not, when I came home from school, the bowl of kibbles had barely been touched.

"What's the matter, old boy?" I murmured, sitting down on the floor beside him and stroking his silky brown head. But all he did was lay his muzzle in my lap and look up at me with dark liquid eyes, whimpering softly.

17

"Denny?" I said, wandering into the living room Friday night after Amanda had gone out babysitting. "I think we need to take Willie Wonka to the vet. He hasn't been eating, and he's been whimpering a lot. But I don't know what's wrong."

Denny put down the sports section. "I think he's just getting old, Jodi. What is he now — fifteen? sixteen? We got him when Amanda was still floor-scooting, mopping up dust bunnies better than Dial-a-Maid."

"Yeah. What were we *thinking*?" I sank down on the couch beside my husband. "A puppy and a baby — it was like having twins! Guess we can empathize with Ben and Ruth, huh?"

He chortled. "Yeah. Except both of their twins poop in diapers, not on the kitchen floor!"

We both started to laugh, remembering our attempts to housebreak a two-month-old Lab — but the next moment I was feeling teary. "Amanda's grown up with Willie Wonka. Don't know what she'll do if he . . . if he . . ."

"Hey, we don't need to go there yet, babe. See what the vet says! Look at your mom. She's got arthritis and had a bad bout of pneumonia last year, but she's still chugging along."

Oh, great. Thanks, Denny. That's real helpful.

But I tried to be matter-of-fact when we loaded Willie Wonka into the back of the Dodge Caravan for the trip to the vet the next morning. "He's probably just getting old," I told Amanda when she got up that morning. "But we should let the vet check him out."

Amanda climbed into the back with the dog, crooning, "Poor baby. You don't feel so good? Don't worry. The doctor's going to make it all better. That's right. Don't be scared, Amanda's here . . ."

I gripped the steering wheel and headed for the animal hospital on McCormick Boulevard. I hardly knew how to pray. Dogs and people . . . we all had to die sometime. *But we're not ready to let Wonka go, God! Please let it be something the vet can fix.* I hated my next thought: *How much is this go-*

ing to cost? We barely had enough medical insurance to cover our family, much less the dog.

But maybe Denny was right. Wonka had been healthy up until now, except for going deaf and his joints getting stiff. We'd just have to see what the vet said.

"The vet thinks it's *cancer?*" Denny's jaw dropped when I gave him the news.

"*Might* be cancer." I peeked down the hall, where Amanda had headed with the dog, and saw that her bedroom door was shut. I sank into a chair at the dining room table and wrapped my hands around the steaming cup of coffee Denny had poured. "He's got a growth in his abdomen about the size of a tennis ball. She can't know if it's benign or malignant unless they do a biopsy and run a bunch of tests."

"And these tests — ?"

I sighed. "Expensive. And if we want the tumor removed, well, they *could* do surgery. But . . ."

Denny's face sagged. "Yeah, I know. Mega bucks."

We sat at the dining room table in silence for several minutes, letting our coffee get cold. *Sheesh.* Made me mad that "what it cost" was even a consideration, if that's what Wonka needed! But God knew we didn't have a couple thousand dollars just sitting in the bank. Even Denny's raise barely covered cost of living increases.

Denny sighed. "So what did the vet recommend?"

I took a sip of the now-lukewarm coffee and made a face. "Well, I kinda expected her to push for the biopsy and then surgery if the tumor is malignant. That's how she makes her living, for Pete's sake! But she didn't really. Said it was a toss-up at Wonka's age. And surgery is, well, *surgery*. Always a risk. It's up to us, of course, she said. But I kinda got the feeling she thought making him comfortable and not doing anything drastic was a decent way to go. In fact . . ." I dug around in the tote bag I'd tossed on the table and pulled out a couple of pill containers. "She gave me some sample meds that will help with his arthritis pain. Also, something" — I squinted at the label of another bottle — "to help him digest his food easily. She recommended we give him a small amount of canned food twice a day rather than the dry kibbles, see if that helps." I shrugged. "She wrote a prescription for the meds and put it with his chart. She said we could take a few days to think about it and let her know."

Denny nodded, rubbing the back of his head. Proof positive he didn't know what to do. "Okay. Let's give it a few days." He pushed back his chair. "Want me to run to the store and get some canned dog food?"

I let slip a grin. "Sure. And while you're at it . . ." I handed him the grocery list I'd made out while sitting in the waiting room, surrounded by meowing cats in plastic carriers and dogs so nervous they were shedding all over me.

The phone rang the next morning while we were doing our usual Baxter hurry-scurry, trying to get out of the house in time to make it to church by ten o'clock. The caller ID said Chanda George. "Hey, Chanda, what's up?"

"So when you going to invite mi to dat new church?" she sniffed over the phone. "You got som'ting special coming up? Men's and Women's Day? Pastor's anniversary? Why you not let mi know?"

"Uh, if that's part of New Morning's traditions, I haven't heard about it yet. We're still trying to decide on a name! But if . . . wait a minute. Why don't you just come to visit today? It's the second Sunday of the month, and we have a potluck after service. That'd be fun to have you there. Except, we're having a business meeting after the potluck. It's like the Chicago Marathon: only the strong survive!" I snickered. "But don't worry. You can duck out at that point."

"*Dis day?* But you said *potluck.* Anyting I cook take at least half a day."

"Just come, Chanda. I'm bringing a taco salad — plenty for you too. Besides, they don't expect guests to bring food. It'll be fun to see the kids."

"Mm." She considered. "What dey wear to dat church? Maybe mi have to shop first."

I laughed, remembering the parade of hats at Paul and Silas Apostolic Baptist, where Chanda, Adele Skuggs, and MaDear were members. "Believe me, Chanda. *Anything* you have in your closet will be fine."

Well, almost anything. Chanda showed up at our shopping center sanctuary in a long red wool coat with a fur collar — probably real — and a fur-trimmed red hat. Underneath she wore a red wool suit, the skirt above the knees and tight around her ample hips, and black, high-heeled boots.

"Wow," I said, and turned my attention to Dia and Cheree, cute as catalog cherubs in matching taffeta frilly dresses, lacy ankle socks, and patent leather Mary Janes. Both of them clung shyly to their mother's hands while twelve-year-old Tom trailed behind, running a finger around his stiff shirt collar and tie. But when the children saw kids they knew — Cedric and Carla Hickman, Marcus and Michael Sisulu-Smith, and Little Andy Wallace — it didn't take long until they were running around with the rest of the rat pack.

As the praise band warmed up and we all found our seats on the folding chairs, I noticed Dia cuddling with Amanda, reaching up and twisting Amanda's butterscotch hair into little ringlets, coaxing a smile out of my teenager. I smiled too. I'd practically had to drag Amanda to church this morning; she'd wanted to stay with Willie Wonka. "He *needs* me, Mom!" But when he ate half the soft canned food we'd put in his dish that morning, I assured her he would be fine without her for a couple of hours.

We didn't have a choir swaying down the aisle like Paul and Silas Apostolic Baptist did. Our preachers didn't wear black robes with Afro-centric stoles. We didn't have cushioned pews. But Chanda seemed to enjoy herself, throwing herself into the praise and worship as though she felt right at home. At one point, she leaned over to me and whispered, "Ooo, dat saxophone player is *fine.*" I wasn't sure if she meant his music, or if she noticed that he was young, good-looking, and dressed smart. "What dat mon's name? He from de islands. Uh-huh. Mi know it."

I had to admit I didn't know his name, but said I'd find out.

Pastor Clark preached that day. Well, "teached." I'd kind of hoped Pastor Cobbs would preach today, since his style would be closer to what Chanda was used to. But as Pastor Clark taught from the life of David, about how God prepared him to be a powerful warrior and a worshiper while he was still a nobody, out in the fields by himself, watching his father's sheep, Chanda nodded and called out, "Amen! Dat's right, Preacher." Young David, Pastor Clark pointed out, killed a lion and a bear when they threatened his sheep, never knowing that God was preparing him to slay giants. He learned to play the lute and sang praises to God when no one was watching, unaware that God was preparing him to soothe the king when he was troubled by evil spirits, and to write psalms that still inspire and comfort us today.

"What about you?" Pastor Clark said, looking around the room. "How is God preparing you in the situation you're in right now, because He has a bigger job for you down the road? Are you being faithful? Using your gifts *now?*"

Chanda leaned toward me again. "Now dat's some good teaching. But dese chairs . . . uh-uh. Dey *killing* my bottom."

I stifled a giggle. "Stu's started a Chair Fund. But it might be awhile."

Immediately after the service, tables were set up and I lost track of Chanda while helping to set out the food — the usual array of rice and beans, fried chicken, potato salad, greens, oxtails, macaroni and cheese, and my taco salad with lettuce, spiced hamburger, chopped tomatoes, onions, cheese, black olives, and crushed tortilla chips on top. The teenagers scarfed that up.

I looked around for Chanda, to be sure she and the kids got food, and saw her talking to the saxophone player. "His name is Oscar Frost," she smirked at me a few minutes later. "De mon has family in Kingston, like mi. Now what you tink about dat?"

Well, at least now I knew his name.

Chanda and kids scooted when the tables were pushed back and chairs lined up for the business meeting. "Mi coming back, dat for sure," she giggled suggestively, pulling the fur-trimmed red hat firmly down on her braided head. "You let mi know when dis church get itself some new chairs."

Pastor Cobbs called the business meeting

218

to order and asked for the minutes from the last meeting to be read. Debra Meeks stood up with a notebook and read the items that had been approved: *Pastor Joe Cobbs and Pastor Hubert Clark to be copastors of the merger of Uptown Community Church and New Morning Christian Church . . . The combined elders from both churches would continue to serve for one year, half serving the first six months, the other half serving the following six months, with a new election in one year . . . However, Mark Smith had withdrawn from the elder board for medical reasons . . . The worship band would incorporate musicians from both churches . . . Current worship leaders would rotate for the next six months, then form new worship teams . . .*

Debra looked up. "Last item of business: Names for the church were still being accepted. We decided a paper vote would be taken in two weeks to whittle the list down to the top two; a final vote at the next business meeting — today."

Pastor Cobbs cleared his throat and grinned sheepishly. "As everyone knows, we had an emergency situation two weeks ago and never got that paper vote. What would people like to do — take a paper vote of the list of names today, and put off the final vote until the next meeting? Or . . . yes,

Sister Florida?"

Florida bounced to her feet. "Don't mean to be pushy, Pastor, but I move we vote on a name *today.* Take two or three votes to narrow it down, I don't care. But calling this church by both names for even one more day be like that Chinese water torture you hear about. *I'm* 'bout to go crazy, know what I'm sayin'?" She sat down to general laughter and not a few hearty amens.

Pastor Cobbs was smiling too. "All in favor?" The ayes clearly carried. "All right. Let's get the list of suggested names passed out. Any discussion before we do the first paper vote?"

The discussion picked up right where we'd left off a month ago. "Seems like we ought to merge the two original names somehow." "Nah, we need a new name, like Sister Avis said." "Sister Jodi, could you tell us what that Hebrew word means again?" "Do we really want a name you have to explain to people all the time?" . . .

I tuned out the discussion, realizing it wasn't looking good for *Yachad,* and read down the list of possible names. *Wait a minute.* A new one had been added since last time. I looked up, about to ask about it, when Rick Reilly stood up.

"As you can see, a new proposal has been

added. When we didn't take the paper vote a couple of weeks ago, the youth group said they'd like to come up with a suggestion. The pastors said fine since, technically, the floor was still open." He looked around at the teens. "Anyone want to explain it? Amanda?"

My daughter ducked her head, but several of the other teens hissed, "Go on, go on." She stood up, giggling with embarrassment.

"Well, like, it's kind of self-explanatory. SouledOut Christian Church . . . or maybe SouledOut Community Church. We couldn't decide. Somebody saw a bookstore with that name — SouledOut Christian Bookstore, or something like that — and we thought it would make a cool name for a church. You know, *souls* and *sold out* — like a double meaning, 'sold out for Jesus' and 'winning souls to Jesus.' But also kinda jazzy."

"You go, girl!" Florida crowed. The congregation laughed. Back at the soundboard, Josh grinned, as if proud of his sister. Flustered, Amanda sat down, her face bright red.

It only took one paper vote. "SouledOut Community Church" got over 50 percent of the vote the first time around. The teens were excited, shouting "Woo woo woo!" as they pumped their fists and then gathered into a spontaneous huddle, slapping hands and yelling, "SouledOut! SouledOut!" like a team ready to go into action on the court.

Amanda slipped over to me as I packed up my empty taco salad bowl. "Sorry, Mom. *Yachad* was kinda cool, too, but like, the whole teen group came up with —"

I gave her a quick hug. "Honey, it's fine! Really. It's a good name. Now go on, shoo, before I put you to work washing dishes."

I wanted her out of there before she saw the tears watering my eyes. Sure, I had a twinge of disappointment that the name I suggested got left in the dust. But that wasn't the reason I felt teary. Even though I'd barely had thirty minutes to get used to the new name, I realized something profound had just happened.

The *teenagers* — black and white — had suggested a name for *their* church.

The congregation *voted for* their name.

Could anything say louder to these young people, *"You are important. We respect your ideas. You contribute to our church"*?

And *SouledOut?* Wow, what a concept! "Oh God," I whispered under my breath, taking another swipe at the serving table I'd already cleaned, "let it be true for me too."

18

Curiosity got the better of me once we got home. "So, um, what name did you vote for, Denny?" He waggled a finger in front of my face. "Uh-uh-uh! No fair. We don't tell each other who we vote for in presidential elections. Why would I tell you how I voted at church?"

"Oh. So you didn't vote for *Yachad.*" I caught the warning look in his eye. "Okay, okay, you don't have to tell me . . . *if* you go roller-skating with me on Valentine's Day."

He threw up his hands. "Jodi! That's practically blackmail! Are you sure you don't want me to take you out to a nice restaurant? Or go see a play or something? Something where the odds are in our favor for staying on our feet?"

I giggled. "Nope. Besides, this will be cheaper. *And* lots of fun." I grabbed his arm and pulled him close, rubbing noses with him. Eskimo kisses, we used to call them as kids. "Aw, c'mon, Denny. Otherwise I'll have to sit out all the 'couples skates' by myself — or end up skating with some dark-eyed lothario in tight leather pants."

Maybe it was the "tight leather pants" that did it, but I squeezed a reluctant promise from my hubby of twenty-one years to accompany me to the Super Skatium the following Saturday. I called some of the other Yada sisters to see if any of their guys were coming. Yo-Yo said her brothers wanted to know "Who else is comin'?" — meaning kids their age, which I couldn't tell her. My own kids had ignored the invitation so far. Florida said she was still working on Carl, but he might be more open to it if he knew Denny was going. "Kinda depends on how Chris's hearing on Wednesday turns out. An' I need another favor . . ."

"This Wednesday?" I peeked at our kitchen calendar. I'd written "FLO 38" in red marker across February 11. "But that's your birthday, Flo!"

She snorted in my ear. "Yeah. Some birthday present, huh? But if the judge doesn't assign Chris to adult court like those other perps, that'd be about the best birthday gift anyone could give me right now."

"You want me to take Carla home with

224

me after school again?"

"Yeah. That's what I was gonna axe ya. Would give me some space to handle whatever comes down before I have to relate to the other kids."

"Oh, Florida." My heart ached for my friend. "Come on, let's pray about it. We gotta keep faith that God's gonna work this out. If Chris didn't do this —"

"*If*, Jodi?"

I stopped. Why did I say "if"? Well, I didn't *know*, did I? And Chris had been hanging out on the edges of the Black Disciples all year. Wasn't that why the Hickmans moved to Rogers Park from their old neighborhood? Only there wasn't any place in Chicago "safe" from gangs if you were looking for trouble. Wannabes like Chris got pressured into lots of petty crime — and some not so petty — just to prove they were "down" for their homeboys.

But Chris insisted he'd only hopped in the car for a ride home. Did I believe him? Would a judge believe him? If that's what happened, someone better tell him, "With friends like that, who needs enemies!"

I blew out a breath. "I'm sorry, Flo. Poor choice of words. Let's pray that God will give Chris favor with this judge and assign him to juvenile court."

"Yeah, Jodi." She sniffed. "Do that."

So I did, right there on the phone, prayed that God would be present at that hearing on Wednesday, prayed that Chris would not only be assigned to juvenile court, but that God would bring him out of the JDC and restore him to his family. "Oh Jesus! Put a hedge of protection around that boy while he's separated from his family! And when he comes out, Lord, give him honest opportunities to develop that artistic talent You've given him!"

Florida was silent when I finished. "Flo? You still there?"

"Yeah." Another silence. Then, "You really think Chris got him some talent?"

Carla came home with me after school on Wednesday. Willie Wonka, who seemed to have perked up on his new diet of canned dog food and two pricey prescriptions, lumbered to his feet when we came in the door and gave Carla a tail wag and a lick on the face, much to her delight.

Over hot chocolate and toast with cinnamon sugar, we plotted the afternoon. "Can I make a card for my mommy? It's her birthday today, but . . ." Carla's face fell. "I don't got no present for her."

I grinned. "You absolutely can make a

card for your mom. Not only that — ta da!" I pulled a chocolate cake mix out of the cupboard. "And not only that . . ." I flashed her my recipe card for craft "salt dough."

For the next hour, we were busy mixing the cake, licking the bowl and the beaters, and making salt dough. Before I could warn her, Carla stuck her finger in the salt dough and popped it in her mouth. "Yuck!" Much spitting followed, while I tried not to laugh. But by the time the cake came out of the oven, Carla had crafted five rather lumpy napkin rings out of the salt dough on a cookie sheet, which we popped into the oven for twenty minutes while I scrounged in my craft supplies for poster paints, paint brushes, and a bottle of varnish.

Denny arrived home, gave me a passing peck on the cheek, and headed for the front room and the TV news. Right on his heels, Amanda dumped her jacket and school bag on the floor, gave Wonka his kissy-face greeting, and leaned over the dining room table. "Hey! Salt dough. Whatcha makin', Carla?"

Carla beamed and held up one of the brightly painted napkin rings. "See? It gots Chris's name on this one." She picked up another. "An' this purple-an'-pink one's for Mommy. See? M-O-M. For her birthday!"

"Cool." Amanda peered into the plastic bowl of dough. "Can I make something?" She scooped out a blob of dough and went to work.

I hid a smile as I disappeared into the kitchen to ice the cooled cake. If I had *asked* Amanda if she wanted to play with salt dough, she would have given me The Look, absolutely sure her mother still lived in the Dark Ages.

The phone rang. I barely got out a hello when Florida screeched in my ear. "Praise Jesus, Jodi! The attorney didn't even hafta make a big case. Judge looked at some papers, said somethin' like, 'This kid's got no priors . . . wasn't identified as the gunman . . . he's only fourteen . . . whatever the court decides at his disposition, there's no way I'm going to send this case to adult court.' Then he set a court date for April somethin', an' *bam!* That was it! Oh, hallelujah! Praise Jesus!" Florida's voice faded temporarily while she did some serious praising in the background. When she came back on the phone, she said, "Carl is so relieved, I might even get him to the roller rink on Saturday."

"That's great, Florida! See? God really answered our prayer!" But I was thinking, *April? That's two months away! If Chris was just in the wrong place at the wrong time and he's not guilty, they've still had him locked up for five months of his life.* But I didn't say any of that to Florida. One day at a time, and this day the news was good.

As we got cake, craft, and Carla ready for the half-mile ride home, she suddenly gave me a big hug. "I like third grade," she announced, grinning up at me. "I wish you could be my teacher next year too."

I was so surprised, it took me several seconds to find my voice. "That," I finally said, returning her hug, "is just about the nicest thing anyone's ever said to me."

Amanda was painting a couple of salt dough hearts when I got back from taking Carla home. "What are *you* making, Michelangelo?"

No answer. More delicate painting. Then she held up two hearts on key rings. "Which one do you like, Mom?"

One heart had delicate white flowers painted on the red background; the other had funky polka dots. Both had **AB** + **JE** in the center. I pointed to the one with flowers.

She lifted the polka dot heart. "I like this one. It's for José. You know, for Valentine's Day."

My choosing the one with flowers had probably sealed its fate. "That's nice."

"Yeah. But I'm gonna give it to him *after* the roller-skating party, in case he falls down or something and breaks it." She hopped up. "Thanks for the salt dough, Mom."

I watched her go and shook my head. By the time I figured out how to step with my teenagers, they'd be gone and I'd have to start all over learning a new dance. *Empty nest . . . adult kids . . . grandchildren . . .*

Whoa. Did she say roller-skating party?

As it turned out, Josh also decided to go roller-skating because Edesa was bringing the Enriquez kids — including José, hence Amanda's change of heart — and he borrowed the church van to pick them up. I was hoping Ben Garfield would bring Yo-Yo Spencer and her brothers, but Ruth just snorted. "Skating, schmating. Broken necks we don't need, Jodi. Who would bring up Isaac and Havah?" So Denny and I picked up the Spencers and met the rest of our party at the Skatium for the four o'clock skate.

Had to admit, Chanda's Lexus and Stu's silver Celica seemed a bit overdressed for the parking lot full of five-year-old Hondas and Fords. Nony and Mark had declined, but they sent Marcus and Michael in their minivan with Hoshi, who also picked up the Hickmans. I never did hear from Avis and Peter, but they didn't show. No surprise there. Couldn't really imagine Avis on roller skates — but given all they were dealing with right now, letting loose with a little undignified fun might've been just what they needed!

Oh, well, we had a good turnout anyway.

I felt almost giddy lacing up my rented roller skates. As Denny said, it'd been more than twenty years since I'd been to a skating rink! The live organ music was gone, replaced by an unseen DJ spinning unfamiliar CDs, stopping the music now and then to announce in a throaty voice, "All Skate" . . . "Ladies Choice" . . . "Couples Only" . . .

My first few times around the rink during All Skate, I had serious doubts about my declaration, *"It's like riding a bike! You never forget!"* Picking me up after a spill, Denny laughed and took my hand. "Come on." Hand in hand, I gradually found my "skate legs" and started to enjoy myself . . . until the DJ sent us off the rink saying, "Guys Only. Ladies, if you value your life, leave the floor . . ."

I didn't remember that one. But I clumped

together with my Yada Yada sisters behind the railing, making irreverent comments about Pete Spencer, Josh, and José racing each other around the rink like a trio of speed demons. The DJ had even cut the music. We applauded the younger boys — Marcus and Michael Smith, Chanda's Tom, Cedric Hickman, and Yo-Yo's brother Jerry — holding their own against the tide of bigger teenage boys and twenty-somethings. Denny and Carl, meanwhile, wisely took the opportunity to duck over to the concession stand and get a Coke.

Another All Skate, then Couples Only. "It's Valentine's Day, lovers," the DJ smirked. "Get out on the floor and get your groooove on." The music wasn't exactly the good ol' sixties love songs we used to skate to, even in the late seventies and early eighties. In fact, I didn't recognize any of the music, if you could call it that. Mostly noise to my ears. But it was fun seeing Carl skating with Florida, nothing fancy, just hand in hand, grins on their faces. Denny took my left hand and put his right arm around my waist. I leaned against him, and we floated around the curves . . . *left, glide . . . right, glide . . .*

We passed Josh and Edesa skating together slowly — she'd said this was her first time ever. I didn't see Amanda and José on the floor, but didn't give it much thought. Didn't want to rush them, anyway.

I half-closed my eyes, aware of Denny's arm snug around my waist, pulling me gently along, holding me up without seeming to. No wonder the Bible said, *"Two are better than one . . ." Oh God, this is so much fun!*

When the Couples Skate was over, I took a break and joined a few other Yada Yadas sipping Cokes and munching on nachos. "Kinda surprised they playin' these kind of songs with all these little kids here," Yo-Yo was saying.

I blinked. What kind of songs?

Edesa nodded. "*Sí.* The words make me feel ashamed."

"Uh," I stammered. "Have to admit, I can't understand the words. What's going on?"

Stu rolled her eyes knowingly. "Probably just as well, Jodi."

I sat down on a bench and tried to listen. Still didn't understand much . . . but by concentrating I caught enough to feel my face redden.

Good grief. My kids are here, listening to this crap? The other Yadas had brought their kids at *my* urging! I saw nine-year-old Carla and Chanda's girls, Dia and Cheree, out on the floor, wiggling their behinds suggestively and giggling.

Edesa must have seen the shocked look on my face. "Do not be upset, Sister Jodi. You did not know. None of us thought about it. But if the other *mamacitas* don't mind, maybe it will be good to cut our time short."

I stood up. "Well, sure. But before we slink out of here with our tails between our legs, I'm going to talk to the DJ. This just isn't appropriate for a Family Skate."

I had to ask three different people before I found where the DJ was hidden behind his glass wall, and then had to wait while he announced, "Ladies Choice. This is Ladies Choice, gents, so suck in that gut and your Valentine just might ask you to skate." He punched a button and looked at the window where I gestured at him to open the door. "Yeah?"

My little talk lasted about sixty seconds. It did not go well.

"Look, lady. I play these songs all the time, and you're the first person who's complained about it. This is what the kids are listening to. It's what they want to hear. If you don't like it, take it up with the manager . . . Gotta go." The door shut in my face.

Ooo! Now my blood was up. I clumped my skates on the threadbare "carpet" back to my friends. The lights were down; Ladies Choice was still on the floor. I saw Chanda flash by hand in hand with a guy in his thirties, a pretty good skater. Becky had asked Carl Hickman, with Florida's blessing, I guessed. But to my surprise, Amanda was sitting on a bench, arms crossed, glaring at the darkened skating rink with the spinning colored lights flickering around the walls and ceiling. I squinted at the circling skaters.

A dark-haired Latina skated past, arm in arm with José Enriquez.

I darted a glance at Amanda. *Uh-oh.* Should I say anything? It was Ladies Choice, after all. The other girl had probably beaten her to it. But I knew she wouldn't want my sympathy, not in public anyway.

After the skate, I saw José make his way over to Amanda and plop down on the bench next to her, laughing, but she turned her face away, mouth pinched. For a few minutes, he seemed to be arguing with her, but finally he threw up his arms and left her alone.

I sighed. *Oh, Amanda.*

We didn't stay for the end of the Family Skate. Some of the younger set griped about it, until we reminded them we were heading for Giordano's for pizza and root beer. All twenty-six of us, adults and kids, crowded into Giordano's party room, generating a lot of laughter and happy bedlam.

Make that twenty-five. Amanda said she had a stomachache and wanted us to drop her off at home. No, she did *not* want us to bring her any pizza.

Denny and I didn't get home until after nine o'clock, after dropping off our passengers. Josh was still out, driving Edesa and the Enriquez crew back to Little Village. The house was dark. Denny and I entered quietly, not wanting to disturb Amanda if she was asleep. I listened at her bedroom door.

Muffled sobs broke the silence.

I stood uncertainly in the hallway, wondering if I should go in. And that's when I saw it in the hallway, broken into pieces as if it had been stomped on.

The heart-shaped key ring Amanda had made for José for Valentine's Day.

19

The next morning Amanda appeared briefly in her rumpled sleep shirt, hair tousled, mumbling that she didn't feel good and wasn't going to church. She disappeared back into her bedroom. "Let her be," Denny advised. "Timing is everything."

As we drove to church, I watched the gray streets go by without really seeing them. I felt badly for Amanda, but my feelings were mixed. She and José had been sweet on each other for over a year already, and they were only sixteen. A year ago this month José had come up with the big idea to throw a *quinceañera* for Amanda — a formal "coming out" fifteenth birthday party, a Mexican tradition, though by that time Amanda was fifteen-and-a-half. Delores's son was a sweet boy, but they were really too young to get serious with each other. Some distance wasn't a bad idea in my book.

"Hey. Look at that," Denny said, pulling

into a parking space facing our shopping center church.

I looked up. Painted across the wide glass windows in a bold red script were the words: SOULEDOUT COMMUNITY CHURCH. A few early shoppers paused and read the sign before heading for the large Dominick's grocery store that anchored the shopping center. Well. There it was. The new name of our church. I smiled. *I think I like it.*

I found it hard to concentrate on worship that morning, though. Roller-skating had been fun, and fun was what we needed, but I also felt embarrassed, inviting my Yada Yada sisters and their families into a situation I hadn't really checked out, music-wise anyway. That language! I cringed just thinking about the few phrases I'd caught. A far cry from the sweet love songs of my parents' generation. Even rock and roll was tame by comparison. Made me mad that the DJ had blown me off, telling me to speak to the manager if I had a problem . . .

Hey. That was a thought. I could gripe . . . or I could do something about it. My brain started composing a strongly worded letter. Maybe I should start a petition —

A nudge in my spirit pulled me up short. *Jodi? Where are you? Did you come to worship Me today? Let's spend some time to-*

gether . . .

I squeezed my eyes shut. *I'm sorry, Lord. Yes, I want to worship You.* I pigeonholed the letter I'd been writing in my head and focused on the song the praise team was singing . . .

Knowing You, Jesus, knowing You . . . There is no greater thing . . .

The song was a new one to me, but easy to pick up. We sang it through two more times, and the words began to sink deeper into my spirit. How glad I was to be in a church where Jesus was "the main thing." It kept me centered.

The words of the song continued to whisper in my spirit all that afternoon as I worked on a card for Florida's birthday, reviewed my lesson plans for the coming week, and composed a letter to the roller rink manager.

Knowing You, Jesus . . . There is no greater thing . . .

I sat at the dining room table, chewing on the end of my pen. How easy it was for me to be consumed with everyday busyness, to fret over all the trouble around me, to spin my wheels even over things I could do nothing about — and forget just to spend time in God's presence. Hadn't the Holy Spirit already shown me there was a difference between knowing *about* God and *knowing* God? I'd started on the journey, but I knew how easy it was for me to get distracted.

Thank You, Father, for reminding me that Jesus made it possible for me to have a relationship with You. A relationship that meant taking time to soak up His Word, listen to His voice, rest in His promises, play music that called me to worship . . .

I got up to put on a praise and worship CD, but the phone rang. "Señora Baxter? Can I, uh, speak to Amanda?" José sounded nervous.

"I'll see if she's awake, José. She didn't feel good today." Well, that's what she'd said. And I needed to give Amanda an out if she didn't want to talk to him.

I covered the mouthpiece and knocked gently on her bedroom door. "Amanda? You awake? Phone for you." Then I added, "It's José."

Silence. I was just about to walk away when the door opened a crack and Amanda held her hand out for the phone. But not two minutes later, I heard Amanda yell, "Fine! If that's the way you want it, *don't* call me anymore!" and the phone came thumping down the hall and cracked into the dining room archway.

The basketball game on television suddenly went mute and Denny appeared in the hallway. "What was *that?*"

I waved him back with my hand and headed for Amanda's door. "Amanda?" I knocked but this time didn't wait for an answer before going in. Amanda was sprawled on her bed, sobbing. A school picture of José had been torn in half and thrown on the floor. I sat down on the bed, pulled her head into my lap, and just let her cry.

Delores Enriquez came to Yada Yada at Stu's that night, but if she knew that José and Amanda had had a huge fight, she didn't say anything. In fact, she pulled me aside and asked if Denny was home. When I nodded, she said, "Do you think it is all right if I talk to him a few minutes? *Mi Ricardo . . .*" She bit her lip. "I would very much like it if Denny invited him again to the men's breakfast at your church. He needs the support of other brothers, though he'd never admit it. In Mexico" — she pronounced it *Me-hi-co* — "humph." She rolled her eyes and slapped her motherly bosom. "Our men keep all their feelings locked up here."

I shooed her downstairs to our apartment, assuring her Denny wouldn't mind. She passed Nony, Avis, and Chanda, who were

241

on the way up . . . and by the time Delores came back upstairs, most of the others had arrived. Becky was secretly putting candles on the birthday cake she'd made to celebrate Florida's birthday and managed to smuggle in, even though they'd both ridden over in Avis's car.

A beaming Estelle, clothed in her hand-made top and pants, was introduced all around the circle as Stu's new house-mate . . . until Stu stopped and frowned. "Ruth? Where's Yo-Yo? Isn't she coming tonight?"

We all looked at Ruth. For the past year and a half, the Garfields had been Yo-Yo's sole transportation to Yada Yada. Most anywhere, for that matter. But Ruth stared back blankly. "Um . . . well, we . . ."

"Ruth!" several voices chorused at once. "You *forgot* Yo-Yo?"

Ruth drew herself up. "So much to think about now to leave the house with twins."

"But you didn't bring the babies tonight, Ruth," Stu pointed out dryly.

"You noticed. Ben is taking care of both of them tonight by himself. A good father, he is!"

Stu unfolded herself from the wicker basket chair where she'd been sitting. "Well, I'm going to call the Good Daddy and tell him to go pick up Yo-Yo and get her over here. I can't believe you *forgot* Yo-Yo." Stu was clearly steamed.

"No," Ruth said.

"Excuse me?"

Ruth looked at her watch. "By now he will be back home feeding the twins. He can't take them out again! Feeding. Changing. Burping. Then two snowsuits. Two hats. Four mittens. Strapping them in the car seats . . . an hour it takes!"

"Fine. Then I'll go get her." Stu grabbed her purse and jacket and headed for the back door.

"Uh, Stu?" I called after her. "You're the hostess tonight."

Stu turned. "So? Estelle can be the hostess."

"At least call Yo-Yo first. Tell her you're coming."

Stu let that sink in, then nodded. But she was back in two minutes, frowning. "No answer. I left a message, told her to call here ASAP and we'd come get her." She flopped back into the basket chair and busied her hands twisting her long hair into a single braid.

The silence was awkward. I wished Avis would say something or get the meeting started, but she seemed to be waiting. Ruth studied her hands, twisting her wedding ring. Finally, she sighed. "Oh, all right. We forgot. And I am sorry. I will call Yo-Yo and ask her to forgive us. *Oy!* At my age, when new information goes in the brain" — she tapped the side of her head — "something else falls out. Maybe she should call to remind us . . ."

I doubted if Yo-Yo would do that. One of *us* might have to call to remind them.

Nonyameko placed a hand on Ruth's arm. "We forgive you, Ruth." Nony darted a quick glance at Stu, as if to say, *Don't we, Stu?* "We know you did not forget on purpose. I am glad you are going to call Yo-Yo tonight. I'm sure she will understand." She leaned forward, as if shifting gears. "Hoshi is not here tonight, either, but" — she smiled — "no, I did not forget her. The good news is, young Sara agreed to go with her to the Christian campus group tonight — they call it ReJOYce — and Hoshi wants us to pray."

The bad news is, my brain filled in, *that takes Hoshi away from Yada Yada.* But I shook off the thought. Hoshi was doing a good thing. She had "looked for the possibilities" and found a way to befriend lonely, confused Sara.

Hoshi's prayer request via Nony opened

244

up our prayer time, followed by praise and thanksgiving that Chris Hickman's case had *not* been sent to adult court, and more praise that Nony had helped Avis's daughter find a doctor who specialized in HIV cases. "Yes," Avis agreed gratefully. "We have an appointment to meet with him next week — all of us."

"Guess God's been busy since our last meeting," Adele said, slipping a grin. "Don't know if y'all know Estelle, here, has been comin' over to my house to stay with MaDear while I'm at work." Her grin widened, showing the little gap between her front teeth. "Have to say Estelle is one big blessing."

Estelle acted offended. "You talkin' about my *size?*" Which got a laugh around the circle, even from Stu. The last of the tension seemed to drain away.

We prayed and praised, and then Becky brought out her cake — in a nine-by-thirteen pan. "Why y'all didn't tell me this kind was so easy? Jodi had me makin' them layer cakes, always fallin' over." More laughter. We'd decided to bring individual cards for Florida this time, a virtual card shower, with inexpensive gifts — jar candles, a bookmark, candy bars. Becky gave her safety pins and rubber bands. "Why not?"

she sniffed. "Seems like nobody can ever find a safety pin or rubber band when they need one. Well, now Flo can."

We whooped. "Good idea, Becky!"

Stu left the room to answer the phone, and we all looked at each other, thinking the same thing: *Yo-Yo returning her call.* But when Stu came back, she motioned to Avis. "For you."

Avis disappeared into the kitchen with the phone. When she returned, she quickly gathered up her Bible and purse. "I need to go home. Dexter called the house." She held up a hand, stifling the questions that rose to our lips. "Rochelle didn't think it was him at first because she didn't recognize the caller ID, but thank goodness, Peter had told her to not answer *any* calls until she knew for sure who it was, to let the person leave a message. But when she heard Dexter's voice leaving a message, she got very frightened." Avis slipped into her winter coat that Stu brought to her. "Pray, sisters. He doesn't *know* Rochelle is staying with us, but he's obviously looking for her."

Yo-Yo still hadn't called by the time we left Stu's apartment. Nony, bless her, took Ruth home so Ben wouldn't have to bring the babies out again. Why Ruth didn't just drive herself over, I'd never understand. She'd done it two weeks ago when the Super Bowl started an hour before our Yada Yada meeting. But then again, there was a lot I didn't understand about Ruth and Ben's relationship. Despite Ben's growl and Ruth's ever-rolling eyes, it seemed like they were devoted to each other. And crazy about those babies.

Stu made Ruth promise she'd call Yo-Yo that evening and apologize. "I'm going to call Yo-Yo too," Stu muttered to me as Estelle and I helped her clean up the birthday cake crumbs and paper plates. "I'll let you know if I hear from her."

When I came down Stu's carpeted stairs and let myself in by our front door, the house was dark. *That's strange,* I thought, flipping on the hall light —

"Eek!" I screeched. Denny was leaning against the archway into the living room, arms folded, a long-stemmed rose in his teeth. "Denny Baxter! You scared me half to death. *What* are you doing?"

He took the rose out of his mouth and picked his teeth with the end of the stem. "It's still Valentine's weekend. Wanna go out on the town?"

"Now?" I glanced at my watch. Eight-thirty. I was in my jeans, my hair was a mess, my makeup faded. I didn't feel like

sprucing up on the spur of the moment.

He waggled the rose at me. "Hate to tell you this, babe, but roller-skating with the Yada Yadas and their assorted offspring — plus fifty other shady characters, strangers all — did not cut it as a romantic Valentine rendezvous. Just you and me. And there's no school tomorrow. President's Day. We can sleep in."

He could sleep in. Willie Wonka always woke me at six-thirty, needing to go out, holiday or no holiday. And it was *cold* out there, hadn't he noticed? Frankly, I'd rather crawl into a nice warm bed about now. But I took the outstretched rose, my mind scrambling how to get out of this without hurting his feelings. "Oh, Denny, that's sweet. But could I take a rain check for tomorrow, when I have more time to get ready? Tonight isn't —"

"Didn't think so." He grinned. "Plan B." He took my hand. "This way, darlin'."

Now I was suspicious. He took that rejection too easily.

He opened our bedroom door. The lights were off, but candles flickered from both nightstands, our dressers, even on the floor. The quilt was turned back. Soft music played from the little FM radio we kept in the bedroom. Now it was my turn to grin.

It was obvious what he'd had in mind all along . . .

But I tipped my head in the direction of Amanda's room. "Um, kids?"

"Gone," he murmured, brushing my hair to the side and nuzzling my neck. "Amanda got a call from the youth group, they're watching a movie tonight since there's no school tomorrow. Guess she decided that was better than moping around all evening . . . yeah, yeah, I checked. The movie's PG. Josh took her, said he'd hang around."

I stifled a snort. The car wasn't even here. What if I'd said, *Sure, let's go out tonight!* . . . but all I said now was, "Give me five minutes to jump in the shower, okay? Don't go anywhere."

"*Go* anywhere?" He was already peeling off his clothes. "I'm coming with you!"

20

When Willie Wonka woke me up the next morning, I stretched and yawned. Now *that* was a good night's sleep. Hadn't even heard Amanda and Josh come in! But Josh must have brought his sister home before curfew, because the alarm clock I'd set and left out in the hall had been shut off before midnight.

Might as well plan my day since I was the first one up. A school holiday in the middle of February was usually good for one thing: staying home and catching up on . . . whatever. Laundry. E-mail. Mending. Lesson plans.

Yeah, right. Today I was going to do minimal "ought-to" stuff and curl up in the living room with a cup of gourmet coffee and the gorgeously illustrated book my parents had given me for Christmas about gardening in flower boxes. After all, if students could sleep in until noon, why couldn't we teachers take a day off too? Even Josh had a day off from Software Symphony, though I had no idea why Peter Douglass closed his shop for President's Day . . . unless it was to coordinate with Avis's school holidays.

Then Denny announced he was going to school for a couple of hours to catch up on some work, but he'd be back in time to catch a few college games on TV. I refused to feel guilty. I'd play while he worked, then work while he played.

The book on flower boxes had me salivating. Perfect escapism for a snowy day in February. Besides, if I wanted flowers this spring, I was going to have to plant them myself. Now that Becky Wallace was no longer living with Stu on house arrest, we'd lost our resident gardener.

I ignored the kids when they got up, other than to yell into the kitchen that they had to clean up after themselves and to answer a plea where to find the electric griddle. I knew what that meant. Pancakes. Maybe French toast.

Back to my fantasy flower boxes . . .

But a few minutes later, I realized my coffee was cold. I wandered to the kitchen to get a refill and to see if Willie Wonka had touched his "special diet." So far, it had been iffy with the canned dog food, sometimes nibbling, other times giving it a sniff and wandering away with a sigh. Maybe I should call the vet again . . .

Amanda and Josh were still making their breakfast, stepping back and forth over Willie Wonka, who lay inert in the middle of the kitchen floor. "He said I was getting too *possessive*," Amanda was saying, spitfire in her voice. "Just 'cause I got upset when he skated with some other girl. Well, why shouldn't I? He didn't even *know* her!"

I stopped, uncertain whether to intrude.

"Sure you didn't overreact? Guys get squirmy when girls get demanding."

"Oh, thanks, big brother. Not you too."

"Hey. Hold on a minute. I just mean, do you two have an understanding that you're an official item? Can't date anyone else?"

"Well . . . not exactly. We're just friends. Special friends, though. At least I thought we were."

"Uh-huh." For a few moments, all I heard were dishes clattering.

"You really think I overreacted?" Amanda's voice was more contrite. "But I'd been planning to ask him to skate when it was Ladies Choice, then that . . . that hussy grabbed him first. And he was *enjoying* himself! Made me so mad." Her voice rose

252

again. "And then *he* calls *me* and says maybe we should break things off, not call each other so much! The jerk! Who dissed who at the rink, huh? Tell me that!"

Now the dish banging got louder. Then a sigh. "But maybe I should call him, tell him I'm sorry for jumpin' on him. See if he wants to do anything this afternoon."

"Uh, know what, Mandy? I'd give him some space right now. Don't call. Don't beg. Don't chase him." Josh's tone was surprisingly empathetic. "Trust me on this one."

I looked at my empty coffee cup. Guessed a refill could wait. I turned to go back to the living room but heard sniffles from the kitchen, then Josh murmuring, "Aw, c'mere, bed head." The sniffles became muffled sobs. I peeked. Josh had pulled Amanda against his chest, letting her cry into his sweatshirt. "Know how you feel, kiddo. Loving somebody ain't as easy as it looks . . ."

I felt sad for Amanda. A broken heart at sixteen. Wouldn't help to tell her that most adults looked back at their high school crushes and wondered, what was the big deal? But I wondered how Amanda would manage seeing José at school. After all, he'd transferred from Benito Juarez High School mostly because she was at Lane Tech. Well, because it was a college prep school too. But she didn't say anything all week. Spent most of her time at home doing homework or listening to music.

The phone stayed in its perch on the kitchen wall.

Denny came home Thursday night all excited, saying he wanted to talk to me. After supper, I loaded the dishwasher while he talked and waved a dishtowel around. He and Peter Douglass had been knocking heads about how best to support the Hickman family, and Pastor Cobb told them about a ministry called Captives Free Jail and Prison Ministry that needed volunteers to lead Bible studies at the JDC. "The girls' units are all staffed, but only about half the boys' units" — the dishtowel waved with enthusiasm — "meaning they need men to volunteer, the sooner the better."

"How does that support the Hickman family? I mean, can you request getting assigned to Chris's unit?"

He considered. "Hm. Probably not. But still, if we could get several Uptown . . . uh, I mean SouledOut brothers to volunteer, I think we could add another two or three Bible studies down there at the JDC. Whatever unit Chris is in, it'd be great if there

254

was a Bible study going on, someone from outside to give kids like Chris friendship and prayer support." He shrugged. "We're going to try to get somebody from Captives Free to come talk about the jail and prison ministry at our men's breakfast this Saturday. Carl is pumped! Thinks it's a great idea."

"Can he volunteer? I mean, with a kid inside?"

Denny shrugged. "Doubt it. Still, I think it means a lot that we're talking about volunteering at the JDC . . . *because of* Chris, really."

I handed him a bowl that wouldn't fit inside the dishwasher. "So when are these Bible studies?"

"Thursday nights at seven — which means I'd probably go right from school." He held the dripping bowl in one hand, the towel in another. "Wouldn't get home till nine or ten. I know having dinner as a family is important, but now that the kids are older . . ."

I nodded, remembering something. "Isn't that how Ruth met Yo-Yo? — leading a Bible study for women at the Cook County Jail?" *Yo-Yo and Ruth . . .* My mind rewound to the last Yada Yada meeting. *What's going on between those two? Did Ruth ever apologize for forgetting to pick her up last Sunday? Stu was going to —*

"That's right!" Denny said. "Man, I forgot all about that. Want me to double-check if Captives Free needs female volunteers? Might be something the Yada Yadas could do down the road, now that Manna House is kaput."

"Hey!" I took the still-wet bowl and still-dry towel away from him. "Don't go volunteering me for anything just yet! Now git, Denny Boy. You're useless in here." A series of sharp raps at the back door saved him from getting snapped with the towel. "And by the way," I called after him, "don't forget to call Ricardo and ask him to come to the men's breakfast! Delores asked you, remember?"

I opened the back door. "Estelle! Come in, girl. It's cold out there." I pulled her in and shut the door. "Just getting back from Adele's?"

She nodded, hands jammed in the pockets of her long, secondhand coat, head wrapped in one of her knitted creations. "Can't stay. Just want to ask y'all to be prayin' for MaDear. She . . ." Estelle shook her head. "She's not doing well. My Lord. She's coughin' an' chokin' all the time. Adele was goin' to cancel her appointments tomorrow an' get her to the doc, but I told her I could take MaDear. We can go by taxi and let Adele know if she's needed. But main thing, we got to be prayin'."

"Sure. I'll let the other sisters know. Thanks, Estelle." I shut the door behind her, then leaned against it, my spirit sinking. Pneumonia again? Couldn't be good.

But maybe this was a good excuse to call Yo-Yo myself. I'd held off, giving Ruth or Stu a chance to connect, but I hadn't heard from anybody if they'd gotten hold of her. I dialed her number, let it ring . . . but then her voice-mail message kicked in: *Yo, dude or dudette! Yo-Yo isn't home and neither are the Rug Rats. You know what to do at the beep.*

I smiled as the *beep* sounded. "Dudette yourself, Yo-Yo. This is Jodi. Missed you Sunday night." I almost apologized for Ruth forgetting her, then decided not to go there. "I wanted to let you know that MaDear isn't doing so good. Might be pneumonia again. Estelle's been taking care of her, is asking all the sisters to pray. Give me a call when you can, okay?"

I called Adele's Hair and Nails when I got home from school on Friday, but Takeisha, the other hairstylist, said Adele was at the hospital.

"They admitted MaDear?" I asked.

"Guess so. All I know is Ms. Adele got a call an' she flew out of here like her hair was on fire."

I called upstairs to see if Estelle was home. No answer. I didn't even know what hospital. St. Francis in south Evanston? That would be the closest. I started to hunt for the number, but for the life of me, I couldn't remember MaDear's real name. Everybody just called her MaDear. Started with an S . . . Sue? Sharon? Didn't sound right.

But Denny remembered. "Her name's Sally. Sally Skuggs." His run-in with MaDear a year and a half ago, when her demented mind mistook him for the man who'd lynched her big brother back in the forties, had affected him deeply. Denny asking her forgiveness for that terrible act had bonded the two of them in a deep, mysterious way.

We called St. Francis. Yes, a Sally Skuggs had been admitted to the ICU. No, they weren't allowing visitors. We hopped in our car anyway.

At St. Francis Hospital, we found our way through a maze of elevators and hallways to the ICU family waiting room. A few people gazed absently at the droning TV hanging

258

high in the corner; others flipped through magazines or just sat. At first, I didn't recognize anyone; then I saw Estelle's knitted hat covering the face of a bulky woman dozing in a corner.

"Estelle?" I shook her shoulder. The hat fell off and her eyes popped open.

"Hey, there." She struggled to sit up. "You the second one to come by . . . that Georgia woman been here, maybe a half hour ago."

Georgia? "You mean Florida?"

"Guess that's it."

I grinned. *Well, good. Word was getting around.* "How's MaDear?"

Estelle shook her head. "Nobody's telling me anything." She lumbered to her feet, rubbing her cramped neck. "But I'll go to the desk, have them tell Adele you're here. Adele's sister in there too."

Sissy was here? "That's good." *I think.* Sometimes Adele talked as if having Sissy around was enough to drive *her* crazy.

A few minutes later, Adele came into the waiting room, still wearing her bright green T-shirt that proudly announced "Adele's Hair and Nails" in white script, a hospital face mask dangling by its strings around her neck. "Hey." She gave us each a tired hug. "Thanks for coming by. Florida was here a while ago. But they don't want any

259

visitors right now 'cept family."

"That's okay," Denny said. We found seats together. Part of me desperately wanted to see MaDear, to kiss her leathery cheek with its childish freckles, wanted to ask if Adele could smuggle us in. But I bit it back. "What are the doctors saying?"

"Pneumonia. Again. Lungs all filled up. Mostly they're trying to keep her comfortable." She snorted. "You know what they say. Pneumonia is the old person's 'friend.' Meaning it's better to die of that than some long, drawn-out disease." Adele's face tightened and she clenched her fist. "But I want her to fight back! Beat this thing! That old woman in there, she's one ornery woman, drives me to distraction. But . . ." Her shoulders sagged, fighting back tears. ". . . don't know what I'd do without her."

We sat in silence for several minutes. Then I asked, "What can we do, Adele? Are you hungry? Do you need anything from home?"

Adele jerked a thumb in Estelle's direction. "You can take Ms. Angel of Mercy over there home. I haven't been able to get rid of her."

Estelle jammed the knit hat down over her head. "All right, all right. I'm goin'. But I'll be back tomorrow mornin'. Meantime, you better come up with another 'sistah' named

Estelle right quick on that list of visitors.
'Cause I can sit with MaDear, but I can't
cut no hair at your shop. If I did, you'd be
out of business in twenty-four hours!"

21

We played ring-around-the-rosey with the car the next morning. Denny left at six-thirty to pick up Ricardo Enriquez for the prayer time some of the guys were having *before* the official men's breakfast at eight-thirty. On his way back, Denny swung past the house and picked me up a few minutes before seven-thirty so I could keep the car for a visit to the hospital that morning. When I dropped them off at the church, Peter Douglass's Lexus was just pulling in with Carl Hickman and Mark Smith inside.

Huh, I thought, as I watched our Yada Yada men unlock and enter the dimly lit store-front "sanctuary." *Mark still must not be able to drive after his head injury.* Even though the vicious beating had happened eight months ago, he still experienced occasional confusion and short blackouts — a frustration, Nony had once confided, that made him feel as if his ankles were shackled together and the key lost.

Oh God, forgive me, I prayed as I headed for the exit of the shopping center. *It's so easy to forget to keep praying for Mark. Please God, heal that man one hundred percent!* The driver of the car behind me honked angrily as I suddenly did a U-turn back into the parking lot. Might as well get my weekly groceries at Dominick's as long as I was here.

By nine-thirty, Estelle and I were in the elevator heading up to the ICU at St. Francis Hospital. We had stopped at Adele's apartment — using Estelle's key — and picked up a change of clothes for Adele, her toothbrush, a pillow and afghan, and her personal address book. Stu had sent along a basket of goodies: hand lotion, gel hand sanitizer, facial wipes, a small notebook and pen, trail mix to munch on, a small box of Fannie May chocolates, and breath mints. She'd wanted to come with us but had several DCFS visits to make that morning. "Tell Adele I'll be up there this afternoon!"

Strangely enough, the ICU waiting room was almost empty, except for a dark-skinned woman with bleached-blonde, straightened hair zonked out on one of the couches. Estelle and I went to "ICU Central" — the squared-off desk area with a visual shot of

263

every ICU room — and asked a woman frowning at a computer screen if someone could let Adele Skuggs know she had, um, "family" here.

Five minutes later Adele met us in the waiting room. "Humph," she said, glaring at the sleeping woman on the couch. "That Sissy still 'sleep? She been there since midnight."

I blinked. That skinny wraith was Adele's *sister?* She looked like an aging hooker.

"No matter," Adele said, linking her arm into Estelle's. "Just as well she's out, 'cause *we* goin' *in.*" She handed each of us a sterile face mask and marched us right past ICU Central and into a dimly lit room with its curtains pulled.

MaDear barely took up space in the bed. She was on a ventilator, breathing rhythmically, in and out, but even I could hear the raspy sound of each breath. For a moment, the room blurred because my eyes teared up. I grabbed the hospital-issue box of tissues from the adjustable tray table and mopped my face above the mask. If MaDear were awake, she'd probably tell me I looked like a raccoon with smeared mascara.

The thought made me smile. Estelle was talking quietly to Adele, asking questions. But I just reached out and held MaDear's

264

bony hand, being careful not to disturb the IV tubes taped to her caramel-colored, paper-thin skin. Many of us in the Yada Yada prayer group had parents who lived far away, so we'd adopted MaDear — even though she hardly ever called any of us by our right name. Dementia had scrambled her mind, and she often confused us with cousins or neighbors from her girlhood back in Mississippi.

It didn't matter. We'd loved on her, taking her for "walks" in her wheelchair on nice days to get her out of Adele's shop, even "elder-sitting" from time to time so Adele could get out for an evening. Now I held her fingers and thought about the big box of miscellaneous buttons that kept MaDear busy sorting them by color into an empty egg carton.

"Hang on, MaDear," I murmured, "hang on! Jesus, please let her stay with us a while longer."

On the way home, I had a little spat with God. *How are we supposed to pray for someone at the end of life? Huh?* Avis would say that as long as there's life, we pray for healing. After all, God is the Creator of life, not death! But, my mind argued (ignoring Estelle, who was humming quietly in the passenger seat of the Caravan), we all have to die sometime. Don't the preachers say at funerals, *"The Lord giveth, and the Lord taketh away"*? And death is the only way we pass from this painful, imperfect life to our resurrected life — no tears, no pain, joy forever! Why keep MaDear here on earth with our desperate prayers, when she will have a clear mind and a whole body in heaven?

When I unlocked the back door and realized Willie Wonka's food had barely been touched that morning, the tears I'd been holding back spilled over. I sank down on the floor beside the old dog, stroking his soft head and letting him lick my hand.

Oh God! Why do dogs and people we love have to get old?

Most of Yada Yada stopped by St. Francis Hospital at some point that day. Stu said she'd coordinate meals for Adele and MaDear as soon as they came home from the hospital. In the meantime, she lined up a few volunteers to take some non-hospital food to Adele and Sissy at least once a day: salads, homemade sandwiches, fruit — all the stuff one's body craves after two days of starchy cafeteria fare.

Denny had come home from the men's breakfast that morning with a form he had to fill out from the Cook County Sheriff's Department for a background check before he could sign up with Captives Free Jail and Prison Ministry. That night at supper he said, "At least six guys from SouledOut have volunteered, so that's three more Bible study teams. Assuming I pass the criminal background check" — he waggled his eyebrows — "I signed up to attend a training session next Saturday morning."

Josh helped himself to seconds of beef stew. "I dunno, Dad. Not if they count all the rules you broke in high school."

"Uh-uh. Nobody knows *I* hid the homecoming mascot to this day, bucko. Unless you're talking."

I pretended to ignore their sparring and got up from the table to look at the kitchen calendar. Next Saturday was blank, so I wrote in "Captives Free training a.m." But it was good to hear Josh joke with his dad. He'd been so glum ever since the fire.

After the kids excused themselves, Denny and I lingered at the table over cups of decaf hazelnut coffee. "How was the Bada-Boom Brotherhood this morning?" I grinned.

He groaned. "Don't say that out loud. It might stick." But he leaned toward me, eyes keen. "We had about an hour before the other guys showed up for the breakfast. Ricardo actually opened up, said how desperate he feels about finding a new job. He applied to a moving company that needs long-distance drivers, but it would mean days away from home, and he'd probably have to give up the mariachi band. It's a tough choice. But except for the restaurant gigs, he's been unemployed for over a year and a half."

I winced. *Give up the band?* That was the one sphere where Ricardo Enriquez seemed to come alive. Even though he'd been a truck driver for years, he had the soul of a musician. But Delores's income from her job as pediatrics nurse at the county hospital was barely enough to keep the family of seven afloat.

"Peter had to twist Mark's arm to get him there, though. I'm worried about him, Jodi. Almost feels like he's giving up. Peter got in his face, told him he needs to kick self-pity to the curb and move forward. 'God brought you back from that coma for a reason!' he said."

I widened my eyes. "Whoa. How did Mark take that?"

"Humph. He didn't say much. But he listened. And we prayed over him — yeah, literally. Carl rebuked Satan trying to discourage this man; made a point that the devil was *dissin'* God's man. He asked God to give Mark the courage to fight back, because Almighty God still wanted to use this man in a mighty way . . ." Denny wagged his head thoughtfully. "Never heard Carl Hickman pray like that before."

Wow. Neither had I. But I knew it was true. They say adversity will make or break you. Could the pain of his son be the making of Carl?

Denny collected our empty mugs and headed for the kitchen. "By the way," he said, lowering his voice. "What's with Amanda? She hardly said anything all through supper."

I sighed. "Still hurting because José broke up with her, I think. Maybe she needs some daddy-daughter time, you know, to assure her she's not ugly and unlovable. Mom can't tell her that. Takes a dad."

Temperatures had been rising steadily all that last week of February, melting the ugly snow and leaving behind the trash it had collected in its frozen grip. By the time we arrived at the church on Sunday, the parking lot boasted a miniature lake from the melting mounds of ice that zealous snowplows had piled all around the edges, and the temperature was heading for the high fifties.

But all our laughing comments about getting out our swimsuits and wading to church died at the church door. My mouth dropped open. People stood in little groups, murmuring comments of wonder and delight as we surveyed an amazing sight.

New chairs.

Rows and rows of sturdy new chairs. Each one with an upholstered padded seat and a padded back, with a rack underneath to hold hymnals — not that we had hymnals — that could interlock with other chairs to make a row of any size, or be used individually.

"Good color," I heard someone comment. "That tweedy material picks up the coral and salmon walls, even the blue trim."

"Where's Stu?" I whispered at Denny. "I had no idea the Chair Fund had collected this much money. She didn't say a thing!" I spotted Stu and Estelle coming in just then and made a beeline in their direction.

"Stu!" I exclaimed. "Why didn't you tell us you'd collected enough money in the Chair Fund to do this! It's wonderful!"

But Stu's mouth and eyes were matching O's. "Uh-uh. Not *our* Chair Fund. Last time I counted, we had about ninety-six dollars."

Pastor Cobbs and Pastor Clark had grins as wide as Cheshire cats, watching as people tried out the chairs, breathing out sighs of comfort and contentment.

"Okay, pastors," Sherman Meeks called out. "Let us in on the secret. Where did these chairs come from?"

Both pastors laughed. "We don't know! That's the amazing thing. A truck just pulled up yesterday with this address on their lading bill — and what you see is what they unloaded. All they said was, 'Sign here.' No bill. All paid for."

Now the room buzzed like a queen bee convention. What anonymous person knew we needed chairs and had enough money to give the church an outright gift? Had to be someone in the congregation, didn't it? Heads were shaking everywhere.

"Come on, church, let's give God some praise!" Pastor Cobb boomed.

Someone started to clap, and everyone joined in with spontaneous applause, punctuated with "Praise Jesus!" and "Hallelujah!" from all corners of the room. And just then my brain clicked and my eyes widened. I looked at Stu . . . and caught Avis and Florida looking at us. All of us nodded slightly, reading each other's thoughts.

271

We knew where these chairs came from.
Chanda George.

22

I called Chanda as soon as we got home from church. No answer. *Rats.* I'd forgotten that services at Paul and Silas Apostolic Baptist ran *late.* But I left a voice mail: "Nice try, Chanda. We know you're behind those new chairs that appeared out of nowhere at our church. Gotta say, a lot of weary bottoms thank you *very* much! Don't worry, we won't spill your secret. Maybe." I laughed and hung up.

Then I called back and got voice mail again. "Sorry, Chanda, almost forgot. Avis is suggesting that as many Yada Yadas as possible gather at St. Francis Hospital later this afternoon to pray for MaDear and Adele. See you there if you can make it!"

Next, I called Ruth with the same message. I heard one of the twins squalling in the background. She didn't commit, but thanked me for calling. I almost asked her to call Yo-Yo, but thought better of it and dialed her myself. No answer. *Oh, right. The Bagel Bakery is open on Sunday.* I dialed her work number and asked to speak to Yo-Yo.

Yo-Yo seemed subdued. "Real sorry to hear MaDear's doin' so bad," she said. "But don't think I can make it."

"What time do you get off work?"

"Ain't that. I don't have no way to get there."

"Yo-Yo! Just call the Garfields and see if Ruth's coming. Get a ride with them!"

Silence on the other end. Then, "I'll see what I can do."

I hung up, frustrated. This was getting ridiculous.

Stu, Estelle, and I rode together to the hospital later that afternoon, bringing a shopping bag full of raw veggies, dried fruit and nuts, and orange juice to help get Adele and Sissy through the long days and nights at the hospital. Edesa and Delores had come up by el. When we arrived, Delores was huddled with Adele, translating some of the medical gobbledygook so she could understand what was happening with MaDear. Avis picked up both Florida and Becky at the Hickmans.

Hoshi came in with Nonyameko, eliciting gleeful hugs from the Yadas who attended other churches and hadn't seen her that morning at SouledOut. "I have only missed one Yada Yada," the Japanese student protested. "Not a trip around the world."

"*Sí, mi amiga,*" Delores beamed, "but missing one Yada Yada means we do not get to see you for several weeks! How is your last semester going?"

We chatted — too loudly, I thought — in the ICU waiting room as we waited for any others to arrive. To my surprise, Yo-Yo walked in. Alone.

"How did you get here?" I whispered, taking her parka and tossing it on the growing pile filling up two chairs.

The pixie-haired girl shrugged, hands in the pockets of her faded denim overalls. "Took a taxi. Wasn't too bad."

I opened my mouth to fuss at her, then shut it. Okay, so maybe it was good for Yo-Yo not to rely on the Garfield limo service all the time. Anyway, Ruth wasn't here; maybe she couldn't make it. Yo-Yo headed across the room to say "hey" to Adele, who was giving a rundown — for the millionth time, probably — about MaDear's condition and treatments.

Chanda blew in like Little Red Riding Hood — well, not *little* — in her red wool coat with the fur collar, matching hat, and leather boots with skinny heels. I noticed that none of the other SouledOut church members rushed to say anything to her about the new chairs — had they decided that "anonymous" *meant* anonymous? — but I sidled up to her and put on my singsongy voice. "The new chairs were a big hit this morning."

"Chairs?" She dumped her coat and hat on top of the pile.

"Aw, come on, Chanda. Did you donate new chairs to our church or not?"

She tipped her nose in the air. "Amendment Five. Don't have to answer. Mi learn 'bout dat in citizenship class." Then she dropped her voice near my ear. "Did dat *fine* Oscar Frost like dose chairs?"

My mouth dropped open. "Chanda George! You didn't!" I rolled my eyes. "You ordered those chairs to impress the *saxophone player?!*" I was laughing now. "Don't forget the donor was 'anonymous.' How would he know?"

"Humph. Well den, no matter. Mi just asking." She flounced around the room, giving overzealous hugs.

Avis had just called us to gather around Adele for prayer when Ruth stole in, hair askew, lipstick crooked. "I know, I know, late I am. And I can't stay long. Ben is driving around with the twins in the car." She suddenly seemed aware of Yo-Yo in the circle. "Oh! Yo-Yo. What, you sprouted wings and flew? We could have . . ." Her voice trailed off and she seemed momentarily confused.

Avis wisely took the cue and began to pray as we grabbed hands, ignoring the sullen looks of the few others in the room. For several minutes, we all prayed at once in quiet voices. "Oh Jesus, we need You now" . . . "Come, Holy Spirit, Comforter, fill this place" . . . "We love You, Lord" . . . "Yes, Lord, yes!" . . . "Bless Your name, Father" . . . "You are Jehovah-Rapha, the God Who Heals!" . . .

Then Avis led out in a specific prayer for MaDear. "Father God, Your daughter Sally is fighting a tough battle right now. Sickness and pneumonia are ravaging her body. But life and death are in Your hands, Oh God. You created us to be whole, to be strong, to be about the business of the kingdom! Jesus raised up Peter's mother-in-law from her sickbed, so we know nothing is impossible for You. You can raise MaDear up out of that bed in the ICU and restore her body and her mind."

"Yes, Jesus!" and "Hallelujahs" from others rode under Avis's voice. I squirmed. Heal her mind too? MaDear's dementia was pretty far gone. On the other hand, Jesus *had* healed that crazy guy named Legion running naked among the tombs.

Oh Lord, I breathed silently, *I want to believe.* Could it actually be?

Nonyameko picked up after Avis. "Praise the Lord, O my soul; in my inmost being, I praise Your holy name. Praise the Lord, O my soul! We do not forget all Your benefits. For You are the One who forgives all our sins and heals all our diseases, who redeems our lives from the pit and crowns us with love and compassion, who satisfies our desires with good things so that our youth is renewed like the eagle's! . . ."

Even though I had heard Nony pray the psalms many times, I felt mesmerized as she prayed Psalm 103. *God forgives our sins and heals our diseases — yes! . . . God satisfies our desires with good things — yes! . . . He renews our "youth," giving us strength and energy to fly rather than plod — yes! . . .*

How true that is, I thought. *How easy to take for granted the many small miracles of forgiveness and healing happening daily in this very group, in my own life. Though —* I peeked at Ruth and Yo-Yo — *God knows we could use a few more.*

As the prayers ended, Avis asked Adele if

a few could go into MaDear's room to anoint her with oil and lay hands on her. Adele nodded and marched resolutely out of the room with Avis and Florida in tow. I doubted whether any hospital staff would deny her.

I wanted to see MaDear again and would've asked, but I knew all of us couldn't go in there. Avis and Florida soon returned, saying that a doctor came in and wanted to talk with Adele about switching MaDear to another antibiotic. Florida shook her head. "They talkin' 'bout some kind of chest physiotherapy — somethin' to clear her lungs out, so she can breathe easier. Ain't a pretty sight. But . . ." She grinned. "We got her anointed and prayed over 'fore they chased us out."

We untangled the pile of coats and started to leave the ICU floor. While we waited for the Down elevator, I nudged Ruth. "Ruth," I murmured, "why does Ben always have to drive you? Especially if it means bundling the twins up and taking them out, or driving circles around the hospital. You drove to Yada Yada on Super Bowl Sunday — I saw you!"

Ruth grimaced. "So call me a criminal. What, they expect a mother of twins to remember to renew her license?" She rolled her eyes. "Ben, of course, conveniently 'forgot' my license had expired when he wanted to watch the Super Bowl with his buddies. But his mind is sharp as a fox now. 'Get your license! Get your license!' he says. How, I ask? I drive myself, I break the law, and who wants to take along a grumpy husband and my two little *oysters*" — she kissed her fingers twice, like a little blessing.

The elevator door slid open. Half the group crowded inside. "Yo-Yo, wait!" Ruth waved her hand. "If you want a ride —" But the door slid closed. We heard the car *whirr* and fade. She looked at me and frowned. "What *mishegoss* is that?"

Temperatures dipped that week back into the Ice Age, but at least no new snow. Still, I lusted for spring, when I could send my class full of Tiggers into the playground so they could *boing boing* outside rather than off the walls — sometimes literally.

I was shouting, "Caleb Levy! Sit down!" for the fourth time on Tuesday when my classroom door opened and Avis Douglass motioned to me. Embarrassed, I held up my finger and nodded that I'd be there in a moment, then marched to Caleb's desk and placed my hand firmly on his shoulder. "If you get out of your seat once more, young man," I murmured, "or if I hear your voice even once while I am speaking to Mrs. Douglass, you will sit in the principal's office the rest of the day. Understand?"

The boy gave a slight nod, bottom lip stuck out in a pout. *Like his ears,* I thought uncharitably, as I gave the class instructions to complete the math paper I'd just handed out. "In silence," I added before stepping out into the hallway.

Avis took a deep breath. "She's gone."

"Gone? You mean . . . Rochelle?" I couldn't fathom why.

Avis shook her head. "No. MaDear. She died this morning about six o'clock. I just got a call from Adele."

I took a step back, as if an invisible hand had slapped me. *Gone?* But . . . hadn't we just pounded heaven with our prayers Sunday night? How could she —

Avis touched my shoulder. "We can talk later. I know you need to get back to your class. But I thought you'd want to know sooner rather than later." She gave me a half smile, her eyes sad. She seemed weary. "God knows, Jodi. He's in control."

I watched her walk down the hall toward the school office, her usual erect posture slightly deflated. Was she saying that for my benefit? Or hers?

I tried to get a breath, but I seemed to have a slow leak, draining the energy out of my body. MaDear was gone? *Dead?* In my mind, I saw her wrinkled, arthritic hand gently stroking Denny's head when he'd knelt beside her and asked for her forgiveness that strange day two Christmases ago. The image sent a shudder through my body.

Couldn't go there . . . I had to get through the rest of the day.

I gulped another prayer. *God, this is hard. I know she's old and has to go sometime, but* . . . My whole body felt tied in knots; I shook myself, as if shaking would loosen up my neurons and make them function again.

I pulled open the door to my classroom and stepped inside. Several pairs of eyes peeked at me guiltily, as if wondering if I'd caught them doing . . . whatever. I didn't care. What was a whisper behind hands or a doodle on the math paper or a booger under the desk, when a precious old woman, as much a fixture at Adele's Hair and Nails as the hair dryers and nail art and weekly chatter, was suddenly gone?

No, I couldn't go back to "class as usual." "Caleb?" I called.

The boy looked up, startled, mouth open, ready to protest, *"I didn't do anything!"*

"Would you like to choose a chapter book

from the bookshelf for us to read? Everyone else, come to the Story Rug . . . That's right, just leave your math pages on your desk. We're going to get comfy and listen to a good book . . . *Encyclopedia Brown,* Caleb? Good choice."

As word flew from phone to phone, Stu's meal plan for MaDear's homecoming kicked into action, only the food now was for Adele and out-of-town relatives who started arriving the very next day. Estelle took herself over to Adele's apartment every morning that week and lit into cleaning the house, doing laundry, answering the phone, kicking out visitors so Adele could get some rest, helping Adele find MaDear's insurance papers, and in general holding things together at the Skuggs household so that Adele could fall apart.

Florida had dropped by to see Adele when a male cousin from Memphis — who'd just been told to take his feet off the coffee table — fussed at Adele: *"Baby, that maid o' yours is too bossy. You shouldn't let no maid talk to family like that."*

According to Florida, Adele had reared up and spit fire. *"Estelle is not a maid, and don't you forget it! She's family as much as you are, cousin — more so in my book. I see* you *makin' more work 'round here, 'stead of helpin' out."*

"Couldn't help myself," Florida had written in an e-mail to the Yada Yadas. *"I bust out laughing. Don't want to say Manna House burning down was a good thing, but the day Stu invited Estelle to move in was like a gift from the Wise Men."*

Estelle called from Adele's on Thursday to say that visitation was scheduled for one o'clock on Saturday at Paul and Silas Apostolic Baptist Church, the funeral would begin at two, and Adele wanted Denny to read the scripture during the service.

Denny scratched his chin nervously when I delivered the news. "Uh, I don't know, Jodi. I'm scheduled to do that Captives Free prison training Saturday."

"Denny!" I gaped at him. "You can't mean that's more important than showing up at MaDear's *funeral,* do you?"

"I didn't say that. It's just . . . let me get my information sheet." A moment later, he was back. "Okay." He blew out a breath. "The training is from eight to one. If I go straight from there to the church, I ought to make it in time for the funeral. Maybe even time to spare."

"Except that means you'll have the car," I

grumbled. "How are we supposed to get there?"

The phone rang, cutting us off. "We'll figure it out," he called over his shoulder. ". . . Hello?" He listened for several moments. "Okay, *mi hermano*. That's good news. We'll be praying with you. *Adiós*."

Denny looked at me, a grin slowly deepening his side dimples. "That was Ricardo. His job application was accepted by Midwest Movers. They only cover eight states — so most trips will only take two to three days, both ways."

I felt a pang. *Good news . . . and bad?* "What about his mariachi band?"

Denny shrugged slightly. "He doesn't know. José's going to fill in for him for now if he can't make it. But the good thing is, Jodi, Ricardo said he's taking the trucking job — band or no band — because he knows he has to put first things first. '*Mi familia*,' he said. 'They are most important.' "

23

The day of MaDear's funeral dawned bright, clear, and cold — not a hard-edged, bitter cold, but softened by the sun, hinting at spring.

Still, I shivered inside my robe as I half-pushed, half-carried Willie Wonka up the back porch stairs after his morning pee. But the shiver seemed to come from deep inside, not just the snap in the air on my skin. "Come on, old boy," I murmured, shutting the door behind us and attaching a can of dog food to the electric can opener. "Eat some breakfast, will you? Gotta keep your strength up." For some reason, my eyes misted as I spooned half the can into Wonka's dog dish. "Eat . . . please eat," I whispered.

Willie Wonka looked up at me with his liquid brown eyes, then lowered his muzzle to the dish and nibbled.

"Good boy." I filled a mug with fresh coffee and settled into the recliner in the front room for some prayer time. But my Bible remained closed on my lap. Why did I feel so . . . low? As if Wonka's obvious decline and MaDear's death were pressing my spirit down into the mud. After all, I tried to re-assure myself, Willie Wonka was still his loveable, sweet self, in spite of slowing down. *Waaay down.* But he didn't seem to be in pain, thanks to the meds the vet had given him. And MaDear had lived a long, full life. The last few years had been distorted by mental confusion, which had to have been stressful for MaDear herself, as well as Adele. Shouldn't we feel glad that the end was quick, without a long, painful illness?

With a twinge of guilt, I remembered how relieved I'd felt when my grandmother died. I was barely a teenager when she came to live with us in Des Moines. Gram had dominated our life with her complaints. The whole family had to tiptoe around *her* needs. My older brothers dealt with the Gram Invasion by staying out of the house as much as possible, hanging out with their friends. But as the only girl, I had to share my room with that impossible woman, who felt free to poke around in my dresser drawers when I was at school. I didn't shed a tear when she died. In fact, I would have shouted *"Hallelujah!"* if I'd been a hallelujah-shouting person then.

Was Adele feeling relieved that MaDear was gone? And guilty that she felt relieved?

At least Adele had treated her mother with compassion, bringing her mother as best she could into her life at Adele's Hair and Nails, giving her comforting things to do to keep her busy, like sorting the buttons from the old button jar and looking through old photos . . . old photos that brought up memories, both painful and sweet, even in MaDear's confused mind.

A tear slid down my face. "Oh God," I groaned, "forgive me for being such a selfish pig when I was a teenager, never once thinking about life from Gram's point of view. All I thought about was how she disrupted *my* life." For the first time ever, I wished I could hug my grandmother once more, ask her to tell me stories from her life as a girl, ask her to forgive me for not understanding what it meant to get old.

I blubbered for a few minutes, my feelings all mixed up because I'd loved MaDear more than my own grandmother. Finally, I mopped my face, blew my nose, and headed back to the kitchen, still feeling depressed. But I needed to get some laundry done so we'd have clean clothes for MaDear's funeral.

As it turned out, Denny got a ride with Peter Douglass to the Captives Free Jail and Prison Ministry training that morning, so we were able to take our minivan after all. Josh drove, looking like a Gap ad in a rumpled shirt and tie, his increasingly shaggy hair caught back in a small, sandy ponytail at the nape of his neck.

From shaved head to ponytail . . . didn't this boy-turning-man know about that lovely concept called moderation? I sighed and kept my mouth shut.

We picked up the Hickman family and Becky Wallace. That put eight in the car and we only had seven seatbelts. Carla and Cedric clamored to ride in the "way back," but I insisted on them having seatbelts. I finally allowed Amanda to ride back there and prayed all the way to Paul and Silas that no one would slam us in the rear.

Even when we found the church on Kedzie, we had to drive around a couple of blocks before we found a parking space. I had visited Paul and Silas Apostolic Baptist a year earlier with Yada Yada, but this was a first for the rest of my family. I'd warned Amanda about the head coverings, but even though there was a basket available with the little "doilies," as Flo called them, for those without a hat, no one was offering them to the many guests coming that day. We waved at Avis and Peter Douglass across the foyer and caught a glimpse of Chanda George arriving with her children, but the foyer was too crowded to actually meet up.

After hanging up our coats in the coatroom, a female usher with white gloves handed us an order of service with a picture of a young Sally Rutherford Skuggs on the front, and directed us to join the long line moving along the far right aisle. I spotted Delores Enriquez and Edesa Reyes in the line ahead of us. As the line approached the front of the church, people were greeting the family sitting in the front rows and paying their respects at the open casket, which was flanked by a lush garden of roses and white carnations. Most of the crowd was black — though after generations in America, "black" was hardly the word for the rich, rippling shades of brown and tan filling the church, from dark coffee bean to malted milk.

The line moved slowly. I had plenty of time to gape at the stylish women's suits and big hats — most of them silky black on black, or black with white or silver trim. I suddenly felt terribly underdressed in my ordinary blue-and-black print dress. I had a gorgeous black dress at home — the slinky black number Denny had bought for me two birthdays ago — but it was definitely *not* funeral-appropriate.

As the line inched along, I wondered how many of the women present that day had sat in one of the chairs at Adele's Hair and Nails getting cut, processed, permed, straightened, weaved, braided, or curled . . . laughing, chatting, *tsk-tsking* over somebody's child, or complaining loudly about the latest runaround with "the system." Knowing Adele, she had probably functioned as Mother Confessor to hundreds of women who knew she would listen, give a word or two of sympathy or encouragement, even pray for them, and keep her mouth shut.

"Excuse me . . . thank you . . . excuse me . . ." A familiar male voice interrupted my wandering thoughts as Denny squeezed into the line next to me. "Made it," he breathed into my ear. "Tie on straight?" I looked him up and down, grinned, and nodded.

We had almost reached the front. Watching what others did, I shook hands with the people in the front row, murmuring, "Hello.

My name is Jodi Baxter. I'm a member of Adele's prayer group . . . you're Adele's aunt? I'm so sorry for your loss." This went on for five or six people and then I was toe to toe with Adele's overly made-up, bleached-blonde sister dabbing at her eyes. "Sissy? I'm Jodi Baxter, Adele's friend. We met briefly at the hospital." Sissy shook my hand limply, a hankie pressed to her nose.

Adele sat next to the aisle. A stylish black hat with a modest brim and a wide black ribbon around the crown hid her short, black-and-silver natural 'fro. She looked up at me, eyes sad but calm, and smiled, showing the tiny gap between her front teeth. "Jodi and Denny Baxter . . ." When Adele used both my first and last name, I never knew what to expect. To my surprise, she stood up and hugged us both before turning to Amanda and Josh, who were crowding on our heels. They got hugs too.

Then it was our turn at the casket. Two male ushers stood impassively on either side, each with one white-gloved hand behind his back. A shimmering white brocade covered the casket, as if the material had been sprayed on. A spray of pink and white roses with a pink ribbon that read "Dearest Mother" in gold script lay on the closed lower half. The upper half was open, lined with tinted pink crepe, shirred and thick and soft. I willed myself to step close and look at the body lying stiffly on the pillow . . .

MaDear? It didn't look like her. The spark of life that had lit up her glittering eyes, whether happy, sad, or angry, was gone. But the freckles dusting the yellowish cheeks were the same. I reached into the casket and brushed the back of my hand against her cold, waxy skin. "Good-bye, MaDear," I murmured, pushing the words past the lump in my throat. "See you in heaven. I loved you, you know."

I started to turn away but felt Denny's arm go around my waist and hold me there. His other hand gripped the casket. We stayed another long minute until the ushers sternly waved us on.

It took a long time for everyone to greet the family and pass by the casket, but the service finally started with the small organ belting out Tommy Dorsey's "Precious Lord, take my hand . . ." A procession of officials in black robes — pastors, ministers, and visiting pastors — walked slowly and solemnly down the two middle aisles. The choir, in dark green robes and bold, gold-brown-and-red Afro-centric stoles, slow-stepped in their wake. The pastors and ministers stood in a row across the platform while Paul and Silas's senior pastor, listed in the program as "Rev. Arthur B. Miles III," gave the invocation.

As the ministers took their seats, the choir launched into a spirited rendition of *"Some glad morning, when this life is o'er, I'll fly away . . ."* The choir swayed; people clapped. *"Just a few more weary days and then, I'll fly away . . ."*

The church quieted as a lanky man from the family row — probably that Mississippi cousin — stood up and read the obituary printed on the back side of the program. "Born Sally Rutherford, August 2, 1923 in Tupelo, Mississippi, to a hardworking family that endured many hardships in the Jim Crow South . . . Married Emil Skuggs in 1942 . . . Moved to Chicago with two young daughters after the death of her husband, often working two jobs to give them an education . . . She is survived by a younger sister and brother and two loving daughters . . . and leaves a host of family and friends to celebrate her life and miss her physical presence."

My mind stuck on the words, *"endured many hardships."* How many in this congregation knew those hardships included the horrific lynching of her fifteen-year-old brother for being "too uppity" around white folks? Hardships, indeed.

The obituary was followed by a congregational hymn: *"Blessed assurance, Jesus is mine! Oh what a foretaste of glory divine . . ."* Halfway through the hymn, I glanced at my program and realized that the Scripture reading was next. Did Denny remember? Had he brought his Bible? I poked him and pointed it out in the program: *Psalm 27* on the left side, *Mr. Dennis Baxter* on the right. He nodded.

He seemed calm enough. I'd be a wreck about now if I had to get up in front of all these people, a white face in a sea of black, with half the women probably thinking, *"Who's that white chick, and why is she wearing that pathetic rag?"* Kinda funny that Adele had asked Denny to read the Scripture, though. Why not Avis or Nony or one of her other Yada Yada sisters?

". . . will be read by Mr. Dennis Baxter," Rev. Miles was saying. "Come on up here, brother." Well. At least it wasn't me, thank goodness. I gave Denny's back an encouraging smile as he made his way up the aisle, up the two carpeted platform steps, and made his way to the podium. He took a small Bible out of his inside suit coat pocket, glanced in Adele's direction with a

295

brief smile, then began to read.

"Psalm 27 . . . The Lord is my light and my salvation, whom shall I fear? The Lord is the strength of my life; of whom shall I be afraid?" As my husband read the words of the psalm, I suddenly realized it was talking to me. My depression that morning had actually been fear. Fear of loss. Fear that I'd lost my chance to make it right with my grandmother. Fear that all the ongoing prayers we'd been praying in Yada Yada — for Florida's boy and Nony's husband and Avis's daughter and Becky fighting to get her parental rights back — would go unanswered, just like our prayer for MaDear's healing. Even my stupid fear a few minutes ago of what people here were thinking of me.

But what in heaven's name did I have to be afraid of? The *Lord* was the strength of my life — *and* Adele's, *and* MaDear's, *and* my family's, *and* of all my Yada Yada sisters and their families. Hadn't we seen God's hand in our lives again and again? Just like the psalmist had written: *"Though an army may encamp against me, my heart shall not fear . . . For in the time of trouble He shall hide me in His pavilion; in the secret place of His tabernacle He shall hide me; He shall set me high upon a rock."*

As he neared the end of the psalm, Denny's voice grew stronger. "— I would have lost heart, unless I had believed that I would see the goodness of the Lord in the land of the living!" Denny closed his Bible and started to return to his seat. But Adele stood up, stepped in his way, and folded him in a long embrace.

Suddenly I realized why Adele had asked *Denny* to read that psalm at MaDear's funeral! It was her way of laying to rest that painful episode when MaDear's confused mind thought Denny was the white man who had lynched her brother decades ago in Mississippi. Two Christmases ago, Denny had bravely asked MaDear to forgive him for something he hadn't done, because the old lady needed closure. "And because somebody needs to," he had said. And MaDear had laid her hand on his head and forgiven him.

But I knew Adele still struggled with the tragedy that had torn her mother's family apart, and the not-always-subtle bigotry she still had to deal with, like being ignored by the cops when she went to the police station to get her jewelry back that Becky Wallace had stolen. Adele had many reasons to "lose heart" — and yet, in spite of everything, she still believed in "the goodness of the Lord in the land of the living."

That was the strength Adele brought to Yada Yada. That was the strength she gave to me: *"Whatever comes your way, Jodi, deal with it and go on . . . because God is our light and our salvation, and God is good."*

I saw Denny's lips form the words, *"Thank you,"* when Adele released him from her embrace. I touched his arm when he sat down, but he was busy fishing for his handkerchief and blowing his nose.

That's when I understood Adele had offered Denny closure too.

24

I tried to concentrate on the rest of the funeral service. One of the visiting ministers was reading a handful of "resolutions" from various congregations in Chicago and Tupelo, paying tribute to the life of Sally Rutherford Skuggs. They got a little long and repetitious, but my ears pricked up when Rev. Miles took the pulpit to preach the eulogy, using 1 Thessalonians 4:13–18 as his text.

"Brothers and sisters," he thundered, "even though we have to say farewell to our elder sister for a time, we are not full of sorrow like people who have no hope. No! Because we know something the world doesn't know — or chooses to ignore. And that is" — he paused dramatically — "the reality, the *fact,* brothers and sisters, of the resurrection from the dead."

Half the congregation was on its feet, shouting back to the preacher. "Yes!" "Tell

299

the truth, Pastor!" "Praise Jesus!"

"If God the Father raised *Jesus* from the dead, then *we* who call on His name will *also* be raised from the dead, and we will be *reunited* with all the dead in Christ who have gone before us. Sister Adele, you *will* see your mother again, and she'll have a *new* body, one that sickness has not ravaged, and her mind will be *clear and sharp* —"

Now Adele was on her feet, practically dancing on the front row, hand in the air, tears running down her face. "Thank You, Jesus! Thank You! Thank You!"

Watching Adele, it suddenly occurred to me that I would see my grandmother again too. Not the decrepit creature I remembered — shuffling around the house, mumbling to herself — but a strong woman with a vigorous body and a quick mind. I stifled a giggle, thinking about Gram and MaDear matching wits in heaven. Maybe MaDear would tell Gram that I'd grown up a little, and I'd be coming too, one of these days, to tell her I was sorry and could we spend part of eternity getting to know each other again?

"— Then we who are still alive and remain on the earth will be caught up in the clouds to meet the Lord in the air and remain with Him forever. So comfort and encourage each other with these words."

The rest of the church was on its feet now as the organ punctuated the pastor's closing words. In the midst of the praise all around me, I whispered my own praise. *"Thank You for MaDear, Jesus, for giving me a second chance to love a 'grandma' these last two years."* The tears ran again and I used up half my travel packet of tissues mopping my face, probably smearing my mascara.

But my once-heavy spirit had reached zero gravity.

"Mom!" Amanda tugged on my arm as the pastor invited the congregation to go downstairs to the fellowship hall for the repast. "Don't we drive out to the cemetery or something? I mean, don't they have to bury her?"

"— Please allow the family to leave and be served first," the pastor was saying.

"I think the body is going to be cremated and the ashes taken to Tupelo for burial," I whispered back.

Amanda's eyes widened. "You mean, *burn* her bod— !"

"Shh!" I hissed. "Later, okay?"

The closed casket remained at the front of the church as the family of Sally Rutherford Skuggs processed up the aisle and disappeared down the stairs to the fellowship hall. The ushers, crisp and unflappable, allowed each row to follow, starting near the front, and working toward the back.

When we finally nudged our way into the fellowship hall, we headed for the long row of tables at the other end loaded down with hot casseroles, salads, chicken, and cake. When Denny and I finally got our paper plates filled, we made our way through the noisy crowd to a table populated mostly by Yada Yada folks. Denny put his plate down on the end of the table where Peter Douglass and Carl Hickman were digging in.

"Anybody see Yo-Yo?" Becky said between munches on a piece of crispy fried chicken. "She told me yesterday at work that she was gonna try to come." She licked her fingers as the rest of us shook our heads.

"Guess we all used to Ruth and Ben takin' that girl wherever she needs ta go," Florida said, a forkful of beans and cornbread halfway to her mouth. "But I don't see Garfields, neither."

Becky shrugged. "Maybe one of the twins is sick or somethin'. If I had a car, I could pick up Yo-Yo. Could pick up Little Andy on Sundays too — sure would be a lot easier. But . . . guess that ain't gonna happen for a while."

"Huh. You and me both, girl." Florida

jabbed the plastic fork at Becky. "But we got us a *two*-car garage out back of our house, so I'm thinkin' God gonna fill it one o' these days. For both of us."

Becky sighed. "Yeah, but it ain't gonna happen on my part-time salary from the Bagel Bakery. Man! I need me a new job!"

As the chatter resumed around us, Florida leaned closer to me, her voice lowered. "What's with that boy of yours, Jodi, sittin' over there all by hisself? He look as miserable as a wet cat in a bubble bath."

I followed her glance and saw Josh parked in a metal folding chair against the wall, his tie and collar loosened, picking at his plate of food. He did look miserable. In fact, if I thought about it, Josh hadn't been himself since the night of the fire at Manna House. I said as much to Florida.

"He still blaming hisself for that? Ain't nobody else blamin' him that I know of. Girl, if we let our screwups dog our footsteps, we *all* be headin' down a dead-end street."

I snorted. "Tell me about it." Seemed like I had enough "screwups" the past couple of years to sink any "good Christian girl" on her way to sainthood. Maybe Denny and I should talk to Josh, find out what was going on . . .

Just then, I saw Estelle, large, round, and comforting, make her way to the chairs along the wall and sink down beside Josh. He gave her a polite nod, but in a few moments, she had him half-grinning in spite of himself and shaking his head as if trying not to laugh. Did that woman know how to work wonders, or what?

By this time, Nony, Hoshi, and Chanda joined the rest of us as we scooted chairs to make room, and Chanda waved at Edesa and Delores, who had just waded through the line for the first time. "Now, this what mi tinkin'," Chanda said, casting her eyes this way and that, as if making sure she wouldn't be overheard — though it was hard enough to hear ourselves talking face to face. She leaned in. "Now, we sistas know Adele be stubborn as old Billy Goat Gruff when it come to letting us know she need som'ting. So we gotta check on her wit'out letting her know we doing it. What you tink of dat idea?"

We all looked at her. "Think about *what* idea?" Stu said.

Chanda rolled her eyes. "Hair! Hair!" She grabbed her own braided extensions and shook them. "We all make appointments at Adele's Hair and Nails in de next two, t'ree weeks. Give us excuse to see how she doing!"

I felt drained by the time we got home around six, but I checked the kitchen calendar. Next Saturday would work for me. I could use a cut . . . maybe even a color. That'd be fun. Besides, Denny had wickedly pointed out a few gray hairs not two days ago, the jerk. Huh. I'd show him. Go blonde or something — maybe a redhead. Or get my hair cut *short.* Spiky, like Yo-Yo's. That'd freak him out.

Yeah, right, Jodi. You're as likely to go redhead or spiky-haired as get your navel pierced.

I wrote "Haircut?" on the first weekend in March, then flipped back to February. It'd been two weeks since Yada Yada met upstairs at Stu's apartment. Where were we meeting tomorrow? . . . "Wait a minute," I mumbled aloud. "Tomorrow is the fifth Sunday in February. How did the shortest month of the year get a *fifth* Sunday?"

"Leap year, babe." Denny was raiding the refrigerator. "We've got an extra day to use up. Wanna do something?" I'd announced *no supper tonight* since we'd just eaten the equivalent of four Thanksgiving dinners at the repast. How could the man eat again?

I turned the calendar back to March.

305

"Huh. Monday is General Pulaski Day. No school. Sheesh! Didn't we just have Presidents' Day off two weeks ago? How are kids going to learn anything if they keep shortening the school calendar!"

"Don't knock it, kiddo. Chicago's tip of the old *chapka* to its Polish son." Denny raised the can of Pepsi he'd found, as if making a toast. "One of the perks of working for the Chicago school system. A family holiday!"

"*Used* to be a family holiday," Josh grumbled, coming in the back door just then with a wheezing Willie Wonka. "I gotta work on Monday." He opened the refrigerator, not even bothering to shed his winter jacket. "We got anything in here to eat?"

Men. Didn't they ever outgrow the hollow-leg syndrome?

Denny was going to ask Amanda if she'd like to go out to a movie Sunday afternoon for some daddy-daughter time, but we scrapped that idea when Pastor Clark announced a leap year party for the youth that night at the church. "Your ticket to the party is to bring a friend who doesn't attend our church already," he said. A month ago, that would have been a no-brainer for Amanda. *José, who else?* But when we got home after

306

church, she started wailing, "Who can I invite? I don't know anybody!"

Which might be another good reason the relationship with José had dialed down, I thought. Amanda needed a broader circle of friends.

"I just won't go!" she pouted. But with some prodding, Amanda finally called a couple of girls in her Spanish club at school who lived in Rogers Park — and to her surprise, both said they'd like to come. "Josh, can you drive me and pick them up? *Puh-leeease?*"

I didn't see that one coming. With Amanda out for the evening, I'd been hoping Denny and I could talk to Josh. Most days we passed each other like the proverbial ships in the night. On the other hand, might be a good thing for him to hang out with the youth at SouledOut tonight. For a while, he'd seemed ready to jump on board with Pastor Cobb's vision for youth; then Manna House had taken up all his free time. But now, he was bobbing around like a rubber ducky in a Jacuzzi . . .

"Do you know what's going on with Josh?" I asked Denny over hot cider and an appetizer called *Avocado con Salsa y Queso* at the Heartland Café later that evening.

He shook his head, dipping corn chips

307

into the baked avocado. "Figured he just needed some time to sort things out after the fire."

"But that was five weeks ago! He seems so . . . deflated lately."

Denny pursed his lips. "Yeah. Know what you mean. He was so fired up about his volunteer work at Manna House. Of course, part of that was working with Edesa, but who knows where *that* relationship is going. Maybe he'd be ready to talk about going to school next year . . . what? Are you okay?"

A couple of corn chips had suddenly created a traffic jam in my throat. I took a swig of hot cider to wash them down. "Ohmigosh, Denny," I choked. "*School?* I'm sure the deadline has passed for renewing his application to the University of Illinois! Wasn't it January first or something like that when he was sending out applications last year?" I pushed my mug and plate away. *Sheesh! Why didn't we get on his case a couple of months ago!* The thought of Josh hanging around the Baxter domicile another whole year, not doing much, made me lose my appetite.

I pressed my fingers against my temples. *Okay, okay. Old Jodi response or New Jodi?* I could freak out, or . . . I could pray, ask God for wisdom, talk to Josh, cool my jets, pray some more . . .

But for that, I needed time. I ordered another hot cider and changed the subject. "Denny, remember all that crappy music at the roller-skating rink? Still sticks in my craw, thinking of all those kids listening to that sleazy music every weekend. The DJ I talked to that night just blew me off."

He snorted. "Yeah. I remember."

"Well, I've been thinking about writing a letter to the manager, maybe sending a petition from those of us who were there that night, asking the rink to offer at least one skate time every weekend that's truly 'family friendly' . . . what do you think?"

He lifted his eyebrows. "What do *I* think?"

"Yeah." I could feel my face coloring. "I don't want to ride off on one of my 'good ideas' again without getting your input this time."

To his credit, Denny laughed. "Ah. The ol' lemonade stand syndrome." He cleaned out the bottom of the avocado dip with the last few chips. "A letter sounds good. Petition sounds good. But don't get your hopes up too high, Jodi. It would probably take a major boycott of the place to sway management to —"

He must have seen the light go on in my eyes because he suddenly threw up his hands. "Now, wait a minute. I was not *suggesting* a major boycott! I just meant . . ." He blew out a huge breath. "You know good and well what I meant."

25

Yeah. I knew what he meant. We'd gone to the rink *once*. It wasn't as if we were regular customers. But still, maybe the letter and petition would be worth a try. And maybe we'd go back sometime if they didn't have R-rated music to skate by.

So while Denny took Amanda on a daddy-daughter date to Walker Brothers Original Pancake House the next morning (their favorite breakfast haunt), I took advantage of the school holiday to compose a polite but assertive letter to the management of the Super Skatium about our experience on Valentine's Day.

"We brought a large group with us," I typed into the computer, *"including parents, children, teens, and singles, but our entire group left early because of the sexually explicit music, which we thought was highly inappropriate for a general audience that included children and young teens."* Then I suggested

having at least one family-friendly skating session each weekend. *"If so,"* I concluded, *"we would be happy to patronize your establishment more often and encourage others to do the same."* Well, at least *once* more.

I read my letter over several times, then sent it by e-mail attachment to the other Yada Yadas who had gone to our "Valentine skate," asking what they thought about adding their names and addresses to the letter at our next meeting. I hit Send, not sure if anyone else had given the problem another thought after that night. But at least I wasn't jumping on my high horse this time and riding off in all directions.

That done, I was strongly tempted to find the book my parents had given me for Christmas and start planning flower boxes for the front and back porches this spring . . . but with a sigh I pulled out my school calendar and lesson plans to review. *Hm. March. Women's History Month.* What could I do this year besides the typical read-a-biography-and-report-on-it yawn?

And who to highlight? We'd already celebrated Mary McLeod Bethune, whose name graced our school, for Black History Month. I looked at the suggested reading list. Marie Curie, Jane Austen, Gwendolyn Brooks, Florence Nightingale, Clara Barton, Susan B. Anthony, Sojourner Truth, Amelia Earhart, Dr. Sally Ride . . . *Hm. Those last two would appeal to third graders. Airplanes and spaceships.*

I chewed the end of my pen. But what about courageous women like Gladys Aylward, an Englishwoman who became a Chinese citizen, ran an orphanage for abandoned children, and challenged the ancient ritual of binding little girls' feet — a painful custom that had kept women mincing on tiny feet for centuries. But what about the fact that Gladys was a Christian missionary too — did we have to hush that up? Could I include her name, or would the PC police come knocking on my door?

I decided to make up my own reading list and include some notable women of faith like Gladys Aylward, Mother Teresa, and Betty Greene, the World War II test pilot who helped to start Missionary Aviation Fellowship. And instead of book reports, maybe my third graders could pretend to be the person they chose and tell her story in first person. Boys could pretend to be newscasters reporting on a famous woman.

Excited, I turned the computer back on and started my list. But would it fly?

The droning TV in the teachers' lounge

made sure I kept abreast of the news that week, whether I wanted to or not. *John Kerry had virtually wrapped up the Democratic nomination for the presidential election . . . a space probe had discovered evidence of water on Mars . . . and suicide bombers had hit several Iraqi mosques, killing 170 Shiite worshipers.*

I was tempted to turn a deaf ear, but a nudge in my spirit said, *Pray, Jodi. Pray for the news . . .*

Avis was cautious but open to my revised list of "Notable Women Who Changed the World." "Add some Jewish and Muslim heroines to your list, Jodi, and I might be able to defend it if anyone raises questions."

Okay. That would take a little more research. Had to admit I was out of touch with most Middle Eastern history, in spite of America's war in Iraq. *But Jewish . . .* I was tempted to ask Avis how far back I could go in time. There was always Esther, the Jewish girl chosen by King Xerxes to be queen over all Persia in 400-something B.C. — who ended up putting her life on the line to save her people from total annihilation. The story was a great read, even in the Old Testament.

Just for fun, I Googled "Queen Esther" when I got home on Thursday to see what other interesting facts I could come up with — and discovered that *Purim,* the Jewish holiday celebrating Esther's courage, an ordinary woman God had put into the royal palace "for such a time as this," was only a few days away!

I called Ruth Garfield, all excited. "Ruth! Why didn't you tell us Purim was this month?"

"Did you ask?"

Argh. "How am I supposed to know if — ! Never mind. We're celebrating Women's History Month at school, and I was wondering if you . . . would you come to my class one day next week and tell them about Purim and Queen Esther?"

A brief silence. "Me you're asking?"

"Yes, you, you goose! Please?"

"Love to, Jodi. I would. But . . ." She sighed. "I'm still criminal. Can't drive. And Ben is working part time. Who would take care of the babies?"

My mind spun like a top, sorting through possibilities. *Estelle. She'd love to take care of the twins.* "Leave it to me, Ruth. Just tell me a day that's good for you and I'll work out . . . something." I glanced at my kitchen calendar. "By the way, Yada Yada is supposed to meet at your house Sunday night. Still good for you?" And, I noticed, it was

Ruth's birthday the day after . . . the Big Five-O.

"Sure. You come to me, anything works. What's that clicking sound?"

"Oh . . . call waiting. I think it's Denny's cell. Talk to you later." I pushed the Flash button. "Denny?"

"Hey, babe. Just want to remind you that tonight's my first time volunteering at the JDC. My team partner is Oscar Frost, you know, the guy who plays saxophone at church. Nice kid. He volunteered too. Anyway, might not be home till ten or so. Save some supper for me, okay? . . . What's so funny?"

All I could see in my mind was Chanda putting her hand on her hip and saying, "That *fine* Oscar Frost." I was trying so hard to stifle my giggles it came out snorting. "Nothing . . . tell you later . . . I'll pray for you, okay? I want to hear all about it."

But when I hung up the phone, I leaned against the counter and laughed aloud. Wait until I told Chanda who Denny's partner was for the JDC Bible studies. Or maybe I shouldn't. She'd bug Denny to death, wanting to know every little detail. What a hoot!

As I drove to Adele's Hair and Nails Saturday morning, I noticed three young teens standing on a street corner, hunched inside their gray hooded sweatshirts, baggy jeans hanging half off their butts, as if waiting . . . for what? Would this trio end up at the JDC like too many other young men? Like . . . Chris Hickman? Kids with stressed-out families, kids with talent, wanting to belong, but hanging with the wrong friends, "catching a case."

Denny had come home Thursday night so wired we both got to bed late. "What a bunch of sharp kids, Jodi. Most of them polite, too, believe it or not. Not what I expected. Real leadership types, if pointed in the right direction. I came with six New Testaments that Captives Free provided — but at least four other guys begged me to get them one too. Talk about a ripe situation, getting to these kids before they get sentenced to prison — or go back out on the streets."

"Did you see Chris?"

He'd grinned big. "Oscar and I got assigned to his unit! Didn't know that till he showed up tonight, though. He acted a bit distant; maybe he was surprised to see us there. I was friendly but didn't acknowledge I knew him or his family. He stayed for the study."

Just seeing a familiar face must be encour-

317

aging, I thought, pushing open the door of Adele's Hair and Nails, setting off the little bell above the door. The sharp odor of hair relaxer snaked up my nose, making my eyes water. Or maybe it was just the difference between the chilly March wind outside and the moist, warm air inside the salon.

Or maybe because I knew MaDear would not be in the back room today, sorting her buttons.

"Jodi Baxter." Adele caught my eye in the wall mirror, as she stood behind the customer in the first chair. "I smell a conspiracy."

"Hi, Miz Baxter!" piped up a childish voice. Avis's grandson hopped off the couch in the waiting area and tugged on my jacket. "Grammy's over there." Conny pointed at the hair dryers halfway back in the narrow salon. "An' Mommy's getting her hair all pretty." The finger swung to the first chair.

The young woman in the chair also caught my eye in the mirror and gave a little smile. "Rochelle!" I said. "I didn't recognize you all covered up in Adele's plastic."

"Uh-huh." Adele went back to sectioning Rochelle's wet locks and rolling them up on squishy pink curlers. "Just coincidence, I suppose, that you and Avis and Rochelle 'just happened' to come in this morning.

Stu and Estelle were here last night. Chanda's coming this afternoon . . ."

I laughed, stooping down to give Conny a hug. I shrugged out of my jacket and hung it up on the coat rack. "Guess we all need perking up with spring coming."

Conny ran to his mother. "I gotta *go!*" he whispered loudly, tugging on her arm.

"I'll take you, little man." I held out my hand to him. "Your mommy and grammy are kinda busy right now."

"Thanks, Mrs. Baxter." Rochelle smiled at me in the mirror. *Sheesh.* The girl was gorgeous, even with pink knobby curlers framing the deep golden glow of her skin.

"Hey. Call me Jodi. When I have grandkids, too, like your *mom*" — I cast a grin in Avis's direction, who couldn't hear a thing we were saying — "*then* you can call me Mrs. Baxter."

Conny frowned up at me under his mat of loose, dark curls, as if considering whether I could handle this major assignment. Then he gave me his hand, and we threaded our way down the middle aisle of Adele's salon, waving at Avis parked under one of the beehive hair dryers as we passed, heading for the cubbyhole bathroom that said, "Employees Only."

My heart squeezed tightly as we entered

the back room, and I saw MaDear's empty wheelchair. On the floor beside the chair sat the jar of buttons and the empty egg carton she'd used for sorting — colors, sizes, memories . . .

"I gotta *go!*" Conny reminded me, tugging on my hand.

I turned on the light in the bathroom, pulled down his corduroy trousers and "big boy pants," and sat him on the toilet. "You okay?"

He waved me off. "I can do it myself."

"Okay." I grinned. "I'll be right here if you need me." I stepped outside, leaving the door open a crack.

Adele bustled into the back room. "You're in the chair next, Jodi . . . oh, he's not done. No problem. I wanted to give you something anyway."

She bent over with an *oof!* and picked up the jar of buttons. "Here." She thrust the jar into my hands. "I want you to have these. Kind of a thank you for all the times you came to 'play' with MaDear."

Tears sprang to my eyes. I brushed them away with the back of one hand. "Oh, Adele. I . . ." My voice got husky. "Thank you. It's the best memento you could've given me of your mom."

"Thought so. Well, come on up front when you —"

We both heard the bell tinkle up front, both heard the angry male voice bark, "Where is he, Rochelle? Where's my son?"

"Uh-oh." Adele moved so fast out of the back room, she seemed to be moving on roller skates. *My* feet, on the other hand, felt nailed to the floor.

Dexter!

Female voices. Avis . . . Adele . . . Rochelle . . . Then Dexter's voice, louder. "Fine! You don't want to come home. But you can't steal my son from me! Where —"

"Is that my daddy?" piped up a tiny voice from within the cubicle.

I darted into the bathroom, pulled the door shut behind me, and hooked the lock. "Hey, little guy. You done?" *Keep calm, Jodi. Keep calm.*

Conny swung his legs and shook his head.

I turned on the water in the sink, full blast. "Sometimes running the water helps, did you know that? Say, do you know this song?" I held up my hands, thumb to finger, finger to thumb, and started to sing in a whisper voice. "Itsy, bitsy spider, went up the water spout. *Down* came the rain" — I wiggled my fingers like raindrops — "and *washed* the spider out . . ."

Conny giggled. I sang another nursery rhyme, and another, and another, all the while the water in the sink splashed and gurgled. Somewhere up front I could hear muffled shouting. I sang louder. Finally, the little boy slid off the stool. "All done."

"Yea! What a good boy." I washed his hands as slowly as possible, and then the moment I dreaded . . . opening the door. What was happening out there? Was Dexter still in the shop?

"Tell you what, buddy." I put my finger to my lips. "Let's play hide-and-seek. You stay here a minute, while I look for another hiding place, okay?"

He nodded, eyes bright. I listened at the door. I heard voices in the distance, but no one was in the back room. I risked unhooking the latch. "Shhh. Let me see if the coast is clear. Then we can find a new hiding place, okay?" Conny nodded again, crouching down low behind a large, twenty-four pack of toilet paper.

I unlocked the door, stepped out into the back room, and closed it softly behind me. I couldn't see the front of the salon from here, but I heard Adele's commanding voice: "*Out.* Out this *second,* or I call the police. Rochelle has a restraining order against you, and they'll slap your sorry butt

322

in jail faster than you can say 'mama.' "

"Hey, I just happened to be out on the street, saw my lady in here —"

"Like hell you did! Avis, call the police . . . *OUT!*"

The bell over the door jangled. I heard Avis screech, "Lock it!" The next moment, feet came flying and Avis and Rochelle burst into the back room.

I pointed to the bathroom. Rochelle jerked open the door and gathered Conny tightly in her arms. "Oh, baby, baby . . . are you all right?"

Conny squirmed. "Aw, you found us. Wanna play hide-an'-seek?"

26

I don't know who was more upset, Avis or Rochelle. Avis paced back and forth in the small back room, mouth tight, brow furrowed, arms crossed tightly across her middle, while Rochelle rocked a squirming Conny, who was much more interested in playing more hide-and-seek.

We heard banging on the glass door up front. A moment later Adele appeared in the back room. "Uh, Avis and Rochelle? You need to, uh . . . Jodi, can you . . . ?"

I nodded, grabbed MaDear's button jar, and made up a counting game for Conny, sorting buttons into the egg carton cups. "Can you put *one* button in this cup? . . . Good job! How about two buttons in this one?" While he was busy, I peeked out front. Rochelle and Avis were talking to two uniformed police officers, one of them female.

Avis finally returned, a smile for Conny.

324

"Hey. Can I play?" She turned to me. "Thanks, Jodi. The coast is clear, and Adele wants you in the chair. Rochelle's under the dryer. But I called Peter. He's coming to take them home, to make sure . . . you know."

I gave her a wordless hug, left her with Conny, and made my way to where Adele waited for me, plastic cape in one hand, the other on her hip. As I settled in the chair, she whipped the cape around my shoulders and muttered, "I'm gonna rename my shop."

A grin tickled my lips as I watched her in the mirror. "Change it to what?"

"Adele's Rescue Mission. Whaddya think?"

Rochelle wasn't at worship with Avis and Peter the next morning. Probably afraid to take Conny out of the house! Afraid that Dexter was going to find her and snatch her baby. But Avis was worship leader that morning, and her normally robust style seemed even more passionate as she read the call to worship from Psalm 139:

"Where can I go from your Spirit? Where can I flee from your presence? If I go up to the heavens, You are there! If I make my bed in the depths, You are there. If I rise on the wings of the dawn, if I settle on the far side of the sea, even there Your hand will guide me, Your right hand will hold me fast . . ."

She looked up from her fat Bible. "Think about it, church! When you leave your house in the morning, God's presence is there! When you crawl into bed at night, God is there. When you stop at the barbershop or the hair salon" — she closed her eyes, lifted a hand, and interrupted herself — "Oh, thank You, Jesus! Yes . . . God is already there."

I blew out a breath. Denny, who'd heard the story from me, squeezed my hand as the praise team followed the call to worship with a stand-and-clap version of the traditional gospel song, "I Go to the Rock." The "fine" Oscar Frost really wailed on his saxophone as we leaned into the vamp: *"When I need a shelter, when I need a friend, I go to the Rock!"*

My own spirit felt like it was going to go right through the roof as hands and voices lifted all over our storefront sanctuary, repeating the vamp. The experience yesterday at Adele's Hair and Nails had rattled my cage, too, giving me a tiny taste of what Rochelle must feel like all the time, never feeling safe, hovering like a mother hen over her chick, trying to protect it from the fox in the henhouse. But Jesus *had* protected Rochelle and Conny yesterday — using even a toddler's need to go potty as perfect timing. I wished Rochelle *had* come to worship that morning, to be reminded that, *"When I need a shelter, when I need a friend, I go to the Rock!"*

The whole service made me want to shout. I was so glad that SouledOut Community Church put Jesus the Solid Rock right at the center of its praise and worship and teaching. And knowing my own tendency to let everyday worries sift the sand under my feet, I probably needed that reminder *at least* once a week!

The Yada Yada sisters who attended SouledOut got our heads together after the service to see what we could do for Ruth's birthday that evening. "We could order a cake from the Bagel Bakery, ask Yo-Yo to bring it," Stu suggested. "But do we want to do cards? A gift?"

Florida snorted. "Betcha anythang she'd appreciate a package of disposable diapers from each one of us."

Nonyameko frowned. "Oh no."

The rest of us chorused, "Oh, yes!" That would be the perfect gift for the mother of three-and-a-half-month-old twins! "Wrap

327

'em in the funny papers," Becky snickered.

As our huddle broke up, I slipped my arm around Hoshi Takahashi's slender waist and gave her a hug. "Can you come tonight?"

She shook her head, smiling apologetically. "I am sorry, Jodi. But Sara likes the ReJOYce campus group, so as long as she is willing to go, I think . . . no, I *know* God wants me to go with her. But . . ." Her silky black hair fell over one shoulder as she looked away. "I do miss you all."

"Oh, Hoshi. We miss you too. But you're right; you are doing the God-thing."

How long had Hoshi been a Christian? Two short years? And she'd already had to choose between Jesus and her Shinto family back in Tokyo. Her sturdy obedience to God's call put me to shame, and I'd been a Christian for decades. Supposedly.

Then she laughed. "I will send a package of *kami omutsu* — paper diapers — with Nony for the birthday queen. But you Americans are very strange!"

I called Yo-Yo at the Bagel Bakery and told her we were all getting Ruth disposable diapers for her birthday, large or small package, didn't matter, whatever we could afford, and we'd pick her up if she didn't mind squishing into the back of Stu's car with me.

"Uh . . . Ruth's birthday? Where's Yada Yada meetin' tonight?"

"Ruth's house." I kept my voice light, even as a red flag poked up in my brain.

"Ah, I dunno, Jodi. Jerry, uh, he need some help with his homework when I get off work. Tell everyone 'hey' for me though."

She hung up before I could say we wanted to order a cake from the Bagel Bakery. *Sheesh*. What was that word Ruth sometimes used? . . . *Mishegoss*. Crazy behavior. Yeah. What in the world was that *mishegoss* all about!

With no special cake from the Bagel Bakery, Estelle, Stu, and I picked up a two-layer carrot cake from the grocery store — still cost almost fifteen bucks — when we picked up the disposable diapers. We gift-wrapped the diapers in the car on the way to the Garfields' house. Ha! The manufacturer should add to the car manual: *"The backseat of the Celica is not suitable for gift-wrapping."*

But backseat gymnastics aside, we were the first ones to pile through the front door of the Garfields' brick bungalow, squealing like teenagers when we saw the twins sitting in bouncy seats in the middle of the living room. Isaac and Havah were dressed in matching denim jeans and little T-shirts that said, "I'm the Brother" and "I'm the Sister," both waving noisy toys that didn't look like any rattles I'd ever seen. Ruth noticed our puzzled faces. *"Graggers* they are. Traditional noisemaker during Purim." She winked at me. "Your third graders will love 'em."

Ack! Should I have second thoughts about Ruth coming to my class?

"Ooo. I need a baby fix *bad*," Estelle said. She reached out for Havah, then stopped and eyed Ruth. "May I?"

"Not if you've had a cold in the last two weeks!" Ben hollered from the next room.

"Don't mind him," Ruth sniffed. *"He's* the one with the cold. I made him stay away from the twins a whole week!"

I picked up and cuddled little Isaac, who looked at me solemnly with his big, dark eyes, the large red birthmark vivid on his otherwise perfect face. "You, little guy, are going to be a heartbreaker when you grow up." Though, knowing the cruelty of children, my heart ached, realizing the birthmark would invite teasing when he started school. I kissed his soft forehead, drinking in the clean smell of baby powder. But I didn't get to keep him long, as other Yada

Yadas arrived and everyone wanted a "baby fix."

But we finally got started by bringing in our generic grocery store cake with five flaming candles — one for each decade — and bestowed a pile of wrapped packages on Ruth. She protested when she saw all the "gifts," but after unwrapping the first three and realizing what we'd done, she laughed with glee. "Diapers, Ben!" she yelled into the next room. "Enough diapers for another set of twins!"

If Ben responded, he was drowned out by gleeful laughter in the living room.

A few people had brought silly cards declaring, "Over the Hill!" and "Congratulations at the Half-Century Mark!" Opening one, Ruth took out a gift certificate, and her eyes widened at Chanda. "What are you, a stockholder at Talbots Kids?" Ruth *tsk-tsked* through her teeth. "Too much it is, Chanda."

Chanda shrugged one shoulder. "Not so much. Dem babies grow so fast, dey outta dey cloes in one minit."

The rest of us had fallen silent. Didn't we agree on bringing disposable diapers? What was Chanda trying to do, upstage the rest of us? I felt a poke in my side and heard Florida hiss, "We gotta rein that girl in."

Stu disappeared into the kitchen and returned with a plastic garbage bag, gathering up wrapping paper, newspaper comic pages, plastic forks, and paper plates with cake crumbs. Avis smiled. "I guess it's time to start our prayer time. 'Martha' has taken care of everything so now we can be 'Marys' and sit at Jesus' feet."

"Huh?" Becky Wallace looked bewildered. "Is that Stu's real name? Martha?"

The room dissolved in laughter. Becky's face colored. Finally Avis gasped, "That wasn't fair to you, Becky. I was referring to a story in the New Testament about two sisters, Mary and Martha. Martha was the efficient one, who made sure everything and everybody was taken care of. She fussed at Jesus, because Mary was ignoring the dishes and just sat at Jesus' feet, listening to him teach. But Jesus said Mary had chosen well."

"Hm," Stu grunted. "Always did think Martha got a bum rap."

Her comment was met with hoots and clapping. From the other room Ben shouted, "Hey! Pipe down in there! I can't hear the TV."

"Sisters, sisters." Avis held up both hands and quieted us down. "I did not mean to get us off track. And Stu, I did not mean to disparage your quick cleanup. I don't think

Jesus belittled Martha's gift of service either. Only when she let her good deeds keep her from sitting at Jesus' feet, soaking up His words. So . . . let's just worship Him a few minutes before moving into our sharing time."

We sang a couple of quiet, worshipful songs, and I noticed that Isaac had fallen asleep over Delores's shoulder. Havah, cuddled in Adele's arms and sucking two fingers, was fast on her way out too. When it was time to share requests, Estelle piped up and said she needed a job. "But I loved caring for Adele's mother. I'd like to do more elder care. Does anyone know if I need to get certified or go to school or . . . ?"

"I could find out for you," Stu said.

Florida pumped a hand in the air. "Somebody else's MaDear gonna be sayin' *thank ya, Jesus,* when you show up on her doorstep, Estelle."

That was followed by "Amen to that" and "That's right." Adele nodded, but she simply jounced baby Havah on her knees, as if she didn't trust herself to speak.

Avis glanced around the room. "Edesa? How can we pray for the future of Manna House? Are all the former residents cared for?"

I leaned forward. Josh had said next to nothing about Manna House for the past few weeks, and I'd hated to ask, not wanting to rub it in that the place had burned down. What *was* happening to the women's shelter?

"*Gracias.* Thank you for asking." Edesa, her dark curls pulled away from her high forehead, sighed. She seemed emotionally tired. "Yes, shelter has been found for all the residents —"

"*Dios es bueno!*" Delores cried, beaming.

God is good, I translated mentally. Maybe I could learn Spanish after all.

"— but even before Manna House burned down," Edesa frowned, "the need for more shelter for homeless women was very great in this city. Manna House had to turn some away. Now . . . it, too, is gone." She shook her head sadly. "Maybe they will rebuild. The last I heard, the board wants to build a new building on the old site. But . . . where to get the money?"

"Could take a long time if you don't want government money," Stu murmured. "You need a foundation or something."

"Edesa threw up a hand. *Sí.* And in the meantime, our women bounce around from shelter to shelter, which are already overcrowded. It feels like too little, too late —

but just pray, sisters. Just pray." She pressed her fingers against her eyes.

Avis cleared her throat. "We will pray, Edesa. And please include Rochelle in the prayers." She briefly shared Rochelle's close call at Adele's Hair and Nails the previous day. "Even though Peter is willing to have Rochelle and Conny continue staying with us, Rochelle says Dexter knows where we live. She's afraid that one day, somehow, he'll get in the building and take Conny from her when we aren't home. I don't know . . ." Avis massaged her hands with her long, tapered fingers, as if working the kinks out of her thoughts. "If she keeps the doors locked . . ."

"Dat girl can't live dat way, no how," Chanda sputtered. "Hiding behind locked doors? She need to come live wit me."

"What? Oh, no, Chanda, that's not what I was asking —"

"But dat *is* what mi a-sayin', Sista Avis. For true. Me new 'ouse is big, eh? Four bedrooms, but we only need t'ree. Dia an' Cheree, dey always end up sleepin' in de same bed anyway, don' like to sleep by dem-selves. Your grandbaby can sleep in Tom's room — he'd like dat. Tom never did like bein' de only mon in de 'ouse. Rochelle can have her own room, pay no money till she get a job. An dat Dexter mon, he don' know where we live. An' if he find out . . ." Chanda drew herself up, crossing her arms across her chest. "Dat mon have to get by *mi!*"

27

Chanda was serious. When our prayer meeting broke up, I saw her buttonhole Avis again. "It's very generous of you, Chanda," I heard Avis say. But she seemed flummoxed. "I — I'll have to talk to Rochelle. And Peter too."

"You do dat. You pray 'bout dat too."

Everyone else was bundling up in the foyer, talking all at once. *"Adiós, mis hermanas!"* . . . "See you in two weeks!" . . . "Where are we meeting?" . . . "Chanda's house!" . . . "Anyone talk to Yo-Yo?" . . . "Yeah. Said she had to help her kid brother with homework tonight." . . . "Huh. I bet."

I hung back, wanting to double-check with Ruth about coming to my classroom this week to talk about Queen Esther and Purim. Estelle was willing to take care of the twins — but how to get Estelle *here* and Ruth to the *school* if Ben was working?

Florida grabbed my arm and pulled me

aside as the others tromped out the front door. "Jodi. Whatchu doin' Saturday? Yo-Yo's day off, right? I think a couple of us sistahs oughta kidnap that girl, find out what's goin' on. She 'bout ready to slide right on outta Yada Yada."

"Good idea. Gotta check my calendar. It should be okay, though."

"Jodi!" Stu yelled from the sidewalk. "Are you coming? It's snowing!"

"Just a minute!" I yelled, waving out the door. A flurry of the white stuff sparkled in the light falling from the Garfields' front window. "*Sheesh.* She's right."

"Oh no!" Florida peeked over my shoulder and groaned. "It's *March.* It's not supposed to *snow.* I'll never get to sit outside on my white wicker porch furniture."

"It's snowing?" Chanda bustled up, pulling on her snazzy red coat and hat. "What crazy sista tinking 'bout sitting in she porch furniture?"

Becky, waiting for Florida, snorted. "Hickman, here. Except she don't *have* any wicker porch furniture."

"Humph. I can dream, can't I? . . . Oh, hey, Avis. We're riding with you, right?" Florida and Becky ducked out into the snow flurry with Avis. "Call me 'bout Saturday, Jodi!" Florida called back.

338

Chanda frowned at the snow. "Uh-uh-uh. Mi don' like to drive dat new car in snow. Dis might be a good time to soak up some Jamaica sunshine!"

"Don't worry, Chanda. It's not sticking. This won't last half an hour." Suddenly an idea tickled my brain. *Chanda.* Chanda had a car . . . and a license. And she wasn't working anymore, not since she'd won the lottery . . .

I was right. The snow was gone by the next morning. And Ruth was coming to my classroom! I was so excited on my way to school the next morning, I felt like a little kid humming along with Jiminy Cricket: *"Zip-a-dee-doo-dah, zip-a-dee-ay!"*

Spring was coming! A sure thing — in spite of today's temperature, which hovered in the low forties. *Hm,* I thought. *I ought to have that same kind of confidence in God's promises in the Bible. A sure thing — even if the circumstances don't look like it at the moment. Same God, isn't it? Spring Creator and Promise Giver?*

"Zip-a-dee-do-dah!" *Yikes!* Did I sing that out loud? Giggling, I gave up and warbled, ". . . wonderful feeling, wonderful day!" Not a typical "praise" song, but to me it was.

When I got to school, I told my class that

in honor of Women's History Month, we were going to have a special visitor this week — Queen Esther of Persia. I saw Caleb Levy's eyes widen and his hand shot up. "I know that story! We just celebrated Purim this weekend!" He nodded knowingly at his classmates. "It's a Jewish holiday."

"That's right, Caleb. Queen Esther lived many centuries ago, but her story is told and retold every year right up to the present day."

By the time Ruth arrived on Wednesday, excitement was practically at fever pitch. She had told me she was going to tell the story of Queen Esther in first person, to make it come alive, but I had to grin when she came into the classroom dressed in a long gauzy gown, a "cloak" with a gold brocade trim down the front, and a thin silver crown on her head. My class gasped in unison as she came in.

Chanda — who'd picked up Estelle, dropped her off at the Garfields to take care of the twins, and brought Ruth to Bethune Elementary — slipped into the room behind Ruth and sat down on a chair in the back of the room. She grinned at me and put a finger to her lips, as if promising she'd be quiet.

"An old woman I am now," Ruth began

— a smart beginning, since she didn't exactly look young and beautiful as one always imagined Queen Esther — "but I will tell you how I came to be Queen of Persia, and why Almighty God put me in the palace."

Not one child cried, *"Foul! Separation of church and state!"* They were hanging on every word.

As I listened to her tell the familiar story — well, familiar to me — Ruth indeed seemed to transform into a majestic queen, keeping her story alive for future generations. "Well! When Queen Vashti ignored her husband, the king decided he needed a new queen. All the beautiful girls" — Ruth batted her eyelashes, setting off giggles all over the room — "were called to the palace, and one by one we were taken to see the king."

She didn't mention that each one spent the night and ended up in the king's harem. *Smooth move, Ruth.*

"But I — a Jewish girl who had been taken captive from my own country — found favor with the king and I became the new queen of Persia. But that didn't mean I was safe."

My students' mouths hung open as they listened to the story of Queen Esther's

"Uncle Mordecai," actually Esther's older cousin, who wouldn't bow down to anyone but God, which made the king's chief adviser very angry. "This man's name was Haman. Can you say that?"

All the kids yelled, *"Haman!"*

"That name you must remember, because Haman was a very bad man. In Jewish homes, when the story of Queen Esther is told and Haman's name is mentioned, everyone boos and makes noise with a *gragger* — like this." Ruth reached into a bag she'd brought with her, and pulled out one of the noisemakers the twins had been waving the other night. She gave it to me with a smirk. "Here. We'll let your teacher rattle the *gragger,* and all the rest of you, *boo* whenever you hear Haman's name. Ready?"

"Boooo!" everyone yelled. I swung the *gragger* and grimaced. We'd be lucky to make it through Queen Esther without some teacher poking her head in and telling us to be quiet. But at least she'd brought only one of the noisemakers — not thirty!

Ruth took a deep breath. "Well. Haman" — *"Boooo!"* — "hated the Jews, and he especially hated Mordecai. He decided he would ask the king's permission to kill them all! But neither Haman" — *"Booooo!"* — "nor the king knew that I, Queen Esther, was also a Jew." She put her finger to her lips, as if telling the children to keep her secret. "Uncle Mordecai told me I must go to the king and beg for the lives of my people. 'Maybe this is the reason God let you become queen — for such a time as this,' he said. But I was afraid! Very afraid. No one was supposed to go into the king's court unless the king asked him to come — not even the queen. I could be killed! But it was either my life — or the lives of all my people."

Meanwhile, Ruth said, the king remembered that Mordecai had once saved the king's life but had never been rewarded. The king asked Haman *("Boooo!")* what he should do for a man he wished to honor. Stuck-up Haman *("Boooo!")* thought the king wanted to honor *him.* So he slyly suggested putting the king's own robe on this man, let him ride the king's own horse, and tell a nobleman to lead the horse all over the city, crying, *"This is how the king honors this man!"*

"Good idea!" said the king. "Go and honor Mordecai in this way."

The kids laughed and laughed as Ruth nodded solemnly. "Now Haman" — *"Boooo!"* — "was *really* mad."

As Ruth continued her story of brave

Queen Esther, I suddenly remembered that telling Old Testament stories at the Cook County Jail was how Ruth had first met Yo-Yo. Yo-Yo, hardly more than a kid herself and trying to bring up two younger half brothers, had forged a check to put food on the table and clothes on their backs . . . and ended up serving an eighteen-month prison sentence.

All of us Yada Yadas knew the story. How Ruth and Ben had helped Yo-Yo get on her feet after her release, got her a job at the Bagel Bakery (where nobody seemed to mind the denim overalls she always wore), and became substitute "grandparents" to Pete and Jerry, her teenage brothers. Ruth had brought her protégé to the Chicago Women's Conference almost two years ago, even though Yo-Yo had been dubious about the "Jesus thing" back then. We all thought our smother-mother Ruth and Yo-Yo the ex-con had forged a bond tighter than family. Yet lately that bond seemed to be unraveling —

Sheesh. I hadn't called Florida yet about Saturday. But she was right. We needed to get to the bottom of this mess . . .

My class clapped and clapped when Ruth finished her story. They really whooped when she passed out the traditional Purim cookie called Hamantaschen, shaped like the three-cornered hat Haman supposedly wore as chief adviser to the king.

I gave her a hug as she gathered up her props. "Thank you so much for coming, Ruth. My students will never forget Queen Esther."

Chanda gave *me* a hug before she followed Ruth out the door. "Dat story hit me right 'ere." She tapped her fist over her heart. "God took dat girl out of de poor 'ouse an' put her in de palace. *Irie, mon!*"

"Just like you, Chanda," I whispered. "Maybe you won that lottery for a reason."

"Humph." She rolled her eyes. " 'Cept it didna come wit no king."

I picked up Flo Saturday morning at ten, and we drove into the parking lot of Yo-Yo's apartment building twenty minutes later. She must have been watching for us, because her door popped open, and she leaned over the railing of the walkway that ran the length of the second-story, like a two-story motel. "Be right there!" she hollered.

Two minutes later, she hopped into the minivan. "Where we goin'? Starbucks?"

"Thought we'd hit Kaffe Klatch on Lincoln Avenue. It's close. Okay with you?"

Yo-Yo shrugged. "Don' matter ta me. I

don't really like coffee."

Florida guffawed. "Well, we do. They got other stuff. How's Pete and Jerry?"

We did catch-up on our kids as we headed for the coffee shop and parked along the street. Comfy couches and overstuffed chairs clustered around coffee tables invited customers to sink down and stay a while. "Cool," Yo-Yo said, flopping down on a couch by the front window. Flo and I ordered a white chocolate mocha and a cappuccino. Yo-Yo settled for soup and a sandwich.

"Thanks for invitin' me out," Yo-Yo said, blowing on her soup. "Haven't seen you guys for a while."

"Uh-huh. Whose fault is that?" Florida got right down to business. "Fact is, that's what me and Jodi wanna talk to you about. Whassup with you ditching Yada Yada lately?"

Yo-Yo shrugged. "Oh, you know. Stuff. Chasin' after Pete an' Jerry. My mom's in rehab, thinks she can get the boys back. Drivin' me nuts."

I took the bait. "All the more reason to come to Yada Yada, Yo-Yo. We've all got 'stuff.' That's why we pray for each other."

"Now hold on here," Florida said. "Let's not dance in the mud and cloudy up the water. What I wanna know is . . . whassup with you an' Ruth? You've been ducking out ever since the twins was born."

Yo-Yo squirmed and looked away. Finally she muttered, "Nothin'. Things change, is all."

"Got that right. Things changed big-time for Ruth an' Ben when the twins was born." Florida's voice softened. "But that don't mean they don't care about you any more."

"Oh, yeah?" Yo-Yo spit her words out like rotten teeth. "Do they ever call the boys any more? Take 'em places? How 'bout forgettin' ta pick me up for Yada Yada, huh?" She cussed right out loud. "They don' know I exist any more!"

I wanted to protest. Of *course* Ruth and Ben still cared about Yo-Yo and her brothers! But . . . it might be hard to prove. Had to admit the twins consumed their time and energy. But why couldn't Yo-Yo understand that? Having babies at their age was a big deal. I was sure it wasn't personal.

Half a minute — it felt longer — had gone by and we'd all been silent after her outburst. Then Yo-Yo pushed away her mug of soup, leaned back against the sofa cushions, and folded her arms across the bib of her overalls. "But it don' matter. The boys an' me, we all right. We don' need them two anymore."

Ouch. Yo-Yo had leaned hard on Ruth and Ben the past few years as she patched her life together again after getting out of prison. And, now, suddenly, her props weren't there and she was hurting, big-time.

"But maybe they need you." The words were out of my mouth before I had time to think about what I wanted to say.

Yo-Yo's eyes narrowed. "Whaddya mean?"

Florida leaned forward. "What she means is, Ruth and Ben have been there for you and your brothers a long time now, an' now they ain't. We'll grant you that. They off in the ozone somewhere." She flittered her hand and rolled her eyes, then got serious again. "But maybe that's good."

Yo-Yo snorted. "What's good about it?"

"Hear us out, girl. I said good, 'cause sometimes God knocks the props out from under us when we get too used to leaning up on people for ever'thang. People-help is good, far as it goes. But people gonna let you down. They just human; we all are. Maybe it's time you start leanin' on God for a change."

Yo-Yo slouched even further down on the couch, hands jammed in her overall pockets, brow furrowed, as if mentally chewing on what Florida was saying. "Maybe."

348

"No maybe about it," Florida said. "You been spoon-fed on the Word up till now. An' that's okay, 'cause you just a baby Christian. But seems to me God is sayin' it's time for Yo-Yo Spencer ta grow up. Walk yo' own walk. Talk yo' own talk. Give back some o' what you been given."

Yo-Yo picked up her soup mug, stared into it for several long moments. Finally she muttered, "Guess I see what you sayin' 'bout needin' to lean on God more. Just" — her face suddenly got blotchy, and she wiped the back of her hand across her eyes — "kinda hurts, ya know? Ruth gettin' pregnant, Ma gettin' high . . . it's always somethin'. Somethin' more important than me and my brothers. Mom dumped me and my kid brothers ever' time she shot up, which was most of the time. Then Ruth and Ben showed up — now, *poof!* They gone too. What was I expectin'? That things would be different?"

Florida's eyes and mouth twitched, as Yo-Yo's words touched a wound not quite healed. "Yeah. Know what you mean, baby," she said softly. "But I'm here to tell you the truth. God don't abandon nobody. Ever."

We all sat in silence a long time. Finally Yo-Yo looked up, a frown etched between her eyes. "Flo said somethin' 'bout givin'

349

back. But don' seem like Ruth an' Ben need nobody these days. It's all 'Havah this' and 'Isaac that,' actin' like them babies the only people in the world. What do they need me for?"

I grinned. "Well, I've got one idea. Ben's still driving Ruth everywhere 'cause she let her license expire, who knows when. But if Ben takes her to the driver's license facility, they have to take the twins with them, and you know *that's* not going to happen. What if we" — I pointed to Yo-Yo and myself — "offer to babysit the twins next weekend so she can get her license? Could be fun! Whaddya say?"

I pulled up in front of Florida's house after taking Yo-Yo home. "Thanks, Flo. Glad you asked me to go with you to talk to Yo-Yo. She's really lonely, poor kid. But I think she . . . what?"

Florida hadn't heard a word I said. She was staring at the front of her house. "What are all them big boxes doin' on the front porch? Somebody just dump they trash on us?" She was out of the car, up the walk, and onto the porch in two seconds.

I followed. "What is it?"

The name *Wickes Furniture* was stamped all over the boxes. We looked closer. "Contents: One wicker loveseat, four cushions" . . . "Contents: One wicker chair, two cushions" . . . "Contents: one side table with shelf" . . .

Florida stared at me, mouth dropping. And then we both said it together:

"Chanda!"

28

I had just come out of the church kitchen the next morning, after popping my "No Fail Chicken-and-Rice Casserole" into the oven to slow-bake for the Second Sunday Potluck ("no fail" when I remembered to *turn on the oven,* as Stu likes to remind me), when I saw Chanda George parking her Lexus. The next moment, Rochelle and Conny climbed out of her car along with Chanda's three kids. I zipped over to the glass doors to greet them as they all came in, but Chanda held up her hand as she breezed past. "Mi know whatchu tinking, Sista Jodee: not enough seatbelts. But de girl only move in yesterday! Goin' to take mi at least a week to get a bigger car."

I closed my mouth and grinned. That wasn't what I was thinking, but it was a good point. I slipped over to Avis, who was getting a big hug from Conny. "I sleeped in a big-boy bunk bed, Grammy! On the top!

An' I didn't fall out, 'cause it gots rails."

"Oh you did, did you?" Avis let him go and watched wistfully as the little boy skipped away.

"So. Rochelle accepted Chanda's invitation?"

She nodded. "Yesterday. Rochelle had a long talk with Chanda, looked at the house, realized Conny would have playmates, and she'd have her own bedroom . . . didn't take her long to say yes." Avis sighed. "I don't know how long we can keep it a secret from Dexter. Too many people know. Or they will." She tipped her chin toward Conny, who was excitedly telling Carla Hickman about sleeping in a big-boy bed.

"Well, we should at least tell the Yada Yada sisters not to be talking out of school — to anyone. But speaking of Dexter, does he know yet about . . . ?" I deliberately didn't finish my sentence.

She shook her head. "No. A health professional has been trying to contact him and set up a meeting, but so far he hasn't returned any of her calls. But it needs to happen soon. Like *yesterday.* No telling how many other . . ." Her voice dropped off.

How many other women he's infected, I mentally finished. I doubted Dexter was going to quit fooling around, though, even if he did find out he had HIV and had infected his own wife.

The beckoning chords of the song "Here I Am to Worship" announced the beginning of the morning service. Avis squeezed my elbow and whispered, "Just pray, Jodi," before slipping into the empty chair beside Peter.

Florida grabbed my hand and cornered Chanda right after the service as the tables were being set up for our Second Sunday Potluck. "Okay, out with it. Did you order me up some wicker porch furniture this week?"

"Why you 'ave to know? So what if mi did — dat not sound like 'tank you' to mi."

Florida rolled her eyes. "Chanda! Of *course* I'm gonna say thank you — but you gotta stop raining down expensive gifts on your friends. It's . . . awkward. You know we can't do nothin' like that for you."

"Humph. Don't de Bible say it more blessed to give dan receive? Just wanted to bless you, Florida Hickman. Send dem back if you don't want dem." Chanda pushed past us and headed for Oscar Frost, who was putting away his saxophone.

Florida scowled as she watched her go. "Humph. Messed that up, didn't I? Now she thinks I'm an ungrateful jerk."

I was distracted by Chanda talking to the saxophonist, her smile big, waving her hands, then pointing out her kids scattered around the room. What was she *doing?* Oscar Frost had to be ten years her junior — at least! But the twenty-something musician was talking pleasantly with her, his face relaxed and smiling. Not flirting, just friendly. Guess the kid could handle himself. Except . . . he wasn't the one I was worried about. I didn't want Chanda to get hurt. Again.

I turned back to Florida. "So what are you going to do? Send the stuff back?"

"What?" She shook her head, setting her 'do of little twists bouncing. "I might be a jerk, but I'm not stupid." She lowered her voice and leaned in. "Next Sunday, Jodi Baxter, is the first day of spring. Week from today, you can find me sittin' on my porch in that new furniture — rain or shine!"

Or snow.

A sloppy mix of rain and snow started right in the middle of our church business meeting, while we still sat around the lunch tables. I watched shoppers outside dashing for their cars in the parking lot. Chanda and Rochelle, neither of whom were members of SouledOut, had already left right after the potluck with their kids.

". . . to kick off our youth outreach this spring," Pastor Cobbs was saying. "And I don't just mean the youth of families in this church." He swung an arm wide, indicating the streets all around the church. "We've got a mission field right here on our door-step, half a mile in every direction. Gangs, drugs, dropouts, pregnant teens, STDs . . . you name it, kids out there are swimming in it. Brother Rick, you want to say something?"

Rick Reilly, who'd been the youth group leader at Uptown, stood up. "Oscar Frost . . . Oscar, stand up. That's right, this young man hides behind his saxophone, but he's coming out with his hands up!" Everyone laughed as Oscar stood, grinning sheepishly. "Anyway," Rick went on, "Oscar recently volunteered with Captives Free Jail and Prison Ministry, along with some of our other men — Denny Baxter, Peter Douglass, several others. That experience opened his eyes to the importance of getting to these kids *before* they end up at the JDC. But we need more volunteers and we need new ideas."

He picked up a clipboard and handed it to the nearest table. "We're devoting our

March men's breakfast — next Saturday, brothers — to praying for God's wisdom and direction for our youth ministry. Right after the breakfast, at ten o'clock, we're having a youth ministry brainstorming meeting here at the church. If you're interested — sisters, this includes you — put your name and phone number on the sheet that's coming around. And if you don't put your name on the sheet but change your mind next Friday" — more laughter — "come anyway." Rick sat down.

I watched the clipboard as it made its way around the room. Josh had been so gung-ho about the potential for youth outreach when our churches merged. But Rick Reilly hadn't mentioned his name today, and frankly, Josh hadn't said anything about youth ministry since he and Edesa got up in church and asked for volunteers for the Manna House shelter in January. Well, that was understandable if he couldn't do both.

But now that Manna House is defunct . . .

Two tables over, I saw Josh take the clipboard and hold it in both hands for what seemed like a long time. Then he handed it on.

My insides mushed. What in the world was going on with our son?

As usual, the Hickman/Wallace household

needed rides after the meeting, so we took Becky Wallace and Little Andy, though Andy begged to go home with us so he could play with "the nice brown doggie."

Becky sighed. "Not today, Andy. We only got a couple more hours till you hafta go back to your" — she practically gagged — "other house."

"Another time for sure, Andy," I said. "Willie Wonka doesn't play much anymore, but I know he'd love to see *you*."

As we dropped Becky and Little Andy off in front of the Hickman's, I noticed the large boxes were still on the porch. "What's that?" Amanda piped up from the third seat. "The Hickmans aren't moving *again,* are they?"

"Nope. Porch furniture, actually."

"Oh. Cool. Why don't we get a porch swing, Mom?"

I left that one unanswered, wondering whether to say something to Josh, sitting in the front passenger seat next to Denny. As Denny navigated the one-way streets between the Hickmans' and our house, I spoke my thoughts. "Josh, I noticed you didn't sign the sheet about youth outreach. I thought that possibility interested you most when our two churches merged." At the wheel, Denny glanced at me in the rearview mirror, but I couldn't read what it meant. Too late now.

Josh turned his head away and looked out the side window. Finally, he said, "Dunno, Mom. Need some time to think about it, I guess."

Another glance from the rearview mirror. *Okay. I got it. 'Don't push it.'*

Stu clattered down the back stairs, heading for work early Monday morning in semi-darkness, just as I was trying to coax Willie Wonka out into the backyard. "Hey! Happy birthday!" I grabbed her on the porch and gave her a big hug. Good thing I'd already looked at the calendar this morning. "What is this? The big thirty-six?"

She made a face. "Sheesh, Jodi. Can't I get older without you announcing it to the whole world? Say, you want help getting Wonka down the stairs?"

"Sure." With me tugging gently on Wonka's collar and Stu half-pushing, half-lifting from his tail end, we managed to get the old dog down the four steps from our porch to the backyard.

"I get home at five-thirty if you want help getting him back up the steps," she dead-panned over her shoulder as she headed for the garage.

"Ha! They're predicting snow tonight. Make that an hour later." I watched her go. Even at thirty-six, Stu cut a youthful figure with her long, ash-blonde hair flying from beneath her red beret, belted jacket, and pants tucked inside lace-up boots.

I was still waiting on Willie Wonka, shivering inside my jacket under a heavy cloud cover, when I heard, "*Psst.* Jodi. Is she gone?"

I looked up. Estelle was leaning over the second-floor porch railing, dressed only in a large loose caftan. Another Estelle sewing project. "Yes, ma'am." I grinned.

"I'm fixin' a birthday dinner for Stu when she gets home. Can you Baxters come up at six o'clock? That would make it a party."

"We'd love to." Just knowing I wouldn't have to cook dinner tonight was a gift to *me.* "But get back inside, Estelle! Just looking at you blowing in the wind up there makes me feel like an ice cube."

She laughed and disappeared inside.

The day remained gloomy, with gusts up to fifteen miles per hour. *Sheesh. What a dreary day for a birthday,* I thought, glancing from time to time out my classroom windows. But if Estelle could cook as well as she could sew, we were in for a treat. Maybe that's what we all needed — some friend time together, candles, good food, laughter . . .

I picked up the mail on my way into the house after school and rifled through it as I headed for the kitchen. *Oh, great.* A letter addressed to Josh from the University of Illinois. *Humph.* Probably a form letter saying his acceptance a year ago is now out of date and it's too late to apply for this year, so too bad, forget it. Disgusted, I tossed the letter on the dining room table — and that's when I saw it.

Doggy diarrhea all over the kitchen floor. I groaned.

But where was Willie Wonka? I called his name, even though I knew that didn't do any good, deaf as he was. But I found him soon enough, crouched under the dining room table, head on his paws, his worried eyes looking up at me as though I'd caught him red-handed with his paw in the cookie jar.

"Oh, Wonka. Poor baby. Come here, boy . . . come on. It's all right. You couldn't help it." The dog inched his way out from under the table on his belly, still cowering. "What's the matter, baby?" I stroked his head reassuringly. "You don't feel good?"

Then the smell hit me, and I realized that not only the floor needed cleaning up, but the dog too.

By the time Denny and Amanda came in the back door stomping off slushy snow from their shoes, holding a hot-pink hibiscus plant for Stu, I'd given Wonka a bucket bath, the kitchen and dining room floors smelled of disinfectant, and our old child safety-gate now barricaded the doorway between kitchen and dining room. "What happened?" they chorused, looking from the gate to the dog penned into the kitchen.

I made a face. "I'll spare you the gory details. But we better keep him in the kitchen until he feels better — and take him out more often."

Josh still wasn't home from work by six o'clock, so I left a note for him on the dining room table to come upstairs when he got home, and the three of us braved the half-hearted snow flurry to hustle up the outside back stairs to Stu and Estelle's apartment. Estelle had outdone herself: tablecloth, candles, Stu's china, and a savory meal of chicken and dumplings, Cajun red beans and rice, green beans swimming in butter, and steaming hot cornbread.

Stu shook her head at the spread, embarrassed and pleased at the same time. "You cooked. You found my china. My parents sent me a card and a package — first one in years. Somebody brought me flowers. It doesn't get better than this!"

"Well, put that overgrown bush in the middle of the table and let's get started," Estelle fussed. "Food's gettin' cold."

We were halfway through the meal when Josh came in the back door. "Sorry. Got a ride, but traffic was awful. Uh, happy birthday, Stu." He slid into the empty chair, tattooed arm peeking out of his cut-off sleeveless sweatshirt, hair pulled back into a ponytail. "Don't let me stop the conversation."

Stu waved her fork. "Uh . . . thanks. I was just about to give Estelle some good news. Found out that organizations providing in-home elder care often use Certified Nurse Assistants. And several colleges in the Chicago area have CNA programs."

Estelle frowned. "College? How many years do I hafta go to school?"

"Not years. Months. Maybe two or three."

Estelle brightened. "Really? I could do that."

"And *experience* doing elder care is a real plus, so your work with MaDear should be a good reference."

"Lord, Lord." Estelle rolled her eyes. "The Lord knows I got *experience*. Took care of my mother, God rest her soul, *and* my great-aunt . . . *humph*. MaDear was a kitten compared to my great-aunt. *Mm-mm*. Sure glad I don't believe in reincarnation."

We laughed and helped clear the table — except for Josh's plate — while Estelle brought in hot peach cobbler and set it in front of Stu. "Had to use canned peaches," she grumbled. "Just ain't the same, ain't the same a'tall."

Couldn't prove it by us. We cleaned up the peach cobbler and sat back with over-stuffed sighs. "This was fun," Amanda said. "We oughta do this more often. I mean, we don't have to wait for a birthday, do we?"

"That's a great idea," I said. "In fact, I was thinking we should invite Precious and Sabrina to come for supper some weekend soon." Was it my imagination, or did Josh wince? He busied himself finishing up his peach cobbler and said nothing. I ignored His Sullenness. "Estelle, do you know if they're still at the Salvation Army shelter? You and Stu can come, and it'll be a party."

"Good idea," Stu said. "Except let Estelle and me help with the cooking. That'll be fun."

We said goodnight and drifted downstairs behind the kids. "Estelle seems to be a good housemate for Stu," I murmured to Denny as we came in the back door. The floor was still clean, thank God. "And looks like Wonka is holding his own."

We stepped over the safety gate into the dining room. I noticed that the envelope from the University of Illinois had been opened and the letter stuffed halfway back inside. I pulled it out, expecting a generic form letter. But my heart suddenly tripped a light fantastic.

"Dear Joshua Baxter," it said. *"Congratulations! You have been accepted into the undergraduate program for the 2004–2005 school year . . ."*

29

I handed the letter to Denny. He skimmed it, eyebrows going north. "Wait a minute. This isn't U of I. It's UIC . . . Josh? Come here a minute!"

What? I picked up the envelope. Denny was right. This wasn't from the University of Illinois in Champaign/Urbana. The letterhead said UIC — University of Illinois Chicago Circle campus.

A moment later, Josh appeared in the archway of the dining room. "Yeah?"

Denny waved the letter. "Were you going to tell us about this?"

Josh shrugged. "It only came today. Found it lying on the table."

"I mean, tell us that you'd applied to UIC. When did that happen?"

Another shrug. "Right after New Year's I guess. Deadline was January 15."

Denny and I looked at each other. "You'd already been accepted at U of I," I said.

"Why did you decide to apply to the Chicago campus? I mean, wouldn't it have been simpler just to submit your intent to enroll at U of I? What about the application fee?"

"I'm working, Mom. Figured it was up to me."

I nodded, still flummoxed. "Guess I, um, owe you an apology. I thought you'd just let the college deadlines pass — or decided not to go next year."

"Don't sweat it." He turned to go.

"Wait a minute, Son. Sit down for a minute, okay?" Denny pulled out a chair from the table. The three of us sat. "Does this mean you've decided to go to school this fall?"

Josh diddled with his fingers on the tabletop. "I don't know. Maybe."

"But . . . why did you apply if you're not sure?" I asked.

Another shrug. "Well, I was leaning that way. When I applied, I mean. But . . ."

"And now?" Denny prodded.

Josh sighed. "I dunno, Dad. Things change, that's all." He threw open his hands. "Look. I know you guys want me to cough up my five-year plan. But I don't know what I want to do next fall. I don't know what I want to do *now*. At least give me credit for sending in the application."

367

He pushed away from the table. "Can we leave it now?"

Denny waved him off. "Yeah, okay." But I could see he was ticked off.

When we heard Josh's bedroom door close, Denny leaned forward. "I don't get it, Jodi. What's going on? What did he mean, 'things change'? What?"

I was tempted to smile. "You sound like me." But I was thinking. "Okay. He sent that application in early January. Back then, Josh was upbeat, working his job at Software Symphony, volunteering at Manna House with Edesa, eager beaver about the church merger and Pastor Cobbs's vision for youth ministry. A few weeks later . . . the fire leveled Manna House. Since then, he's been like a cardboard cutout of himself. That's what, I think."

"Okay. You're right. I've been trying to allow for that. It was traumatic for a kid his age. Traumatic for a lot of people, frankly. Good grief, Jodi, when I got the call, I was so scared, thinking about what could have happened to my wife, my son . . ."

I stared at Denny. I didn't know he'd been scared.

"But life happens! The world doesn't stop while we mope around. We pick ourselves up and go on. Why can't he see that?"

Denny slumped back in his chair.

I shook my head. All the things I'd been thinking the past few weeks were coming out of my husband's mouth. Laid back, easygoing Denny, spouting off like a Jodi-whale.

Then, to my astonishment, his voice got husky. "Now, someone like Mark Smith, he's got good reason to be spinning his wheels. After the beating those punks gave him, he's not sure he can teach again. Maybe he's afraid to try, afraid to find out he can't. But even with Mark, it tears me up to see him not even try. He has so much to offer — *still* has so much to offer."

"Wait a minute, Denny. Weren't we talking about Josh? We shouldn't —"

"I know, I know. I just mean, Josh is a kid who's got a lot going for him. But here he is, acting like he's hit a brick wall the first time he hits a bump in the road. Frankly, I don't care what he does — go to school, don't go to school, do this, do that. Just . . . set a goal and go for it!" He threw up his hands. "But what are we supposed to do?"

I felt a strong nudge in my spirit. There *was* something we could do. I laid a hand over my husband's. "I don't know either, Denny. But let's pray for Josh — you and me. Right now. Maybe in our bedroom. You know, 'where two or three are gathered together in My name' — that kind of praying. Asking God for wisdom. Asking God to move mountains. Trusting God . . . all that stuff it says in the Bible but is so hard to do."

A small smile cracked his tense features. "You're right. Again. Gee, twice in five minutes." He stood up, our fingers interlocked, and we headed toward our bedroom. "I kinda like this, Jodi."

If nothing else, our prayer time together set me free emotionally. Or spiritually. It was sometimes hard to separate the two. But agreeing with Denny Sunday night to put Josh in God's hands helped me loosen up the rest of the week. I didn't need to keep bugging Josh. I didn't need to keep bugging God. God was at work. God was in control.

And okay, had to admit I was proud of Josh for applying to UIC *without* us bugging him. *Sheesh.* That alone ought to give me hope that my firstborn was going to grow up.

Denny and I really should pray together more often, I thought several times that week. But in the helter-skelter of everyday life, it was harder than I thought. Thursday night rolled around, Denny was down at the JDC leading a Bible study for kids awaiting trial, and we still hadn't prayed together again. He'd mentioned one kid, who had to decide whether to take a plea bargain and serve two years, or fight his case and go to trial. And another, who rarely spoke up but came every Thursday . . . and another who seemed a natural-born leader. And then there was Chris Hickman.

We should pray for all these boys by name together! See what God would do! *Well, maybe Saturday morning would be a good time . . .*

I forgot that Saturday was the men's breakfast at SouledOut, and Denny had to leave the house early. Correction. *Earlier.* In order to hob-nob and pray with "the Bada-Boom Brothers" an hour before the breakfast, which meant picking up Ricardo Enriquez down in the city, who "just happened" to be home for the weekend in spite of his long-distance trucking job. I felt a twinge of resentment at not having *any* mornings that week together — and then wanted to slap myself upside the head. *Hoo boy!* I should talk. Denny probably felt that way every time Yada Yada met on Sunday evenings.

Well, we just had to find a way where it wasn't either/or.

"I need the car when you get back," I told Denny, as he did an awkward hop over the child safety gate still penning Willie Wonka in the kitchen. "Yo-Yo and I are going to babysit the twins so Ben can take Ruth to get her driver's license."

"Ben? That's later, right? Because I think he's coming this morning to —" Just then Denny caught his pant leg on the gate and nearly did an end-zone tackle with the toaster. "Good grief, Jodi! Can't we get rid of this gate? Wonka hasn't had any more accidents this week, has he?"

I rolled my eyes at him. "Two. You just weren't here to clean them up."

"Well, put him outside then. It's supposed to get up to sixty today. Maybe we need to build a doghouse or something."

As if knowing we were talking about him, Willie Wonka slunk over to the air vent that heated the kitchen and sank down on top of it with a sigh.

The outdoor thermometer went up, but a drizzly rain came down. When Denny returned with the car, I left Wonka in the kitchen with the gate still in place. "Take him out a couple of times, will you?" I asked, grabbing my purse and the car keys. "Precious and Sabrina are coming tonight for supper, and I don't want the house smelling like disinfectant."

"Better than the alternative," Denny snorted, head inside the refrigerator. He came out with a carton of orange juice. "Have you seen Josh? He didn't show up for the youth ministry meeting at Souled-Out — at least not by the time I left. I didn't stay; knew you needed the car."

I shook my head and jerked a thumb toward the bedrooms. "He came out once, looked at the rain, and went back into hibernation."

"Humph." Denny swigged straight from the orange juice carton, then wiped his mouth on his sleeve as he capped it. "Hey, guess what. Ben came to the men's breakfast this morning — actually, came to the prayer time beforehand with Peter, Mark, Carl, and Ricardo. I invited Oscar Frost too — that made seven. I think he'll fit in. Last Thursday night when we rode back from the JDC, I sensed he'd really like a mentoring relationship with some older guys."

I suppressed a smile. *The Bada-Boom Brothers . . . nope, nope. Gotta quit that, Jodi. It might stick.*

"Anyway," Denny said, replacing the orange juice back in the fridge, "Ben took us by surprise. Peter asked how we could pray for him, and he got all croaky, said he just wanted to thank God for his babies. Before the twins, life was kind of like the old black-and-white TVs. Now everything is in living color."

"*Ben* said that?" I edged toward the door.

"Yep. And . . . oh, right. You've gotta go. But remind me to tell you something else when you get back."

Oh, great. I did have to go, but now that "something else" would bug me for the next three hours.

I picked up Yo-Yo, and we arrived at the Garfields' house around eleven. Ruth's usually neat flower garden bordering the front of the brick bungalow was a tangle of last year's dead flowers and weeds. Being "huge with child" last fall, she didn't do her usual surgical fall cleanup. But I had no doubt she'd have the twins out here in a month or two, teaching them — at the tender age of five months — the fine points of gardening.

"Maybe she changed her mind," Yo-Yo said nervously as I punched the doorbell.

The door opened. "*Ay ay ay!* You come at last." Ruth gave Yo-Yo a mama bear hug, as if she hadn't been sure we'd show. Then, ignoring me entirely, she bustled off into the next room, tossing off a half-dozen instructions over her shoulder.

"Don't worry," Ben snorted, standing in the foyer holding her coat. "The *shtick* is all written down. You'd think we were taking off for a week in Honolulu." He rolled his eyes. "She's had the *shpilkes* all morning. *Oy vey.*"

I slipped Yo-Yo a tissue and hinted that she should use it on her cheek where Ruth had left a lipstick-red smudge. Yo-Yo rubbed furiously. It was the only time I'd seen anything close to makeup on her clear, boyish face.

Ben finally dragged Ruth out the door. Yo-Yo and I stood at the picture window, each holding a twin, and waving good-bye. Ruth hollered something at us, but Ben practically stuffed her into the big Buick and pulled away.

Yo-Yo and I looked at each other and burst out laughing. "*Sheesh.* The rest oughta be a piece of cake," I gasped.

Yo-Yo jiggled Isaac on her shoulder. "Hey there, big guy. You ready to go to sleep or somethin'? . . . Whoa. Jodi! What was that? My shoulder is all wet!"

Isaac had thrown up his last meal all over Yo-Yo's T-shirt and his own sleeper.

I laid Havah tummy-down on a blanket in the living room with a few toys and did my best to sponge off Yo-Yo's clothes with a washcloth from the bathroom. Found a clean sleeper for Isaac and changed his wet diaper while I was at it. He kicked and wiggled, but I sang a couple of rounds of "Six Little Ducks" and finally managed to get him clean and packaged once again.

"Hey." Yo-Yo stood in the doorway, hands stuffed in her overall pockets. "You're good at that. I never did babysit or nothin' when I was a kid."

I grinned. "I'll show you. It's not too bad one at a time."

"Yeah. But *two?* Glad we doin' this together."

According to Ruth's list, we were supposed to feed the twins baby food at noon, then put them down for a nap. The jars of peas and carrots ended up all over their faces, the high chairs, and us — sort of like vegetarian finger paint. The peaches went better, but the whole process meant another change of clothes for both babies this time. I changed Havah, then held her while I led Yo-Yo step by step through the process with Isaac . . .

Take off the soiled sleeper. Peel back the sticky tabs of the disposable diaper, throw it in the diaper pail, and wipe his bottom with a baby wipe. Dust on baby powder, while making sure he doesn't nosedive off the changing table. Now pick up his feet with one hand, slip the new disposable under his bottom, and press the tabs. Wrestle his arms and legs one at a time into the sleeper, snap the snappers . . .

"Whew!" Sweat beaded Yo-Yo's forehead. "I had no idea it was so much work!"

I nodded. Frankly, I'd almost forgotten.

We put the twins down in their cribs, darkened the room, and wound up their musical mobiles — but the babies immediately set up a wailing duet. "Ignore them. They'll get quiet," I said as we tiptoed away.

They didn't. The wailing got louder. Yo-Yo couldn't stand it. "Forget the list," she said. "Let's just hold them. What's wrong with that?"

We tiptoed back into the room and each picked up a baby. The wailing dwindled to hiccups by the time we got back to the living room. "Put on some of that high-falutin' music they got," Yo-Yo said, settling down into a rocking chair with Isaac. "Aw, look, he wants to suck my finger."

Cradling Havah with one arm, I found a Mozart clarinet concerto, stuck it in the CD player, then settled down in Ben's recliner. Nestled in the curve of my arm, Havah looked up at me with her large dark eyes.

"You're a beauty, little one," I murmured . . . and watched as her eyelids flickered, dropped, and closed.

I glanced over at Yo-Yo. She was watching the baby in her arms, a look I'd never seen there before. Tenderness? Longing? Awe?

"He's asleep," she whispered, still staring at Isaac's face, gently rocking.

"Havah too," I whispered back. The music, turned low, blanketed the room. I almost drifted off myself.

The clarinet concerto finally ended. "Thanks, Jodi," I heard Yo-Yo say.

I opened my eyes. "Thanks? For what?"

"For what you an' Flo said, about how it's time to give back." She looked down at the baby sleeping in the nest she'd made with one ankle crossed over the other knee. "Didn't know givin' back was like gettin' too."

30

"How'd it go?" Denny looked up from the computer when I got back.

"She's legal. Finally! Ben looked like he had a few more white hairs, though."

Denny laughed.

"But it was a big deal for Yo-Yo to help take care of the twins. I think she and Isaac bonded. A good thing." I opened the fridge and pulled out the two lasagnas I'd made that morning. *A very good thing — like sticking a finger in the dike of her crumbling relationship with Ruth and Ben.* I turned on the oven to preheat. *No, more like picking up a slipped stitch and knitting it back into a seamless whole.*

I glanced at the clock. Four-thirty already. Stu was supposed to pick up Precious and Sabrina and bring them about five-thirty. Estelle was baking homemade French bread and pie. Guess all I needed to do was set the table and add a tossed salad. Wine with

Italian food? No, better not.

"Amanda!" I yelled. "Did you clean the bathroom? . . . Denny, would you vacuum the living room before they get here? And where's Josh? He needs to take Wonka for a walk around the block."

By the time we heard the garage door go up, I'd lit candles on the table and the lasagnas were bubbly. Estelle came in the front door with her bread and crumb apple pie ("Don't like them back stairs in rain or snow, uh-uh," she complained) just as Stu and our two former houseguests came in the back.

"Precious! Sabrina! I'm so tickled to see you guys again!" I gave Precious a hug, then held her at arm's length. Both had their hair braided into long extensions. "Girl, you are looking *good*. Gee, you two look more like sisters than mother and daughter."

Precious laughed and poked Sabrina. "Uh-huh. Hear that, 'Brina?"

Sabrina, dressed in tight jeans, skimpy tank top, and a body-hugging sweater, turned her eyes away, as shy as the day she first came to our house — and then she saw Willie Wonka. "Aw, there's my baby." The teenager squatted down and hugged the dog, who obligingly licked her face.

We took down the child gate until everybody got in and the food was on the table, then penned Wonka back in the kitchen. He whined at the gate.

"Can't we let him in?" Sabrina petted him over the gate. "He don' scare me anymore."

"It's not that, Sabrina." I tried to be delicate. "He's having some, um, bowel difficulties. We keep him in the kitchen lately, close to the door."

"Eww." Sabrina made a face and found a chair on the far side of the table. Amanda looked disgusted. I wasn't sure if it was because I said the "B" word, or because Sabrina's loyalty to her dog was so shallow.

After holding hands around the table and singing "Thanks! Thanks! We give You thanks!" — though we didn't sound quite as good as when T. D. Jakes sang it — the lasagnas disappeared at an incredible rate. Good thing I'd made two! The conversation bounced from one person to another, as we caught up after almost two months.

"We've got a new name for our church," Stu offered. "SouledOut Community Church. The teenagers came up with it . . . Can I have some more garlic bread?"

Precious passed the breadbasket. "Now that's cool. I like that. Sabrina an' me, we worship now an' then with the Salvation Army. But I'd like to find us our own church. Whatchu doin', Estelle? You ever finish that vest you was crochetin' for your grandboy?"

Stu laughed aloud. "That, and two more, plus about ten outfits for herself."

"Humph. Gotta do somethin' to keep these hands busy. Won't be doin' much sewing for the next few months, though. I'm goin' back to school — at my age!" Estelle beamed. "I applied this week for the Certified Nurse Assistant program at Chicago Community College."

"That's where Edesa goes to school!" Amanda piped up.

"*Did* go to school," Josh murmured. "She transferred to UIC. Getting her degree in Public Health now, remember?"

"Oh. Well, aren't they connected or something? They're both in the Loop."

"Speakin' of school, Sabrina gettin' almost all Bs now," Precious bragged. "Some of them Salvation Army folks helping tutor her, praise Jesus."

"Ma, don't." Sabrina rolled her eyes.

"Well, baby, we got lots to be thankful for. Even that Manna House fire gonna reap good things, you wait an' see."

"Well, now, that's right," said Estelle. "Reverend Miz Handley called me up this week, said the board wants to set up an advisory board made up of former residents and volunteers, an' asked me who I thought would be good to ask." She pointed her fork at Josh. "I told her she should ask you, Josh. You one of the few mens who volunteered, and you always had good ideas."

This time I did not imagine it. The color drained right out of Josh's face.

"Uh . . . I don't think so." He laid down his fork.

"Now, why not?" Precious jumped in. "You an' that girl Edesa really livened up Manna House. The kids was always excited when you two showed up. That's what that advisory board needs — some youthful blood." She looked around the table. "Now wouldn't that be grand if Manna House rose from the ashes, like the Phoenix bird, bigger an' more beautiful each time? The old had to go so the new could come."

I gaped at her. "How'd you know about the Phoenix bird?" A homeless single mom from the streets of Chicago didn't seem the type to read mythology.

Precious simpered at me. "Girl, you could put me on that *Jeopardy* show with what I know."

"Uh, could I be excused?" Josh didn't wait for an answer but picked up his dishes, stepped over the gate in the doorway to the kitchen, came back empty-handed, and headed for his room.

"Josh? Wait a minute." Estelle, for all her bulk, was up from the table and heading off our son in the hallway in less than two seconds. A moment later, she crooked her finger at Precious and the three of them headed for the living room.

"Well, if we're done . . ." Amanda pushed back her chair. "Wanna listen to Audio Adrenaline in my room, Sabrina?" The two girls disappeared with only, "Call us when you serve the pie, Mom."

Denny, Stu, and I looked at each other. "Uh, what just happened here?" Stu said.

I folded and unfolded my napkin. "Estelle wants to talk to Josh, I guess."

Denny scratched the back of his head. "Hm. Hope she knows what she's doing. He's not been the talking type lately. Guess I'll make coffee."

For the next several minutes, the three of us puttered in the kitchen, loading the dishwasher, cutting Estelle's crumb apple pie, getting out dessert plates, pie forks, and coffee mugs. "Don't get out the ice cream yet," I said. "I'll go see if they're ready to come back for dessert."

I slipped off my shoes and padded silently down the hallway toward the living room, not sure if I should interrupt. I heard Josh's voice. Well, at least he was talking.

". . . should never have let the kids talk me into plugging in the tree again. I *knew* it was a fire hazard. My mom and I talked about it."

I stopped, realizing this was not the time to go in.

"But, oh yeah, I wanted to be Mr. Nice Guy to the kids. Everybody says, don't be hard on yourself. It wasn't your fault, Josh." Josh's voice turned bitter. "Well, you know what? That doesn't help! I *feel* like it was my fault. If I'd taken out that tree, it never would have happened! What if . . . what if someone had gotten hurt that night? Or killed? It could've happened. Kids, women, who had nothing in the first place, ended up with *less* than nothing! Oh, God . . ."

The last words were muffled. I peeked around the corner of the archway into the living room. Josh's head was in his hands. Estelle and Precious sat on either side of him on our couch. Tears puddled in my eyes and spilled over. *Oh, my son, my son . . .* I wanted to rush into the room and gather him into my arms. *Don't keep blaming yourself!*

And then I heard Precious say, "Sounds like you need to be forgiven."

Josh lifted his head and looked at her. "Yes." His voice sounded strangled, but he nodded. "Yes . . . yes . . ."

"Well, now." Precious put her arm around my son. "*I forgive you.* I know what you done — or didn't do — wasn't on purpose, an' we all make mistakes. But you right, it coulda been a whole lot worse than it was, only by the grace of God. But He got that grace for you, too, baby. He knows you sorry, and He forgives you. An' so do I."

Josh's shoulders began to shake. Suddenly he was sobbing into his arms. I could hardly stand it, but I knew God was holding me back. *It's not for you to do, Jodi,* said the Voice in my spirit. *He needs* their *forgiveness, the residents of Manna House.*

"I forgive you, too," said Estelle, also putting an arm around Josh. "Now go on, let it all out. It been too long a-comin'."

As quietly as I could, I fled to my bedroom, shut the door behind me, and fell on my bed. *Oh, God, Oh, God!* my heart cried out. *Why couldn't I see it?* The brick wall that had been closing in on my son ever since the fire was his own sense of responsibility and guilt. He *could* have prevented what happened. He didn't. He didn't need to be told it wasn't his fault.

He needed to be *forgiven.*

31

The weather turned windy and cold again on Sunday with snow flurries predicted — the first day of spring, ha! — but I didn't even care. The cold spell in Josh's heart had broken last night. I could feel it in the atmosphere.

Josh had excused himself from pie the night before, but when it was time for Precious and Sabrina to go home (well, if you can call a shelter "home"), he came out of his room and offered to drive them. He still wasn't back when we went to bed — we hadn't set any curfew since he'd graduated from high school — but he was up early the next morning and jogged the short mile to the Howard Street Shopping Center to set up the sound board. And when we got there, I saw him talking to Rick Reilly. *Interesting.* Josh had blown off the youth-ministry brainstorming meeting yesterday. What now?

"We celebratin' Stu's birthday tonight?" Florida asked me after church.

I blinked. We'd already celebrated Stu's birthday at our house — but that wasn't Yada Yada. "Um, sure. Got any suggestions?"

"Stu been a good friend to Little Andy an' me," Becky popped in. "I'd like ta make the cake. But not one o' them round things. Flat. *In* the pan."

I laughed and gave Becky a hug. "You got it. I'll pass the word. We meet at Chanda's tonight. You guys want a ride?"

But when I pulled up in front of the Hickman house later that afternoon, I had to laugh. Florida, bundled in her winter coat, was sitting like a snow queen in her new wicker furniture on the porch. "Tol' ya I was gonna sit on my porch the first day of spring, rain or shine!" she yelled. But when Becky came out with a cake pan, Flo ran for the minivan. "Turn that heater up, girl! My fingers is froze."

Avis was already at Chanda's house when we arrived, getting the VIP tour of Rochelle's new bedroom and "the boys' room," which Conny was sharing with Chanda's boy, Tom. Florida and I ran up the stairs to peek, too, while Becky took her cake to the kitchen.

We had a good turnout at Yada Yada that night, including Ruth, who drove herself and Yo-Yo, and didn't let us forget it. "What? You are surprised? If I can birth two babies at my age, what's a little ol' driver's license?"

Yo-Yo rolled her eyes behind Ruth's back. "Huh. The license was easy; it's the driving that needs a little work," she muttered.

Our other surprise was Hoshi, who arrived with Nonyameko. "Most of the Northwestern students have gone home for spring break." Hoshi grinned, returning our hugs. "ReJOYce Campus Club meeting was cancelled."

"What about dat Sara?" Chanda asked, as she and Rochelle brought in a tray of coffee mugs along with a pot of good Jamaican coffee. The aroma was heavenly. "Did you bring her? Don't she only live a couple burbs nort' of 'ere?"

Hoshi shook her head. "She says no every time I invite her. But I told her we pray for her and are grateful for what she did, turning in those men who hurt Dr. Smith." Hoshi's lip suddenly trembled, and she busied herself looking for a tissue in her pocket.

Nony put an arm around Hoshi. "It is all right, my sister. God is working out His purpose in spite of what happened. One day Sara will come so we can love on her."

"Mm-hm," I heard Adele murmur. "So I can get my hands on that hair too."

I gaped at Adele. "That's it! That's what we can do."

Adele frowned. "Do what?" Others were looking at me, too.

"Hoshi, do you know when Sara's birthday is? Something to celebrate. We could collect money as a gift to give her the works at Adele's Hair and Nails — haircut, color, set, manicure, pedicure . . . you know, the works! Hoshi can tell her it's from all of us, to let her know she doesn't have to be afraid."

"Dat's a good idea." Chanda reached for her purse. " 'Ere's a twenty to start."

I felt like rolling my eyes. She didn't have to announce *how much.* But others nodded, liking the idea. I took Chanda's twenty. "Whatever people want to contribute. We can collect next time too."

Just then, Becky entered with her cake in an aluminum nine-by-thirteen pan, candles flaming. "Happy birthday to Stu . . ." she warbled, and we all joined in. Estelle had brought a card "From the Whole Gang," which we all signed. But Becky had the best idea of all.

"I just wanna say, Stu's somethin' else. I don't know many folks who woulda taken me into their house, just to give me an address so I could get out on parole. I know I ain't the easiest person ta live with —"

Stu put a hand over her mouth, hiding a grin.

"— but she took a chance on me anyhow. Now I'm in my own place, but she still workin' the system to help me get Andy back. So on her birthday I just wanna say, I love ya, Stu girl." Becky Wallace grabbed Stu in a bear hug while we all clapped.

Flo spoke up. "Yeah, well, Stu found Carla, when DCFS lost track of *my* baby. An' she treated my man like a *man*, asked him ta help her move, let him know she needed him, trusted him with the job. Men like Carl, they need ta be needed. So I thank ya, too, girl." Another big hug.

"I wasn't sure if I wanted Stu to move into the apartment above us," I admitted. "Even though I'm older than Stu, I always felt like a little kid around her, she's so . . . so good at everything."

A chorus of "Hear, hear!" went up, laughter and clapping.

"But I have to say, Stu is nothing if not a loyal friend. She might make me feel like a dork" — more laughter — "but, frankly . . ."

391

I stopped, realizing that what I was about to say was actually true. "Frankly, she's more like the sister I never had growing up." I stepped over to Stu and gave her a tight hug, amid more clapping. "I love you, Stu," I whispered in her ear.

"I love you, too, Jodi," she whispered back. She looked around at all the Yada Yadas sitting all over Chanda's living room. "Frankly, *you all* have been the family I didn't have for so many years — and you still are, even though God's starting to give my natural family back to me. Now that God and I got honest." She took the tissue Hoshi handed her and blew her nose.

Avis smiled. "Looks like we have a lot to give thanks for tonight. Why don't we continue with our thanksgivings?" Her glance fell on her daughter Rochelle, perched on the arm of Chanda's leather couch. "*I* want to praise God and thank Chanda for offering her home to my daughter and grandson." Now *she* got teary. More tissues. "In the midst of a tough time for Rochelle, God is also pouring out His blessings. Mm!" Avis raised a hand in the air. "Thank You, Jesus! You are so good! So *good!*"

Rochelle smiled shyly at her mother's spontaneous praise. "I'm thankful to

Chanda too. But I also want to say I'm grateful to Nonyameko, who is helping me see that HIV isn't something to be ashamed of. Fear and silence will only keep me from getting the help I need. Many women and children are suffering from this disease through no fault of our own. Though *some* people . . ." A flash of anger burned in her eyes.

Whew. That's deep, I thought. I had never heard Rochelle speak so boldly.

The moment of anger passed. "One more thing I am thankful for. My *stepfather,* Peter Douglass" — Rochelle used the word deliberately, tossing a teasing smile at her mother — "is starting a Manna House Foundation to raise money to rebuild the shelter."

I heard a gasp from Edesa. "Oh! *Es verdad?* It is true?"

Avis smiled. "Yes. Peter came home from the men's breakfast at SouledOut yesterday with this great idea. The last few months, some of our husbands have been meeting before the monthly breakfast to pray for one another, that God would use them in new ways. For Peter, starting a foundation to rebuild the shelter that had taken in our own daughter seemed like a way to give back."

"Gloria a Dios!" Delores Enriquez beamed.

"Ricardo came home and told me about the foundation." She grimaced apologetically to Edesa. "I knew you would be so happy, *mi hermana*. But I did not know if the news was mine yet to tell."

Excited comments flew. I wondered if that was the news Denny had wanted to tell me. Nony clapped her hands together, then burst out laughing, like a little girl dying to tell her secret. "Has a holy fire baptized our men, sending them into the marketplace like on the day of Pentecost?"

"Hm. Don't know about *that*," Florida murmured. "Ain't heard Carl speak in no tongues and don't think I will."

We joined Nony's laughter, but Adele always could read between the lines. "You got more 'holy fire' to tell us about, Nony?"

Nony nodded, pressing her hands flat together in front of her smile. "Yes . . . yes. Mark *also* came home from the men's breakfast yesterday and asked me to go out for coffee so we could talk. Sisters . . ." She blinked back sudden tears, but her smile stayed fixed. "It has been many months since my husband did that. He said he had not planned to tell me yet, not wanting to disappoint me if he failed, but the brothers encouraged him to include me in his plans."

Adele rolled her eyes. "*What* plans? Girlfriend, you better tell us quick."

Nony's smile widened. "He decided — no, *we* decided — we should move forward with our plans that were so viciously aborted last summer, unless God shuts the door."

A universal gasp greeted this announcement. "Ya mean, like, you guys goin' to South Africa again?" Yo-Yo asked bluntly.

Nony nodded. "Mark has decided to apply once more to the University of KwaZulu-Natal as guest instructor. Yes, he is afraid — afraid they will reject him because of his recent medical history. But Carl and Peter and Denny told him — how do Americans say it? — to 'get off his duff' and live again." Now the tears spilled over, but Nony lifted her face in praise. "Oh, Lord God, thank You! You are making a way out of no way, a stream in the desert, a path over the mountain!"

For several minutes, the rest of us joined Nony's praise, which became prayers for God's favor on Mark Smith's application and the birth of the Manna House Foundation. But as we praised and prayed, I struggled inside. Mark Smith "getting off his duff" was a *huge* answer to our prayers. But if the Sisulu-Smiths *did* move to South Africa, we might be saying good-bye to them for . . . for who knew how long!

Oh God! How can it be good news and hurt so much at the same time?

The Voice in my spirit nudged me. *Your Yada Yada sisters are a gift, Jodi Baxter — not a possession. You know how Nony has longed to return to her homeland, how her heart aches for the suffering caused by HIV and AIDS. Would you keep her from My plans for her and Mark?*

Well, of course the answer was no — but that didn't help my feelings any.

Besides, the Voice within continued, *I have plans for you, too, Jodi — but you must keep your heart and your mind open. My plans are not your plans. Be alert; My Spirit is moving. Think of the possibilities . . .*

"Hey. Earth to Jodi. You collecting the money for Sara's makeover?" Becky Wallace stood in front of me, trying to give me a wadded-up bill.

With a start, I realized the prayers were over and people were starting to leave. "Oh, yeah, sure. Thanks, Becky." I stuffed the bill in my pocket along with Chanda's twenty and started to put on my jacket.

"Sister Jodi?" Edesa pulled me aside. "Does . . . do you think Josh knows about the Manna House Foundation?"

I thought a minute. "I don't know. He didn't go to the men's breakfast yesterday.

Denny might have told him, but I don't think so. The first I heard about it was tonight." Her eyes seemed imploring. *What is she really asking me?* "Estelle did tell him about the advisory board. He . . . wasn't interested. But that was before . . ." I hesitated. What happened last night was probably not my news to tell.

But she nodded. "I know. He came to my house last night." She looked up at me, her dark eyes huge, black diamonds in her sweet mahogany face. "He asked me to forgive him for his part in the Manna House fire."

So. That was what Josh did after taking Precious and Sabrina home! "And?" I asked gently.

"I forgave him. I was glad! You see, I had been blaming him in my heart, holding it against him. We are very traditional in my country. To me, he is a man, even though he is young. And a true man always protects the women and children, but his careless-ness put us all in danger. Those women had nothing but lost everything. But . . . I, too, asked him to forgive me, for holding blame in my heart. I was not honest with him; I only held him away."

She sniffled, and I found a clean tissue to give her. As she wiped her eyes and blew her nose, I felt a tenderness toward this young woman I'd never felt before. God's Spirit had told me to be alert, that His Spirit was moving. That His plans were not my plans. *To think of the possibilities* . . .

"He loves you, you know."

I don't know who was more startled by my murmured words — Edesa or me. She stared at me, eyes rounded. And then her chin quivered beneath a small smile. "I know," she whispered.

32

Whew. So much had happened over the weekend, I felt like an amateur juggler, trying to keep all the prayers in the air but dropping half of them in the hurry-scurry of a muddy school week. I was a tad jealous of Hoshi's week off from classes between her winter and spring quarters. What I wouldn't give for even one day off, just to catch up with myself! — not to mention the weekend laundry that still needed folding. But Chicago schools still had three weeks to go before our spring break.

On the other hand, I told myself that Thursday, while navigating a chain of sidewalk puddles and trying to keep dry under our old black umbrella, it'd been raining most of the week, even though the temperatures had finally climbed into the sixties. Maybe having spring break after Easter would give us some warm, sunny days to enjoy, time to plant some flower boxes for the back porch . . .

Unfortunately, another puddle in the kitchen greeted me when I got home from school. My initial frustration evaporated when I saw poor Willie Wonka, curled up in a corner, looking at me miserably. "Aw, it's all right, Wonka," I murmured, getting out the bucket and disinfectant. I mopped up the mess with a rag and dried the floor, then lowered myself beside Wonka and pulled his head into my lap. The tip of his tail patted quietly as I stroked his head and scratched behind his ears. "Guess it's time for another trip to the vet, eh, old boy? Don't worry," I crooned. "The vet's our friend, remember? Maybe she can help us with this problem."

A thunderclap rattled the windows. I decided against trying to take the dog out, and just sat on the floor with my back against the wall, petting his once silky brown fur that had grown dull and thin, showing his ribs — until the phone rang. I scrambled to my feet and caught it on the third ring. "Mom?" Amanda sounded desperate. "Can you call Dad and ask him to pick me up at school on his way home?"

I looked at the clock. "You're still at school? I was expecting you any minute."

A loud crack of thunder drowned out her next few words. "— language lab, but I can't

400

go outside now to wait for the bus. It's raining buckets!"

I squeezed my eyes shut. "Sorry, honey.
Tonight's the night Dad goes to the JDC.
He's probably on his way downtown al-
ready."

"But Mo-om! I'll get soaked standing at
the bus stop!"

"Oh . . . ask the school office for a phone
book and call a cab."

"Really?" She sounded interested. "A
cab?"

*Well, why not? What could it be — five dol-
lars? Ten?*

"Fifteen dollars!"

Amanda, casting anxious looks out the
front door at the blinking hazard lights of
the Yellow Cab, rolled her eyes. "Mo-om.
You *told* me to call a cab. The meter said
eleven-something — almost twelve. And
you're supposed to give a tip, you know."

Somehow, I scrounged up the money,
thinking ruefully that fifteen dollars was half
a night out for Denny and me — maybe a
whole night out if we went to CrossRhodes
Café where we could split a large Greek
salad with gyros slices and a large order of
lemony Greek fries and still have enough
left over to rent a video. *On the other hand,* I

thought, as Amanda grabbed an umbrella and ran out to pay the cab driver, *she's home safe and dry. That's worth a lot, thank You, Jesus.*

Josh called to say he was working late to get a big software shipment out before the weekend, and not to wait supper for him. So I served up two plates of Pad Thai from a box, saving a plate for Denny, while Amanda tried to coax Willie Wonka into the dining room for a half-hour reprieve from his kitchen jail cell. But the dog just wagged the tip of his tail, sighed, and laid his head down on his paws.

"Mo-om! What's the matter? He won't come!" The next moment, she took her plate and flopped on the floor beside the brown Lab. "I'm gonna eat in the kitchen with Wonka."

I shrugged. "Huh. Guess it's either eat by myself in the dining room or join the sit-in." I sank to the floor beside my daughter and the dog with my plate, making Amanda laugh. "Say, got any ideas for Dad's birthday next week?" April first, his birthday, was a week from today. "Oh, wait. That's a Thursday! He won't even be here for supper."

Amanda dug into her Pad Thai noodles. "Don't sweat it, Mom. Just celebrate on Friday. Dad won't care. He probably gets tired of April Fool's jokes on his birthday anyway."

Denny was pumped when he got home from the JDC, as usual. He leaned against the counter, eating his plate of Pad Thai standing up, while he related the latest saga of the Bible study in Unit 3B. "Two of our regulars weren't there tonight. Found out one was found guilty of first-degree murder at his hearing and has been shipped out to the Joliet Youth Center. Makes me sick, Jodi. I don't think he was the shooter, but because he was present at the time of the shooting, they got him on the accountability law. He cooperated, told what he knew, but they used it against him. The *shooter,* on the other hand, had enough street smarts to keep quiet — and he was acquitted for lack of evidence." He shook his head and fell silent, eating his microwave-warm noodles.

Oh God! Is that what will happen to Chris Hickman? No, Lord, please . . . I swallowed. "How do you know this? I thought you weren't supposed to talk to the kids about their cases."

"Oscar Frost, mostly. He's been trying to follow the cases as they're reported in the newspaper, buried somewhere in the *Metro* pages, and online."

"What about Chris? Was he there to-night?"

Denny nodded. "Yeah. He looks good. Has lost that sullen look he'd been affecting, and from all I can tell, doing good in his schoolwork too . . . though, man!" He waved his fork. "The kids can't take any textbooks out of the school area. They're not even supposed to have pencils in their cells — anything that could double as a weapon. So much for homework and studying. But . . ." Denny chewed thoughtfully. "Don't think school is uppermost in his mind. His disposition is coming up at the end of the month. He asked me to pray."

Definitely. I really needed to check in with Florida and find out how she was doing. Funny how easy it was to forget that her mother-heart must be weeping every day Chris was in jail. She seemed so strong; "life goes on" and all that.

"Hey. Almost forgot." Denny pulled a sheet of paper from his briefcase. "Don't know if you'd be interested, but the school at the JDC is looking for a volunteer English teacher to help the boys produce a play for their parents. Their regular teacher got mono and won't be back for several weeks. I thought of you."

"Me?" Was my husband crazy? "I have a

full-time job, Denny. And I teach *third grad-ers.* What do I know about teenagers?"

He chuckled. "You've got two of your own. And half your friends have teenagers — Florida, Yo-Yo, Delores. These boys aren't that different. Well, yeah, true, they've come from some tough situations, made some bad choices. But under the skin, they're just kids. Just kids . . ." He squatted down and scratched Willie Wonka behind the ears. "Hey, old buddy. I hear you're go-ing to see the vet this weekend." He ran his hand thoughtfully over the dog's thin body. "Anyway, think about it, Jodi. You're a teacher — a good teacher. This would be something different, a way to reach out. It could be a lot of fun. You might have to do it during spring break, though."

Give up my spring break?

Think of the possibilities, Jodi . . .

"Man, I don't know, Denny." I held out my hand for the sheet of paper. "Is that some information about what they want?"

He grinned up at me. "Uh, not exactly. It's a form from the Sheriff's Department for a background check."

The rain woke me up just minutes before the alarm. "Ohh," I groaned. *More rain!* Four days in a row! And it wasn't even April yet. That would make taking Willie Wonka outside miserable for me *and* the poor dog. But — I swung my legs out of bed — it had to be done, or we'd have another puddle in the kitchen *before* school.

I pulled Denny's bathrobe around me and stuck my feet into my slippers, shuffling toward the kitchen. I missed my "Wonka alarm clock," snuffling his nose into my face, letting me know he had to go out. But since he'd started to have bladder and bowel problems, we couldn't let him sleep in our bedroom anymore.

"Wake up, sleepyhead," I said, swinging one leg over the safety gate in the kitchen doorway, then the other, and turning on the light. I sleepily filled the coffeepot with cold water, scooped coffee into the basket, and punched the On button. The coffee might as well be dripping while Wonka and I had our big adventure into the wet-and-wild outdoors.

The dog hadn't moved, curled up on his doggy cushion near the door. "Hey, c'mon, Wonka," I said, shaking him gently. "Let's get this over with."

He still didn't move.

Suddenly, fear grabbed my throat. My heart started racing. "Wonka!" I yelled, this time shaking him roughly. No response.

"Oh God, Oh God, oh nooooo . . ." I fell backward, as if I'd been shocked with an electric current. *"Denny!"* I screamed, scrambling to my feet. "Come here! Quick!"

Footsteps thudded from the bedroom. Doors opened, more footsteps. Within seconds, Denny, in sleep shorts and T-shirt, had yanked the safety gate from the doorway and was at my side. Josh and Amanda, their hair tousled, their eyes wide, were right behind him.

"Wonka . . ." My voice barely came out in a whisper. Denny immediately squatted down on one knee and held his fingers to the dog's neck.

"Oh, Mommy! . . . Oh no! He's not . . . he's not . . . is he?" Amanda started to cry. Josh reached out and put his arm around his sister, pulling her close.

Denny, still down on one knee, turned and looked up at us . . . and nodded slowly.

I burst into tears. Amanda threw herself down and covered Willie Wonka's body with her own. "Wonka! Don't leave me! Don't leave me!" Her whole body shook with sobs. "You're my only friend, Wonka! Please, *please,* don't go . . ."

And then our arms reached out for each other, all four of us surrounding our beloved

dog, our friend, whose love was uncondi-
tional . . . and we cried.

33

I didn't go to work that day. I couldn't. We let Amanda stay home too. We called the high school and said we had a death in the family — which was true. But when I called Bethune Elementary, I simply told the office I had a family emergency and needed a substitute. "And could you leave a message for Mrs. Douglass to call me?"

The rain was still coming down hard. Denny stood on the porch, hands in the pockets of his jeans, watching the rain cascade off the garage roof, forming a wet trench on the ground. Finally, he motioned to me to join him outside and to close the door. "I suppose we could call Animal Control and they would —"

"No, Denny! They'll just . . . just 'dispose' of him in some garbage pit. A dead animal doesn't mean anything to them. We can't let Willie Wonka . . ." I choked up.

"I know. That's what I was going to say.

Maybe we're supposed to call Animal Control, but I want to bury him ourselves. Only problem . . ." Denny tipped his chin at the soggy backyard. "We can't dig a grave in weather like this. Weather report says it's supposed to clear later this afternoon, though. Might be all right tomorrow." He shook his head. "But I don't know, Jodi. Think Amanda can deal with it? Wonka's body in the house all day, I mean. Especially if she's not going to school."

"Better than the alternative!" I snapped — and immediately repented. "I'm sorry, Denny. I just can't bear the thought of strangers taking Wonka away."

"I know." His voice was tender. He pulled me into his arms and we just held each other for a few minutes.

"Whoa! Look at the lovebirds." Stu came clattering down the back stairs, half hidden under her umbrella. "I'm late. See you later." She dashed for the garage.

Just as well. I wasn't ready to talk about Wonka yet. We'd tell her tonight.

When we came back into the kitchen, Amanda had wrapped her bright yellow comforter with the black geometric designs around the dog's body — way too much blanket for our small kitchen. But I quietly toasted some bagels for Denny and Josh,

410

who decided to go on to work. "We'll bury him tomorrow, sweetie," Denny said, kissing the top of Amanda's head as he came back into the kitchen, dressed in slacks, shirt, and tie. "When the rain stops, okay?"

She nodded mutely.

He tipped up her chin. "You going to be okay?"

Amanda pulled away and didn't respond. He let her go, grabbed a bagel and a travel mug of coffee, and headed for the garage, Josh right behind him.

Suddenly the house felt cavernous. Yawning like an empty mouth, and nothing to fill it. What was I going to do all day? I couldn't put on some loud gospel music to drown out my sorrow, as I usually did. It wouldn't feel right, not with Wonka's motionless body wrapped in his yellow-and-black shroud on the kitchen floor. Maybe not going to work was a bad idea. I could go in late. . . . no. I should stay with Amanda.

The phone rang. "Jodi?" It was Avis. "Ms. Ivy said you had a family emergency! What happened?"

I told her about Willie Wonka. "Amanda's a wreck. I need to stay with her. And to be honest, I'm pretty much a basket case myself. I'm sorry, Avis. Just today."

"Oh. Well . . ."

I could almost hear her struggling between the professional Mrs. Douglass (*"What? You want to stay home because your dog died? What about your third graders, who are very much alive? I'm putting you on professional probation!"*) and Avis, my friend.

Avis won. "All right, Jodi. Family emergency it is. And . . . I'm really sorry for your loss. Give Amanda a hug for me."

Her words wrapped themselves around me, and I had another cry after we hung up. *Get hold of yourself, Jodi Baxter. You didn't cry this much when MaDear died!* I blew my nose and stood looking at the garish yellow-and-black pile in the corner of the kitchen. Should I try to find another blanket? Something smaller and —

"Mom?" Amanda came into the kitchen, noiseless in her socks, and stood beside me. Our arms slid around each other's waist. "I don't wanna put Wonka into the wet ground just wrapped in a blanket. Can't Daddy and Josh make a box or something? We could line it with something soft, maybe cut up my comforter, and sew it to fit."

Cut up her comforter! Suddenly it didn't matter. Why not? What was one comforter anyway, compared to a decent burial for Amanda's lifelong friend?

■ ■ ■ ■

The rain stopped shortly after noon. That evening, Josh and Denny built a box — basically, the deep bottom drawer from an old chest of drawers sitting unused in the basement, with a new lid that fit snugly over the top. Amanda and I cut up her comforter and sewed it together on two sides, vaguely resembling a dog-size sleeping bag. Amanda then sewed a pillowcase out of the same padded material, stuffing it with pieces of wadded-up comforter to make a pillow for Wonka's head to rest on.

It was time to let Wonka's friends know. I dialed upstairs when I heard Stu arrive home. "What?" she cried into my ear. "Why didn't you tell me this morning? I rushed right past you . . . Oh, Jodi, I feel so stupid."

"It's all right, Stu. We weren't ready to talk about it."

"I'm so sorry, Jodi. You want me to call anyone? The rest of Yada Yada?"

Relief sighed in my spirit. "Yes, please. We're going to bury him in the backyard tomorrow morning at ten — in case anyone wants to come. Like maybe Becky. She and Wonka were good buddies when she lived with you." *Becky* . . . I felt like bawling all over again. Little Andy had wanted to come play with "the doggy" a couple of Sundays ago, and it hadn't happened. Now it never would.

Josh and Denny lifted Willie Wonka's limp body into the soft bag, then laid him in the box, head on the pillow. "Don't put the lid on, not yet," Amanda begged. She bent down and kissed Wonka's still-silky ears — then fled to her bedroom.

I checked on her before going to bed. She lay curled up in her bed, her old faded comforter, once pink, now barely beige, in service once more. As I leaned over to kiss her, she grabbed my arm and pulled me onto the bed. "Mom? Why is God taking everything away from me?"

I could barely breathe.

"I mean, first José left me . . . and then MaDear died, and, and, she was practically a relative . . . and now Willie Wonka." The sobs started again. "I mean, *why,* Mom?"

I didn't have an answer. So I just held her and let her cry.

Sometime during the night, the clouds disappeared and the early morning sun kissed rooftops, trees, and bushes, inviting the world to come outside. Josh and Denny dug a hole out by the garage, where Becky had worked so hard to make a flower garden last year. I stood and watched them, suddenly aware of the sparrows flittering through the still-bare tree limbs. A few landed on the bird feeder Denny had hung for me last year, pecked hopefully, then flew away, still hungry.

But I turned away. I couldn't think about the birds. Not yet.

At ten o'clock, Stu and Estelle came down the back stairs and joined us in the back-yard. A huge white-and-silver SUV I didn't recognize pulled up in the alley behind our garage. A moment later, Florida, Cedric, and Carla tiptoed respectfully into the back yard, followed by Chanda's three kids and Becky Wallace — carrying Little Andy! "I get Andy two full weekends a month now, not just Sundays," she whispered to me, set-ting the curly-headed boy down. "Ain't God good?"

Andy made a beeline for Denny. "Hi, Big Guy!" he squealed, throwing his arms around Denny's leg. And then he saw the open box. The little boy stared. "Why is the doggy in the box?"

Denny shot a quick glance at Becky, who mouthed above Little Andy's head, *I didn't know how to tell him!*

Denny nodded at Becky, gathered all the

children around the box, and started talking to them in a calm voice. "When dogs get very old, one day their body just stops working, just like people. But that doesn't mean we forget about them . . ."

I leaned toward Becky. "How'd you get here? I mean, whose monster SUV?"

She snorted. "Chanda's. She leasin' it for a few weeks ta see if she wants somethin' that big. Came in handy today, fer sure."

Chanda joined us in the backyard ten minutes later, muttering, "De parking all *chacka-chacka* in dis neighborhood." But she hushed when she realized Denny was inviting the children to say something about their friend, Willie Wonka.

"He never bited me," Little Andy said solemnly.

"Sometimes he licked my face," Carla added.

"Whenever we came to see him, he wagged his tail." Dia wiggled her skinny rump. "I wish I had a tail to wag."

We laughed softly, then fell silent around the box holding our beloved Willie Wonka. "Amanda?" Denny prodded gently.

Amanda pulled something out of a paper bag. It was her old, favorite stuffed Snoopy dog, more grey than white now, one eye missing, one ear sagging. She laid it in the box with Wonka's body. Her lip trembled. "I . . . guess I have to grow up now."

Just then, footsteps came running on the walk alongside our house. José Enriquez burst into the backyard, followed by a gasping Edesa. "Are we too late, *Señor* Baxter?" he cried. The teenager's dark eyes took in the circle of adults and children around the hole, the pile of dirt, the box still sitting on the winter-dead lawn. "Amanda, I —"

Amanda didn't let him finish. She threw herself into José's arms and burst into tears. "Oh, José! You came!"

The backyard was quiet now. Chanda's vanload decided to go to the zoo and thank God for all the animals. The pile of dirt had been shoveled back into the hole and smoothed over the top. Becky promised she'd be back to plant some special flowers over the grave. "We'll call it Wonka's garden, right, Andy?"

I peeked out the kitchen window as I chopped vegetables for soup. José and Amanda sat cross-legged on the damp ground, shoulders hunched, picking at the brown grass, talking. On the porch, Josh and Edesa sat on the porch swing, soaking up spring's first rays, sometimes talking, sometimes just sitting quietly as the swing squeaked gently.

"God," I murmured, putting the lid on the pot and turning up the heat, "thank You for little graces, even in the middle of sad times like today . . . for José showing up, just when Amanda needed a friend . . . for Edesa and Josh able to sit comfortably together — though You might be the *only* One who knows what's going on with those two." I don't think prayers are supposed to end with rolling eyes, but I did it anyway.

When the pot was bubbling and the smell of garlic and basil filled the kitchen, I opened the back door. "Edesa! José! You want to stay for lunch? Got plenty of soup."

José jumped up. "Oh no, I can't, *Señora* Baxter. I have to rehearse with the band at one o'clock. My father's on the road today, so I am filling in. What time is it?"

I glanced at the kitchen clock. "Fifteen minutes to twelve."

Amanda danced on her toes hopefully, but José shook his head. "*Gracias,* Señora Baxter. But we came by el and —"

"Chill, José." Josh pulled out his car keys and playfully tossed them in the air. "I'll take you guys home. We only need thirty minutes to get there — forty, tops. Stay for Mom's soup."

34

Denny said he didn't want a big hullabaloo for his birthday, not so soon after losing our dog. So even though Stu and Estelle offered to come downstairs to help us celebrate on April first, I said no thanks, we were putting off his birthday until the weekend, and then we were going out to dinner, "just family."

It had been a strange week. The tears had dried up, but the hollow feeling in our lives remained. No Willie Wonka to trip over when we came in the door. No *click-click-click* of his nails on the hardwood floors. No muzzle pushed into our laps as we watched TV or sprawled in the recliner. And especially no kissy-face ritual when Amanda came home from school.

But I couldn't let Denny's actual birthday go past unnoticed, even though we'd put off going out until Friday. So while he was at the JDC Thursday evening, I made a chocolate tunnel cake. It even came out of the bundt pan in one piece, shiny and firm, belying its gooey center. I lit candles in the living room, put the cake on our old oak coffee table that was "fashionably stressed" after years of snacks and feet — with and without shoes — and made a pot of decaf coffee.

"What's this?" he said, coming into the living room after his long day, dropping his briefcase and loosening his tie. He lifted an eyebrow suspiciously. "You promised no April Fool's jokes this year."

"No joke. Just cake. I promise."

The front door banged. "I smell chocolate," Josh said. He stopped at the living room door. "I thought we weren't celebrating Dad's birthday till tomorrow."

"Well, um, I cheated. Get your sister. We're having cake."

A funny peace settled over the living room as the four of us dug into the cake by candlelight. "Mm," Amanda said, ignoring her fork and breaking her slice into gooey pieces, licking her fingers after each bite. "You haven't made this for a long time, Mom — oh!" She looked at her father guiltily. "We didn't sing 'Happy Birthday.' "

He gave a dismissive wave. "That's okay. Just eat."

"But can we say *happy* birthday? Even if,

you know, we're kinda sad?"

Denny chewed thoughtfully. "Sure. Because I am happy, you know."

"You are? But —"

"Well, I'm sad because we're missing Willie Wonka. But, I'm happy we got him when *you* were just a pup, snickerdoodle" — he reached over and pinched Amanda's nose — "because it was fun watching you two grow up together. And I'm happy because my wife, who's put up with me for twenty years —"

"Twenty-*one*," I corrected. "Twenty-four if you count dating."

"— and my two best kids —"

"You only *have* two kids," Josh pointed out.

Denny ignored the interruptions. "— are here with me right this moment, eating 'tunnel of fudge' cake. It doesn't get much better than that."

"Da-ad." Amanda rolled her eyes.

"I'm serious. Who knows if we'll all be together next year? Actually . . ." Denny put down his empty plate and leaned forward, forearms resting on his knees, looking around our small circle, ". . . Willie Wonka's death marks the end of an era for the Baxter family. I realized that was true, 'Manda, when you put your Snoopy dog in the box with Wonka's body and said, 'Guess I have to grow up now.' "

She made a face. "Yeah. But I was kinda mad. I didn't want any ol' stuffed dog if I couldn't have my real one."

Denny reached for our daughter and pulled her close to him on the couch, wrapping one arm around her shoulder. "But it's true, you know. You've had a rough time this winter. José broke up with you. MaDear died. Now Willie Wonka's gone. Familiar props have been knocked out from under you."

"But José came back! Well, not really. He said he's missed me, wants us to still be friends. Not like, you know, before — all tight and exclusive and stuff. But . . ." Amanda shrugged. "It's okay. I'm glad we can be friends."

Denny smiled at her. "Exactly. I think God knows you're strong enough to forge ahead even without the familiar props. In fact, tonight at the JDC, our study group came across this verse." He fished in his briefcase for the Bible he'd taken that night, and flipped pages. "Okay, here it is. First Corinthians, chapter thirteen: 'When I was a child, I talked like a child, I thought like a child, I reasoned like a child. But when I became a man' — you know, grown — 'I put childish things behind me.' "

He looked up. "Oscar and I talked to the boys that part of growing up is learning to face up to the consequences of mistakes and bad decisions. But it's also learning to overcome disappointment, even the loss of friends or family. Life isn't always fair. Bad things happen. But life keeps rolling. We have to keep rolling, too. Roll with the punches, roll with God's help."

"Can I see that?" Amanda reached for her dad's Bible and studied the page. Then her eyes widened. "Look at the next verse! It says, 'Now I know in part; then I shall know fully, even as I am fully known.' " She looked up thoughtfully. "It's kinda saying we don't always know *why* things happen, but we will someday — because God knows everything about us."

I watched my husband and daughter, gratefulness squeezing my heart. Amanda had cried, *"Why, Mom? Why?"* I didn't feel badly that I didn't have any answers that night. That wasn't the night for answers. But tonight, she was listening. Listening to the Word.

Josh cleared his throat. "Uh, can I cut in? I know you guys have been waiting for me to grow up, leave the nest, whatever."

I hid a grin. *Well, yeah.*

"But what you said, Dad, about God sometimes knocks the props out from under us . . . guess that sums up what I've been feeling. When Dr. Smith was attacked by those racists, well, that knocked the rosy color off my world, that's for sure. But I kept doing this, doing that, thinking I wanted to save the world, college could wait, all that stuff, until . . . well, the fire, you know. Kinda burned up my self-confidence."

The candles were starting to drip wax on the coffee table. But I couldn't take my eyes off my son, sandy hair falling over his ears and curling down onto his neck, blue tattoo peeking out from under the sleeve of his T-shirt, both knees of his jeans ripped. Jesus was right. It was what was on the *inside* of a person that counted with God.

"But Edesa and I, we've been talking, and she kinda showed me God takes things away sometimes, so all we have left to lean on is God. Funny thing, though, those women and kids at the shelter — they lost a lot more in that fire than I did. But women like Estelle and Precious, they still had something I didn't . . . confidence in God. Ya know?"

My eyes blurred. Amanda was watching her brother with her mouth half open.

Denny pulled out his handkerchief.

Josh threw out his hands. "But I think God's telling me He can guide a rolling stone better than a stick-in-the-mud. So I went ahead and enrolled at UIC for the fall semester, you know, the Chicago Circle campus. Maybe international studies, not sure yet. Relating across cultures, that kind of thing. But staying in Chicago means I can get involved with the youth outreach at SouledOut on the weekends — maybe even sit on that advisory board for the new Manna House shelter." He cast an impish look at me. "Don't worry, Mom. I'm gonna look for an apartment or somethin'."

"Sounds good, Josh. Real good." Denny lifted an eyebrow. "But you were going to tell us this . . . when?"

Josh grinned. "Hey. Happy birthday, Dad."

I crawled into our queen-size bed, propped myself up with both pillows, and watched Denny pull off his tie, then his belt, then his shoes. He saw me watching him and grinned. "Best birthday I've ever had."

I nodded. It had been a magical night — the kind of magic created when God breaks into our everyday world with angels making announcements and stars bringing wise men. The kind of magical night when you're just grateful you were present to see God at work, even though you didn't have anything to do with it.

Well, maybe the chocolate cake helped. Got us together, anyway, unplanned and unrehearsed.

"I've been thinking," I said. "What you said about life keeps rolling. So when stuff happens, we have to roll with the punches and keep going with God's help."

He raised a quizzical eyebrow at me as he finished undressing and pulled on his sleep shorts and T-shirt.

"I mean, not *just* 'keep going,' but moving outward. You know, like Mark Smith applying again to that university in KwaZulu-Natal. Nony is so excited — not just about the possibility of going back to South Africa, but because Mark is 'rolling' again, moving forward, instead of telling himself he can't."

Denny crawled into bed beside me and stole his pillow back. "Yeah. God is good. *Real* good."

Which was true, though I could hardly imagine Yada Yada without Nony. She was the one who taught us about praying the Scriptures right back to God, claiming His promises, something I was still learning. But . . . I couldn't let myself think about losing Nony right now.

I propped myself up on one elbow and faced Denny. "But that's going to be a big change for Yada Yada. And it's not the only one! Hoshi graduates in June. What's *she* going to do? Especially if the Sisulu-Smiths leave and sell their house. That's been her home for the past year. And our family is facing big changes too. Like you said, in a way Wonka's death marks the end of an era for our family. Our kids are growing up. Josh will be moving out, Amanda graduates next year . . . that whole empty-nest thing."

"Mm-hm." Denny breathed out a sleepy sigh. "And your point is?"

I hesitated. Was I really ready to take the plunge? But wasn't that what God had been saying to us tonight? Time to uncircle the wagons. Time to get rolling!

"The point is . . . I think I want to do that drama thing with the kids at the JDC. If the position is still open."

"You gonna do *what?*" Florida said before worship started on Sunday morning. Daylight Savings had dragged us out of bed an hour earlier that day, but the fact that it was Palm Sunday and the beginning of Holy Week helped ensure that the majority of

SouledOut members made it by the new time.

"I'm applying to the Nancy Jefferson School at the JDC as a drama coach volunteer." I grinned. "The English teacher got mono or something."

Florida stared at me. "Since when you a drama coach? I thought you taught third grade. An' one thing I *know,* they ain't got no third graders at the JDC. Huh. Not yet, anyway." She wagged her head. "But I tell ya, Jodi, they got some kids up in there young as ten. Breaks my heart."

Now it was my turn to stare. *"Ten!"* Ten was fifth grade.

"Yeah," she said glumly. "Those gangs are recruitin' shorties at a younger an' younger age — then these babies end up holdin' drugs for the big dudes, or smugglin' weapons, or even usin' 'em to make themselves feel big an' bad. Maybe it's good they get caught; keeps 'em off the street for a while anyway. But I dunno, the JDC ain't all it s'posed ta be — oh! Hey there, Nony. Hey, Mark."

We both got warm hugs from the Sisulu-Smith family, who had just come in. "Yada Yada tonight at my house, sisters?" Nony shrugged off her coat. "Help me pass the word that we are still collecting money for that gift certificate for Sara. Hoshi found out Sara just had a birthday in March — but thinks our idea would still work as a belated birthday gift."

Carla Hickman's age group was busily handing out palm fronds, and Avis set her big, falling-apart Bible on the small wooden stand that served as a pulpit, ready for the call to worship. "Talk to you later," I whispered to Flo, then took a palm frond and scurried to my seat beside Denny. But my mind was backpedaling. *What did Flo mean, the JDC isn't all it's supposed to be? What am I getting myself into? Have I leaped before I looked?*

But Avis's strong voice pulled me into the reason we had gathered that morning. "Blessed is He who comes in the name of the Lord!"

We all repeated her words: "Blessed is He who comes in the name of the Lord!"

Little Andy's voice piped up, "She *s'posed* to say, 'Good mornin', church.' " Becky Wallace's face turned a bright pink as the other children tittered.

Avis smiled. "Imagine for a moment that we are worshipers on our way to the temple in Jerusalem. And then the whispers start. 'Jesus of Nazareth is coming!' . . . 'You mean the Healer?' . . . 'Could He be the

429

Messiah?' Excitement mounts. And then they see Him coming down the road, riding a humble donkey. 'He's coming! He's coming!' Suddenly people are breaking off palm branches to wave." Avis began to wave the palm frond she held in her hand. "Others take off their cloaks and lay them in the road. The children began to sing; soon the cry was heard all along the road into Jerusalem —"

As if on cue, the praise team and instruments launched into a song: *Hosanna! Hosanna! Blessed is He who comes in the name of the Lord!* Palm fronds waved all over the blue-and-coral-painted room. I hadn't heard this particular song before, but it was easy to pick up.

As we repeated the "Hosanna" lines at the end of the song, Oscar Frost put down his saxophone and picked up a pair of maracas. The drummer laid down his sticks and began a thudding beat with his hands on a set of congas. Suddenly the praise team was singing the song again — in Spanish:

Hosanna! Hosanna! Bendito es Él que viene en el nombre del Señor!

I saw Amanda's face light up. *Hosanna! Hosanna! Bendito es Él que viene en el nombre del Señor!* Children jumped up and down, waving their palms. In fact, it was impossible to stand still. People began moving away from their seats, forming a processional around the room. The waving palms, throbbing drums, and joyful words did seem as if we were welcoming the One we'd all been longing for — the Messiah, the Savior, the Son of God who came to live among us.

But even as we sang and waved our palms, we passed the plain wooden cross on the wall of our storefront sanctuary. And it hit me with renewed clarity: between two joyful Sundays — Palm Sunday and Easter — came the Cross.

35

Whoa. That whole Cross thing stayed on my mind all afternoon. *Hope and joy. Suffering. Resurrection.* Jesus said, *"Take up your cross and follow Me."* That meant we went through that cycle too. *Hope and joy. Suffering. But never despair, because then came the promise of resurrection.*

But at least I remembered to bring the money we'd already collected for Sara's "belated birthday present" as Yada Yada gathered at Nony's house that evening. To my delight, Hoshi was still at the house since the ReJOYce campus meeting she and Sara attended started an hour later. Hoshi beamed as others added to the collection.

Ruth was the last one to arrive, lugging a baby carrier. "A cold her brother has," she announced, lifting a pink-cheeked Havah out of the swaddled blankets, leaving us to figure out whether that was the reason she didn't bring Isaac, too, or whether leaving one fussy baby with Ben was more than enough. Seeing what Hoshi was doing, Ruth dug in her purse, stuffed several bills into Havah's tight baby grip, and cooed, "See? Havah wants to help Sara too . . . okay, sweetie, let go now . . ."

Finally, Hoshi shyly handed the basket of bills to Adele. "Will this be enough for — how do you say — a 'makeover'?"

Adele pocketed the money without even counting it. "Just right." She handed a gift certificate to Hoshi in exchange. "Tell Sara to call that number for an appointment."

Nony, her sculpted braids freed from the African headwrap she'd worn that morning, poured tea and passed a plate of sugary lemon bars as the conversation drifted to Holy Week celebrations.

"Easter sure was the biggest day of the year when I was comin' up Baptist," Florida said. "Didn't matter how poor we was, my mama decked us out in lacey anklets, patent leather shoes shined with Vaseline, ruffled dresses — and new underwear in case we got run over. And an Easter hat! Mm-mm. I felt so grown-up wearin' a big ol' Easter hat like all the big mamas."

Adele fanned herself with a small paper plate. "You forgot hair. Mama pressed mine — first straightened it with Vaseline and a

433

hot iron comb, then curled it with iron curlers heated on the stove. Ouch. I think that's when I decided I wanted my own salon, to save little girls from all that torture."

Florida was shaking with laughter now. "Same, same. But first, we had to make it through Good Friday. Always had seven different preachers, preachin' the Seven Last Words of Christ. Sometimes lasted till midnight!"

Stu grinned. "And I thought *our* Good Friday service was long. In the Lutheran church, we prayed the fourteen Stations of the Cross. We walked solemnly from station to station around the church, where somebody read the relevant scripture: Jesus condemned to death . . . Jesus carrying His cross . . . Jesus falling under the weight — all the way to His death and burial. After each station, everybody said, 'Lord have mercy, Christ have mercy, Lord have mercy,' and someone blew out the candles at that station, until the whole church was dark." She twisted a strand of long hair around one finger. "Easter, of course, was full of light and joy, lots of banners and big organ music."

Yo-Yo rolled her eyes. "Huh. Only time I ever remember goin' ta church with my mama was Easter. Oh, yeah. Couple of times we went at Christmas. Kinda got the idea if you showed up on Easter and Christmas, you could forget it the rest of the time."

"At least you went to church," Becky said. "I thought Easter was Easter eggs and Easter bunnies. My dad took me to an Easter egg hunt once when I was little. A couple of months later he split, an' I don't remember ever seein' him again."

Florida squeezed Becky's hand. "That's why Jesus came, girl, to heal all that."

"At least the Easter bunny has not made it across the border into Mexico!" Delores huffed. Then her eyes got wistful. "But the whole country celebrates from *Domingo de Ramos* to *Domingo de Gloria* — Palm Sunday to Easter. Every year on *Viernes Santo,* Holy Friday, there is a big procession through the streets in every town. A man wearing a bloody crown of thorns carries a cross, escorted by men dressed as Roman soldiers. Everyone ends up at the Catholic church to repent of our sins that sent Jesus to the cross."

Chanda shook her head. "In Jamaica, Easter just a big party, like a carnival. Mi remember mama looking so sad, down on she knees, praying for all dem heathens, not even know what dey do. But she not so sad she not make Easter buns and cheese!"

435

Chanda closed her eyes and sighed. "Mm. Dem buns so sweet and spicy and *full* of raisins! Mm-mm."

"Sounds like hot cross buns," I said. "My mother used to make them — sweet rolls with a cross of white frosting. You can get them in the grocery stores, but they don't taste anything like homemade — not that *my* kids have ever had the homemade version." Everyone laughed. "But what I remember most is sunrise services. I always thought that was so exciting — getting up while it was still dark on Easter morning, going to a local football stadium, a bunch of churches all together usually, and watching the sun rise, then singing some glorious hymn, like 'Christ the Lord Is Risen Today!' "

Heads nodded. Several had been to at least one sunrise service.

Yo-Yo squinted thoughtfully. "At the Bagel Bakery, we're makin' a lot of foods for Passover. Funny that the Jewish folks have a holy day same time as the Christians."

Ruth, who was jiggling Havah over her shoulder, practically choked. "Same time as . . . !" She rolled her eyes. *"Oy vey."*

"What? What'd I say?" Yo-Yo threw out her hands.

"Here." Ruth handed the squirming baby

436

to Adele. "What? You don't read your Bible?" She tapped her noggin with one finger. "What feast was Jesus celebrating with His disciples the night Judas betrayed Him?"

"Huh. Passover, of course," Florida said. "But that's Old Testament stuff, Ruth — pardon me sayin' so. We ain't under the Law an' all that anymore, thank ya, *Je*sus!"

Yo-Yo snorted. "You said it. I have a hard enough time keepin' the Ten Big Ones, much less all them itty-bitty rules in the Old Testament."

Ruth *tsked-tsked* through her teeth. "*Oy, oy, oy.* It's time all you *New Testament* Christians celebrated a *Seder,* along with Jesus, who seemed to think it was important to show His disciples the hidden meanings in the ancient Passover meal."

Most of us looked blank. "Seder?"

"Seder — the Passover ritual celebrated in Jewish homes all over the world to remember God's deliverance from Egypt." Ruth's exaggerated patience sounded like she was talking to my third graders. "For Messianic Jews, the Seder takes on a deeper meaning, foretelling the coming of the Messiah." Ruth got up and paced around Nony's family room. "Hm. Hm. How could we do this? . . ."

Hoshi glanced at her watch and started to slip out of the room.

"Hoshi, wait one moment," Nony said quickly. "Let us pray with you before you go to meet Sara." Nony turned to Ruth. "Please forgive the interruption, my sister. But Hoshi must leave."

Ruth nodded, still deep in thought, murmuring to herself.

Nony stood with an arm around the slender Japanese student and prayed that Sara would receive our gift as an offering of our love. Adele, still holding Havah, who had fallen to sleep over her shoulder, added a prayer of blessing over Hoshi for "walking her talk" by loving Sara.

Hoshi whispered, "Thank you" and slipped out . . . but the prayers just kept coming. Florida asked God for mercy at Chris's final hearing later that month, when his fate would be decided by a judge in the juvenile court.

"Thank you, God, that he wasn't sent to adult court," Stu murmured.

"Yes! Thank ya, *Je*sus." Florida had to blow her nose.

"Nony?" I heard Avis ask quietly. "Has Mark heard from the university yet?"

Eyes opened. Nonyameko shook her head.

438

"Not yet. We are trusting God to do what is best."

But Avis prayed that Mark would receive favor from the University of KwaZulu-Natal, and that we could send out this couple with gladness in our hearts.

Well, that last part might be a stretch, I thought with a pang.

"And bless de whole Baxter family," Chanda said suddenly, "feeling so sad wit' losing dey sweet dog."

She took me by such surprise, a lump grabbed me in the throat. I reached over and squeezed her hand. But it reminded me that I had something to share. "Um, sisters? I'd appreciate your prayers, because I volunteered to help the school at the JDC put on a play. The regular English teacher got mono and had to take a leave. Denny told me they were looking for a substitute, so . . ." I sucked in a big breath. "That's how I'll be spending my spring break. It's a big stretch for me, but with one of our own children at the JDC, seems like a responsibility I need to own too."

"Jesus, Jesus . . ." Florida grabbed the tissue box.

Adele chuckled. Couldn't blame her. It was pretty funny. Me, Jodi Marie Baxter, taking on a classroom of juvenile delinquents — well, guess they were "innocent until proven guilty" — even if it was for a short time. But, still chuckling, Adele prayed for me. "Lord, don't know who's gonna learn more, the boys and girls at the JDC, or Sister Jodi here. But it's so unlikely, it's gotta be one of Your ideas. And whatever comes out of this drama thing, Lord, wash it all over with Your love."

Avis wrapped up our prayers, and we started to break up the circle when Ruth said, "All right. Gonna be tight but we'll do it."

We all looked at her. What in the world was she talking about?

"Seder. At our house this Thursday, the night Jesus celebrated Passover with His disciples before Judas betrayed Him. Six o'clock. Bring your children. It is very important that the children understand — that is the Jewish way."

"At your house?" I blinked. "What about Ben? I mean, how is he going to feel about a bunch of Christians celebrating a traditional Jewish feast?"

"That," Ruth said, a puckish gleam in her eyes, "might be the whole point."

36

Ruth had bustled out to her car with Havah snugly strapped into the carrier before what she'd said sunk in. *Thursday night? With kids?* That was a school night!

Except it wasn't — which I discovered when I got home and looked at the calendar. Spring vacation began next Friday — which "just happened" to be Good Friday. *Mm-hm.* The Chicago school system's way of accommodating a religious holiday without risking a lawsuit.

Okay. So how to sell my family? Denny was out; he'd be at the JDC Thursday night — *with* the car. Maybe Chanda could pick us up in her monster SUV. But getting a ride was the easy part. Convincing Amanda and Josh to come with me, when I didn't have a clue what to expect, was the bigger challenge. But I had one ace up my sleeve.

I called Delores. "Are you, um, coming to the Garfields' for that Seder thing on Thursday with the kids?"

"No, I am sorry, *mi amiga.* I work three to ten this week. But Edesa said she would bring the *niños.* José will help her."

Bingo! I hung up, smiling. That's what I wanted to know. My kids would come.

I tried to keep my students on task that week, but it was a losing battle. They could smell spring vacation in the air. But the idea of sharing holiday traditions, as we'd done at Yada Yada Sunday night, might keep their interest. Was I pushing the line between church and state too far? Shouldn't be, if I included other faiths. I did a search online but came up zero for any Muslim holy days during the month of April. But I asked Caleb Levy to come prepared to tell us about the Jewish Passover, and asked for other volunteers to describe how they celebrated the Christian "holy days" of Good Friday and Easter. That sparked a sea of waving of hands — the usual litany about yellow marshmallow chicks, Easter egg hunts, and the Easter bunny.

Mercedes LaLuz waved her hand. "*My* mama says there's no such thing as the Easter bunny. Easter is when *Jesucristo* got raised from the dead."

Lamar Jones snorted. "Another fairy tale."

"Just a minute, Lamar." I chose my words

442

carefully. "For some people, Easter is a way to celebrate that spring is coming. But Christians believe something very important happened many years ago at this time of year. Jesus Christ, whom Christians believe is the Son of God, was killed by His enemies, buried, and rose from the dead — and that's why *they* celebrate." *How am I doing, God?*

But before I got in too deep, I steered a corner. "The Jewish faith also celebrates Passover at this time of year. Caleb, can you tell us what 'Passover' means?"

Caleb walked to the front of the room, pushing his glasses up on the bridge of his nose. I tried to keep a straight face. This kid was destined to be a college professor. "Well. Thousands of years ago, the Jewish people were slaves in Egypt." The class got quiet. "God chose Moses to lead the people out of slavery. But King Pharaoh didn't want to let them go. So God sent all kinds of terrible plagues — frogs and lice and flies *and* the Nile River turned to blood."

"Blood! *Eww.*"

Caleb looked triumphant. "But Pharaoh *still* wouldn't let the slaves go free. So God got mad and sent the Angel of Death to kill the oldest son in every house. But Moses told the Jews that if they splashed the blood of a lamb on the door of *their* houses, the Angel of Death would *pass over* that house and nobody would die. That scared King Pharaoh so much he finally let the Israelite people go. That's why Jewish families celebrate Passover, to remember how God rescued them from slavery."

Caleb dipped his head like a little bow and sat down. For a moment, the class stared open-mouthed. Then they started to clap.

"Wow!" Bowie Garcia shouted. "They oughta make that into a video game!"

I kicked myself later. Why didn't I point out that there is a connection between the Christian celebration of Good Friday and the Jewish celebration of Passover? *"Jesus was a Jew, and He and His disciples were celebrating the Passover meal in Jerusalem the same night He was captured and killed by His enemies."* Would have been educational, that's for sure.

Funny thing was, I never thought much about that connection. Most of the Christians I knew didn't either. After all, that last Passover meal had become "The Lord's Supper" or "Communion" — what we celebrated once a month in the church I grew up in by eating a broken cracker and a plastic thimble of grape juice or wine to represent the broken body and blood of Jesus. I certainly didn't connect it much with the Jewish Passover. But Ruth had said the connection was built in from the beginning . . .

I found myself looking forward to celebrating Seder with Yada Yada.

Of course, Ruth managed to rope all of us into the preparations. "Jodi," she'd barked into the phone early that week with no preamble. "You want you should make potato kugel or matzo ball soup? Never mind. Yo-Yo can pick up some kugel from the Bagel Bakery. Make the soup. Just follow the recipe on the back of the box of matzo meal. Cook a chicken first; you need chicken broth."

Two minutes later, the phone rang again. "Add carrots, celery, and some of the chicken. Just make sure you have plenty of broth to cook the matzo balls. And tell the other Yada Yada sisters to pray for Ben."

Pray what for Ben? Didn't he want us to come? And how many was I cooking for, anyway? I only had one large soup pot, so I decided one pot would have to do. So Wednesday night found me boiling a large stewing hen with carrots and celery. When I got home from school on Thursday, I mixed matzo meal with egg and a bit of broth and dropped the balls into the boiling broth. By the time Chanda tooted her horn out front, I had a pot of hot matzo ball soup — I hoped. What did I know?

Josh and Carl Hickman were catching a ride from work with Peter Douglass and Avis, so Amanda and I and the soup pot climbed into the Yukon Denali along with Chanda's three kids, Rochelle and Conny, and Florida and her two youngest. Eleven passengers. Still two over the nine-passenger limit for this huge SUV.

"You need a bigger car," I *umphed,* squeezing in between Dia George and Carla Hickman, and setting the soup pot, wrapped in a heavy bath towel, on the floor.

Chanda, in the driver's seat, grinned into the rearview mirror. "Mi know dat. Driving dis baby is fun. Mi should be a city bus driver!"

When we pulled up in front of the Garfields' home, the house already looked jam-packed through the front window. Inside, a string of card tables and collapsible portable tables snaked from the dining room, through the front hallway, and into the living room, covered with white plastic tablecloths, and set with colorful paper plates, matching paper napkins, and clear plastic tumblers. Tall white candles, small bouquets of flowers, and bottles of wine and sparkling grape juice on each table added a festive touch. Laughter and curiosity filled the small, brick bungalow.

With a touch of guilt, I realized I hadn't called anybody to "pray for Ben," as Ruth had asked. But he seemed comfortable enough to me, teasing the kids and showing off the twins, each one sporting a new tooth and matching crawlers. Only Isaac's raspberry-colored facial birthmark told them apart.

"Sit! Sit!" Ruth beamed when everyone had arrived. She set a china plate displaying several food items on the table in front of two chairs in the middle of the long line of mismatched tables as Ben, wearing his traditional yarmulke, joined her.

We all found places to sit. Counting kids and adults, there must've been thirty of us! I glanced around. Josh was holding baby Havah, a sight that unsettled me a little bit since he and Edesa were sitting together with the Enriquez kids clustered around them. They looked like a family with a passel of kids. *Sheesh, Jodi! Don't go there.*

As parents shushed children, Ruth solemnly lit all the candles, murmuring a Jewish blessing. Then Ben Garfield cleared his

447

throat. "Welcome to our Passover meal. It's not often we share this meal with Gentiles. In fact, in my case, never." That got a laugh. "This meal is called a Seder, which means 'order' — but hardly applies to the raucous Jewish family I grew up in." Another laugh. We were starting to relax.

Ben picked up a set of pages stapled together. "You can follow along the simple Seder service beside your plate. But you're getting off easy. Two nights ago, we celebrated the first night of Passover with my relatives, using the traditional Haggadah. Thirty-two pages it is — in Hebrew! Sixty-four when they include the English translation."

Now groans mixed with the giggles. Ruth poked him to get on with it.

"All right, all right." Ben cleared his throat again, reading from his Seder service. " *'We celebrate the Passover in obedience to God's command in the Torah'* — that's the Old Testament, to you *goyim*. *'In days to come, when your children ask you, What does this mean? say to them, With a mighty hand the Lord brought us out of Egypt, out of the land of slavery.'* "

"Hallelujah!" Florida said. "Guess that gives your people an' my people somethin' in common — 'cept our people was freed less'n a hundred fifty years ago. We still tryin' to put it all behind us."

Ben scowled. Ruth smoothed over the interruption. "To remember is good, so we can thank God for His deliverance." She nudged her husband.

Ben cleared his throat again. To his credit, he did a neat summary of the story up to the point where the Egyptian Pharoah refused Moses' demand to let the Jewish slaves go. "For this next part," he said, "everybody needs to have a little wine or grape juice in their glass — but don't drink it."

Bottles were tipped, filling the plastic glasses half an inch. Now Ben told the story of the ten plagues. "When I call out one of the plagues, dip your finger in your wine, and flick it onto your plate while you repeat it. Ready?" He dipped his own finger. "Blood!"

Fingers dipped all around the table, flicking wine or grape juice onto the paper plates. "Blood!" we echoed.

"Frogs!" *Flick, flick.* "Lice!" . . . "Flies!" . . . The kids were really getting into it now. "Boils!" *Flick, flick* . . . "Hail!" . . . "Locusts!" The shouts were getting louder. "Darkness!" . . . "Death of the firstborn!"

The tables suddenly got quiet. It didn't

seem fun anymore.

"Finally," Ben said solemnly, "Pharoah let the Jewish people go."

Ben continued leading us through the shortened Seder service. We all turned our pages. "Who's the youngest child here? Not counting Havah and Isaac. They can't read. Dia, sweetheart? You want to ask that question on the next page?"

Seven-year-old Dia squinted at the paper. "Too many hard words."

"I'll do it!" Ten-year-old Michael Smith, sitting beside Nony, waved his hand wildly. "Here? Okay. *'Why is this night different from all other nights? On all other nights we eat all kinds of bread, but tonight we only eat matzo.'*" He looked up. "What's matzo?" His mother pointed to the matzo crackers on the table. "Oh. Okay. *'On all other nights we eat many kinds of vegetables and herbs, but tonight we only eat bitter herbs.'*" He made a face. " *'On all other nights, we don't dip one food into another, but tonight we dip the parsley in salt water, and we dip the bitter herbs in . . . in . . .'* What's that word?"

"*Charoset,*" prompted Ruth. The "ch" was guttural. She beamed at Nonyameko. "A *boytshikl* he is, Nony. You should be proud."

Dia pouted. "I wanted to read. I just didn't know them big words."

450

Ben opened his mouth but Ruth took over. "Questions are asked at every Seder — it's tradition. So . . . feel free! But first we give answers to Michael's questions." She picked up the china plate in front of her and pointed to the three matzo crackers. "Matzo reminds us that when the Jews left Egypt, they had no time to bake bread with yeast."

"Tastes like cardboard . . . just my opinion," Ben cracked behind his hand.

Ruth ignored him, continuing to explain the items on the plate. The sprig of parsley dipped in salt water, "a reminder of tears shed during slavery." The *charoset,* a mixture of chopped apples, nuts, and wine, "a reminder of the clay used to make bricks for Pharoah's buildings, which was eaten with bitter herbs" — she pointed to a mound of ground horseradish — "because our days in Egypt were bitter."

"What's that bone for?" Yo-Yo pointed at the plate.

Ben picked it up. "A lamb bone —"

"I know *that* part!" Carla interrupted. "Caleb Levy told us at school. God was going to kill all the firstborn boys in every family, but He secretly told the slave people to kill a lamb and smear its blood all over the doors of their house. When the Angel of

451

Death saw the blood, it was s'posed to *pass over* that house. *Pass over,* get it?"

Ben grinned. "Very good, *bubeleh.* Now, let's do the *afikomen* —"

"Wait, wait. Back up a minute," Becky said. "I've been reading my Bible, like ya tol' me to, Avis, and that John the Baptist guy called Jesus 'the Lamb of God.' " She turned to Ben. "So was that blood-of-the-lamb thing, ya know, some kind of prophecy about Jesus or something?"

Nods and murmurs went around the tables.

Ben colored. "Uh, well, now . . ." He glared at Ruth helplessly. And suddenly I realized why Ruth had wanted us to pray for Ben — that he would see the truth behind the Seder meal he had celebrated every year of his sixty-odd years of life.

Oh God! I'm sorry I didn't pray, sorry I forgot to ask others to pray. But I'm praying now . . .

Ruth whispered to Ben, and handed him the three matzo crackers from the plate. "All right," he growled. "Let's move on so we can eat. The middle matzo we break" — which he proceeded to do — "and wrap it in a special cloth, and hide it." He wrapped the broken piece of matzo in a cloth napkin. "This is called the *afikomen.* Now . . ." His voice took on its former bounce. "All the

452

children close your eyes. Tight. No peeking!"

Laughing, all the adults sitting near children made sure they didn't peek, while Ben snuck around the two rooms pretending to hide the napkin here, then there. I never did see where he finally hid it.

"After the meal," Ruth said brightly, "the children may hunt for the *afikomen.* The one who finds it can hold it for ransom until Ben forks over some money."

Yo-Yo butted in. "Wait. We can ask questions, right? So, like, do the three matzos represent that Trinity thing — God the Father, God the Son, and God the Holy Spirit? Ben just broke the middle one — is that what Jesus was doing when He broke the bread at Passover and said, 'This is My body, broken for you'?"

José grinned. "Whoa. And then broken matzo gets buried . . ."

"I know, I know!" Cedric Hickman waved his hand. "An' when we find it, Mister Garfield has to pay a ransom, 'cause Jesus paid the ransom for our sins! 'Cept Mister Garfield ain't God, but I guess that's okay."

We couldn't help it; we broke up with laughter. Even shy Carl Hickman had to chuckle. Ruth beamed. "Are these children smart, or what?" But Ben looked flustered, as if he was losing control of the situation.

Ruth said, "Now eat! Eat!" as if it was an order. My matzo ball soup came out hot from the kitchen, along with sturdy paper bowls. Then roasted chicken, potato kugel, and cooked carrots swimming in butter and dill. We laughed, ate, made faces at the gefilte fish, and passed the babies from lap to lap.

All except Ben. Ben had turned quiet.

37

" 'Next year in Jerusalem'?" Denny raised a curious eyebrow as I told him how the Seder service had ended, with the traditional cry of displaced Jews all over the world. "And how many glasses of wine did you say you had? *Four?*" He was clearly enjoying goading me.

We were sitting at the dining room table, while Denny finished the plate of chicken and potato kugel I'd brought home and heated up for him. I rolled my eyes. "The wine was mostly symbolic. Little sips. Seriously, Denny. I wish you could've been there. It was . . . I can't explain it. It helped me understand Jesus the Messiah, the fulfillment of prophecy, in a new way. But Ben got pretty uncomfortable with some of the questions Becky and Yo-Yo asked. Hope he's not mad."

"Hm. Sorry I missed it." He got up and tossed the paper plate in the trash. "Sorry I missed your matzo ball soup too. Oh, before I forget. The principal at the JDC school would like to meet with you personally — tomorrow if possible. They're hoping to pull off this play in the next couple of weeks." He grinned at me. "You're on, Jodi."

I stared at him. It wasn't as if I was surprised. Avis said she'd gotten a call from the JDC, wanting a reference. My background check had checked out — second time this year. But hearing Denny say, *You're on, Jodi,* made my mouth go dry.

"Uh, sure, I could go tomorrow. It's Good Friday, no school — oh. You know that. Can I get there by el? Where am I supposed to go? What's the principal's name again? Do I need to take anything with me? Or . . . anything I *shouldn't* take with me? Do they want me to actually start tomor—"

Denny reached out and put his fingers on my mouth to stop my prattling. "Hey, hey. Tell you what. I'll go with you tomorrow, okay? We'll go by el to map out the way; maybe some days you can take the car. We'll figure it out. You're going to do great, Jodi." He pulled me out of my chair into an embrace. "I'm proud of you."

I let myself relax against Denny's chest as his arms held me close. I wasn't sure about "great." But if Denny went with me tomorrow and helped me figure out where to go, *that* was definitely great.

No school. The wonders of a Friday without the usual Baxter hurry-scurry made me feel delicious when I woke up. I no longer had to get up before everyone else to let Willie Wonka outside, either . . . though I'd give anything to feel his nose snuffling my hand once more, even if I *did* have to get up early, even on holidays. But today, I could go back to sleep . . .

Then I remembered. I was going to the juvenile detention center today. Today, of all days, I definitely needed some prayer time!

Coffee cup, Bible, and afghan in hand, I curled up in the recliner near the front windows. At times like these, I really did miss Wonka. His brand of loyalty meant I was never really alone in the house; he was always faithfully underfoot. Early mornings had been our special times — me in the recliner, Wonka splayed out on the floor under the footrest.

But today it was just me and God. Cuddled in the afghan, I found where I'd last stopped reading — Paul's letter to the Philippians. I needed an encouragement for today. Had to admit I was nervous. This whole thing wasn't my idea. But seemed as if God had dumped it in my lap and nudged me to say yes. Wasn't I learning that if God was in it, I didn't have to be afraid? All I had to do was be faithful, and God would take care of the rest . . . right?

I tried to focus on my reading. In chapter three, the apostle Paul said if anyone qualified for bragging rights about how "religious" he was, he was the man. But then he said none of that self-important religious stuff counted. Only knowing Jesus Christ and what He could do in our lives — that's what counted.

Kinda like me, when I let my "good Christian girl" pride get in God's way.

"But one thing I do," he wrote. *"Forgetting what is behind and straining toward what is ahead, I press on toward the goal . . ."*

Press on. Wasn't that what Denny was trying to tell our kids the night of his birthday, that sometimes we had to let go of what was behind us and *press on?* Well, he said, "get rolling," but same difference. My old King James Version used the phrase, *"press toward . . . the high calling of God."*

I closed my Bible and stared out the window. Suddenly I realized that the limbs of the trees along Lunt Street were no longer bare. I brought the recliner's footrest down with a bang — a move that used to send Willie Wonka scrambling — and pressed my nose to the window. Thousands of swollen buds created a shimmering green fuzz along each limb, ready to burst into life. The old leaves were dead; the new ones were waiting in the wings, eager to dance along every branch, catching the wind.

A funny joy bubbled up in my chest. *Today is full of possibilities. Press on, Jodi, press on. Do it for God and His children at the JDC.*

Denny and I got home from the JDC in time to eat a bowl of soup out of the Crock-Pot and make it to the Good Friday service at SouledOut that night. It was a simple service, not long, with various "readers" reading the story of Jesus eating the Passover meal with His disciples for the last time . . . the prayer of agony in the Garden of Gethsemane . . . Judas's betrayal . . . the desertion by the other disciples . . . the trial of Jesus . . . and His execution on a Roman cross. Throughout, the music group wove songs — mostly old hymns — about "the blood of Jesus."

I have to admit I had a hard time keeping my mind focused on the service. My mind was still so full of the Seder service the previous night, with all its prophetic symbolism, pointing to these very events we were

459

singing about — the saving "blood of the lamb" splashed on the wooden door-posts . . . the broken matzo, hidden, and then "resurrected" . . .

And then there was my visit to the juvenile detention center just a few hours ago. I hadn't realized it was just a few blocks from the Cook County hospital where Delores worked. Denny and I had to take the Red Line el all the way past the Loop to the Roosevelt Road station, then catch the west-bound Roosevelt Road bus. Took over an hour! It wasn't so bad doing it with Denny, but I couldn't really imagine doing it by myself five days a week next week.

Glancing at Avis and several of my other Yada Yada sisters soaking up the Good Friday service, I thought of the Yada Yadas who did not have cars. *Oh God. Is that what it takes for Delores and Edesa to come to Yada Yada every time? Neither one has a car . . . and they're so faithful.* I squared my shoulders. *Suck it up, Jodi. Press on.* If they could do it, so could I.

As we sang, "What can wash away my sin? Nothing but the blood of Jesus . . ." my mind drifted to my interview with the school principal at the JDC that afternoon. After we'd gone through a metal detector and taken the elevator up to the second floor, we sat in a waiting room with molded plastic chairs until the principal came out to greet us. She gave us visitor tags, then we were buzzed through the glass-paneled security area — not one, but two doors, where security personnel could see all directions — into the main part of the second floor, which housed the school.

The principal had given us a short tour of the school, which wasn't in session, since it had the same holidays as any other Chicago public school. The windowless rooms had the regular stuff of classrooms — desks, marker boards, maps, textbooks. "Classrooms for boys and girls are separate. Each residential floor is color-coded," our host explained, "so your students will be wearing purple, green, or blue DOC uniforms. Our youngest residents and the girls occupy the top floor."

Our last stop had been the large, all-purpose room where "school events" were held. No stage. No lights. Not what I'd imagined when I volunteered to supervise a school play. "What about props? Costumes?" I ventured.

The principal shrugged. "You can ask. Not making any promises, though."

Then we sat in her office, while she explained basic rules ("Do not ask your students about their case") and my temporary responsibilities. I was bursting with questions about the children and teenagers within these walls, but did my best to listen to my volunteer assignment.

"We do two or three drama or musical presentations for parents and staff every year. This year, our English teacher was trying to introduce the kids to some classic literature through drama. Then she came down with mono! The other teachers are covering her classes, but no one had time to take on the drama too." The principal gave me an encouraging smile. "We're happy you've volunteered, Mrs. Baxter."

"Will I meet the students today who are doing the drama?" I'd asked.

She shook her head. "But I will give you a copy of the scripts she was going to introduce. There are a couple you can choose from. Next week is spring break, so the students who signed up to do the drama don't have classes next week. We can give you three hours, nine to twelve, each morning."

"And if we need more time?"

The principal shrugged. "You'd probably lose half your kids if they had to give up afternoons. They like to play softball or basketball outside, now that the weather's getting warmer."

I'd blinked at her. "Outside?"

Denny grinned. "Oh, yeah. Forgot to tell you. The top three floors are built like a square doughnut, with the residential units around the outer ring and an open recreation area in the middle." He pointed to the ceiling of the second floor. "Right up there."

I'd tried to picture it in my mind — and got the picture. Open to the sky — but completely surrounded by the building. Whatever way one looked at it, this was a jail for juveniles, kids, waiting for their hearings, waiting to hear whether the state judged them guilty or not guilty, waiting to hear their "dispositions" or sentences.

Kids like Chris Hickman . . .

I'd been able to walk away today. But not Chris. Now, as I sat in the "sanctuary" of SouledOut Community Church singing the closing song, "At Calvary," I glanced over at the Hickman family, sitting together in the dimly lit room. Wet streaks glistened on Florida's face as Oscar Frost's saxophone rode under the words of the chorus . . .

Mercy there was great, and grace was free;
Pardon there was multiplied to me;
There my burdened soul found liberty,
At Calvary!

How would I hear those words if I were in

463

Florida's and Carl's shoes? Would their son be "pardoned" for his sins? Would he be given liberty?

Oh Jesus! my heart cried. *Your mercy to me was great when I was accused of vehicular manslaughter in the death of Jamal Wilkins. Please have mercy on Chris. He says he had nothing to do with the holdup of that 7-Eleven, and . . . and I believe him. His only crime was bad judgment in the friends he chose. Oh God, please, let Your blood cover his transgression and bring him home to his family.*

When the Good Friday service was over, the pastors encouraged us to leave quietly, reflecting on our Savior's death. But outside in the parking lot, I saw Hoshi getting into the Sisulu-Smith minivan. I ran over and poked my head inside. "Hoshi! Did you give our gift certificate to Sara? Did she accept it?"

A smile lit up Hoshi's long, thin face. "Oh yes, Jodi. She was much flustered, but we met at the student center for lunch yesterday, and she said she'd made an appointment at Adele's Hair and Nails for Saturday."

Saturday! That was tomorrow — and Adele's Hair and Nails wasn't that far from our house. Did I dare "just drop in"? I'd been praying for Sara so long, ever since that fateful day our eyes had met at the plaza on Northwestern's campus. I wanted to tell her how God had changed my heart when she went from "that girl in the sundress" to "Sara" . . .

Which gave me an idea.

38

The bell over Adele's shop door tinkled as I pushed the door open. Was I doing the right thing? Or was this another one of my "brilliant" ideas that could blow up in my face? I'd felt a little sneaky, calling the shop first thing this morning to find out what time Sara's appointment was, hoping Takeisha or Corey would answer the phone. But wouldn't you know it — Adele picked up.

"Jodi Baxter," she'd said suspiciously. "You want to know Sara's appointment time . . . why?"

I blew out a breath. With Adele, honesty was always the best policy. "Because I made something for her — a small gift. I want to give it to her."

Silence. Then, "Suit yourself. Ten o'clock." And she hung up.

I waited until ten-thirty to give plenty of time for Sara to get in the chair. I'd had too many *trauma-dramas* at Adele's Hair and

Nails to want to precipitate another one. But the last time I'd seen Sara — when Hoshi had tried to bring her new friend to Yada Yada when we'd met at the Sisulu-Smith home near the NU campus — Sara had taken one look at the house, at Nony and Mark, and run the other way.

The bell tinkled again as the door wheezed shut. Adele glanced up and acknowledged me with a nod — a nod that seemed to say, *Just sit a while.* So I did. I sank onto the couch by the front window, picked up a copy of *Essence* magazine, and flipped through it, my eyes not on its pages but on the young woman in the chair.

Adele snipped and shaped. Sara watched the process in the mirror with sober eyes. *When should I talk to her?* I wondered. But I felt a check. *Not yet.* The not-quite-wedgie cut — shorter in the back, a little longer in the front, sweeping forward, bangs brushed to the side — already freshened her plain features. But she was so . . . colorless. A touch of lip gloss, some plum blush on her cheeks, and mascara to darken her pale lashes would —

Ha! Listen to yourself, Jodi. A lot you know about makeup.

Adele handed Sara a hair-color chart, which Sara studied while Adele swept up the dishwater-blonde hair on the floor. Finally, she pointed, and Adele mixed the color chemicals, shaking the rubber bulb while running her fingers thoughtfully through the girl's hair. Adele chatted with other customers and staff — though she ignored me — while she saturated the girl's hair with the color mixture, as though allowing Sara a reprieve from being the center of her attention.

Finally, Adele piled Sara's wet hair on her head, covered it with a breathable cap, and pointed to a plastic chair in the hair dryer section. "Sit there," she said. "No, not under the dryer. We need to leave that on for twenty minutes." As the young woman moved to a chair behind the partition, Adele gave me the eye and tipped her head.

I picked up the plastic bag I'd brought with me and peeked around the partition. "Sara?"

Her head jerked up at her name. "Do I know you?"

I pulled over an empty chair. "My name is Jodi Baxter. We have a mutual friend, Hoshi Takahashi."

She reddened. "Oh. Yes, I've seen you before. Your p-prayer group . . ." She touched the cap on her head. "You all g-gave me this gift certificate, Hoshi said."

I smiled and nodded. "Yes. It's our way of saying thanks."

Her color deepened. "Don't know what for." Her eyes found her lap.

I tried to keep my voice easy. "All of us are deeply grateful for your courage, for going to the police, and —"

"Don't want to t-talk about that." Her hands clenched, and her mouth pinched into a thin, straight line.

"No problem. Actually, that's not why I spoke to you. I wanted to give you this." I laid the plastic bag in her lap.

She stared at the bag. "What is it?"

"Before you open it, I want to tell you something. It's not my intention to drag up painful memories, but —"

"Then don't."

"All right. But after the, um, first time I saw you" — I didn't mention it was at the so-called freedom of speech rally on the NU campus where the leader of the White Pride group she'd been part of proceeded to insult "mud races" and everyone else who wasn't white — "God told me to pray for you. But I didn't know your name. So for a long time, I just prayed for 'that girl in the sundress.' Not very polite, I know, but I kept praying for you anyway."

She said nothing, but seemed to be listening.

"And then Hoshi told us about meeting a new friend named Sara. Of course, I didn't know it was *you*, not until, uh . . . later." Again, I deliberately didn't mention the day she came with Hoshi to the Sisulu-Smith home, which had ended in such disaster. "But God kept telling me to pray for you, so now I could pray for you by name. Sara."

I pointed to the package. "Now you can open it."

At first, I thought she wasn't going to. But after a moment's hesitation, she pulled the bag off and held the eight-by-ten-inch frame in her hands. I had used the computer to write her name, "Sara," in a beautiful script on some fancy vellum paper, and right beside it the meaning of her name. "Princess."

She snorted. "What is this, some k-kind of joke?"

"No, no. That's what the name Sara means — 'Princess'! In our prayer group, we like to find the meaning of each person's name. Hoshi's name means 'Star.' Mine means 'God is gracious.' "

She frowned. "Well, somebody g-got it wrong somewhere, because I'm certainly no p-princess. Cinderella, maybe."

I almost laughed. Maybe she meant Cinderella sitting in the ashes while her nasty stepsisters went to the royal ball. But Cinderella became a *real* princess. Well, as real as it gets in a fairy tale. "No, I don't think the meaning of your name is wrong. Because that's how God sees you. His princess. His royal daughter."

To my surprise, tears suddenly dripped down her cheeks, and she fished in her pockets for a tissue. She blew her nose. Then, she peered closely at the smaller words within the frame. "What's this?"

Thought she'd never ask! "It's from the Bible." I reached out and turned the frame slightly so I could see the words. "I paraphrased it just a little, but you can read it yourself in the book of Isaiah, chapter forty-nine: *The Lord called me before my birth; from within the womb He called me by name. . . . [I said], 'The Lord has deserted me; the Lord has forgotten me!' [But God said,] 'Never! Can a mother forget her nursing child? Can she feel no love for a child she has borne? But even if that were possible, I would not forget you! See, I have engraved your name on the palm of my hand.' "*

As I read the words aloud, I momentarily forgot about Sara. That last phrase! When I chose those verses, I just wanted to let Sara

471

know that God knew her personally, *by name*. But suddenly it seemed like another prophecy in the Old Testament about Jesus! God told Isaiah He'd written his name — and mine, and Sara's, and everybody's — *on the palms of His hands.* And just yesterday, Good Friday, we'd all been reminded that His Son, Jesus, stretched out those hands, the ones with our names on them, on the cross, taking the punishment for our sins —

"How d-did you know?" Sara's tight whisper broke into my thoughts.

"What? Know what?"

"About my mother. I never t-told Hoshi." She looked at me accusingly. "Have you been d-digging up stuff about me?"

I was stunned. "No! I don't know anything about you. Except . . . I know that God loves you. And I've been praying for you almost a whole year."

Adele's large form loomed above us. "Time's up. Need to rinse that color out 'fore it takes you someplace you don't wanna go."

Sara stood up and put the frame back in the plastic bag. I gave Adele a look, which, properly interpreted, told her to go jump in the lake. Didn't she realize something important was happening here?! Adele gave me a look right back that said not even the end of the world was going to stop her from rinsing out her customer.

But Sara held the bag close to her chest as she followed Adele to the sinks. Halfway there, she turned back and mouthed silently: *"Thank you."*

I sat in the car a full five minutes before I turned on the ignition. Half of me wanted to whoop and holler, *"Praise Jesus!"* that Sara whatever-her-last-name had received my gift. I was glad, *so glad,* that I'd obeyed the prompting of my heart to research the meaning of her name for her and to frame it, glad that God had given me those verses in Isaiah to include.

The other half of me was dying of curiosity. What in the world did she mean, did I know about her mother? What about her mother? Something in those verses, the part that said, even if a mother *did* forget her child, God never would . . . Had Sara been abandoned by her mother? Didn't she live up on the North Shore somewhere, in the hoity-toity suburbs north of Chicago?

And, I had to admit, I wanted to see the final transformation of Sara's makeover. All I'd seen so far was the haircut and color application — and even then, her hair had been wet. Hadn't been set, dried, or combed out. No makeup, no manicure or pedicure. Should I go back in? Offer her a ride home? I had no clue how she got here. Maybe she had her own car.

Just go home, Jodi. The Spirit Voice within seemed to put a quiet hand on my shoulder. *You gave your gift. Now give Me room to work.*

A knock on my window made me jump. A Chicago police parking enforcement uniform made a circular motion with her finger. I rolled down the window. "You plan to sit here all day, lady? Because your parking meter has run out, and if you don't move or feed the meter in the next thirty seconds, I've got to give you a parking ticket."

I nodded and rolled the window back up. "Okay, okay, Lord. I heard you the first time," I muttered as I stuck my key in the ignition. "You didn't have to send a cop too."

Five minutes later, I pulled the Caravan into a parking spot in front of our house and headed inside, picking up yesterday's mail, which was still in the box — *what's this?* A business envelope addressed to me from the Super Skatium. *Hoo boy.* Still standing on the porch, I ripped open the envelope. It'd been over four weeks since

474

I'd written. Had our petition done any good?

I pulled out the single sheet of paper. "Dear Ms. Baxter," I read aloud. "Thank you for informing us of your concern. We are proud of our ten years in the Chicago community, serving a widely diverse clientele and providing quality entertainment for young and old alike." *Yeah, yeah, yeah.* I skimmed on. ". . . sorry for any inconvenience or disappointment you experienced. We hope you will come again and —" . . . *blah blah blah.*

I sighed and sank down on the top step of the front porch. Huh. So much for that. The Skatium manager had probably had a good snicker-fest with the DJ before shooting off his thinly veiled reply: *"Change our music? You gotta be kidding, lady!"*

Made me want to gag.

Now what? Organize a boycott? *Yeah, right.* It wasn't as if I knew a hundred people who went skating every week. The Skatium wouldn't even notice. Go out to the Skatium with a protest sign? *"The Skatium plays X-rated music!"* Not really my style. Maybe a letter-writing campaign. If they wouldn't pay attention to one letter, what about ten letters, or twenty, or thirty, or —

Whoa. Slow down, Jodi.

What? Oh, right. I was doing it again, Old Jodi response, jumping on my high horse and riding off in ten directions. *But, God, it makes me mad, thinking about the raunchy music they're feeding to all those young kids! Is it too much to ask for one, measly, family-friendly skate night? Do I just give up at the first resistance?*

The Voice in my spirit cut into my thoughts. *Not too much to ask. It's a good idea. But . . . is this your battle right now? Didn't you just agree to spend your spring break at the juvenile detention center, starting Monday?"*

Well, yeah. Good point. I felt pretty clear that saying yes to the JDC was something God wanted me to do. When would I do any of that other stuff?

I squeezed my eyes shut and crumpled the letter. *Okay, God. I think I get it. But God? This business of hearing the Holy Spirit — knowing what's from You and what is just distracting me from doing what You want me to do . . . it's hard, You know?*

I stood up and unlocked the front door. I had Easter dinner to plan and a couple of scripts I needed to read.

39

When we arrived at SouledOut the next morning, a row of Easter lilies graced the front of the low stage, a bevy of little girls in pastel dresses darted about in patent leather shoes, and people came in greeting each other happily: "The Lord is risen!" "He is risen indeed!"

I was trying to feel resurrection-ish, but after reading the scripts that had been handed to me two days ago — a short, modernized version of Shakespeare's *Much Ado About Nothing* and a dramatized version of Washington Irving's *Legend of Sleepy Hollow* — I felt more like someone who'd be facing a firing squad the next day. I'd *never* pull this off!

But I now had an inkling — just an inkling — of how Mary Magdalene must have felt when she ran into Jesus walking among the tombs that first Easter morning. Someone she never expected to see there. She couldn't believe it. But such a welcome sight!

Because when I came in the door, the girl named Sara stood by the hot drink table with Hoshi Takahashi, sipping coffee from a paper cup. Not the Sara I'd last seen at Adele's salon with gooey wet hair piled up on her head. No, *this* Sara had warm honey-blonde hair with sunny highlights and a fresh bounce, with just enough curl to tuck the ends under sweeping below her ears. Yes, and just enough makeup to highlight her pale eyes and give some color to her usually lifeless skin.

Lord, You sure are an Almighty God. What kind of miracle had brought crowd-shy Sara to *church?*

Hoshi was introducing her simply as "my friend from school." But when I slipped over to the coffee table, she beamed. "Sara, this is Jodi, one of my Yada Yada sisters."

Sara nodded shyly. "I know. We m-met yesterday." A small smile tipped the corners of her mouth.

"Oh?" Hoshi's eyebrows raised.

Let Sara tell Hoshi if she wanted to. I just grinned and said, "I'm so glad to see you again, Sara. Welcome to SouledOut. And you look great. Really great." I wanted to grab her in a big ol' hug, "that girl in the sundress" I'd prayed for so often the past year — but decided not to push it. I didn't know what God was doing with Sara, but the Holy Spirit had clearly told me to back off now and give Him some space to work.

Pastor Clark's voice called out over the general hubbub. "Church, find your seats!" Adults and children scurried to stand by their chairs. "The Lord is risen!"

"He is risen indeed!"

And with that cue, the praise team with keyboard, drums, electric bass, and saxophone launched into the wonderful Easter hymn: "Christ the Lord is risen today! Ah-ah-ah-ah-ah-le-eh-lu-u-ia!"

I opened my mouth and belted out the *alleluias*, grinning so big I thought my earrings might pop off. *Lord, I know it's not a go-down-in-the-history-books miracle, but . . . thank You! Thank You!*

It wasn't until we'd welcomed visitors and sat down again on the comfortable, cushioned chairs from an "anonymous friend," that the firing-squad feeling loomed once more. *Oh Lord,* I moaned silently. *I'm going to need another miracle tomorrow.*

I had to leave the house by seven-thirty the next morning in order to be at the juvenile detention center by nine o'clock. Denny, bless him, walked me to the Morse Avenue el station. The temperature was once again sagging in the low forties.

"You sure you feel okay taking the el?"

I nodded. But I lied.

"You got the cell phone?"

I nodded again. "Don't worry. I'll call if I need to, but I ought to be home by one-thirty or two." *That's right, Jodi, press on. Keep rolling.*

The ride was long, especially with no one to talk to. As we jostled from station to station, I read and reread the scripts the English teacher had wanted to introduce. Brave woman. Maybe in a fully equipped school with honor students. Kids who'd already read Shakespeare and Irving. But kids off the street, in trouble with the law, struggling to get their GED? Not to mention we were already weeks behind schedule. The production was supposedly on the calendar for April 24 — barely two weeks away.

If I weren't so terrified, it'd be hilarious. Crack-up, take-me-away-in-a-straitjacket funny. *God, You got me into this. You've gotta get me out!*

But I guess God decided not to spirit me away in a fiery chariot like the prophet Elijah, because at nine o'clock I was standing in front of the rows of chairs in the all-purpose room on the second floor of the JDC, sweating in my armpits as a handful of boys shambled through the door, followed by two men I presumed were guards. The boys, ranging in age, I guessed, between thirteen and sixteen and dressed in various colored DOC uniforms, flopped into chairs and slouched on their tailbones.

"Sit up, gentlemen!" barked one of the guards, who proceeded to park himself on a chair at the back of the room along with the other guard, arms folded.

I looked at "my" students — and blinked. Chris Hickman sat among the boys, his eyes averted. I almost didn't recognize him with his almost shaved head. I wanted to shout. *Thank You, Jesus!* But if Chris didn't want to acknowledge our relationship, I'd respect that.

"Good morning."

A few of the boys mumbled, "Mornin'."

"My name is Mrs. Baxter, and I understand that we're here to produce a play." A few nods. "But tell you what. This isn't a lecture. We need to get acquainted, and we need to figure out how we're going to do this play. Each of you, grab a chair from the front row and pull it into a circle . . . that's it." I took a chair and started the circle. As the boys slowly complied, I counted noses. Ten.

"Let's start with names." I could remember ten names.

Ramón . . . Jeremy . . . Chris . . . Terrance . . . James . . . T-Ball —

"Not your street name!" yelled the guard at the back. "Real names, gentlemen!" Snickers from the boys.

. . . T.J. . . . Mike . . . Kevin . . . Rashad . . . David. Mostly African-American or Latino. Only James was obviously white. Rashad was probably black but had a Muslim name.

Given my restrictions on asking anything about their personal lives, I got down to business. "Your English teacher selected two possible plays to put on for your parents. It's your choice." I gave a brief summary of both plays, starting to relax. *Just stick to business, Jodi. Do what you can do. They're just kids . . .*

"*Legend of Sleepy Hollow?* Yeah, saw that on TV once." T.J. grinned. "I wanna be that headless dude who smoked the ol' scarecrow guy, what's-his-name."

"Ichabod Crane," I said, but T.J. was pretending to screw off his head and "throw" it like a fastball at Kevin. The boys laughed.

"*Bam!* Busted, man!"

"Yeah. Forget that Shakespeare crap." Jeremy, who seemed to be the oldest — or at least the biggest — of the group, nailed that one into a coffin.

"All right." I dug into my tote bag and handed out photocopies of the *Sleepy Hollow* script ("No staples, nothing sharp," the principal had said). "Let's just read through it. Don't worry about who's who. We can assign parts later. Ramón? You want to start? Just go around the circle."

But we hadn't even made it to the bottom of the first page when I realized we were in trouble.

"Katrina? A *chica*? I ain't readin' no girly part."

I read the part of Katrina.

A couple of the boys read well. I was surprised and pleased. They were smart. Bright. But Mike stumbled over every other word. Chris read tonelessly. And by the time we got to the third page, Jeremy tossed the script to the floor. "Aw, this is dumb. Who cares about some ol' ghost story? What's this gotta do with us?" His outburst drew a chorus of "Yeah, man" and "Got that right" from the others.

Frankly, I had the same question. *Maybe*, if we had two months, these boys might catch a vision for classic literature. *Maybe*, if their English teacher wasn't down with mono, she could pull this off. But they had me, I had two weeks, and we didn't have a play.

Don't panic, Jodi. Think!

"All right." I laid down my script. That surprised them. "Talk to me. What do you want to do?"

The boys looked at each other. No one spoke for several seconds.

T.J. was the first with an opinion. "Action, man! We wanna do some action." He pulled out an imaginary pistol. "Ya know, *bam bam bam!* Blowing da cops — uh, da rivals' heads off."

"Hey! None of that!" snapped one of the guards.

Thank you, mister. I took a breath. "Okay. Action. What about the rest of you?"

"We could, ya know, do some rappin'. I got Snoop Dogg's latest *down,* man." Terrance stood up, affecting the hunched shoulders and distorted fingers of a rap artist, and letting go with a string of snappy words I could hardly understand, though I caught the S-word a few times.

"Uh, okay. Rapping. Though I bet you could write your own. What else?"

The group fell silent.

I had no idea where I was going with this,

but I asked, "What do you want to do when you get out of here? What do you want to be when you grow up?"

Now eyes rolled and heads began to shake. "Huh. We ain't goin' ta grow up," Rashad muttered. "Ain't you heard? We destined for prison or da ice house. If da cops don't pop us, some rival will."

I stared at the young faces around me. No one contradicted Rashad, a good-looking young man, seemingly bright. He should be going to college. But he'd already given up.

I made another stab. "You don't have to be a statistic. Who are your heroes? Somebody you look up to, who overcame diversity to do great things. Dr. Martin Luther King? He was a great man. He had a dream for young people like you — and it didn't include prison or the, um, 'ice house.' "

Jeremy shrugged. "So? They popped him too."

His words hit me like a fist in the mouth. I couldn't breathe. Had no words. I just stared at Jeremy until he broke our gaze and looked away.

Tears stung my eyes. Suddenly I was mad. Angry that these young men, one of whom was the son of my Yada Yada sister, thought they had no future. Maybe I'd believe it, too, if I was thirteen, fourteen, or fifteen

485

and already in trouble, sitting here in the Juvenile Detention Center . . . except I *knew* Chris could have a future. He had *talent*. He was *smart*. He had parents — a whole lot of people, in fact — who *cared* about him. And if it was true for Chris, it could be true for the rest of them.

A vague idea started to spin a web in my brain. I found my voice. "Look. It might seem like we've wasted our first day, and we don't have that many days. But it's not wasted. You decided what you *don't* want to do. That's a start. And you gave me a lot to think about. I'm going to go home, and when I come back tomorrow, we're going to put together a play, a show — whatever — ourselves. Don't know what yet. But" — I cast a wry grin at T.J. — "it'll have some action. *Maybe* some rapping. Something that'll make your parents or guardians sit up and take notice. I just need one thing from you."

Ten pairs of eyes shifted from one to the other, then back at me. "What's that, Mrs. B?" Jeremy said.

"Promise me you'll come back tomorrow. All of you."

Shrugs, a few grins. "Yeah, why not." "Yeah, we'll be here." The boys filed out — all except for Chris Hickman, who lagged behind.

I wanted to hug him. But I just said, "Hey, Chris."

"Uh, thanks, Mrs. B, for not lettin' on our families are tight. But . . . I dunno about comin' back tomorrow. I heard it was you comin' ta do a play, I thought it might be fun. But I can't talk or act or any of that stuff."

The idea web in my head was catching more flies. "Don't worry about that. I have an idea for you — but can we talk about it tomorrow? Will you come?"

He thought it over. "Okay. Tomorrow. But that's all I promise."

I don't even remember walking to the bus stop. Barely remembered the ride home on the el. My mind was buzzing. Jeremy was right. A lot of "heroes" had been shot and killed, even in my lifetime. Dr. King, President Kennedy, his brother Bobby. Civil rights workers like Medgar Evers. Earlier American heroes, too, like Abraham Lincoln, who was from Illinois. Just like the prophets of old.

That's what we do to prophets, Jesus said.

Pieces of ideas floated and collided in my head like meteor fragments. I needed a connection, something to piece all the pieces together. *Wasn't Dr. King killed in April? What else happened in April?*

I leaned my head against the window of the northbound el as it creaked and groaned around the Loop, then headed north toward Rogers Park. "God," I whispered, "You said if we lack wisdom, to ask for it. I need a whole lot of wisdom right now! I *know* I can't do this in my own strength. This whole situation is way over my head. But I have a crazy confidence that You put this in my lap, so I've gotta trust You're going to come through. I just . . . don't see how yet."

My breath was steaming up the window; a couple of passengers nearby looked at me strangely. So I shut my mouth but continued my talk with God. *Don't mean to tell You what to do, Lord, but . . . I've got less than twenty-four hours to get my act together.*

I felt better as I got off the el at Morse Avenue and headed home. God put this in my lap, but I'd just put it back in His.

When I got home, I found a note from Denny. *"Amanda and I went to a movie. How'd it go? Love, D."* They weren't home. Good. And Josh was at work. Good. Because I didn't want any distractions.

"Wouldn't mind if you were home, though, Wonka," I murmured to the silence as I turned on the computer and waited for it to boot up. Yeah, I missed Wonka lying on

my feet when I had some serious praying
and thinking to do.

40

I was genuinely glad to see all ten boys saunter into the JDC school all-purpose room the next morning. Even Chris. I motioned them to sit in the same circle of chairs. "Thanks. I know you didn't have to come. But I have an idea for a play — actually, the idea came from you." I grinned. "God helped a lot too. Here's the deal . . ."

I leaned forward. Curious, the boys all leaned in. I shared my idea, sneaking a peek now and then at the two guards who sat cross-armed at the back of the room. One glared at me, frowning, as I passed out the stuff I'd found online to provide background; the other chewed absently on his nails.

So far, so good.

"Okay," I said. "We need four volunteers to make these speeches. You can't read them; you have to memorize them. We can make them shorter, though — I've marked the main thoughts."

"Huh!" T.J. snorted. "James is the only one who can play a white dude."

"Hey! Don' matter to me," Ramón smirked. "Might be my only chance to be prez-i-dent." The others laughed.

"Exactly," I said. "These heroes belong to all of us — white, black, Latino. Don't think of it as giving a speech. Become your character. Speak as though these thoughts, these feelings, these ideas came from inside *you*." I looked around the circle at the ten boys, clothed in their purple, green, and blue uniforms. "But we need some action scenes too."

T.J. raised a fist. "Aiiiight!"

Once again, we huddled. Their laughter punctuated the process. By the end of the three hours, we'd selected our four main characters, selected the villains, and brainstormed the final act. When the guards looked at their watches impatiently, I released the boys, but asked for another minute with Chris.

"Yeah, I can do that gangbangin' stuff, Mrs. B., long as I don't hafta give one o' them long speeches."

"Sure. You'll do fine in the action scenes. But that's not the main part I have for you." I pulled out some drawings and photographs and gave them to him. "Think you could paint these characters?" My arm swept from one end of the wall behind me to the other. "Big as a wall?" I grinned. "I've actually seen your work on a wall before."

His eyes nearly popped. "They'd *never* let me do that here! Man! I'd be in so much troub—"

"Whoa, whoa!" I laughed. "I don't mean actually on the *wall*. I mean a backdrop for our play. You've heard the idea. Work with it. Include these characters somehow."

He looked at me sideways, frowning dubiously. "You could do that? Get me stuff to paint with, I mean? Stuff to paint *on*?"

Good question. I was going out on a limb here . . . way out. "To be honest, Chris, I don't know. But I'm going to try. But there's something you can do."

"Me! What?"

"Pray about it. Let's leave it to God to move the mountains."

A slow smile leaked over his features. He balled up his fist and held it out. I balled up mine and we touched, fist to fist. "I'll do that, Mrs. B."

I spent all afternoon trying to get permission from the "powers that be" at the JDC to allow Chris Hickman to use spray paint and airbrushes under strict supervision. No dice. Chalk. That was their compromise. Colored chalk. Did they have a budget for this play? No budget. Okay . . . I wasn't going to let a little thing like money stop this production, even if my husband and kids had to eat rice for the next few weeks.

Once I arrived home, I got on the phone with Josh in the mailroom at Peter Douglass's business. Could he rustle up some very large cardboard boxes that could be flattened and taped together with duct tape to make a wall?

"Sure, Mom. Whatcha doin'? Putting me out in the doghouse?"

"Hm. Good idea. But, sorry. This doghouse isn't for you."

To my delight, a trip to Goods, the huge art store in Evanston, yielded big, fat colored chalk, and a whole palette of smaller poster chalks in intense colors. Who needed spray paint? Almost giddy, I drove our minivan on Wednesday to lug everything down to the JDC. Even got those two bored guards involved in flattening and taping.

Chris's eyes popped again when I handed the various chalk sets to him. "Really? Really? I can use these? I mean, legal-like?"

I couldn't help it. I gave him a hug. They could lock me up, for all I cared.

■ ■ ■ ■

"What? You're going to spend Saturday at the JDC too?" Denny asked me Friday evening. We were in the backyard grilling steaks to celebrate the last day of spring vacation, which had finally shaken off the doldrums and hit the eighties. "You fly out of here every morning like you're meeting a secret lover." He stuck out his lip. "I'm jealous. Spent all week by myself working on tax forms."

"Denny Baxter!" I swatted his backside with the barbecue tongs I held in my hand. "You're the one who took the kids to New York last year and left *me* home during spring break." Well, I'd had doctor's orders not to travel, but hey, I could use guilt too.

Denny stuck a fork in the sizzling steaks and turned them over. "So it's going good? You seem excited about the whole project."

I was bursting to tell Denny what we were doing. But on the off-chance he might be able to attend the performance along with other "staff," I wanted him to be surprised.

"I am! It's going great — I think. Not sure I know what I'm doing, but I'm having fun." I turned a big grin on Denny. "Best part, I think the boys are having fun too."

Denny sat down beside me on the steps. "So what now? School starts next week."

He wasn't going to like this part. "Uh, I'd like to go down to the JDC after school a few days, maybe Monday, Wednesday, and Friday, to make sure the performance holds together. The boys are putting it on for family and staff next Saturday. If I could, um, take the car, maybe I wouldn't get home too late."

He frowned. The silence was filled by a dozen sparrows happily flitting about the back yard. Finally, he said, "Guess so. You taking the car tomorrow? Can you wait till I pick up Ricardo for the men's breakfast? And what time are you getting back? I have some errands I need to do."

Irritation nibbled at the edges of my peace. *Don't feel guilty, Jodi. He's had all week to do his stupid errands!* But I bit back the smart remark. "Sure. I can wait. And I'll be back by two or three. Earlier if it's really important."

He shrugged. "No, that's okay. Just so I know — oh, heck!" He leaped for the grill. "The steaks!"

I would've let Denny drop me off at the JDC when he drove to Little Village to pick up Ricardo Enriquez the next morning, and

495

taken the train home, but I was sure the JDC didn't want me coming in at six-thirty. But I got there at ten, and we did a run-through of the whole performance. It was rough, but we still had a week to smooth it up.

What pleased me most, though, was Chris's backdrop. One hardly noticed that it was done on cardboard boxes that had been flattened and taped together. "It's beautiful, Chris," I said, watching him work on the four scenes that blended into each other.

Chris grinned. "Thanks, Mrs. B. But don't tell my folks about it, okay? They're comin', ain't they?"

"You bet." *They'd better.*

As I drove home via Lake Shore Drive and Sheridan Road, windows open, enjoying the balmy weather in spite of the thunderstorm building up over the lake, I tried not to think about all the stuff I *didn't* do during spring vacation — like putting away winter clothes, doing spring housecleaning, filing all the bills and tax forms. But for some reason I didn't care. I doubted I would say fondly in my old age, "Oh yes, that was the spring I cleaned out the closets." But I didn't think I'd ever forget the spring break I spent putting together a drama at the JDC.

Pulling into the garage, I felt half-giddy with the warm weather, imagining how surprised the Hickmans would be next week, and — finally — realizing I *did* need to spend the rest of the weekend working on lesson plans for the next two months and grading papers. I was halfway up the walk to the house before I noticed my family clustered on the back porch watching me. Denny had a silly grin on his face.

"Oh! Hi guys. Uh, what's up?"

"Mo-om!" Amanda rolled her eyes. *"Look!"*

I looked. And then I saw. A row of solid wooden flower boxes, painted a deep forest green, ran the length of the back porch railings. Sprays of cheerful white daisies decorated each one. My mouth fell open. "What . . . ? When . . . ?"

"That's not all, Mom." Amanda ran down the back steps and pulled me around the side of the house to the front. More flower boxes ran the length of the front porch.

My men followed. "Dad figured if we were going to get any flowers this year, we better get you some flower boxes," Josh said. "After all, we don't have anybody on house arrest this year to tackle the flower beds."

"But . . . but . . ." I ran up onto the porch and examined the boxes closely. "These are handmade!"

Denny's grin widened. "You were kind enough to abandon us completely this week. We had plenty of time to make them. Amanda stenciled the daisies."

Amanda blushed. "The boxes needed something to look pretty till you can plant some flowers. Would've bought you some, but the greenhouses say it's still too early."

"We got potting soil, though." Josh jerked a thumb back toward the garage. "Bags and bags of it."

I was speechless. I'd barely thought of my family all week — and all week they'd been plotting and making something special for me. I threw my arms around Denny, then hugged my kids. "Thank you so much," I finally managed. "All of you. Really. It's the best gift you could've given me — and it's not even my birthday, or Mother's Day, or anything!"

"Sure, Mom." Amanda and Josh each gave me a quick peck and disappeared inside. But Denny walked me hand in hand around to the back again and sat us down in the porch swing.

"Not quite the best gift," he said.

"What do you mean?"

His side dimples deepened. "Well, thought you might like to know. This morning, Ben Garfield came to the prayer time we've been having *before* the men's breakfast, and asked about coming to church at Souled-Out. I think his exact words were, 'Would they accept a crusty old Jew like me?' "

Now my mouth really did drop open.

"According to Ben, he was pretty upset by all of the 'Jesus questions' at the Seder last week. But he started to read the New Testament to see if all that stuff was true — something he'd never done. Then he started in on the Old Testament. And a lot of things started to make sense, just like Yo-Yo and others were pointing out."

Oh, that was funny. Yo-Yo, of all people, teaching Ben Garfield a thing or two. "But doesn't he go with Ruth to Beth Yehudah sometimes? That's a Messianic congregation. Hasn't he heard that stuff before?"

Denny shrugged, still grinning. "All I know is, the brothers prayed with Ben Garfield this morning, who said he wanted to stop messing around the edges of faith and really believe that the Messiah has come."

41

The best gift, indeed! Ben Garfield had become a *Christian?!* I was so excited I wanted to call all the Yada Yada sisters and tell them. Then I realized Yada Yada was meeting this weekend . . . somewhere. I checked the list taped to a kitchen cupboard door. At my house, yikes! They'd find out tomorrow anyway. Let Ruth tell them.

If Ben told her. Communication between those two was weird at best.

But when we got to church the next morning, sure enough, Ben and Ruth's pearly green Buick was already in the shopping center parking lot. And there they were, taking up half a row with two baby carriers, two diaper bags, and the twins, dressed in — what else? — matching knitted sweaters and caps, though Havah's was yellow and Isaac's blue.

But what I noticed most was that Ben was wearing his yarmulke. What was that about?

By his own admission, Ben hadn't been a very religious Jew. But maybe his Jewishness made even more sense now that he saw the fulfillment of the Old Testament prophecies about a coming Messiah.

I was so moved that Ben and Ruth had come to church together, all I could do was give Ben a big, long hug. "Welcome," I whispered in his whiskery ear. And I didn't just mean welcome to our church. By the look he gave me, I think he understood.

Chanda and her kids showed up, too, along with Rochelle and little Conny, the cutie. What was going on? Chanda was a member of Paul and Silas Apostolic Baptist, like Adele. On the other hand, Rochelle's parents were members here. Maybe Chanda's household was taking turns at both churches, since Rochelle had moved in. Or —

Sheesh. I sure hoped Chanda wasn't chasing that *fine* Oscar Frost.

Avis led worship that morning. Peter must have told her about the "Bada-Boom Brothers" praying with Ben yesterday, because she couldn't stop smiling, couldn't stop praising. The call to worship was from Psalm 125: "Those who trust in the Lord are like Mount Zion, which cannot be shaken but endures forever!" she cried. "As

501

the mountains surround Jerusalem, so the Lord surrounds his people both now and forevermore."

Beautiful, I thought. *Let Ben know our faith is rooted in his.*

The praise team followed with the spiritual, *"Tell me, how did you feel when you come out the wilderness? . . ."* The whole congregation leaned into the song, clapping and singing it again and again. I snuck a glance at Ben and Ruth, each bouncing a five-month-old on their hips in time to the rhythmic music. *"Did your soul feel happy when you come out the wilderness? . . ."* Neither one was singing the words, but both had the kind of wobbly smile that betrayed a well of happy tears.

Between clapping, singing, the sunshine streaming in through the wall of windows, and temperatures predicted in the high eighties — *hot* for April — a lot of handkerchiefs came out to mop sweaty faces, and a couple of men propped open the glass double doors. During the lengthy service, several of us walked and jiggled the babies in the back of the room when they got fussy, since we didn't have a nursery yet.

Afterward, the Garfields were mobbed by greeters, both friends and strangers. Ruth took me by surprise when she sought me out and pulled me aside. "You prayed; God answered, Jodi. *Toda raba* . . . thank you."

I flinched. "Um, to be honest, Ruth, I forgot to pray for Ben until the middle of the Seder. Worse, I forgot to tell the other Yada Yadas to pray like you asked."

She patted my arm. "Do not worry. God answered, *yo?* My prayers, your prayers, all the Yada Yada prayers that have gone up for my Ben. God is faithful."

I grabbed her in a hug. "Yes, God is so faithful," I murmured as Stu and Estelle joined us. "Uh . . . hi guys. See you all tonight? Yada Yada's at my house. Pass the word, will you? I've gotta zip home and clean house" — I groaned — "not to mention finish lesson plans and grade a zillion more homework papers."

Estelle wagged a finger in front of my face. "Slow down, Jodi Baxter. Stu and I will bring snacks tonight, won't we, Stu?" She elbowed Stu in the ribs. "An' I'll be down an hour early to run yo' vacuum cleaner or whatever else you think needs doin'." The finger wagged some more. "An' don't you be oh-no-ing *me.* You should know by now I'm a stubborn old woman. Now" — She eyed the room from side to side — "where are them babies? I'm not leavin' till I get me some sugar."

By the time the Yada Yadas started arriving at five o'clock, I had finished the stack of papers I had to grade, my lesson plans would at least get me through the next two weeks, and Estelle had swept through our house as if her hair were on fire. Stu brought down her homemade cranberry bread, still hot from the oven — though Josh and Amanda sweet-talked her out of two whole slices on their way out the door to the SouledOut youth group at the church. "Your cranberry bread is my favorite, Auntie Stu," Josh teased.

"Don't you 'Auntie Stu' me, you over-grown sheepdog," she grinned, flicking his shaggy hair out of his eyes.

I was surprised to see Hoshi come in with Nonyameko. I peered behind them. "Is Sara with you?"

Hoshi shook the silky black ponytail at the nape of her neck. "No. But she wants me to tell all of you thank you very much for the gift certificate."

"Mm-hm. That Adele sure did work wonders on that girl," Florida murmured, her mouth full of crumbly cranberry bread.

Hoshi laughed. "Yes. It has given her more

504

self-confidence. So, today I tell her, 'Sara, you will have to go to ReJOYce tonight without me. I cannot come.' It will be — how do you say? — good for her." Hoshi winked impishly.

Nony slipped an arm around the girl's slender waist. "The truth is, sisters, Hoshi misses Yada Yada more than she lets on. And tonight she needs prayer for her future, after graduation. But we will share later, yes, my sister?" She gave Hoshi a tender kiss on her long, smooth cheek and sat down in our overstuffed chair.

Whoa. I kinda sorta remembered that Hoshi was scheduled to graduate from Northwestern University this year, but I hadn't given any thought to what came after. Would she return to Japan? Or . . . what?

Ruth bustled in *without* any babies, but we mobbed her anyway. Those of us from SouledOut knew the good news already, and everyone else found out soon enough that Ben had prayed with "the brothers" to receive Jesus as his Messiah. I waited until the hugs and hubbub died down to satisfy my curiosity. "Um, Ruth, why did Ben want to come to SouledOut? Don't get me wrong — I'd love to have my favorite grouch at our church." Ruth and I both laughed.

"But, what about Beth Yehudah? I mean, that's Christian *and* Jewish. I've learned so much about my own faith from you two."

Ruth rolled her eyes. "Beth Yehudah yesterday, SouledOut today. A church marathon we did this weekend!" She thought a moment. "But for Ben, he considers Denny and the other Yada Yada husbands as true brothers, who accepted him, even valued him, for who he was. He wants to worship with them for a while . . . or 'hang,' as Yo-Yo would say. *Oy-oy-oy.*"

By now, most of the group had arrived, and Avis rounded us up, encouraging us to start our praise and worship time. Chanda slipped in scowling as we sang one of our old favorites: *"Hold to His hand, God's Almighty hand . . . !"*

"Are you okay?" I whispered to her.

She muttered something dark about the terrible parking. I wanted to guffaw. *Well, yeah, Chanda, if you're going to insist on driving that monster SUV.* But I didn't. She'd bought the thing so she could haul kids and families around, bless her. So I just gave her a hug and brought in another chair from the dining room.

As I sat down again, Avis was opening her Bible. "I want to share a scripture from Hebrews, chapter twelve," she said.

" 'Therefore, since we are surrounded by such a huge crowd of witnesses to the life of faith, let us strip off every weight that slows us down, especially the sin that so easily hinders our progress. And let us run with endurance the race that God has set before us. We do this by keeping our eyes on Jesus, on whom our faith depends from start to finish.' "

My ears perked up. *Whoa.* More verses about running the race, moving forward, like the ones God had showed me in Philippians last week.

Avis closed her Bible. "It occurred to me as I read these verses that they speak both to the one running the race of faith, and to the 'crowd of witnesses' urging the runner on. Each one of us in this room finds herself in both roles — running the race of faith, and encouraging each other when we falter." A gentle smile bathed Avis's face as she looked around the circle. "I just want to say thank you, my sisters, for being there for my family this year. It has been so hard to see my precious daughter suffer abuse in her marriage, and now have to deal with HIV. Thank you especially, Chanda, for taking Rochelle into your home."

Chanda squirmed. "Aw, *irie, mon!* It's all good. For we too!"

Edesa, her nutmeg skin glowing in the warm evening, leaned forward with a wide smile. "I, too, want to say *gracias* to Chanda for her encouragement. She made a generous donation to the new Manna House Foundation, and promised matching funds to anything else we can raise in the next two years. We can start building this summer!"

"Awright, Chanda!" Yo-Yo punched the air, spurring a general round of clapping and hooting and praise to God.

Chanda was genuinely embarrassed. "Mi tink dat was supposed to be *anonymous*, Edesa girl. But since you got such a big mout', mi say dat dis group help mi see dat lottery money belong to God anyway." She folded her arms across her bosom as if to say, *An dat's dat.*

I watched Chanda, realizing what a wonderful, funky sense of humor God had. He could use anyone and anything, no matter how ordinary or unlikely — in fact, He seemed to like "ordinary" and "unlikely" the best! — to work out His grace in this world.

Nony spoke. "That word is for me tonight, Avis. To press toward the goal. To set aside every weight. To run with endurance." She pulled a long envelope from her bag. "Mark got a reply from the University of KwaZulu-Natal —"

Eyes widened. "Did he . . . ?" several started to say but did not finish.

Nony smiled and shook her head. "No, he has not yet been accepted. But they are interested, and would like to interview him in person, so we —"

We? I had expected her to say, *"So he is flying to South Africa for an interview."*

"— are leaving for South Africa as soon as the boys are out of school in June, as we had planned before."

A collective gasp seemed to suck the air out of the room for several moments. But Nony's heart was in her smile. "Mark says it does not matter if he is offered a job at the university or not. If God is calling us to South Africa as a family, we will better know what our options are if we are there in person. All of us. Northwestern has extended his sabbatical for two more years. Praise You, Jesus." Her eyes closed and her hand lifted in silent praise. Just as suddenly, her eyes opened, and she turned to Hoshi. "We have asked Hoshi to consider going with us when she graduates in June. She has become a much-loved member of our family, and there is quite an international community in KwaZulu-Natal, many Asians as well. But . . . it is up to her, of course."

Now my heart really started to flutter. *Nony and Mark leaving? Hoshi maybe leaving too?* What was going to happen to Yada Yada? I knew God wanted us to reach out beyond our little group. But did that have to mean *losing* each other?

Someone said, "Hoshi? What are you thinking?"

Hoshi seemed surprisingly calm at such a momentous crossroad. "That is why I wanted to come to Yada Yada tonight, to ask all of you to pray with me about my future. I had always planned to return to Japan, but" — her almond eyes saddened — "as you know, my family has turned against me. I am grateful for Nonyameko and Dr. Smith's invitation to accompany them. It is true; they are my family now. But . . ." She grew thoughtful. "Befriending Sara and getting acquainted with what ReJOYce is doing on campus has touched me deeply. There are so many lonely, empty souls on the Northwestern campus. I feel drawn to work with them, but . . ." She took a deep breath. "I don't know what God wants me to do. So I ask you, dear sisters, to pray."

"Exactly what we should do." Avis reached for the hands on either side of her. "What other prayer requests do we have tonight?"

"Oh, help me, Jesus!" Florida's cry made me jump. She'd been strangely silent all evening, but suddenly pent-up words burst out. "Pray with me, sisters. Chris's final hearing is a week from Wednesday, last week of the month. I can hardly sleep nights, worried about my baby." Her head wagged from side to side; she thumped her chest. "He didn't do nothin', I know it. I believe that with all my heart. Pray, sisters. Pray that the judge will see the truth." Her head wagged harder. "Don't know what I'll do if he —"

The tears started to flow.

I felt torn. I'd almost forgotten that Chris's hearing was coming up! He hadn't said anything to me during play practices; maybe he wasn't supposed to talk about it. I wanted Florida to be excited about coming to see the play, but Chris hadn't wanted me to tell her what he was doing. With Florida all torn up about the upcoming hearing, how could I share my excitement at what God was doing with this "home-grown" play — in my life, in the lives of the boys taking part? And I needed prayer. Oh boy, did I still need prayer! God would have to pull it together or it would fall flat.

But several sisters had surrounded Florida; others were laying hands on Hoshi and Nonyameko and starting to pray. I blinked back hot tears, joined others on their knees beside Florida, and laid a hand on her shaking shoulder as Yada Yada pelted heaven.

Lord, hear my prayer too. Please, don't forget this play . . .

As we broke up our circle, Ruth asked, "So. We meet where next time?"

"I'm next on the list," Avis admitted. "But that's the weekend of Peter's and my first anniversary, and we might —"

"Your anniversary?!" Yo-Yo screeched. "Hey, guys, know what that means? It's Yada Yada's anniversary too! Two years — and we haven't killed each other yet." People started to laugh. Had it really been a year since Avis "jumped the broom" with Peter Douglass? *Two* years since God had thrown us together at the Chicago Women's Conference as Prayer Group 26?

"*Our* anniversary, too, Yo-Yo." Becky grinned. "We got baptized in Lake Michigan right after Avis's wedding last year — remember?"

"Yowza." Yo-Yo high-fived everyone within reach. "We gotta do somethin' special. *Really* party — hey! Delores. Your man doin' a gig at La Fiesta that weekend?"

Delores shrugged. "Not sure. I'll find out."

Florida shook her head. "I dunno . . .
might not feel like partyin' if Chris's hearing don't go right."

I grabbed her and whispered in her ear.
"Have faith, sister. Have faith!"

42

I knew putting in a full day at Bethune Elementary, and then driving downtown to the juvenile detention center would stretch me thin as razor wire. Before I collapsed into bed Monday night, I e-mailed a frantic SOS to Yada Yada for prayer support, then buried myself beneath the covers.

On Wednesday, I grabbed a few *Israel and New Breed* CDs to keep my praise going on the commute. But when I bumbled into the all-purpose room at the JDC with my bag of scripts and a box of props, nine sour faces waited for me — and the principal.

"What? Where's Jeremy?"

"That's what I came to tell you. He had his disposition yesterday. The judge gave him two years for dealing; second offense. They took him to the Illinois youth prison in Joliet this morning."

"But . . . he was doing the Dr. King speech!" My heart felt like it was flopping down around my ankles. "Couldn't they have waited till next week?" I sank into the nearest chair. "Sheesh. Way to take the guts right out of our play."

The principal gave a sympathetic shrug. "I'm really sorry, Mrs. Baxter. Do the best you can. I'm sure the parents will understand." She slipped out of the room.

I closed my eyes and pressed my fingertips against my temples. *Yeah, right.* What were we going to do now? Me get up there and read Jeremy's part? That'd be a comedy, for sure.

Wait a minute, Jodi. Jeremy was sent to prison for two years — and he's only sixteen. And you're worried about your play?

I sighed. *You're right, Lord. I'm sorry. But I really don't know what to —*

I felt someone tapping on my shoulder. I opened my eyes. "What is it, T.J.?"

The boy gave me a lopsided grin. "I'll do Dr. King."

"You?" I managed an appreciative smile. "I thought you just wanted to do the 'action' parts. Besides, the play's only three days away. How would you memorize —"

"I already done it."

I blinked. "You've *already* memorized the Dr. King speech?"

T.J. nodded, still grinning. "Yeah. Jeremy

was in my unit, so he used ta make me listen to him say his part over and over, an' —" He shrugged. "I dunno. I jus' learned it."

I couldn't help it. I started to laugh. Then I stood up and clapped my hands once. "All right. Thank you, T.J. Let's do a run-through of the whole thing . . ."

All the way home, I confessed my lack of faith and praised God for preparing T.J. ahead of time — our "ram in the bush," just like He did for Abraham and Isaac. T.J. had done a passable job with the Dr. King speech. Ramón, James, and Rashad had their parts memorized too. The action parts . . . well, I just hoped the audience wouldn't laugh. My actors got a little carried away sometimes. But Chris's backdrop was finished and helped pull the whole mishmash together. "Thank You, *Jesus*!" I yelled at the top of my lungs right in the middle of homegoing traffic on Lake Shore Drive.

I thought my next hurdle would be convincing Florida and Carl that showing up Saturday night for the "spring play" at the JDC was important to Chris — without actually telling them what it was about or what Chris was doing.

But that was before I arrived at the JDC

516

Friday afternoon. This time the principal met me outside the all-purpose room. Our eyes locked. *Uh-oh.* I tried to steel myself. "Who's gone now?"

She shook her head. "No one's gone. They're all inside, but . . . we've had an incident. I just wanted to prepare you." She opened the door and I walked in, my heart flopping around my ankles again.

The two guards parted as I walked between them. The boys sat slumped in the chairs, shoulders hunched. Except Chris. Florida's son paced back and forth in front of the backdrop, fists clenched, muttering every cuss word he'd ever heard. When he saw me, he hurtled toward me in three angry strides. "See?" He flung a hand toward the backdrop. "See? It don't matter what I do, Mrs. B. I ain't gonna go *no-where*."

I stared at the backdrop. Four long gashes snaked across the four beautiful figures he'd drawn on the cardboard "wall." Slashes with something sharp. Knife? Box cutter? Fingernail file? I whirled to face the principal. "How could this happen?!" I was one pitch short of shouting. "Isn't this door kept locked?!"

Get a grip, Jodi. Satan would really like you to lose it right now. Is God faithful, or not? I

517

took a deep breath and lowered my voice. "I'm sorry. Never mind. I . . . . just need some time with the boys. Yes, all of them. We need to decide what to do together."

I heard the door close as the principal left. The guards respectfully withdrew to the back of the room. But I walked slowly along the backdrop, tracing the slashes with my finger, like Thomas touching the wounds in Jesus' hands and feet and side. *Wounds . . . that's what these are . . . wounds . . .*

I turned to face the boys who were watching me. "Chris? I'm truly sorry this happened. I don't know why someone would do this. Maybe something ugly happened to them and they took out their anger on your artwork because it's beautiful. I don't know. But I do know this: what the devil intended for evil, God can turn into something good."

Chris snorted in disgust. The other boys rolled their eyes.

"Wait — hear me out." I sat down and motioned the boys to draw their chairs close. "Whoever did this thought he was going to ruin our play. But without knowing it, this backdrop perfectly fits what we've been trying to say all along. We're not going to fix it. We're going to use it just the way it is. And this is why . . ."

The next day Denny and I arrived at the JDC two hours early. The performance was scheduled for seven o'clock, but I wanted to be sure the room was set up, give the boys a pep talk, make sure we had no last minute "surprises" . . . and to pray.

"Go early and pray over the room," Avis had urged me on the phone. "Touch each chair, pray for each parent or staff who comes tonight. Pray for the boys. Pray *with* the boys if you can. Peter and I will be praying for you here at the house." I grinned as we pulled into the parking structure next to the JDC. Avis had done more than pray. She'd loaned her car to the Hickmans, who didn't want to ride with us and have to sit around for two hours.

I wished Amanda and Josh could've come, but Denny barely squeaked in, because he was the husband of the "play director" *and* a JDC volunteer. By now the security *schtik* was routine, and we hurried to the all-purpose room with the few props I'd managed to scrounge up from Bethune Elementary's costume box.

To my surprise, the room was already unlocked. I heard voices inside. *Oh no. What now?* With a sense of dread, I opened the door . . . and stopped dead in my tracks.

The two guards who had accompanied the boys for each play practice were mounting spotlights on tripods, adjusting them to fall on Chris's damaged backdrop and various spots in front of it. The one the boys called Mr. Wheeler turned his head. "Oh, hey, Mrs. Baxter. This your husband?" He came over and shook Denny's hand.

"What's this?" I raised my hands toward the lights on left and right.

"Oh, Gonzalez over there . . . he swiped 'em from his church. Thought you could use 'em tonight." Wheeler scratched his jaw. "We've been watching what you're doin' with the boys for this performance. We'd like to help. We'll be your light techies tonight, if it's all right with you."

"All right with — ! It's wonderful! That's what we really needed to highlight the different parts! But, uh, we don't have time to practice with the lights, to work out —"

"Aw, don't worry about that, Mrs. B. We got it down. Don't forget, we've been watching you practice for days. Gonzalez over there — he does this all the time for big performances at his church."

Denny chuckled in my ear as we left them to their work. "Any other surprises, 'Mrs.

B'?" I just shook my head, and got down to the praying business before my actors arrived at five-thirty. It was a little awkward with the guards-turned-light-techies there, but no way was I going to skip over this part. If it wasn't prayer holding this play together, I didn't know what was!

The room was packed by seven o'clock. I saved a couple of seats for Florida and Carl in the second row; good thing, because they slipped in at six-fifty-five. The principal welcomed the parents, administrators, staff, and visitors, including someone from the mayor's office. She introduced me briefly, but all I did was introduce each one of that night's cast by name. "The stage set for tonight's performance was designed by Chris Hickman, age fourteen," I added, and sat down.

The lights went out. Well, not completely, for security reasons, I guessed. But dim enough so that David slipped onto the "stage," and seemed to suddenly appear, illumined by one spotlight. David was articulate, and the boys had unanimously elected him to be narrator. "Welcome," he said. "Tonight we bring you 'Voices from the Past — Voices for Our Future.' Sit back, enjoy — but most of all, listen."

The spotlight died. When the lights came up again, two "gangs" came at each other from opposite sides of the room, three purple uniforms against three green uniforms, yelling insults, making dares, calling names. I could see parents squirming, glancing at each other. As they met in the middle, Kevin (purple) pushed T.J. (green). Suddenly T.J. drew a fluorescent green water gun (I'd been firmly told not to use anything that looked realistic), pointed it at Kevin and yelled, *"Bam! Bam!"*

Kevin fell in a heap to the floor. The other boys ran in two directions. Left lights died. Right lights followed the "shooter" and his homies. "Why'd you pop him, man?" Mike yelled at T.J. "You didn't hafta kill him!"

"He was dissin' me, man. Didn't ya hear? *Nobody* disses me, man."

The spotlight came up again on Kevin, still sprawled on the floor. David, who hadn't been one of the gangbangers, knelt down beside him, shaking his head, moaning. "He was goin' ta go to college. He wanted ta build bridges and skyscrapers. *Why* do we kill our brightest and best? Won't we ever learn?"

The audience was clearly uncomfortable. I heard murmurs and chairs squeaking as the spotlights dimmed. When the spot came up again, James — even paler under the bright light — stood in the middle of the stage with a "stovepipe hat" on his head and an Abe Lincoln beard anchored to his chin. I heard a few titters, but they quickly died when James spoke. "I, Abraham Lincoln, President of the United States, by virtue of the power in me . . . do order and declare that all persons held as slaves within these States and henceforward shall be free!" The room grew even quieter as he paraphrased the Emancipation Proclamation. ". . . And I hereby charge the people so declared to be free to abstain from all violence, unless in necessary self-defense . . ." James drew himself up, needing no mic as he boomed the last words. "Upon this act, sincerely believed to be an act of justice, warranted by the Constitution . . . I invoke the considered judgment of mankind and the gracious favor of Almighty God!"

People in the audience began to clap — but just then Terrance came out of the shadows and pointed the fluorescent green water gun at "Abe Lincoln." *"Bam! Bam!"* James dropped to the floor. I heard several gasps around me. The spot moved to Chris's chalk drawing of President Lincoln with the ugly slash across it, lingered . . . then died.

When the spotlight came up again, David

stood with his head hanging. "Why do we kill our brightest and our best? Won't we ever learn?"

Lights out . . . lights on. Rashad was "on stage" wearing a shirt and tie. "My name is Medgar Evers. Thank you for giving me this opportunity to speak by radio. I speak as a native Mississippian, educated in Mississippi schools, serving overseas in our nation's armed forces against Hitlerism and fascism. I mention this because I believe I am typical of many loyal Mississippians of color, who are equally devoted to their State and want only to see it assume its rightful place in the democratic scheme of our country."

The room was completely silent as Rashad, quoting Medgar Evers's speech, painted a tough picture of the Jim Crow years. Finally "Medgar Evers" said, "What does the Negro want?" Rashad ticked off the end of segregation . . . to register and vote without handicap . . . more jobs at all levels . . . desegregated schools. "The Negro has been in America since 1619, a total of three hundred and forty-four years. He is not going anywhere else; this country is his home. He wants to do his part to help make his city, state, and nation a better place for everyone regardless of color and race."

Denny took my hand and squeezed as Rashad said, "Thank you," and started to walk off. I heard an "Oh no!" behind me as the shadowy figure appeared, pulled out the fluorescent green water gun and — *"Bam! Bam!"* — "shot" him in the back. "Medgar Evers" fell to the floor. The spotlight moved to Chris's drawing of the civil rights leader on the backdrop. In the strong light, the ugly gash across the drawing stood out even more glaringly.

David moved into the spotlight. This time he threw his hands up. "*Why* do we kill our brightest and our best? Won't we ever learn?"

The third scene featured Ramón wearing a white shirt and tie. No one would have guessed who he was supposed to be, except that he stood next to Chris's drawing of President John Kennedy for a moment before he moved to center stage. "My fellow Americans." He didn't quite make the stretch from Latino accent to Bostonian inflections, but he tried. "The oath I swore before you and Almighty God — as the thirty-fifth president of the United States — is the same solemn oath our forefathers prescribed nearly a century and three-quarters ago." People were leaning forward. "The world is very different now . . . yet we hold the same revolutionary belief — that the rights of man come not from the generosity of the state, but from the hand of God."

I was so proud of Ramón. Amazed that he had dropped all his S-words and F-words for the stirring words of this inaugural address. ". . . And so, my fellow Americans: ask not what your country can do for you — ask what you can do for your country."

But no one clapped. The audience tensed. Sure enough. Out came the shadowy figure and the water gun. *"Bam! Bam!"* Ramón dropped to the floor. And David repeated his sorrowful line: "Why do we kill our brightest and our best? Won't we ever learn?"

By the time T.J. took the stage, even Denny's grip on my hand was tight. T.J., too, had on a shirt and tie. The spotlight followed him as he paused by the drawing of Abraham Lincoln, looked up into that craggy face, then moved to center stage. When he spoke, I was amazed how he deepened his voice, rolling his words, sounding very like Dr. Martin Luther King. "Five score years ago," he started, "a great American, in whose symbolic shadow we stand today, signed the Emancipation Proclamation. . . . But one hundred years later, the Negro still is not free."

I held my breath. But T.J. had spoken the truth; he knew this speech backward and forward. "*I have a dream* that one day this nation will rise up and live out the true meaning of its creed: 'We hold these truths to be self-evident: that *all* men are created equal.' *I have a dream . . .*" At the end of Dr. King's "I have a dream" litany, T. J. finally raised his arms proudly. "When this happens, when we allow freedom to ring from every state and every city, we will be able to speed up that day when all of God's children, black men and white men, Jews and Gentiles, Protestants and Catholics, will be able to join hands and sing in the words of the old Negro spiritual, 'Free at last! Free at last! Thank God Almighty, we are free at last!' "

The audience couldn't help it. They burst into applause. But once more, the shadowy figure appeared with that evil water gun. *"Bam! Bam!"* T.J. crumpled to the floor. The spotlight moved to Chris's drawing of the great man, with its ugly gash.

But this time the original "gangbangers" of the cast (minus T.J.) came slowly out of the shadows from both sides, once more in their purple and green uniforms, and stood sorrowfully on either side of the "body" of

Dr. King. They looked at one another across T.J.'s crumpled form. The Purples said, "Why do we kill our brightest and our best? Won't we *ever* learn?"

The Greens replied, "Maybe it could start with us." Hands reached out. Purples and Greens touched fist on fist, up, down, then slapped open hands in the familiar street greeting, friend to friend.

The lights dimmed. The actors slipped to the back of the room. Now I expected the lights to come on, and the audience would clap for the wonderful job the boys had done. But the lights stayed dim; no one clapped. The audience sat silently, as if stunned. And then I heard a sound coming from the second row where Florida was sitting.

The sound of someone crying.

43

I got teary myself the next few days, every time I remembered how Florida and Carl had walked slowly along the backdrop after the performance, whispering together, as if seeing Chris's talent for the first time. I don't know what she said to him, but I saw her hug her boy a long time, and he had to brush the back of his arm across his eyes.

But the next day at church, she planted herself in front of me. "Hate to admit it, Jodi Baxter, but you was right about Chris. I didn't see no use for all that scrawlin' he was doin', but after seein' what he did for that play? Now I *know* God got His hand on my son, an' He gonna raise him up to *be* somebody. I'm thinkin' it's time I quit tellin' God what He's s'posed ta do, and just start askin' God to work out His own purpose for my boy, no matter what happens next Wednesday!"

Had to laugh, though, at the message she

left on our answering machine on Monday. "I meant what I said yesterday, Jodi, 'bout trustin' God for Chris no matter what happens at the hearing Wednesday. But that don't mean *you* ain't s'posed to keep prayin' that the judge do right by my boy an' send him home!"

I did pray — as I walked to school, every time I saw Carla, every time I saw Chris's name on the sticky note I'd stuck to the bathroom mirror. But I was also having withdrawal pangs after spending two weeks with "the boys" at the JDC, and now suddenly . . . nothing. It seemed like a dream. *God? What was it all about? Will I ever see those boys again? What's going to happen to T.J. and Ramón and David . . . and Chris?*

As Wednesday's hearing approached, my anxiety level heightened, as if Chris were my own son. What if he was sent away to Joliet, like Jeremy? *Oh God! . . .*

I tried to be a reassuring presence for Carla, offering once more to take her home with me after school if Florida and Carl were delayed for some reason. When the dismissal bell rang on Wednesday, she hung around my desk after the other kids piled out of the room while I packed up my things. "Can I erase the board, Miz Baxter?"

"Sure, honey. Just leave today's homework assignments."

"Hey, Carla," a male voice growled. "Ready to go home?"

Both of us jumped. I hadn't heard the door open. Nor did I expect to hear that voice in my classroom —

"Chris!!!" Carla screamed, scattering papers, books, and stumbling over chairs as she threw herself into her brother's arms. I was so astonished, I just watched in a daze as he swung her around and around, laughing so hard I thought both of them were going to fall over.

When Chris finally did put her down, Carla kept hopping up and down and hanging on him, so that finally he dragged her along like a ball-and-chain to where I stood, my mouth hanging like it'd been propped open with a toothpick. "Hey, Mrs. B." He laughed. "You glad to see me?"

"Glad?!" Now I laughed, grabbing him in a hug. All that fear and worry and prayer and hoping came blubbering out of me all at once. Then I held him at arm's length. "But . . . you're out? Home? Free? Just like that? No sentence?"

"Nope. Judge believed me, that I didn't know nothin' 'bout that robbery till after it happened. Dropped the armed robbery

531

charges. But she tol' me I was headin' for big trouble if I hung out with them gang-bangers anymore. Said if I got picked up again, she'd put me in the slammer so fast, my ears would be ringin'." He made a face. "Man, felt as if she'd blistered my behind by the time she got through."

Carla tugged on his arm. "C'mon, Chris! Let's go home!"

"Yeah. My folks are waitin' outside for us. Come on out, Mrs. B, say hi."

I walked down the hall with Chris and Carla and out the school's double doors, once again wondering why I was so sur-prised when God answered our prayers. I'd told Florida, *"Have faith, sister"* . . . but when it came to my own —

"Hey, Jodi!" Florida waved out the passenger-side window of a navy blue Toyota Corolla. "Ya like it? Tol' ya God was goin' ta put a car in that garage of ours. One of Carl's coworkers sold it ta him. Only ninety thousand miles — pretty good for a '97."

"Is it ours, Mama? Really, truly?" Carla pulled open the backseat door and hopped in. Chris slid in after her.

Carl waved at me from behind the wheel and the car started to move. Florida just laughed. "God is good, Jodi!" she yelled back at me. "All the time, God is good!"

The weather forgot to look at the calendar that weekend. May Day — the first of May — fell on Saturday, but the warm temperatures of April had fallen once more into the forties, along with a chilly rain.

Who cared! We were going to La Fiesta Restaurant that evening with the rest of Yada Yada and our families to party our socks off.

"Where's Josh? Isn't he coming?" Stu asked as she and Estelle piled into our Caravan with Denny, me, and Amanda.

I rolled my eyes. "Yeah, I think so. He disappeared around noon today, said he'd meet us there."

"I hope they don't put us off in some party room an' make us listen to Mr. Enriquez's band piped in or somethin'," Amanda grumped.

"That's why we didn't *say* we were coming as a group. Ricardo told us to come early and just fill up the place!" I glanced at Denny. Sure hoped that worked. The whole point was to listen to Ricardo's mariachi band, dance, eat, laugh. Celebrate!

Because we sure had a lot to celebrate that night — not the least of which was that the whole Hickman family would be there. All five of them.

Most of us arrived around five-thirty, give or take fifteen minutes. By the time Ricardo arrived with his band at six o'clock — an hour earlier than usual, his "gift" to the restaurant, but really to us — we had filled up half the main room of the restaurant with its festive magenta walls, orange stucco ceiling, and terra cotta tiled floor. The wait staff, attired in white shirts, black pants or skirts, and black string ties, rushed about getting menus, water glasses, and silverware for everyone. When a young server spilled water all over Delores's lap, Delores patted the air in a calming gesture. *"Ninguna prisa. Estamos muy bien."*

"What'd she say?" I murmured to Amanda.

Amanda shrugged. " 'No hurry. We are fine' . . . something like that."

By the time most of us had our food — plates heaped with flautas, enchiladas, burritos, quesadillas, and more, along with the necessary rice and beans, tortilla chips, and salsa — the band was well into their first set, a string of mariachi favorites such as *"Tú Sólo Tú"* and *"Volver, Volver."* José was playing a mandolin in the band tonight, and brought the house down with a mandolin solo on *"Dos Arbolitos"* — "Two Little

Trees." Amanda clapped so hard I thought she was going to break her chair.

Chanda and her kids arrived late, as usual — though parking her monster SUV couldn't be the excuse tonight, since the restaurant had a good-size parking lot in back. I was happy to see that Rochelle and Conny came too. I craned my neck and skimmed the tables nearby. Was everyone else here? The five Hickmans and Becky filled one table, with Little Andy climbing all over Chris . . . Delores and her four dark-eyed *niños* sat with Avis and Peter . . . Ruth and Ben *noshed* with Yo-Yo and her brothers, who each held a twin . . .

My eyes lingered on the Sisulu-Smith table, where Mark and Nonyameko and their boys laughed and talked with Hoshi and Adele. Would we ever gather like this again, all the Yada Yadas with our families, to celebrate what God had done for us? What would the next year look like for Yada Yada? Becky and Estelle had been added this last year — one saved from prison, the other from the fire. *Sheesh, Lord. If You have new sisters for Yada Yada, couldn't you send them in less dramatic fashion next time?*

I tackled my quesadillas. Well, at least we were all here right now. I should just be thankful for the moment — wait a minute!

535

My head jerked up. Everyone was *not* here.

Josh and Edesa were missing.

I was so flummoxed that I almost missed Ricardo Enriquez at the mic, wearing the elegant *charro* suit of the mariachi band, introducing the next song. ". . . for my wife, Delores, who had a birthday this month." He stepped off the small stage and stopped at Delores's table with his large *guitarrón*, making her blush and sending the Enriquez children into giggles.

Stu poked me. "Good grief! Yada Yada forgot Delores's birthday!" Huh. Did she mean Yada Yada — or *me?* Whatever. We'd make it up to her.

Ricardo's serenade was beautiful. "What is he singing?" I whispered to Amanda.

"It's *'Las Mañanitas',*" she whispered back. "Something about 'the lovely psalms sung by King David . . . today we sing them to a loved one who happy will be.' "

Delores was beaming when Ricardo rejoined his band on the stage. But once again, Ricardo leaned into the mic. "We have another special occasion to celebrate tonight. A young couple who have an announcement to make, but I don't see them — oh, there they are. Ladies and gentlemen . . ." The entire band began strumming their guitars and violins like a stringed drum roll. ". . . may I present Joshua Baxter and Edesa Reyes."

I clutched Denny's arm. *Young couple? Announcement?* My heart nearly stopped as Josh and Edesa walked into the room hand in hand, as if they'd been waiting in the wings of a stage. Edesa, wearing a lovely white eyelet dress and fringed black-and-rose shawl, smiled radiantly beneath a halo of tiny black ringlets framing her mahogany skin. An audible gasp traveled around the tables. Amanda squealed.

Josh, looking manly and grown up in spite of the sandy hair curling down over the collar of his open-necked shirt, quickly took the mic and grinned our way. "Hey, pipe down, sis. Don't steal my show." They stood together in the spotlight, my tall Caucasian son and the beautiful young black woman from Honduras. Josh put his arm around Edesa. "I asked her to marry me —"

Edesa laughed and took the mic away from him. "And I said yes. In a year or two." She held up her left hand. A simple diamond on her third finger flashed in the light.

The entire room erupted in a volcano of cheers, clapping, squeals, and laughter. I was so stunned I could hardly breathe; Denny's tight grip around my waist didn't help.

The band began to play. Ricardo took the mic. "Josh and Edesa have requested *'Amar Es Para Siempre'* — 'To Love Is Forever.' For you gringos, the song says: 'You're my reason, my peace, my faith, my light . . . your smile is the sun of every dawn.' "

The band began to play. Josh took Edesa in his arms and, grinning at each other, they danced. It looked like a combination of a waltz and a salsa, but what do I know? But in the midst of the sweet violins and the floating figures in the spotlight, I heard that still, small Voice in my spirit . . .

Trust Me, Jodi. Trust My Spirit within these young people. Time for you to let go. And — think of the possibilities!

THE YADA YADA PRAYER GROUP GETS ROLLING CELEBRATIONS & RECIPES

LET'S CELEBRATE!

The wonderful thing about a prayer group of Yada Yada sisters who come from different Christian traditions and cultural backgrounds — whether fictional, as the sisters in *The Yada Yada Prayer Group,* or a group of real-life sisters-in-Christ (maybe like yours!) — is that we can share the rich rituals and celebrations that come from our various spiritual and family heritages.

And then there are times when we simply have to create our own traditions and celebrations! Even during the tough times. Maybe especially during the tough times.

HOSPITAL HOSPITALITY

The phone rings. A friend or family member is scheduled for surgery. When the time comes, you pop in during visiting hours and bring a card or some flowers, and like a good guest, you don't stay too long.

541

But hospital stays can be as exhausting for the family as for the patient. Long hours at the hospital. Lost hours of sleep. Cafeteria food. The nurses and doctors are taking care of the patient — but who's taking care of the family caregivers?

And as you probably know, being the *patient* isn't exactly the funnest way to spend a perfectly good week of your life.

But with a little thought and putting heads together with friends, there are a number of ways to make a hospital stay a bit less fearful, a bit less frazzled, a bit less lonely, a bit less unhealthy for *both* the patient and his or her family.

Hospital Guest Book

Purchase a simple notebook with lined pages. (If you use an actual guestbook, be sure it has space for visitors to write notes, not just space for names and addresses.)

Make a title page on the cover or first page, using colored markers, stickers, or fun fonts on your computer, e.g. one ten-year-old decorated the notebook cover and titled it: "Grandpa's Hospital Guest Book."

Write "Date & Time" on the top left of each page, followed by "Name & Notes."

Encourage each person who comes to the waiting room during surgery and recovery

— when the patient is decidedly out of it — to write notes of greeting, good wishes, and prayers in the guest book.

Keep the book going with visitors who come each day: pastor, in-laws, buddies, kids, grandkids. If a visitor comes when the patient is asleep or out for testing, the patient will still be able to know who came to visit.

The book can also be used as a log by the spouse or primary caregiver of progress each day, feelings, and things said that might be forgotten.

The Hospital Guest Book will be a treasure to read and re-read once the patient is home and recovering.

Care for the Caregiver

Family members aren't always prepared for a hospital stay, especially in an emergency. Here are some things you can do . . .

Bring a pillow and light blanket for those long nights in a waiting room.

Bring some healthy snacks: small bottles of orange juice, fruit, nuts, granola bars, even some raw veggies. And replenish those snacks from time to time.

Offer to go to the home and pick up their toothbrush, toilet kit, shaver — whatever will make them feel human after a long day and night at the hospital.

Once the patient is back in the hospital room, offer to sit with him or her to give the spouse or caregiver time to go home for a shower or get out for a walk.

Ask if plants at home need to be watered, kitty litter scooped, or the dog walked.

Cheer for the Patient

Print out the patient's favorite Scriptures in large letters on colorful 8 × 10-inch paper and tape them around the hospital room. Or even just words of encouragement: "God Loves You" . . . "This Is the Day the Lord Has Made" . . . "God Is Your Rock," etc. (You'll often find that the nurses and cleaning staff are encouraged, too!)

Bring a small, portable CD player and some of the patient's favorite worship CDs for those long hours when he or she needs encouragement and comfort.

If you bring cut flowers, be sure you also bring a vase to put them in! (The nurses might throw a conniption if you try to use the plastic water pitcher!)

A basket to hold Get Well cards will be appreciated. (Space to display cards is limited in a hospital room.)

Once the Patient is Home

Arrange for a week's worth of meals to be brought in by friends, church members, neighbors. Disposable containers are best, so the patient's family doesn't have to return a stack of dishes to half a dozen different folks — but if that's not possible, make sure each "angel" clearly labels his or her dishes. And *you* offer to return them.

Again, offer to patient sit, so the family caregiver can get out to do errands, go for a walk, go to church Sunday morning, even take in a movie.

A cleaning crew might be appreciated to do a once-over of the house: bathrooms, kitchen floor, vacuuming. One hour by a few good friends can certainly give a house or an apartment a quick but much-needed face-lift.

You get the idea! You'll probably think of other gifts of hospitality specific to your friend's situation. And don't think you have to do all the above by yourself. That's where you "yada yada" with your prayer sisters and spread the care and the cheer around.

Who knows, next time the patient might be you.

A CHRISTIAN SEDER

In *Gets Rolling,* the Yada Yada Prayer Group celebrates a Jewish Passover meal (a "Seder") with the Garfield family. This is one of the feasts commanded by the Lord in Leviticus 23:5–8, to commemorate God's deliverance from their bondage in Egypt.

For many Christians, the Jewish Passover meal has been relegated to Old Testament practices, and has been replaced with a simple "Lord's Supper" or "Communion" or "Eucharist" (depending on your denominational affiliation) — primarily "drinking the cup" and "breaking the bread" which we do in remembrance of our Lord's shed blood and broken body. End of story.

But there are a growing number of Christian churches and families who have rediscovered the yearly Seder meal, with its rich traditions and — best of all — with its spiritual significance for us as Christians. So hold on to your Bible and let's take a fast journey backward through time . . .

Why Should We Celebrate Seder?

First, because it was important to Jesus. In the week leading up to His arrest and crucifixion, Jesus was *persona non grata* in Jerusalem. He had ridden into Jerusalem with all the people cheering, which upset the religious leaders to no end. (Who did He think He was, anyway?) Then He strode into the temple grounds and threw out the money changers and sacrificial animal vendors who were ripping off the people. Jesus then withdrew to Bethany to let things cool down a little, even while the religious leaders began plotting ways to get rid of Him.

So why did Jesus return to Jerusalem a few days later, when things were still so hot for Him? In Luke 22:15, Jesus tells His disciples, "With fervent desire I have desired to eat this Passover with you before I suffer." Jesus was eager to eat the yearly feast commanded by God in Leviticus and sent His disciples ahead to prepare it.

Secondly, because Jesus told us to. During the Passover (Seder) meal, when it came time in the ritual to pour the cup of wine and then to break the bread, Jesus gave deeper meaning to the symbolism of these events. As the Lamb of God, the cup symbolized *His* spilled blood. The broken bread, *His* body. Then He told His disciples, "Every time you do this, do it in remembrance of me" (I Corinthians 11:23–26).

The early Christians took this instruction seriously, and the Seder meal was celebrated with joyous wonder for the next three hundred years. Their eyes had been opened to its layers of significance, not only for what this feast symbolized regarding God's deliverance of His people in the past, but for how it pointed to the continuing work of God's salvation through the life, death, and resurrection of His Son, Jesus, delivering *all people* from the bondage of sin.

Certainly, we should continue to celebrate the "Lord's Supper" once a month (as many congregations do), or the "Eucharist" every Sunday (as liturgical churches do), but why not *also* celebrate that rich prophetic Seder meal once a year, along with Jesus and His disciples?

Preparing for Your Seder Meal

Invite guests! Especially guests with children or teens. The purpose of the Seder meal is to invite questions from children.

Set the table for a festive meal — a tablecloth, flowers, candles (important), and your best dishes. (If you've invited more people than you have dishes, and have to use paper goods, use colorful paper plates or Chinet.)

Set the table for one more than the number of guests expected (if possible) — this is for Elijah.

Each place setting should have a wine

goblet or glass.

A bowl for hand washing, along with a small towel, should be placed near the head of the table or nearby.

Place a *Haggadah* (the Order of Service) at each place setting, or every other place so guests can share. (See pp. 553–555 to obtain copies of a Christian Haggadah. You will want to decide whether to use a long version or a shortened version. The online versions can be printed out and photocopied for your guests.)

Optional: You might want to put a pillow or cushion on each chair for leaning on, in the spirit of the Four Questions (see pg. 553).

The Seder Plate

Near the head of the table, place a fancy serving plate with the following symbolic items:

A shank bone of a lamb — represents the lamb that was slain to obtain blood to put on the doorposts of every Israelite home.

Bitter herbs (grated horseradish) — represents the bitterness of their lives as slaves in Egypt.

Karpas (a green vegetable, usually parsley, good for dipping in the salt water) — the salt water represents the tears shed while the Israelites were in bondage.

Charoset (a mixture of chopped apples, chopped nuts, moistened with wine or grape juice) — represents the mortar they had to make to hold bricks together.

Three pieces of *matzo* (wrapped within a cloth napkin) — for the Christian, represents the unity of One God: Father, Son, and Holy Spirit.

What Else Goes on the Table

Place several of the following on the table within everyone's reach:

- Small bowls of salty water
- Enough parsley sprigs so each person can have one
- A plate of matzo (unleavened crackers, available in your grocery store)
- A bottle of wine or grape juice (for every four to six people, if you pour only "symbolic" amounts)
- Extra serving bowls of the bitter herbs (horseradish) and the *charoset* (apples/nuts/wine mixture)

What Happens During a Seder (General)

When your guests arrive, seat them at the table, and give each one the *Haggadah,* or

Order of Service. (The *Haggadah* for a Christian Seder will highlight the Messianic "foretellings" which were fulfilled in Jesus the Messiah.) Tell your guests that even though you are going to follow the Order of Service, it's all right to interrupt and ask questions.

The mother or hostess lights the candles with a blessing.

The father or leader washes his hands. (But when Jesus did it, He washed the feet of His disciples!)

The youngest child (or four children) asks the traditional Four Questions, which the leader answers, explaining the meaning of the symbolic items on the Seder Plate and why things are done a certain way (see pg. 553).

The leader retells the story of the escape from Egypt from Exodus 12. Read the story ahead of time so you can tell it in dramatic fashion.

Your story might also include a summary of the Ten Plagues God sent as judgment of Egypt for not letting His people go. As the plagues are mentioned, each person can dip a finger into their cup of wine or grape juice, and flick a drop onto their plate as each plague is mentioned: (1) Blood! . . . (2) Frogs! . . . (3) Lice! . . . (4) Flies! . . . (5)

Livestock disease! . . . (6) Boils! . . . (7) Hail! . . . (8) Locusts! . . . (9) Darkness! . . . (10) Death of the firstborn!

Bitter herbs (horseradish) are eaten with a small amount of *charoset* on the matzo crackers.

The leader unwraps the three matzo and breaks the middle one in two. He wraps one of the broken pieces in a separate cloth, then hides it for the children to find later. This is called the *Afikomen*. (The broken middle matzo represents the broken body of Christ, which was buried — hidden — until God raised Him from the dead.)

Throughout the service, four glasses of wine are poured and drunk, each with its own blessing. Since this is symbolic, you might want to pour just a little bit of wine or grape juice in each glass — at least until the actual meal!

The festive meal is eaten! This might include Matzo Ball Soup (see pp. 565–566); chicken or lamb; potato kugel; gefilte fish (a delicacy — not!); etc.

After the meal, the third and fourth cups of wine are poured and blessed.

The door is opened for the prophet Elijah.

The children hunt for the *Afikomen*. The child who finds it can ransom it for a price (which means the leader has to dig in his pockets for a few coins!) — just as Jesus paid our ransom price.

At the end of the Seder meal and service, everyone says: "Next year in Jerusalem!" (Expressing, for many displaced Jews, the hope that one day they would celebrate Passover in Jerusalem once again. For Christians, we look forward to a New Jerusalem, where we will live with Christ forever.)

The Four Questions

It is important for children to be included in the Seder celebration. During the service and before the meal, the youngest child (or four different children) asks the following questions, which are answered by the head of the table:

Q. 1 — On all other nights we eat all kinds of breads and crackers. **Why do we eat only matzo at Passover?**

A. 1 — Matzo reminds us that when the children of Israel left Egypt, they had no time to bake bread. They took along raw dough and baked it on hot rocks in the desert — represented by the matzo we eat today.

Q. 2 — On all other nights we eat many kinds of vegetables and herbs. **Why do we**

eat bitter herbs at our Seder meal?

A. 2 — The bitter herbs remind us of the bitter and cruel way King Pharoah treated the Israelite slaves in Egypt.

Q. 3 — On all other nights we don't usually dip our food, but at our Seder meal we dip parsley in the salt water, and the bitter herbs in the *Charoset*. **Why do we dip our foods twice tonight?**

A. 3 — We dip parsley in the salt water to remind us of the tears shed during slavery. We dip bitter herbs into the *Charoset* to remind us how hard the Israelite people worked to make bricks for Pharoah's buildings.

Q. 4 — On all other nights we eat sitting up straight. **Why do we lean on a pillow tonight?**

A. 4 — Tonight we lean on a pillow as a reminder that once we were slaves, but now we are free!

Resources for Your Seder

A 24-page reproducible Haggadah from a Messianic perspective is included in the book, *A Family Guide to the Biblical Holidays* by Robin Sampson and Linda Pierce (Heart of Wisdom Publishers). Available online at www.biblicalholidays.com, www.amazon.com, and other sources.

More ideas from the above book for celebrating Seder can be found at www.biblicalholidays.com.

A Christian Haggadah is available for just a few dollars at www.christianseder.com.

"The Passover Seder for Christians," a *Haggadah* adapted by Dennis Bratcher, is available at www.crivoice.org/haggadah.html. You may download and photocopy this Seder service for no charge (with certain restrictions). Includes responsive readings, blessings, prayers, etc. More information and ideas — including ideas for celebrating Seder with a large church group, or celebrating only a *symbolic* Seder — can be found on the same site at www.crivoice.org/seder/html.

A Jewish Seder

One more thing . . .

If you have an opportunity to attend a traditional Jewish Seder with a Jewish family or at a Jewish synagogue, by all means GO. Much of the *Haggadah* may be in Hebrew, but if you have a general idea of the various parts of the Seder meal, you'll get the idea. And feel free to ask questions! Your friendship and interest — even if you are a *goy* — will be appreciated.

But don't assume this is the time to point

out all the Messianic implications of the Passover meal. However, if you have a Jewish friend with whom you feel free to discuss various points of Judaism and Christianity, it could be a very enlightening discussion! Start with how eagerly Jesus wanted to celebrate Passover with His disciples, and go from there . . .

Lashanan Habaÿah Bi Herusahlayim!
Next year in Jerusalem!

RECIPES

Did you make it through *Gets Rolling* without drooling on the pages? Man, every time you turned a page, the Yada Yadas were feasting. Again. It was a hard call, which recipes to include in this batch, but here they are. Quick, into the kitchen, so you can do something besides drool!

Jodi's Lasagna Spinach Roll-Ups

Got vegetarian friends? Or ready for something a bit lighter? Spinach roll-ups are devoured even by carnivores (and even by kids who think they don't like spinach).

Serves 6 when accompanied by a green salad and hot garlic bread.

16 lasagna noodles (a 1-lb. package)
2 bunches fresh spinach, chopped, or 2
   small boxes frozen *chopped* spinach,

thawed, drained, and excess water pressed
out

1/4 to 1/2 cup grated parmesan cheese

1 pint small-curd cottage cheese

1/2 tsp. nutmeg

1 (28-oz.) can tomatoes

1 (6-oz.) can tomato paste

4 cloves garlic, minced or crushed

2 tsp. basil

2 tsp. oregano

1 tsp. marjoram

1 medium onion, chopped

2 cups mozzarella cheese, grated

[*] metric conversion chart on page 569

While you cook the lasagna noodles according to the instructions on the package to
the *al dente* stage, chop and steam the fresh
spinach until limp or, if frozen, thaw it in a
microwave. Press out excess water from the
spinach. Place the spinach in a bowl and
add the parmesan cheese, cottage cheese,
and nutmeg. Mix this filling well.

Blend the tomatoes, tomato paste, and
spices in a blender into a smooth sauce.
Note: This sauce does not have to be cooked
ahead of time.

Lay out the individual noodles side by side

on your counter and spread a heaping tablespoon of filling along the length of each noodle. Adjust until all the noodles are covered evenly. Roll each one up and lay it on its side in a greased 9″ × 13″ baking pan. Arrange evenly and sprinkle the chopped onions and mozzarella cheese over the roll ups. Cover with the tomato sauce and bake at 350 degrees for about an hour.

Calico Beans

Forget plain ol' baked beans. These beans are pretty (all those colors!) and tasty, with a bit of sweet-and-tangy sauce, and makes enough for a crowd. Just be prepared for everyone to ask you for the recipe.

Serves a crowd.

1 (15-oz.) can green lima beans
1 (15-oz.) can large lima beans (or butter beans)
1 (15-oz.) can black beans
1 (15-oz.) can red beans
1 (15-oz.) can great northern beans
1 (28-oz.) can pork and beans
1/2 lb. bacon
2 medium onions, chopped
3/4 cup brown sugar
2 tsp. salt

1 tsp. dry mustard
3 cloves garlic, minced
1/2 cup vinegar
1/2 cup ketchup

Cut the bacon into about 1-inch pieces and fry. Meanwhile, drain the cans of beans, reserving the liquid, and put them in a large casserole dish. Just as the bacon begins to crisp, add the onions and fry together. Then add all the other ingredients to the fry pan and bring to a simmer for 5 minutes. Pour this over the beans and mix thoroughly. Add enough reserved bean liquid to barely cover the beans and bake at 325 degrees for 1 1/2 hours, checking periodically and adding more liquid as needed to keep the beans from drying out.

Makes many people happy at your picnic or potluck.

Estelle's Peach Cobbler
Estelle says her mother used to make this with fresh peaches, but canned peaches will do nicely. And it's yummy either way.

Serves 4–6.

1 stick butter
1 cup flour

1 1/2 tsp. baking powder
1 1/4 cups sugar
3/4 cup milk
1 tsp. vanilla
1 (28-oz.) can sliced peaches
1 tsp. cinnamon
1/4 cup chopped pecans (optional)

Melt butter in a 2-quart casserole dish in a 375 degree oven while combining flour, baking powder, and 1 cup of sugar (reserve the rest for the top). Add milk and vanilla to the dry ingredients and stir until blended. Pour the batter into the melted butter. Dribble peach juice into the mixture and arrange the peaches evenly over the batter. Scatter pecans on the top and sprinkle with cinnamon and sugar. Bake 30 to 40 minutes until golden brown at 375 degrees.

Can be made utterly decadent with scoops of vanilla ice cream.

Jodi's "Tunnel of Fudge" Chocolate Cake
Denny has been known to get down on his knees and beg for this cake. It probably won a prize somewhere, but variations of this recipe pop up everywhere. Here's Jodi's version. But beware. You can't make just one and forget it. If you love chocolate, it will haunt you in your sleep.

Serves 8–10 lucky people.

3 1/2 sticks butter, softened
1 cup granulated sugar
1/2 cup brown sugar
2 oz. unsweetened chocolate, melted and
  cooled
6 eggs
2 cups powdered sugar
2 1/4 cups flour
1/2 cup cocoa
2 cups walnuts or pecans, chopped

Cream the butter, granulated sugar, and brown sugar in a large mixing bowl at high speed until light and fluffy. Add melted and cooled chocolate, beating until combined. Add eggs, one at a time, beating well after each. Gradually add the powdered sugar, and continue creaming at high speed. Stop the mixer and, by hand, stir in flour, cocoa, and nuts until well-blended.

Pour batter into a well-greased Bundt® pan. Bake at 350 degrees for about 50 minutes or slightly longer until the top begins to show a shiny, brownie-type crust. During cooking, some of the fudge will migrate to the center to create a yummy, gooey tunnel, so testing doneness in the traditional way with a toothpick is ineffective. (Note: nuts are essential to the success of this recipe.)

Cool for 2 hours before attempting to remove from the pan. Dust the inverted cake with powdered sugar and allow to cool completely before cutting.

Chanda's Easter Buns and Cheese (or Hot Cross Buns)
Chanda and Jodi compared notes and realized that Chanda's Jamaican "Easter Buns" and Jodi's mom's "Hot Cross Buns" were almost identical — except for the cheese.

Makes 16 buns.

2 pkgs. dry yeast
1/3 cup milk
1 stick butter
1/3 cup sugar
3/4 tsp salt
4 eggs
4 cups flour
2/3 cup raisins or currants
1 Tbsp. cinnamon
1 1/2 cups powdered sugar
1 1/2 tsp. lemon zest, finely chopped
1/2 tsp. lemon extract
2 Tbsp. milk
Cheese

Dissolve the yeast in 1/3 cup of warm water and set aside for 10 minutes until the yeast foams to prove it is active. Scald the milk and then combine with butter, sugar, and salt in a large mixing bowl. Stir in 3 beaten eggs (the fourth egg is for egg white to brush on top of the buns), 1 cup of the flour, the activated yeast, and raisins or currants. When smooth, add the remaining 3 cups of flour and the cinnamon. With dough hooks on your mixer or by hand knead until smooth and elastic. (Add a little extra flour if the dough is too sticky to handle.) Cover and set in a warm place to rise for about 2 hours until it doubles in size.

Punch down the dough and divide in half repeatedly until you have 16 pieces to form into buns. Flour your hands and roll each bun into a ball. Arrange them on a greased cookie sheet with space to rise. Cover with a towel and allow to rise 1 hour. Just before baking, brush with egg white mixed with a teaspoon of water until frothy. Bake for 12 minutes or until light golden brown in a 375 degree oven.

Blend the powdered sugar, lemon zest, lemon extract, and milk. When the buns are cool, drizzle the glaze into the cross on top of each bun.

You might want to make a double batch and give some away to your neighbors. And for that Jamaican touch, serve with cheese.

Ruth's Matzo Ball Soup

You don't have to be Jewish to enjoy Matzo Ball Soup! (Not to mention that matzo balls floating in a yummy chicken broth is probably the most edible way to enjoy matzo!)

Serves 8.

Soup:
1 chicken
1 large onion
3 carrots, cut in 1 1/2-inch segments
4 stalks celery, cut in 1 1/2-inch segments
2 Tbsp. chicken bouillon
1/4 tsp. pepper

Place the chicken in a large pot. Cover with water (at least 2 qts.). Add the vegetables, bouillon, and pepper, and boil 1 to 1 1/2 hours until the chicken is almost falling off the bones. Add additional bouillon to achieve desired saltiness. Remove the chicken and set it aside. Allow the soup to cool and the grease to rise to the top. Skim it off, saving 1 tablespoon of the fat.

Matzo Balls:

2 eggs, separated
1 Tbsp. *schmaltz* (the chicken fat)
1 celery stalk, diced
1 small onion, diced
2 cloves garlic, diced or crushed
1 cup chicken broth (heated to boiling in a saucepan)
1 cup matzo meal
1 Tbsp. fresh parsley, chopped
1 Tbsp. fresh dill (or 1/2 tsp. dry)
1/2 tsp. baking powder

Beat the egg yolks and set aside. Beat the egg whites until stiff and set aside. Fry the celery and onion in the chicken fat until translucent. Near the end, add the garlic. Then add the boiling chicken broth, stir, and allow to cool a few minutes. Stir in the matzo meal, egg yolks, parsley, dill, and baking powder. When evenly mixed, fold in the egg whites, and put in the refrigerator for 1 hour to solidify into a workable dough.

Reheat the pot of soup to a rolling boil. Remove the matzo mix from the refrigerator and form heaping tablespoons of the mix into ping-pong size balls (no larger). Drop into the boiling soup. Cover and simmer for 30 minutes.

At the last minute, Jodi de-boned the chicken and added some of the meat to the soup. Probably wasn't kosher, but it sure was good!

US TO METRIC CONVERSION TABLE

CAPACITY

1/5 teaspoon = 1 milliliter
1 teaspoon = 5 milliliters
1 tablespoon = 15 milliliters
1 fluid ounce = 30 milliliters
1/5 cup = 50 milliliters
1 cup = 240 milliliters
2 cups (1 pint) = 470 milliliters
4 cups (1 quart) = .95 liter
4 quarts (1 gallon) = 3.8 liters

WEIGHT

1 ounce = 28 grams
1 pound = 454 grams

READING GROUP GUIDE

1. Have you ever attended a Jewish holiday celebration or ceremony, such as Rosh Hashanah (Jewish New Year), Yom Kippur (Day of Atonement), Purim (Story of Esther, Festival of Lots), Sukkot (Feast of Booths), Pesach (Passover), or Hanukkah (Festival of Light)? Or maybe a ceremony such as a *brit mila* (ceremonial circumcision), *bar mitzvah* (a boy's coming of age), *bat mitzvah* (same for a girl), or a Jewish wedding? Share your experience. In what way might these celebrations enrich our own faith?

2. How do you respond to the "blending" of Uptown Community and New Morning Christian Church? What do you see as the strengths/weaknesses of being a "homogeneous" church? What do you see as the strengths/weaknesses of being a "heterogeneous" church? How important do

you think it is to reflect some of the diversity that is the body of Christ within a local body?

3. In this novel, what name for the blended church would you have voted for? Why? Have you ever been part of naming a church or group? Was it a good experience? How important is *naming* an organization? A new baby? Your own name?

4. In what way do you identify with Jodi's struggles with Old Jodi responses (worry, stewing, acting first and praying later) and New Jodi responses (praying first, waiting on God, listening for God's voice, seeking counsel from others)?

5. Now that you've read Book 6 in the Yada Yada series, what *growth* do you see in the other characters (e.g., Chanda's attitude toward money; Nony and how she handles her desire to return to South Africa; Yo-Yo and Becky, the "baby Christians"; Florida facing myriad challenges in her family; Avis's seeming "perfection" becoming more "real")? What character's growth do you identify with most — and why?

6. When the Holy Spirit speaks within Jodi,

does that seem real to you? How is Jodi learning to hear the Holy Spirit? In what way does God's Spirit speak to you? How can you discern between "God's still, small voice" and your own thoughts and feelings?

7. Denny tells his almost-grown kids that sometimes we have to let go of the past in order to go forward. Are there events or people in your past you are hanging on to that are keeping you from "rolling" with God?

8. Two of the Yada Yada sisters are ex-cons. Both came to faith because someone visited them in prison. In *Gets Rolling*, both Denny and Jodi volunteer at the juvenile detention center and are surprised at the eager responsiveness of these young "criminals." *Read Matthew 25:34–36 and Hebrews 13:1–3.* What priority do Jesus and Paul give "prison ministry"? Have you ever visited someone in prison? What do you think would happen if you did?

9. In *Gets Rolling*, the Yada Yada Prayer Group begins to reach beyond their group in new ways. Is God nudging *you* to "reach out" beyond your own circle of

family and friends? In what ways? What are the challenges for you? How can you support one another?

10. Throughout this book, the Holy Spirit nudges Jodi, *"Think about the possibilities!"* What does that mean for her? What might that mean for you?

For more information about *The Yada Yada Prayer Group* novels or to contact author Neta Jackson, go to www.daveneta.com.

A NOTE FROM THE AUTHOR

Dear Sister Readers,
I hope you've enjoyed this Yada Yada Prayer Group Party Edition!

As I was writing the stories of the Yada Yada sisters and following them around, I realized a wide variety of foods and multi-cultural celebrations and holidays were appearing. I thought, "Wouldn't it be nice to collect some of these and expand them so readers could enjoy them, too?"

Well, now you can! The creative team at Thomas Nelson Fiction encouraged me to share my collection of celebrations and recipes for this special Party Edition. Hopefully, this will be an encouragement for dear sister readers to discover and celebrate the wonderful diversity within the Body of Christ!

So . . . enjoy! If you're a newcomer to the Yada Yada Prayer Group series, I hope you hang on for the ride through all seven of the novels! God may use these feisty, praying Yada Yada sisters to change your life, as He has used them to change mine.

As for what's next, I'm working on a new series titled Yada Yada House of Hope, due to premier in December 2008 with a cast of new characters. But remember that old camp song, "Make new friends, but keep the old . . ."? You'll find some of your old Yada Yada friends woven into the new series, too!

Visit my website at www.daveneta.com to sign up for updates. See you next time around!

Your sister on the journey,
Neta

ABOUT THE AUTHOR

Neta Jackson's award-winning Yada books have sold more than 400,000 copies and are spawning prayer groups across the country. She and her husband, Dave, are an award-winning writing team, best known for the Trailblazer books. They live in the Chicago area.